BETWEEN
HEAVEN & HELL

≪ WELCOME TO A NEW *OLD WEST* ≫

JACQUI
NELSON

To my mother and father who gave me a magical childhood on a cattle farm in the middle of nowhere—a perfect place for a girl to dream and a writer to remember.

You are always in my thoughts.

PREFACE

A journey between Heaven and Hell, and back again, can begin in many places.

For America's First People and their children, the strength to begin such a journey often came from legends.

— *Jacqui Nelson*

The Legend of Grandfather Spider

One day, an Osage chief went into the forest hunting for a symbol to give his people strength. All of the other clans had found such symbols, all but his.

He stumbled across the tracks of a deer of great size. In his desire to catch this deer and harness its power for his people, he ran faster and faster, his attention fixed only on the tracks.

He collided with a huge spider's web strung across the trail.

Down climbed the web's creator. "Grandson," the spider said, "why do you race through our world looking at nothing but the ground two strides ahead?"

"I am following the path of a great deer. Only one as mighty as he can be a symbol strong enough to help my people."

"Strength can be found in many places," replied the spider. "If I were your symbol, you would see this."

"I see only one thing. You are small and weak. I didn't even notice you as I chased the deer." The chief turned away from the spider, searching for a way around the web blocking him.

"Grandson," the spider said again, "look closer. While I spin the web that forms my life, I watch and I wait. I am patient. All things come to me when the time is right."

PROLOGUE

Kansas—1839

One minute the men were talking to her papa, the next they shot him dead.

Barely tall enough to see over the window sill, nine-year-old Hannah watched the tattered band of militiamen celebrate by riding circles around her family's cabin, whiskey bottles in one hand, roaring pistols in the other. Their whooping laughter conveyed the pleasure they took in taunting those left alive inside.

Terror kicked Hannah's legs out from under her, leaving her huddled on the dirt floor of her home. She clamped her hands over her ears, tried to shut out the gunshots, the pounding hooves, the jeers and calls for her and her mother to come outside.

But Mama did not heed them. Instead, she crouched beside Hannah and fired her own gun to keep their attackers at bay.

Suddenly, all sound ceased.

Mustering what little courage she had left, Hannah rose on trembling legs to once again peer out the window. The men had stopped circling. Had they grown bored of galloping around in the midday sun amid the clouds of churning dust?

Their sweat-streaked faces were lowered as they

stuffed scraps of cloth down the necks of their whiskey bottles. Had they grown tired of drinking, too?

Bright orange flames burst from the bottle tops. Putting heel to horse, the renegade mob rushed the cabin. Hannah jerked back in disbelief. The men tossed their makeshift torches onto the roof and then withdrew to a safe distance, knowing she and her mother were still inside. Mama's rifle had told them so.

Dreading what she might see, Hannah's gaze rose to the ceiling. A slash of red ripped across the wood planks, then another and another, like the eyes of a dozen demons. With a shriek, she flung herself into her mother's outstretched arms. The cabin crackled and hissed. The flames snaked all around her, making her skin hurt like she'd come too near a boiling pot.

A shroud of charcoal covered the sunbeams in her mother's hair, and her voice was hoarse with the same ash that choked Hannah's lungs when she spoke. "Climb out the back window. Run faster than you've ever run. Head for the ravine. Hide under its brambles."

Hannah nodded. Mama always knew what to do. She would save them.

Her mother's cornflower-blue eyes glistened. Her gaze slid slowly over Hannah's face as if memorizing it. Then she blinked and her gaze locked on the window. "I'll keep firing. They won't know you've left. They won't come after you if they think we're still inside."

Hannah hesitated.

"Go on now." Mama's push was gentle, but her tone had turned firm. "I'll come as soon as I can."

Reluctantly, Hannah obeyed. She ran until her lungs ached. When she reached the bramble bushes a hundred yards away, she ignored the thorns that tore her clothing and cut her skin. She crawled under the tangle of twigs until she could go no farther. Lying on her belly with her cheek pressed against the hard earth, she listened to the comforting crack of her mother's rifle.

Soon she'd come out and join her...wouldn't she?

Uncertainty pinned Hannah down. So did the brambles above her. She couldn't breathe. She had to get out. With a gasp, she clawed the dirt, tried to scramble back the way she'd come. Her home burst into a roaring ball of fire. *Mama! You have to come out!*

The cabin buckled in on itself and collapsed.

Clutching her knees to her chest, Hannah let her tears burn her cheeks. The militiamen's yelling faded as they left. They left her with no reason to move or live. She stayed under the brambles and gave in to the sweet oblivion darkening the corners of her vision.

The pounding of hooves startled her awake. She squinted through the twigs. The towering funnel cloud of black smoke had faded to a wisp of a memory. A band of raven-haired riders halted between her and the charred remains of her home. Even though she was embedded deep in her hiding place, one of them turned in her direction. And pointed.

They were Indians! Fear constricted her throat. White men had shot Papa and burned Mama alive. What would these people that everyone called savages do to her?

They dug her out. When they reached her, she screamed and fought like an animal. The men drew back as if bewildered by such fierceness in one so small. They didn't go far, though. They formed a circle around her. Dark statues with sharp-cut features, they uttered not a word as the lines of their faces settled into impenetrable granite.

Their silence unnerved her as much as the white militiamen's noise. She darted around her cage, seeking an escape. She found none. Gasping for air, she fell to her knees.

A woman pushed through the wall of bodies holding her captive. Hannah tensed, wanting again to flee. But her legs wouldn't obey. All she could do was stare through stinging eyes.

Tall and straight as any queen, the woman wore no jewels or garments of grandeur. Her mane of glossy black hair was her crown, her simple buckskin dress her mantle. She didn't watch Hannah with the curiosity of a stranger or the calculating look of a superior. Instead, her dark eyes glistened with compassion...with understanding.

Surrounded by a ring of emotionless faces and the stench of her smoldering home, the smallest ember of hope flickered inside Hannah. Acting on instinct, she raced forward, throwing herself into the woman's arms—and into a whole new world.

CHAPTER 1

11 years later…
Fort Leavenworth, Kansas—Spring 1850

Lord help her, for she had entered Hell. That Hannah had sought guidance from the God of her past made her loneliness increase tenfold. She should've prayed to Grandfather Spider.

"Well, what'a we got here?" someone yelled from behind her. The voice was rough with malicious undertones.

"Don't reckon I know," replied another man. "Though she be a purty lil' yellow-haired thing."

"Maybe, but we'd hafta get them injun' clothes off her to tell fer sure."

Hannah stiffened in her saddle but kept her buckskin-clad knees tight against White Cloud's sides, urging him forward. She fought the need to tug down the frayed cuffs of her wool coat or touch the beads and feathers in her belt for comfort.

Don't react, she told herself. *Don't make eye contact. Don't turn back.*

A mountain man, the size of a bear, spat a foul-smelling stream of brown chewing tobacco in front of White Cloud's path. He sneered at Hannah with lips stretched over rotting teeth.

Behind him on a saloon porch, a trio of dusty cowhands rose from their card game, waved their whiskey bottles at her and hollered, "Ooh-wee, lovey! Come on down from yer horse. Let us show you a good time."

Strident feminine laughter filled the air. Hannah's gaze darted heavenward to discover a row of women dressed in corsets and short calico skirts. They leaned over the balcony railing, watching her with black-rimmed eyes full of disdain.

If she ignored them, maybe they'd leave her alone. Or maybe coming to Fort Leavenworth hadn't been such a good idea. She had no choice. She couldn't turn back.

She drew in a ragged breath and kept White Cloud moving.

From her hiding place in the north, it'd taken four days of riding to reach this frontier outpost and three more to work up the courage to enter its imposing wooden gates. She had to get as far from Kansas as she could, but her mind balked at traveling any further alone.

Fort Leavenworth held the key to her salvation. One of the wagon trains bound for the Western Territories—a land claimed to require three months to reach—needed a scout. Their leader had put out a call for a crack shot, a strong rider with his own horse and someone who could speak Sioux or Pawnee, or at least knew the sign language used by all the Plains Indians. All skills she'd mastered years ago.

He won't believe you. You'll have to convince him.

Self-doubt and loneliness gnawed at her soul. Fear overruled everything. She'd been lucky so far. If she didn't leave, Eagle Feather would find her. He wasn't a man who failed to make good on a vow.

Sensing her growing turmoil, White Cloud broke into a trot.

"Easy now," she said softly, drawing the words out, coaxing him back to a walk. Hurrying conveyed the wrong message. Today, she couldn't afford to appear anything less than confident. Not if she wanted to impress the wagon master in charge of hiring.

Up ahead, a couple dozen people stood in a cluster, talking with their backs to her while they glanced repeatedly at a rough-hewn table under a sheet of canvas. Relief allowed her to breathe again. She'd found the recruitment tent. Soon she'd find the wagon master.

Then what? Surely, he must be tired of listening to candidates trying to convince him of their worth. As she pondered her next move, her fingers traced the puckered scar on the back of her wrist. Realizing what she was doing, she hid her hand under her coat cuff.

The crowd's chatter changed from many excited voices, rippling back and forth, to a single infuriated one. She sat as tall as she could in her saddle and scanned her surroundings.

A barrel-chested braggart with a flushed face was yelling at three men seated behind the recruitment table.

The first man held himself with a distinguished bearing. Neatly trimmed silver hair framed his weathered face and his blue jacket, though faded, fit him well. The sandy-haired individual sitting beside him was more boy than man, judging from his slight build and smooth skin. The pair appeared frustrated and flustered.

Of the third man seated, all Hannah could make out was thick black hair beneath a worn cowboy hat and a wide chest encased in a buckskin jacket. His shoulders were stiff as he held himself motionless, like a mountain lion assessing an enemy. His whole being radiated hardness.

Hannah swallowed around the lump in her throat. Maybe not seeing his face was for the best.

The air crackled with tension as the horde edged closer toward these three men and the barrel-chested ruffian yelling at them.

"Yer cutting me loose?" he hollered, stomping up and slamming a meaty fist on the table. He leaned across its vibrating surface. "You can't. I'm the best damned scout this side of the Blue Mountains."

"So you have informed us many times, Mr. Dawson." The silver-haired man released a weary sigh. "But we have *seen* the opposite. You have shown yourself to be a drunken nuisance every night since we were given the unique pleasure of making your acquaintance. Not, one might say…" he paused to raise a snowy eyebrow, "…an auspicious start to our journey."

Dawson threw back his head and roared with laughter. "Yer angry 'cause I got a lil' roostered up?" He slashed the air with his hand. "Yer dead wrong, Sherwood. You—"

"General Sherwood," the silver-haired man interrupted in a quiet voice.

The correction widened the scout's eyes before narrowing them to slits. "Didn't you quit the army? Well, *General* Sherwood, you may have been a big bug in Texas, but you got no notion how things are done in Kansas. I be deservin' a little bender before this here journey, and none a you can begrudge a man this."

"No, you are wrong," General Sherwood replied in the same mild tone as before. "This may be my first venture into the West, and I may be a general in name only now, but on this wagon train, if you do not take your responsibilities seriously and obey orders—" his voice turned as hard as the stare he now fixed on Dawson, "—then you have no place with us."

Dawson's face darkened an unhealthy shade of purple. "N-now, hold up." He gave his head a shake and shoved away from the table. Thrusting out his chest, he returned to strutting before the onlookers. "Who you gonna get to take my place?" A smug smile contorted his lips. Spinning on his heel, he jabbed a finger at the general. "I'll tell you who: not a soul. You'll come a cropper. 'Cause yer out of time."

"Not quite," an unfamiliar voice bit out in a near growl. "There's still today, and I'm keen to find your replacement." The razor-sharp clip of the man's voice shredded Hannah's remaining composure like wolverine claws. But his words held her fast.

I'm keen to find your replacement.

Hope crept into her heart. She turned toward the voice. Its owner was the black-haired man in the buckskin jacket.

She could see his face now. High cheekbones, full lips and a firm jaw. All shrouded by a harsh scowl. But it was his eyes that stampeded her defenses, caused a surge of alarm to dash up her spine. Never before had she seen such eyes. Metal gray, hard as the cold steel of a gun. Thankfully, those eyes weren't looking at her but instead skewered Dawson.

Dawson's strutting halted. "Callahan." He spat the name like an oath. "You think yer so all-fired smart, as well."

"This isn't my first time in Kansas." The man's voice was as chill as mountain frost.

"I don't give a bushwhacking rip where you've been."

Callahan's unblinking regard remained on Dawson. "You might when things get tough on the trail ahead. Not my first time there either." His eyes narrowed. "Unlike you."

Dawson huffed a breath. "One man can't handle a wagon train. So let fly, find someone to replace me. I dare you. Hell, I'll even help you." He planted himself in front of a gangly youth unlucky enough to be standing nearby. "How 'bout this feller?"

The young man blushed beet red and retreated several paces.

"Didn't think so. Kid's between hay and grass." Dawson swiveled toward a one-legged soldier leaning on a crutch. "And this one?" He didn't pause long enough for a response but instead declared, "He ain't fit to shoot at when you want to unload and clean yer gun." Dawson's crafty eyes sought his next victim. "Wait! I've found yer man." He thrust a finger at a rail-thin fellow with a pregnant woman clinging to him.

The woman shook her head and pulled the man away.

Hannah stole a glance at Callahan. A muscle jumped in his jaw as he continued scowling at Dawson. The scout had built a solid case for reinstatement to his post, but he didn't stop. His gaze kept moving and halted on Hannah. An unholy light brightened his eyes. He strode toward her, forcing the crowd to open a path for him.

She drew back, but luckily White Cloud stood firm. *No retreating,* she reminded herself.

Dawson pointed at her now. "How 'bout the *lady*?" The corner of his lip snaked up. "She may be sittin' pretty on that there horse, but in a pinch I bet she'd tumble off in the dust."

Laughter rippled through the throng. Dawson's guffaws joined in before his gaze raked her one last time and he spun to face his audience. "I'm the only feller for the job. No one here can shoot or ride better 'n me." He thumped his chest to emphasize his point.

Dawson and the people of Fort Leavenworth had dismissed her. But she wasn't without skills. She wasn't without value. Straightening her shoulders, she scanned the crowd for an opportunity, then glanced at the recruitment table—only to be held captive by a pair of gray eyes, now fixed solely on her.

A startled gasp burst from her lips. She felt like he'd cast a lasso around her chest and squeezed all the air out. Struggling to breathe, she shrank from his relentless stare until a spark ignited in her gut. She'd experienced a similar sensation once before. But that was long ago, when she was a child who'd lost her parents. And this feeling wasn't hope. Anger burst into flame and coursed through her veins, breaking the steely-eyed stranger's hold over her.

Her anger wasn't aimed at him, Dawson or the crowd though. She was angry with herself.

Who was this timid person who'd taken up residence inside her? Had she not faced death and come out alive? Not once but twice? She was stronger than this.

"Would you care to test your 'bet'?" Her words were meant for Dawson, but her gaze never left the man named Callahan. He no longer scowled but leaned forward in his chair with an intensity that made her wonder if he might leap out of it.

"Christ Almighty, don't insult me." Dawson gestured at the crowd. "And don't insult these fine folk. You wouldn't last a minute in a competition with me."

"Maybe," she replied. "But there's only one way to find out for sure. If I beat you, then I'm surely the right person to take your place." She'd found the perfect solution. Now she could let her actions and abilities speak for her. She would win a place on this wagon train.

Dawson crossed his arms. "Bah! I need a serious contender."

Disappointment took a bite out of her confidence. If Dawson wouldn't take the bait, her plan wouldn't work. She cast another glance at Callahan.

With his gaze still fixed on her, he leaned sideways and whispered to his two companions. His expression revealed nothing, but the younger man's jaw dropped and the elder's eyebrows shot skyward. After a pause, both nodded.

In one fluid motion, Callahan rose to his feet and stepped out from under the tent to tower over everyone around him. "She seems pretty serious," he drawled. "So am I. A test could be helpful."

The crowd buzzed with excitement.

"A horse race and target shooting, does that suit you, Dawson? Surely you'll win, so what's the harm?"

Dawson grunted and tightened his arms over his chest. "Have it yer way. I'm sure it'll prove right entertainin', watchin' her sorry attempts to keep up with me."

"Fetch your horse then," Callahan ordered.

Dawson stalked away, accompanied by two cohorts who bobbed along beside him, slapping him on the back.

"Let's go." Callahan strode down the street in the opposite direction with the pair from the tent and rest of the crowd trailing after him.

The human surge forced Hannah and White Cloud to follow him as well. If she'd imagined a lot of folks had stared at her when she arrived, she was certain every single occupant of Fort Leavenworth gawked at her as she left. She, on the other hand, only had eyes for Callahan's wide shoulders and long-legged stride.

Spirits Above, she'd never seen a man exude so much confidence and power by merely walking.

After they exited the stockade gates, he led them to the north wall of the fort and halted by a dirt track. Pale-green clumps of grass circled the racetrack, struggling to overtake the brown husks of their ancestors. But the ground of the track was bare, pounded flat by many hooves. Other than one flag, there wasn't much else to the area.

The spectators jostled each other, trying to secure the best view while making sure they stayed clear of Callahan. The scowl had returned to his face.

Even though it was May, the spring rains had yet to come. An unseasonable chill wind nipped Hannah's back. She welcomed it, glad to have escaped the confines of the fort and still be sitting up high on White Cloud. He kept her away from the boisterous gathering.

They'd been together for many years. His head was a rich chestnut until it met his white neck. The only other sorrel marking was a patch running the length of his underbelly. He resembled a pale cloud hovering over the earth. His velvety ears twitched, tracking the noise. She touched one knee to his side, guiding him so Callahan stood between them and the crowd.

Dawson and his companions rode up in a swirl of dust. With a savage jerk on his roan's bridle, he halted in front of the crowd. His mount tossed its head, fighting the bit. Dawson cuffed the animal several times on its neck.

Callahan moved closer to her.

Hannah needed only to tighten White Cloud's reins a fraction to hold him in check. His muscles quivered. With the arrival of the other horses, he'd become as excited as she. They hadn't raced since they'd left the Osage and gone to live in the cabin in the hills.

The crowd's chatter intensified, like blue jays swarming a berry bush.

General Sherwood raised his voice. "Let's have some quiet!" He swept a stern-eyed gaze over those around him before he looked at her and Dawson. "Race to the flag and back. Circle the marker or be disqualified." He drew his pistol from its holster. "The race starts when you hear me shoot. Not before. And no rough behavior. I want a civilized competition."

Callahan's hands were now fisted by his sides. She turned White Cloud to face the track. The flag fluttered in the breeze, beckoning in the distance.

The general raised his arm, his gun pointed in the air. Dawson dug his spurs into his horse's belly. With a squeal, the animal leaped forward. The pistol shot cracked, echoing in the wake of Dawson's premature start.

A holler went up. Hannah crouched low over White Cloud's neck and gave him his head. He jumped forward to chase Dawson. Up ahead, whipping and kicking his mount, the scout was intent on lengthening his lead. Stride by stride, Cloud gained ground until his nose drew even with the red tail of Dawson's mount.

Hannah's blood surged with exhilaration. The withering embrace of two years shared in exile disappeared. She and White Cloud were strong again. With quickening strides, White Cloud pushed forward until he ran neck and neck with Dawson's roan. Then they pulled ahead and ran alone.

When they reached the flag, she spun White Cloud around the pole and made a beeline back toward the start line. Dawson had now fallen a considerable distance behind in the race. He wasn't anywhere near the flag. The two horses raced toward each other. But unlike White Cloud, who hadn't slowed, Dawson's mount lumbered along, struggling to continue. As she neared her competitor, Dawson sat up with a roar and reined his horse into her path.

Hannah's breath stalled in her throat. An image of the future hit her before Dawson could. A bone-jarring collision. A fall beneath the crushing weight of two horses and one extremely foolish man. What if White Cloud broke a leg? She stopped breathing altogether. An injury like that would be the end of him.

Praying White Cloud could react in time, she jabbed one knee into his side and hauled up on the reins. It was a maneuver used by many Indian warriors. In her early days with the Osage, she'd spent hours practicing the exercise in pairs with the village children. But that was just play. She hadn't sidestepped an opponent at full gallop in years.

White Cloud bounded to the right, away from Dawson. He'd remembered, but she hadn't given him the command quickly enough. The shoulder of Dawson's roan struck a glancing blow against White Cloud's flank. The two horses rebounded off each other for several strides before they found their footing. They ended up running side by side. Only the length of her arm separated them.

Dawson lashed out at her with his fist. He missed. She cursed him and everyone at Leavenworth. She cursed herself most of all for being fool enough to have even set one foot inside the fort. Her thoughts ricocheted in a dozen different directions, then snagged on one. Her efforts to evade one furious man had thrown her in the path of another.

Dawson raised his fist again. Her heart raced faster than a doe fleeing winter-thin wolves. Animal instinct came to her rescue. Seizing the horn, she slipped off her saddle to hang on White Cloud's far side by both hands and one foot.

Dawson's fist struck her saddle where she'd sat only seconds before. The hit reverberated through her bones. Her neck whiplashed as White Cloud sprang forward, out of reach of further attack. She couldn't stop her foot from sliding out of her stirrup. Her body jerked downward, anchored only by her hands on the horn.

A cold sweat stung her eyes, moistened her palms. Her grip on the horn loosened. Her toes scraped the ground. Pain shot up her legs and her arms trembled uncontrollably.

One chance. That was all she had. She gathered the last of her dwindling strength. Timing her movements with White Cloud's stride, she propelled herself up and landed belly down on her saddle. She swung her leg over White Cloud's rump, only daring to breathe a sigh of relief when her bottom touched the saddle again.

Amid much whooping from the crowd, they sprinted home first. She slowed White Cloud to a trot, circled around and brought him to a rest near the three judges. As soon as she did, Callahan's fingers curled around her reins down low next to White Cloud's nose. To her surprise, White Cloud nuzzled his hand.

"I shouldn't have allowed this," he muttered. "Dawson's version of a fair competition is the complete opposite of mine."

"Mine too." She'd aimed for a calm voice but her words came out reedy. She should've waited to catch her breath, but she wasn't sure she'd ever breathe easy in the presence of this man. Most disturbingly, she couldn't tear her gaze away from his strong, tanned fingers stroking White Cloud's nose.

"Then we're all in agreement." General Sherwood stood on the other side of White Cloud. "I hope you can shoot as well as you ride. Then we can all be rid of him."

The general's unexpected words of encouragement made breathing easier.

Callahan released her rein. "I only agree that this needs to end."

The raised voice of the young man from the recruitment tent drew Hannah's attention. He was berating her competitor for cheating as Dawson's mount stumbled across the finish line. Callahan strode toward Dawson. His scowl was even more fearsome than before.

Oblivious to the wagon master's approach, Dawson dismounted. "I can't help the actions of my horse. The nag's downright addled-headed, lurching into other mounts." He raised a fist to strike the animal.

Callahan snared Dawson's wrist and inserted himself between the horse and its owner. "If you want to hit someone, try hitting me." He released the man's arm with a shove.

Dawson froze with his fist still raised.

"What are you waiting for?" Callahan drawled. "Don't you trust your skills in a contest with me?"

Dawson lowered his hand and backed away. "A shootin' match is a truer test of a feller's talent. Why, I've been known to hit a bull's-eye at over a hundred paces. Few men, and certainly no girl, can claim an accomplishment like that."

"Gabe," Callahan shouted over his shoulder. The lad who'd berated Dawson moved to stand beside him. "Set a pair of tins at eighty paces."

Dawson drew a shiny Remington rifle from his saddle scabbard. "I'm first," he declared with a glare that froze her hand on her old rifle. He easily put a bullet through one of the two cans. "Beat that!" he crowed, his arrogant grin returning.

His two cronies, confident once more in their champion, came out of the crowd to shake Dawson's hand. The rest of the spectators conversed in whispers.

Hannah jumped down from White Cloud's saddle. Patting his neck, she said in Osage, "Stay."

The crowd went silent. A frown tightened her brow. Did they not want a scout who spoke a native tongue? Or were they reacting to her size? She used to feel that whatever she'd lacked in stature, she made up for in gumption. Now when she folded her arms over her stomach, she only felt her ribs. Within the haven of a tribe, everything had been shared. Alone, the work had drained her, but the loneliness had been the worst.

With a will of its own, her gaze sought Callahan. Spirits Above, he was tall and rigid with an unsettling tension. She sealed her lips against the compulsion to ask what he was thinking. She couldn't stop herself from looking at him, though. No living soul had ever claimed her attention so strongly, or made her blood race when she became the focus of his.

Forcing herself to concentrate on the task at hand, she raised her rifle to her shoulder.

Her audience held a collective breath. Then the silence was pierced by the crack of her gun and swallowed up by a chorus of shouting as her tin can spun through the air.

"Hellfire," Callahan muttered, rubbing his forehead. Just as quickly he dropped his hand to his side. "Gabe, put the targets at a hundred paces."

Dawson set his mouth and sighted down his rifle barrel. He took a long time adjusting his aim. A nervous titter rippled through the crowd. Dawson's gun boomed. Neither of the tins budged.

"Damnation! The crowd put me off. I'll hit the next one." He proceeded to fire a volley of shots. He only stopped when his rifle was empty and Hannah's ears were ringing.

In the distance, the two cans remained where they'd been placed. Their sides glinted mockingly in the midday sun. She stole another peek at Callahan. He'd crossed his massive arms over the broad expanse of his chest. The raw strength conveyed in a pose mundane on most others sent a shiver up her spine.

His gaze remained fixed on his scout. "You're done, Dawson."

A flush darkened Dawson's face again. "No one can hit that target. Let anyone try. It's an impossible shot."

She drew in a slow breath, the future shimmering tantalizingly before her. All she had to do was hit one little tin can.

She was so close now. She could escape her past, maybe her loneliness as well. Fort Leavenworth was a hellish place, but the wagon train might be different. With all of her heart, she longed to be part of a family again. She didn't want to spend another minute without the hope that one day her life could have meaning.

"Nothing is impossible." The resigned look in Callahan's eyes startled her more than his words. Had he assumed her hesitation meant she too deemed the shot impossible? He pulled his revolver from his gun belt. Without pausing to check his aim, he fired a single shot. One can hit the ground.

A sad smile edged his lips as he stared down at

her. "Nothing is impossible," he repeated. "But will you be all right? Staying here in Kansas?"

Staying? Had he written her off already? A sudden tiredness overwhelmed her, making her sway.

The cold steel in Callahan's gray eyes vanished. His gaze now inflamed her like molten iron straight from a blacksmith's furnace. He moved closer, reaching for her. The heat of his body enveloped her, as did his scent. Sweet sage. The tribes collected the grass in bundles for ceremonial use. He smelled like home.

His fingers brushed her arm. The resulting jolt wrenched her free of his spell. For a moment he'd made her think of happier days, but he was still a stranger whose size and strength could as easily break her arm as steady it. She shied away from him, her gaze darting anywhere but him. General Sherwood, the youth named Gabe and the crowd stood nearby while in the distance, suddenly seeming very far away, the last remaining target waited.

Why had Callahan taken his shot? With that act, he'd joined the competition. Had he handed her another challenge? This one between the two of them?

She raised her chin and her rifle. The tremor in her hands made her pause.

Small and weak. That was how she felt. She'd struggled to be patient like Grandfather Spider advised, but only her shame, not her strength, had grown during the two years following Morning Star and Laughing Eyes' deaths. If she stayed here, she'd die as violently as them. Their sacrifice to save her life would've been for nothing.

She forced herself to stand as tall as she could. The line of Callahan's broad shoulders remained high above her. "Nothing is impossible," she said, then sighted down the barrel of her rifle and pressed the trigger.

A single shot echoed across the plains. Strong and resolute. The last tin can flew into the air, somersaulting to land next to Callahan's. Dawson roared in disbelief. The crowd's gasps of astonishment transformed to cheers, overruling him.

She'd earned her victory...but would the man standing next to her agree?

CHAPTER 2

Paden Callahan lifted his gaze skyward. High above him, the pale blue arc didn't even come close to rivaling the eyes of the woman standing beside him. How on earth had she made that shot? He knew only a handful of men capable of the feat she'd accomplished. Most of them were seasoned Rangers. Men from a life he'd left far behind.

He shook his head. A woman couldn't be a scout. The job was chockfull of hazards. But the competition had been dangerous as well. Why had he allowed her to stand off against a brute like Dawson? Why had he behaved so impulsively?

Dawson looked none too pleased either. He clutched his rifle against his chest in a white-knuckled grip. He dropped his voice so only Paden could hear. "Yer not seriously considerin' that white squaw over me."

White squaw. The words impaled Paden like an arrow. He couldn't stop himself from rubbing his chest, from rubbing the sudden ache in his heart. It didn't matter to him how she dressed. It didn't matter that she could ride and shoot. All that mattered was that neither a woman nor Dawson were acceptable scouts. They both had to go.

"*Consider* yourself dismissed." Paden raised his

voice so everyone would hear. "Your services are no longer required."

Dawson's arms fell to his sides, his rifle dangling in one hand. "You can't do this."

"I can, and I am. Get out of my sight."

"You'll be sorry." Dawson's voice was as close to a hiss as any Paden had heard. The man wasn't going to leave quietly.

Paden suppressed a growl of impatience. He hadn't shot anyone in years and meant to keep it that way. He strove for an even tone. "I've got a whole saddle bag full of sorrys. Adding another won't make much difference."

Dawson's free hand twitched, inching toward the loaded pistol strapped to his hip.

Paden drew his revolver, cocking it on the upswing and leveling it at Dawson. The feminine gasp close beside him made him freeze. He suppressed the urge to tell her he wasn't a killer. Why lie? He'd pulled the trigger in the past, and Dawson needed to believe he'd do it again. "Keep the supplies we advanced you. That's more generous than I have to be. But this is the last time I'll tell you—leave."

Dawson slunk off with his two cronies dogging his heels. Paden released the hammer and shoved his revolver back into its holster. Then he spun to face the woman. This time she didn't retreat, but every bone in her slender body leaned away from him. He shouldn't have reached for her earlier when she swayed on her feet. Being almost grabbed by a lout like himself had only added to the storm of emotions he sensed in her: caution warred with curiosity...and something more.

A hand gripped his shoulder. General Sherwood had moved to his side. The old man canted his head toward the hovering crowd.

"Show's over, folks," Paden hollered, putting as much authority into his voice as he could. "Go about your business." He waited for the spectators to disband before he glanced down at the woman again.

She dropped her gaze and fidgeted with the frayed cuffs of her coat. She didn't even reach his shoulder, and he feared a stiff wind would blow her over. Why was she so thin? Dawson could have broken her bones with one punch. It would've been his fault.

With her oversized coat, he couldn't determine much about her body. Only a small section of buckskin-clad leg showed between her coat and her knee-high moccasins. The coat could've been worn by any trapper west of the Missouri. But the belt cinching it was different. It'd been threaded with an intricate number of colorful beads and feathers. It'd been crafted with care.

She finally met his gaze. The urge to hold her, to protect her, intensified. He turned away to prevent himself from doing something idiotic.

"Collect your horse and come with me," he muttered. He adjusted his stride to match hers as he headed for the fort with the general and Gabe following. His thoughts spun, making his head throb. He hadn't felt this lost in a long time.

When Dawson had rammed his horse into her, he'd barely restrained himself from sprinting out and beating the man senseless. Throughout his years as a Ranger, he'd always considered himself a defender of the unjustly attacked. This reaction had been different. A cold dread had twisted his heart. How could that be? He'd known this woman less than an hour.

He couldn't protect her. She was better off far away from him. He had to let her go.

He halted in front of the fort's gates. "I know you

won the competition. But—"

"We need to talk, Paden." Sherwood had retired from the army, but he still knew how to make his voice authoritative as well. It was the first thing Paden had learned under the general's tutelage.

The woman glanced between them. The frown had returned to her now pale brow. Laying her hand on her horse's shoulder, she leaned heavily against the pinto. She looked ready to collapse. She wasn't just thin, she was starving.

He spat out a curse. Her gaze jerked to him. The anxiety in her wide blue eyes tore at his conscience. She must think him no better than Dawson.

"Gabe," he said slowly, drawing out the lad's name in an attempt to make his voice less gruff. "Take her to our wagon and feed her." A peculiar ache tightened his chest as he watched her walk away from him. "Wait." The word leaped out before he could stop it. He must look like a fool. He couldn't remember the last time he'd cared the slightest what someone thought of him.

Now she, Gabe and Sherwood stared at him. Waiting.

He cleared his throat. "What's your name?"

"Blue Sky." He didn't think it possible, but her eyes flared even wider. Shaking her head, she retreated a step. "Please forget I said that. My name is Hannah."

"What's wrong with Blue Sky?" he asked, wanting to keep her talking, wanting to keep her by his side. "It doesn't do your eyes justice, but it suits you."

"Please don't tell anyone I said that name." She continued backing up, glancing around like she was searching for an escape route. Her gaze fixed on her pinto.

What in Hades had he said to make her want to

run?

"Of course, we won't say anything." The general's voice was low, soothing. "Do you want to share your last name with us, Hannah?"

Her breathing turned fast and shallow. "I can't remember it."

"Why not?" The answer hit Paden with the force of a charging bull elk. Blue Sky was an Indian name. That accounted for her clothing. She'd lived with the savages. He knew them only too well from his days in Texas, knew the ferocity of their raids. They'd slaughtered people as if they were livestock. But occasionally they'd stolen women or children and forced them to work in their villages.

If Hannah couldn't remember her last name, they'd taken her young. The name they'd given her linked her to them. She regretted the revelation. She was alone, scared, wanting to run. How badly had they abused her? He couldn't see any scars but that didn't mean they weren't there.

Rage made his blood roar in his ears.

"Mr. Callahan?" Gabe stared at him, a worried expression knotting his brow. "You still want me to feed her, don't you?"

Unable to speak, he nodded his agreement. This time, even though the ache in his chest returned, he let Hannah walk away. Gabe strode by her side, talking a blue streak. Being the sociable young man that he was, it didn't take him long to win her over. Their heads bent closer and closer together until she finally smiled. The sting of jealously pricked his heart.

"I shouldn't have let her go with him," Paden growled into the void her departure had created.

"She'll make a good scout," the general replied.

Paden flinched. He'd forgotten he wasn't completely alone.

"Son, she isn't..." Sherwood's voice was thick with sadness.

Dear God, don't let him say her name. But the old man only called him "son" when he talked about—

"She isn't Jeannie."

"You're right." Paden pushed the words past the invisible hand choking him. Bile followed, burning his throat. "She isn't dead."

"You and I are not the only ones evading the past. Whatever happened to Hannah—" The general sucked in a sharp breath. "She might turn it into something positive if you let her use the skills she gained while living with the Indians. She is stronger than she looks. I never expected her to win against Dawson. Did you?"

Paden scrubbed his hand over the back of his neck. "Of course I didn't."

"Then why ask me and Gabe to agree to the competition?"

"To shake Dawson up. Humble him. Make him easier to deal with in the days to come. He was a pain in the *cojones,* but he could ride and shoot." Paden snorted. "As long as his target wasn't a hundred paces away. For all his faults, Dawson's right about one thing. We're limited in our options for recruits out here. Even if I'd been given a fortnight, I probably couldn't have found anyone to replace him."

"So instead, a new scout found us and proved her worth in a competition you endorsed. Should we ignore that? Can we?" Sherwood's questions came fast, but when he spoke next his voice was heavy with fatigue. "We need her. We should have departed weeks ago."

Hannah and Gabe disappeared behind the scouts' wagon. The boy had better keep her safe if he knew

what was good for him. Cut adrift, Paden's gaze
skimmed the settlers' wagons and the clutter strewn
around their traveling homes. Had someone actually
brought a piano? He hadn't heard anyone play one
since Jeannie had died.

He spun away from the wagons. *It's just a piano.
It's not Jeannie's piano.* What mattered was that the
settlers had decided to bring the fool thing. It'd
weigh even more than the grandfather clock he'd
seen yesterday. He shouldn't have agreed to help
Sherwood shepherd these naïve souls through the
Indian lands between here and the Western
Territories. But General Sherwood had asked for his
help, and the old man was the one person he
couldn't say no to.

His gaze followed the grasslands stretching out
like an endless dusty-brown blanket around Fort
Leavenworth. The barren openness of this flat
country, lacking a single tree or hillock to break its
uniformity, made his shoulders stiff and his feet
restless. Far to the west, Oregon's mountains, full of
trees instead of people, beckoned. He craved the
solitude, but he wouldn't find it until he got this
wagon train safely across half a continent.

Sherwood had a right to be concerned. Spring
was late, but that didn't mean they could also count
on winter being delayed at the tail end of their
journey. The wagon train couldn't afford any further
delays. They needed to move out and make the most
of every day that followed. They needed every scout
they could get.

Having Hannah with them would help. But
would it help her?

His stomach rolled with uncertainty. Food might
settle him. So would seeing how his new scout was
fairing. The new scout he couldn't keep. No matter
what Sherwood said, he had to let Hannah go. For

her own good and Paden's too.

He'd load as much food on her pinto as the animal could carry. Then he'd say goodbye.

Hannah listened intently as Gabe talked about the wagon train, doling out both advice and reassurances. Only when they stood behind the scouts' wagon, out of sight of its leader, did she release a sigh of relief.

Spirits Above, why had she told him her Osage name? Because he made her nervous, and she'd said the first name that came to mind. The name she was most familiar with. Only since arriving in Fort Leavenworth had she once again started thinking of herself as Hannah.

What must he think? She'd given him two names and then revealed she couldn't remember her last name. He must think she'd lost her mind.

General Sherwood had called him Paden. The informal reference, the acceptance of the older man's hand on his shoulder earlier, indicated the pair knew each other well. Right now they were discussing her…and her future. Would they let her stay with them? If they didn't, how long could she hover around Fort Leavenworth before trouble found her?

Gabe bent to start a fire. She tied White Cloud to the scouts' wagon and kneeled beside the young man.

He shook his head. "You must be tired, miss. Why don't you take a seat on that crate over there and let me handle this?"

She mimicked his headshake. "I want to help."

They stared at each for a long moment. Finally, Gabe shrugged, and together they built the fire. They did the same little dance of manners when Gabe brought out the pork and beans. She won that battle as well, and their combined efforts made the meal preparation go quickly. He rewarded her with a huge grin.

Happiness flooded her. If she worked hard, could she earn Paden's smile as well? Indian villages coddled no one, and through sheer determination she'd earned her tribe's approval. She and Laughing Eyes had been equals among the braves. Morning Star had demanded no less for her daughters. They'd been a family. Tears blurred her eyes. She ducked her head, trying to blink them away before Gabe noticed.

"Everything will be all right, miss." Gabe spoke softly, like General Sherwood had a moment ago, like Hannah did when she wanted to calm White Cloud. "Soon as you get some food in your belly, you'll feel better."

She gratefully accepted the plate he held out to her. Her mouth watered at the abundance he'd heaped on it. "Thank you."

Gabe's smooth cheeks turned pink as he sat on the ground and used a saddle as a backrest.

She perched on the edge of the crate he'd indicated earlier. Her hand trembled when she lifted the spoon. All of a sudden, Gabe was awfully quiet. She didn't want his pity. Maybe she could distract him with conversation before she began bolting down her food like a ravenous beast. "Can you tell me more about the wagons?"

"I can tell you it was a challenge getting everyone packed 'n prepared for life on the trail. Can you believe we'll be living out of these wagons, constantly on the move, for five or six months? When Mr. Callahan advised us what would be required, we were amazed."

Gabe's excitement was contagious. Hannah's

smile returned and she concentrated on eating slowly. It wasn't easy. The meal might have been simple, but she'd never been more grateful for it. "Thank you again for the food, Gabe."

He sat up. "I can make you another plate if you want?"

She shook her head. "What I have is more than enough."

"Just ask if you want more. We got plenty." Gabe leaned back against his saddle. "Our wagon's full of provisions. We're only bringing the essentials. Not like some of the others. I hope the oxen 'n mules can handle the load."

She set her spoon on her plate. It'd been a long time since she eaten so much. She hoped the food stayed down. The continued distraction of learning about the wagon train might help. "Which is better, oxen or mules?"

Gabe shrugged in the same easygoing manner as when she'd challenged him to accept her assistance preparing her meal. "Everyone's got a different opinion. Mules are considered smart, quick-moving, real hardy. Oxen can pull heavier loads, are rumored to eat anything 'n don't cost as much to buy. But them beasts plod on terrible slow 'n can add a fortnight to the trail. We gotta get through the mountains before it starts snowing."

She surveyed the nearby wagons. Chickens were housed in makeshift coops strapped to wagons alongside tethered milk cows. "What about the farm animals? Won't they slow things down as well?"

"Yup. But having milk 'n eggs is just too tempting when a person's facing the boredom of pork 'n beans every day. Still, I can't wait to get started." His voice rose with youthful exuberance. "Granddad agreed to let me drive the scouts' wagon."

Her lips twitched. She couldn't stop smiling when she was around Gabe. "I hope I get to meet your grandfather."

"You already have. My granddad's General Sherwood."

She nodded, seeing the resemblance now. They shared similar personalities. It explained how such a self-assured but also easygoing manner could be present in one so young.

"We'll be storing our gear in the scouts' wagon. Mr. Callahan's keeping his in one of the wagons loaded with dry goods he plans to sell to the homesteaders already out west. He's hired teamsters to drive his pair of wagons."

Now that she'd eaten and the food had stayed down, an intense curiosity filled her. If she learned more about Paden Callahan, could she find a way to convince him to let her stay with his wagon train? "How long have you known Pad— I mean, Mr. Callahan?"

"Granddad 'n him fought together in Texas. That was seven years ago, before Mr. Callahan went west. Last year, Granddad wrote asking him to help us with our wagon train. Mr. Callahan got together a supply of furs 'n made the journey back to Fort Leavenworth."

Disbelief tightened her brow. "He traveled the trail alone?"

"Yup, done it all by himself." Gabe's words tumbled out with increasing speed as his excitement grew. "Sold his furs and used the profits to fill the two wagons I mentioned. He's a smart one, Mr. Callahan. Can you believe this will be his third time riding this trail?"

Paden had made quite the impression on the young man, and rightfully so. Hannah was becoming increasingly aware of the enormity of the journey ahead of her. With that understanding came an immense respect for those who tackled the trip. She imagined that after surviving the journey once, most wouldn't contemplate doing it a second time, let alone third.

What amazed her the most, though, was Paden's choice to travel alone. But he must prefer traveling with others. Wasn't that why he was leading this group?

"Don't let the boy sweeten you on Callahan," advised a smooth voice. Its owner sounded like he was singing his words.

She scrambled to her feet. Spinning to look behind her, she came face to face with a black-haired man. She only had to raise her head a fraction to see the grin on this man's face. Deep lines bracketed his mouth, indicating he smiled often. Right now he was smiling at her and staring. Intently. She didn't think it could be possible, but his smile widened.

She cast a glance in the direction of the scouts' wagon. Earlier she'd been relieved to put its wood and canvas between her and Paden's keen-eyed perusal. Now she felt the opposite.

The man before her raised his hands in what he probably hoped would be a reassuring gesture. It wasn't. He had dark brown eyes like the braves of the Osage. The reminder of her past made her heart thump even harder against her ribcage.

"I'm sorry if I startled you, *señorita*, but you have nothing to fear from me. I've known Callahan as long as Gabe's grandfather. After I departed Mexico for Texas, we three rode together for many years. And although I think the general is a man of great distinction—" he winked at her, "—I cannot say there's anything special about Callahan." His gaze roamed over her from the top of her head to the tips of her toes. "You, on the other hand, are very special. You are *muy bonita*."

Heat scorched her cheeks.

Gabe's elbow brushed her sleeve. Hands fisted on his hips, he stood beside her. "Ignore him, miss. He's just jealous 'cause Mr. Callahan's a war hero 'n a bona fide mountain man now as well. You don't measure up to him anymore, Alejandro. This is your first wagon trip, same as me 'n Granddad."

Alejandro's smile remained firmly in place. "Who would want to be compared to a man that half of Texas christened *el Diablo hizo de Humo*, the Devil made of Smoke? Besides, I have not come to discuss the past. I have come to meet the *señorita* the entire fort is talking about." The man's gaze slid to Gabe before returning to her. "I see why you have *everyone* so agitated. But I have failed to introduce myself." With a flourish, he extended his hand, palm up. "My name is Alejandro Ramirez."

She stared at his offering. Was this a customary greeting? Uncertainty made her hesitate.

With a sigh, the Mexican scooped up her hand and raised it to his mouth. His gaze never left hers as his lips brushed her knuckles. "And you are?" he asked, leaning much too close.

She felt her jaw drop before she remembered to jerk her hand free.

"Lay off, Alejandro." The growled words came from Gabe's direction. The voice was too deep to belong to the young man. Hands on hips, Paden stood next to Gabe, mirroring his pose.

The Mexican arched an inky brow. "I was merely saying hello."

Paden's familiar scowl returned. He had yet to look her way though. "Do I have to spell it out? I don't want you touching her."

Hellfire, why had he said that? Paden had no claim over Hannah. He'd never see her again after today.

Alejandro's eyes widened with interest rather than the compliance Paden wished he could've evoked. What had he expected? He and Alejandro had always butted heads.

"As you wish, *mi capitán*." Alejandro gave a mock salute and stepped back to stand at attention.

Paden huffed out an annoyed breath. "I'm no longer involved with the Rangers, and neither are you for that matter. So I'd thank you not to call me that anymore."

"We may have left Texas and the Rangers, but are you not this wagon train's *capitán*?"

"The position's temporary."

"And the title?"

"Didn't want it back in Texas. Sure as hell don't want it now."

"Today you are overflowing with many don'ts, *amigo*."

Spurs jingled, approaching from the direction of the fort. Virgil strode past them and halted on the opposite side of the fire. His lanky body folded up like an accordion as he squatted down and prodded the embers with a stick. "Don't you think you've both bored the young lady enough with your granny bickering?"

Paden sealed his lips against the urge to enter another argument. Virgil was right. He shouldn't be quarrelling with Alejandro. He should be telling Hannah that she couldn't come with them. But his rebellious mouth remained closed, refusing to give the order.

"Since no one's got the manners to make introductions," Virgil drawled, "I'll do it myself." Tugging the brim of his hat, he dipped his head to

Hannah. "Name's Virgil, miss, and I'm pleased ta meet you. How about you have a seat and I'll rustle you up a cup of coffee?" He tossed a handful of coffee beans in a skillet and held the pan over the fire.

Hannah reclaimed her seat, or at least the edge of it, then cast a questioning glance Paden's way.

The tightness in his jaw eased a fraction. She'd looked to him for guidance. How could such a small thing make him feel...lighter? "Virgil's one of our scouts. So's Alejandro."

"I don't know either of these young fools very well." Virgil gestured toward Paden and Alejandro with his skillet. "Still I'd advise you to ignore 'em both." Virgil had a penchant for calling everyone young, but his long brown hair was only slightly streaked with gray. So was his impressive handlebar moustache. "What shall I put in your coffee, miss?"

She leaned forward, eyeing Virgil's preparations with interest. "I've never had...coffee before. What do you suggest I put in it?"

If Virgil thought Hannah's answer strange, he didn't let it show. Instead, he chuckled. "We'll start with lots of sugar. Let you acquire a taste for it gradual-like. By trail's end, you'll be tossing it back black."

"No." The word came out gruffer than Paden had intended. Everyone swung around to gape at him. "She can't come with us," he explained.

Virgil set his skillet on the ground. Resting his arms on his knees, he leveled a sharp stare at Paden. "Why not?"

Alejandro rounded the fire to stand beside Virgil. "*Si*, why not?"

Gabe followed, claiming a spot on Virgil's other side.

With only a handful of words, Paden had united

his team against him. "The journey's too dangerous. So is being a scout. You all know that. She's safer staying behind."

"I'll agree that what lies ahead ain't gonna be a Sunday social." Virgil jerked his thumb over his shoulder. "But is it safer leaving her near that fort…and Dawson?"

Dread iced Paden's veins. He should've shot the bastard when he'd had the chance. "What's Dawson saying?"

"He's retelling the competition, or at least his version."

"Which is?"

Virgil's gaze darted to Hannah then back to Paden. "Ain't sure where to start."

Gabe inhaled a sharp breath as if outraged. "Is he saying we ousted him for a whi—"

"Gabe!" Paden had thought Dawson uttered his foul remark too quietly for anyone else to hear. Or maybe he'd just hoped. He'd be damned, though, if he'd let anyone call her a white squaw again, even if it was just repeating what another had said.

"Dawson claims he knows the tribe the *señorita* lived with." Alejandro's voice had lost its laughing lilt. "He said he recognized the language she spoke."

Paden scoffed. "She only said one word. Dawson isn't that talented with languages."

"He apparently gained wisdom from a man he saw last week." Virgil tilted his head as he studied Hannah's horse tied to the scouts' wagon. "Dawson said an Osage brave was asking about a pinto with those markings."

A clatter of metal made Paden reach for his revolver.

Hannah's plate and spoon lay overturned on the ground. "Spirits Above, he's here?" Once again, her gaze darted around like she wanted to escape.

"Who is he?" Paden released the handle of his revolver and reached for her instead. He paused midway. If he grabbed hold of her, he might hurt her. Or in her panic she might injure herself trying to break free. He'd be no better than Dawson or this Osage brave she was running from. He jammed his hands in his coat pockets. "Tell me who's looking for you. I'll—"

"I've got to get out of here." She clutched her fisted hand against her chest, then slowly opened it to stare down at her palm. Something dark marked her skin. Something he couldn't make out. Whatever it was, she stared at it as if seeking the answer to a great riddle before she clenched her hand again. "It's no use." Shoulders hunched with a grim acceptance, she turned to face the west. "I'll have to go alone."

Paden was pretty sure his shoulders looked the same as hers. "You're not going anywhere alone. This wagon train leaves at first light, and you're coming with us."

CHAPTER 3

The next morning, perched on White Cloud next to Paden and his mount, Hannah tried not to fidget with her coat cuffs as she watched her new employer out of the corner of her eye.

He sat with an easy grace on his tall bay stallion. The animal's Spanish bloodlines were evident in its arched neck and long ebony mane and tail. The horse pawed the ground, eager to go, and then pranced, lifting its feet high.

Paden let the spirited animal blow off some steam before murmuring, "Settle down, Cholla." With a steady hand on the rein, he eased the horse to a standstill. Then he leaned forward, resting his arms on his pommel and scowling even harder at the wagon train in front of them.

Man and beast jockeyed for position in starts and stops, creating total chaos. The pioneers should've been concentrating on getting their wagons into a line. Instead they pointed, they whispered, they openly gawked at Hannah. Word had spread. They'd probably enjoyed discussing her presence long into the night. And who could blame them? In these parts, she was about as common as a snowflake in hell.

After what felt like an eternity, the pioneers

formed a line, a very crooked one.

"All right, move out!" Paden hollered. "No stopping till the midday meal, and no asking when that is. I'll let you know." He turned to the two scouts mounted on the other side of him. "Virgil, take the head. Alejandro, take the tail. Keep everyone moving as fast as you can. I'll be riding the line with General Sherwood doing the same."

"And the *señorita*?" Alejandro peered around Paden to smile at her. "She could ride with me."

"She's staying with the scouts' wagon." Paden's tight-lipped reply made her spine sag.

What help could she be doing that? Virgil and Alejandro rode off to their assigned tasks while she tried to concentrate on the positive. She was leaving Kansas and she wasn't alone.

"Well, you have your wish," Paden drawled. "Now you're stuck with this motley bunch. You're stuck with me too."

This was the first time they'd been together without someone else nearby. She sat up straighter

"You aren't getting everything you wanted, though." The leather of Paden's saddle creaked as if he'd adjusted his seat. "I need your full attention for what I'm about to say. Look at me…Hannah."

His deliberate pause, along with the sound of her name said for the first time in his deep voice, shattered her resolve. She gave in to his request. The small smile that suddenly curved his lips made her blink with surprise and hope. Just as quickly a frown obliterated his good humor, as if he regretted giving her any reassurance.

What else did he regret? And what did he mean when he said she wasn't getting everything she wanted?

"You're not scouting. You're staying with Gabe."

His answer hit her hard. He didn't want her beside him. Her dismay must have shown on her face, because he turned away from her to stare through narrowed eyes at the horizon.

"You're staying safe," he continued. "Safe from whoever you're running from. You won't be seeing Kansas or anyone in it again." He tapped his heels to his stallion's sides and loped toward the scouts' wagon at the head of the line.

Without being told, White Cloud followed. If only it was so easy to leave the past behind. She glanced over her shoulder at the fort. Every muscle in her body stiffened. Three men on horseback hovered by the north wall near the racetrack. The bright light of the sun rising behind them made it hard to see more than their silhouettes, but their stillness filled her with foreboding.

In the chill dawn, the rising sun did little to warm Dawson's back...or brighten his dark thoughts. He glared at the wagon train assembling to leave Fort Leavenworth. Not just any wagon train, his former employers' and his replacement's. He could count the times he'd been bested on one hand. None of those defeats had been by a woman.

It was unthinkable. It was all he could think about. The humiliation ate at him like maggots in an open wound. Only one prospect brought relief.

"Callahan 'n his blond squaw must pay." Leaning sideways in his saddle, he spat on the ground for emphasis. "They think they're so high 'n mighty. I'll show them otherwise."

The shorter of the two men sitting next to him on newly pilfered horses jerked upright and blinked sleepily. "What'd ya say, boss?"

"He said we're gonna try our hand at robbing

wagon trains," replied the other man. His eyes, dark and strange as a bird's, stared soullessly at Dawson from a pockmarked face surrounded by a tangle of greasy hair.

Dawson had only met the two men recently. He understood their kind, though, drifters and opportunists. Like himself.

"Sounds good to me," the first man replied. He was as unkempt as the other man, but he looked like a straight and narrow bible thumper in comparison. He darted a nervous glance at Fort Leavenworth. "Should be easier stealing from wagons than forts."

The second man's night-black eyes held Dawson's for a moment longer before he went back to stroking the edge of his knife. Wickedly long at fifteen inches and two inches broad, the blade glinted in the bloodred rays spilling over the horizon. "It'll be easier doing a lot of other things as well."

Dawson gave a sharp hoot of laughter. A thief and a lunatic. He liked his new friends. Now he just needed to decide the perfect way to repay his enemies. A quick kill wouldn't satisfy. The best revenge was prolonged, painful. Callahan 'n his new scout must suffer.

When the wagons struck camp at midday, Hannah helped Gabe pull the crate from the back of the scouts' wagon and unload the cooking supplies. She couldn't have predicted that Dawson would be the one to help secure her a place on this wagon train. But if she wasn't a scout, what was she?

She helped Gabe prepare the pork and beans. Virgil joined them and commenced the ritual she'd seen him begin yesterday. She and Gabe had already fallen into a comfortable routine, which enabled her to also follow Virgil's creation of his beloved coffee. He roasted a handful of round green beans in a pan, then ground them in a device Gabe called a mill. After pouring the grinds into a pot of water he'd hooked on an iron tripod over the fire, he sat cross-legged on the ground and watched the mixture boil.

Alejandro arrived from his post at the rear of the wagon train. His teeth flashed white in his dust-caked face as he walked toward them. "The air is thick at the back of the line. I think I drew the short straw when Callahan doled out assignments this morning. How did you fair, *señorita*?"

She shook her head. "He isn't letting me work as a scout."

"Do not despair. It's only your first day. Give it some time."

"You think time will help? He'll stop regretting his decision to bring me along?"

"Regretting?" Alejandro's eyes widened before his gaze dropped to his boots. "His acceptance is important to you?"

"Not just him," she rushed to reply.

"*Señorita…*" He inhaled a deep breath. "Hannah. I advise caution. He is incapable of—"

Galloping hoof beats cut him off. Paden pulled his stallion to a halt by the wagon.

"Just be careful," Alejandro whispered and moved to stand beside Virgil.

Be careful of what? Hannah wanted to shout. She tried to focus on the banter Alejandro and Virgil struck up, but every nerve in her body was tuned to Paden. From the corner of her eye she watched him tie his horse to the wagon.

"*Dios,*" Alejandro suddenly hissed. "What's that horse's ass doing with the general?"

Virgil craned his neck to look down the line of wagons. "Thomas Riley? Isn't he the one General

Sherwood said should've stayed in Texas?"

One of the pioneers—a stout man with bushy red-brown hair and a short stride that made him waddle like a determined badger—headed toward their campfire with General Sherwood by his side. An air of reluctance clung to the general, stooping his normally straight shoulders. When Riley saw Paden, he barreled forward to grasp the wagon master's hand. General Sherwood came and stood beside her.

Pumping Paden's hand up and down, Riley proclaimed in a loud voice, "The general said to wait, but he's been saying that for days. I had to shake your hand, Captain Callahan. You're a legend back home."

Hannah tensed at the mention of the title Paden had objected to so strenuously yesterday.

"Tell me Riley's not *loco* enough to bring up San Antonio." Alejandro surged past the general, heading straight for their visitor. "If he does, I'll help Paden tear the man's head off."

Hannah's lips parted with surprise. How could the slightest possibility of a town being mentioned bring Alejandro to Paden's side with such fervor?

The general grabbed Alejandro's arm, halting him. "It's too late. Riley won't be dissuaded."

Alejandro spat out a string of words in rapid Spanish. "Do not let him. Not in front of Hannah."

The sadness in the general's eyes stole her breath. "She shall hear it from Riley, or one of the other settlers, soon enough. I apologize, Hannah. We should have told you. I should have told you. But I hoped you might…" He sighed and turned to face Paden and Riley. "Now maybe it's too late for that as well."

Her throat constricted. Too late for what? Her gaze snapped to Paden and Riley, and stayed there.

Paden used his free hand to extract himself from Riley's grasp. He folded his arms, putting his hands out of reach or maybe restraining them. "Those days are better forgotten," he said from between clenched teeth.

"Not so, Captain! Texas won't forget its heroes or the loss you suffered in San Antonio. Our enemies won't either. They still call you the Devil made of Smoke." Riley said the name in a hushed tone full of reverence, then his voice rose even louder than before. "You should've killed them all. The only good Indian is a dead one."

A shudder racked Hannah's body. She drew her arms deep into her coat sleeves, curling the cuffs over her hands to hide them. He'd killed Indians?

"Thank God," Riley continued, "that you slit their heathen gullets and made it safe for decent folk to sleep in their beds."

Disbelief clawed its way up her windpipe, threatening to erupt in a scream. He'd cut their throats? Like the white trappers had done to Laughing Eyes?

"I never attacked a village." Paden's gaze met hers, but the steel in his eyes had lost its strength. He seemed to look through her as if she were the one made of smoke. "I made war on camps full of armed braves. I killed every one of those men. Then I cut their bodies and burned them with their possessions so their souls would be damned, like they'd damned mine."

Fear contracted her heart. Her nerves snapped tight. *Run! Get out of here! In your soul you are more Osage than white. He will damn you for it as well.* But Paden just kept staring at her with blank eyes. He'd yet to threaten her or even say a disparaging word about her. Her grip on her coat cuffs eased. He knew she'd lived with Indians *before* he'd agreed to let her stay with his wagon train.

Paden raised his gaze to stare at the sky high above her. "We leave in five minutes if…if you still want to travel with us."

"Of course I want to travel with you, Captain Callahan," Riley replied. "Who wouldn't? With you nearby, there's no safer place on the trail. Still, I'd better get back to my wagon. I left my daughter tending our oxen."

Paden's familiar scowl returned as he swung around to glare at Riley. "You left your daughter alone so you could talk to me about San Antonio?" His voice had gone as cold and hard as a winter lake. It was the voice he'd used with Dawson. Why was he reacting so strongly to Riley leaving his daughter alone? Weren't they safe as long as they stayed close to the wagons? Surely there were more dangerous places than here.

Riley backed away, ducking his head sheepishly. "I know, I know. But this isn't San Antonio. She's fine. The most that will happen to her is an ox will step on her foot or some such nonsense."

Paden grabbed Riley's arm and pushed him ahead of him. "You'd better hope she's fine."

Hannah watched in stunned silence as they left. A hand squeezed her shoulder gently. She almost jumped out of her moccasins. Her gaze darted up to find the general staring down at her.

"I hope you won't judge us too harshly." His voice was once again low and soothing.

She didn't know what she should do. Riley's words came back to her. *With you nearby, there's no safer spot on the trail.* What better place to hide than with people who feared and hated Indians? People led by a war hero famous for his combat skills. Paden wasn't a man who'd hand her over to a despised enemy without a fight. But such a battle would result in much bloodshed.

The memory of Laughing Eyes' blood splattering her face surfaced as swiftly as her sister's life had ebbed. Hannah struggled to breathe, to push that horror back into the corner of her heart where it always lurked. This time it wouldn't go. Eagle Feather had every right to blame her for the white trappers killing the two women they'd both loved. She'd rather die than witness his death as well.

The metallic scent choking her finally retreated. No one need die. Not if she did everything she could to stay away from Eagle Feather. They'd grown up together. He'd remember her fears, her reasons for distrusting her own kind. Surrounded by the people of her birth would be the last place he'd look for her.

She drew in a deep breath. No matter what these white strangers said, she must stay with them. She must hide in the shadow they'd created between her two worlds. The wagon master might be her salvation or her demise. There probably wasn't a shadow big enough to conceal Paden and his past. What horrible tragedy had happened in San Antonio?

CHAPTER 4

Out of the corner of her eye, Hannah watched Paden ride toward her and Gabe.

He pulled his mount to a halt beside them. "Every evening we circle the wagons. I've seen both Indian and white men try to steal anything left untended, so anything worth keeping—belongings, livestock, whatever—had better stay inside. After dusk, the same goes for people." His gaze slid to her. "The middle of night isn't the time to leave." With a flick of his wrist, he reined his horse up the line, where he continued delivering his order.

The abruptness of his departure filled Hannah with an unexpected sense of loss. To distract herself, she kept busy helping Gabe assemble the wagons in the requested formation. When the task was complete, bubbly, carefree laughter snagged her attention. A group of chattering women stood nearby in the setting sun. They were gathering their clothing and preparing to head to a small creek to wash.

Another wave of loneliness invaded Hannah. She'd always enjoyed the companionship of the Osage women. They understood that a favorite ritual like bathing, or a backbreaking task like washing clothing, was best shared. The joy found in any kind of friendship had been denied to her for much too long. She grabbed her spare clothing and approached the women.

One by one they stopped talking to gape at her. A brittle silence filled the air.

Hannah reminded herself that she'd come out of hiding not only to break free of Eagle Feather's threat but to redeem herself. Part of that meant casting off her solitude. She pushed aside her doubts and took the final step. "I was wondering if—"

"Tell me she doesn't mean to join us," a young woman with mousy-brown hair whispered and grabbed the arm of the matron beside her.

The older woman drew the girl close against her ample form and glared at Hannah from narrowed eyes. "Of course she doesn't. It's out of the question. She lived with the savages. She isn't decent."

The last word came like a slap, quick and stinging. It rocked Hannah back on her heels.

"Then she's sealed her fate," declared a woman of similar age to the first. Her shining blond curls shook as she spoke, like an angel passing judgment. "She can't come with us to the creek."

"Thank heavens." The first girl waved her hand in front of her as if she'd come close to fainting.

A woman with bright red hair shoved through the women. Hands on hips, she inserted her petite frame between them and Hannah. "Of course she can. Where's your charity?"

"It doesn't extend to women like her," the matron shot back. "That's asking too much, Rebecca, and you know it."

"I know nothing of the sort. Who are we to make a decision better left in God's hands?" Rebecca challenged the women with an unrelenting stare. Gazes dropped, feet shuffled, but no one answered. "She's no different from us," Rebecca insisted.

The matron's gaze jerked up and narrowed again.

"Of course she is. Didn't your mother teach you anything?"

Hannah's defender blinked in surprise. "My mother—"

"Ran off with a snake oil salesman from St. Louis," the angelic-looking blonde burst out and then arched her brow. "Hasn't your poor father suffered enough? What would he say if he saw you talking to a woman even worse than your mother?"

Hannah's mouth dropped open. The women had turned on her one supporter. She tugged Rebecca's sleeve, trying to gain her attention. The arm under the yellow gingham remained stiff. "Miss, I don't want you getting in trouble because of me. It's best if I go back to my wagon."

The woman glanced at her with glittering golden-brown eyes. "No. It is definitely not best." She pressed her lips tight and turned back to the women. "This is about doing what's right. It has nothing to do with me, or my mother and father."

"We'll see about that," the blonde said. "Here he comes."

The women turned as one. A man with bushy red-brown hair advanced on them with a brisk pace, his ample belly leading the way, his arms pumping by his sides like pendulums. The man was Thomas Riley.

Disbelief trapped the air in her lungs. The kind woman who'd come to her defense was Riley's daughter?

"Rebecca!" he yelled. "What do you think yer doing?"

"I wanted to help this woman."

Riley grabbed his daughter's arm and jerked her away from Hannah. "I can't leave you alone for a moment without you doing something foolish." His gaze swung to Hannah, raking her with contempt before returning to his daughter. "How many times do I have to say it? Stay away from Indians. They're heathens."

Rebecca gasped, sounding mortified. "Father, please. She isn't an Indian and even if she was, we shouldn't turn our backs on her."

Riley shook her roughly, cutting off her words. "Yer embarrassing me," he hissed under his breath. "What do I have to do to make you listen?" His free hand had curled into a fist and was starting to rise.

Hannah held out her palms. "Please, Mr. Riley. Your daughter was just trying to help."

Riley turned his glare on her. "You dare to explain my daughter to me? You dare to even talk to me?"

Hannah stared at the sea of angry faces surrounding her and Rebecca. Their hostility and righteousness stole her breath. Rebecca opened her mouth as if unaware of her growing danger. Hannah shook her head and quickly backed away. Hugging her clothing against her aching chest, she trudged back to the scouts' wagon.

Worry squeezed her heart tighter. What if she continued failing to redeem herself? What if she couldn't make herself worthy of Morning Star and Laughing Eyes' sacrifice?

The days took on a routine. Hannah and the scouts rose with the sun. Paden's bedroll was always packed away when they did. Sometimes she caught a glimpse of him patrolling the wagon perimeter, rifle in hand, before the wagons headed out.

Gabe informed her that Paden had set a goal of fifteen miles per day. But no matter the distance covered, Paden always halted their march before the daylight disappeared. After listening to the information Alejandro and Virgil gathered, he selected camps that offered water, better grazing or some natural fortification to increase their safety. His protectiveness seemed to extend to the animals as well as his human charges.

Every evening inside the wall of wagons, they ate by firelight and curled up in their blankets, snug till dawn. All except the men who took a turn on a rotating night guard. And every morning, Paden gave Alejandro and Virgil their orders—one to scout the trail ahead, the other to guard the tail of the wagon train. To Hannah he said nothing. Not even to tell her to stay with Gabe and the scouts' wagon, as he'd done the first morning on the trail.

The pioneers were never friendly to Hannah, but as long as she had Gabe or General Sherwood by her side, they said nothing to her. She stayed close to the grandfather and grandson. She either rode by Gabe and the scouts' wagon or helped General Sherwood ride up and down the line keeping the wagons moving.

She also assisted the general with any Indians they encountered. She translated their words, and the general relayed the information to Paden, who always stood at a watchful distance, radiating a tension that made it hard to breathe. She never asked the general what Paden said in return. She wasn't sure she wanted to know what he thought about a people he'd previously hunted with a vengeance. But he'd told Riley that he'd only attacked war parties.

The Indians they now encountered weren't warriors but beggars who craved the white man's firewater. While they might provide an interesting distraction for the pioneers, some of whom had never seen an Indian before, they saddened Hannah's heart.

She prayed that her band hadn't succumbed to

such a state. For her adoptive family, the white man's ways and the reservation land allotted by him had held no appeal. They'd embraced the nomad's life. That was how they'd found Hannah and why she was familiar with this portion of the trail. While roaming with the Osage, she'd glimpsed it several times but always from a distance.

On the fifth day after leaving Fort Leavenworth, while they paused for the midday meal, a different band of Indians approached. Their eyes were curious, not greedy. They didn't rush the wagons with pleas spilling from their lips. Instead, they waited patiently for Hannah and the general to walk the final yards to greet them.

"We are heading to the northern hunting grounds in search of buffalo," their chief said in the language of the Delaware. "We wish to trade with those we meet along the way."

General Sherwood gave his permission and when the women brought out their trade goods, Hannah felt her lips part with surprise, then delight. From the softest leather they had sewn moccasins and shirts, taking great pains to decorate them with intricate designs fashioned from glass beads and colorful dyes. They bartered shrewdly with the pioneers. When the trading was finished, the Delaware women clustered around Hannah, admiring her belt and moccasins, asking how she'd made them. The pleasure of their company made Hannah buoyant with happiness.

One by one, as their curiosity was sated, they turned back to their ponies and packs, preparing to leave. But the eldest woman delayed and placed a hand on Hannah's arm. Her tiny frame, topped by an explosion of snowy hair, barely reached Hannah's chin. But her eyes were strong and clear as she raised her face of wrinkled walnut to study Hannah.

"May the Great Spirit watch over you and guide you on your journey," the old woman said in the Delaware language. "This land is steeped in sorrow. The wind blows turmoil through it once more." She pointed to the north. "Death has recently visited there again."

The horizon contained a series of hills with a familiar outline. A shudder of dread swept through Hannah, leaving her cold and trembling. This was where she'd last seen Morning Star and Laughing Eyes alive.

The old woman gestured from the north to the west. "I hope those troubles do not spill onto your path."

"What troubles? What death?" a deep voice demanded from behind Hannah.

With a gasp, she spun to find Paden standing so close that her fingers brushed his stomach. His breath hissed in his throat and his eyes glowed with a silver intensity.

"I'm sorry," she blurted. "That was clumsy of me." Why was he here? Why wasn't he waiting for her to talk to General Sherwood and receive his information in the usual way?

"I didn't mean to startle you." He released a slow breath as if trying to hold on to his patience. "Are you going to answer my questions?"

About death? No. Maybe she could avoid answering by asking a question of her own. "How do you know the Delaware language?"

"When I was a boy, there were Delaware living in east Texas. I learned a handful of their words, including the ones for 'death' and 'trouble.'" His gaze narrowed. "Tell me why I'm hearing those words now."

The old woman glanced between them. This time when she spoke she used halting English. "You know valley?"

Hannah knew it. Too well. *Please,* she prayed, *don't let either of them ask any more questions.*

Under a puckered brow, the matriarch's searching gaze held Hannah prisoner. Her snowy head tilted inquiringly as she whispered, "Blue Sky."

Hannah's heart seized with disbelief. Paden opened his mouth, but the old woman spoke first.

"Your eyes. Blue as sky. If not named Blue Sky, should be." Standing in Paden's shadow, the old woman appeared even smaller. Still, not a trace of fear showed in her posture or expression. "That valley…no one stay long, only pass through, go elsewhere. One moon ago, during spring snowstorm, Osage camp there. Attacked. All dead."

Hannah's stomach lurched. An entire band of Osage killed? Which one? Hers? Was that why this woman knew her name?

As if sensing Hannah's turmoil, the woman sighed and shook her head. Voices called out. Her own tribe was leaving and beckoned for her to follow. "I've told you everything I know," she said, speaking rapidly in her own language as she shuffled away. "You must find your answers on your own."

Hannah kept her gaze on the Delaware as they departed. She felt Paden watching her instead of them. Even when the band had become a speck on the horizon, she continued staring after them, anything to avoid looking at Paden. *Please, let his silence continue. Please, no more questions.*

"Hannah." He'd said her name in a low voice that brooked no refusal. "Get your horse. This afternoon you ride out with me."

CHAPTER 5

Hannah had been riding for half an hour—Paden by her side, Alejandro and Virgil behind them—when she came to the base of the familiar ridge. She brought White Cloud to an abrupt halt. The three men reined in their horses and formed a half circle around her as they scanned the hills. The terrain appeared no different than the land they'd already traversed. The wind sighed, rustling the grass, while bees droned nearby. Everything appeared ordinary, peaceful.

There was no peace inside Hannah. Whatever calm she'd gained in the last few days had vanished like smoke in the wind. Gritting her teeth, she pointed ahead. "The valley's on the other side. I won't go any farther."

Paden raised an arched brow. "Why?"

"Because it's as the old woman said, a place of bad spirits and continued suffering. My tribe used to pick fruit there, but then—" She stared at the ground. Morning Star and Laughing Eyes had died in that valley trying to save her from her own kind. "It isn't close enough to the wagon trail to pose a threat to the emigrants," she whispered. "So why go there?"

A long moment stretched out before Paden

spoke. "Virgil. Alejandro. Return to the wagons. You've helped me bring Hannah this far. Now we must continue alone."

Hannah's head came up with a start. Before she could object, the scouts had departed and Paden was riding toward the valley.

She dug her heels into White Cloud's flanks, propelling him in front of Paden's stallion, blocking his path. "No!"

Paden's eyes narrowed. "Tell me why you're afraid."

"I won't let you hurt them."

"Who?"

It was on her lips to say *my tribe*. Keeping the past separate from present had become difficult. Paden's war hadn't been against the Osage. They hadn't done anything to hurt him. But did Paden believe what Riley had said? That the only good Indian was a dead one?

Paden continued staring at her, demanding her answer.

She pressed her palm against her racing heart, striving for the strength to say anything. "I'm worried about whoever's in the valley," she blurted.

"You think I'd hurt them?" Paden clamped his lips tight and a muscle bunched in his jaw. "Riley's a flannel-mouthed blowhard. He doesn't know me. Neither do you."

"Are you now saying you didn't kill those men in Texas?"

His scowl returned. The scowl he'd given Riley and Dawson, but never her. Not until now. Her regret only fueled her anxiety.

"Oh, I killed them," Paden ground out. "But I'm not going on another rampage, if that's what's worrying you. I only want to know why you're so afraid of that valley."

One truth usually led to another. Even if she pushed aside her shame, could she tell Paden and still keep the white men Eagle Feather had killed a secret? She shook her head.

"Yes, I know," he said. "You don't trust me. So I'm resorting to the only option you've left me. I'm going to see that valley for myself, and you're coming with me." He leaned forward until his nose almost touched hers. "But know this, if I have to kill someone to keep you safe, I will."

He rode halfway up the ridge before dismounting. She followed him reluctantly and even more reluctantly left White Cloud behind with Paden's horse. Creeping along half-crouched and then crawling on their elbows and knees, they finally peered over the ridge. Hannah's stomach knotted as she held her breath.

The earth spiraled down in waves of gold and green grass, forming an oval bowl cut in half by a winding stream. Empty. No one was here. The sigh of relief caught in her throat as her gaze kept traveling and halted on the opposite slope.

"Do you recognize them?" Paden asked.

She stiffened, wishing she could avoid answering. They couldn't be her tribe. Or could they? She had to know. She leaned closer. The men wore breechcloths and leather leggings, while the women dressed in deerskin skirts and poncho-like blouses. Some of the rigidity left her body. The designs painted on the flanks of their ponies made her release a pent-up breath.

"Pawnee," she said on the tail end of that exhale. "The Osage traded with them, mostly on good terms."

Her gaze skimmed the valley, searching for more people. The chokecherry bushes still flourished in the same spot. She'd been with the women of her band picking fruit when the white trappers had tried to take her. The recollection of their hands on her wrist, rough and bruising, made her jerk back.

Paden reached out to halt her. "Stay low. We don't want them to get a glimpse of your hair."

"It's not my fault how I look." Her words were as brittle and old as if she were hearing herself say them two years ago.

A frown creased Paden brow. "Who said it was?"

Eagle Feather had. But she wanted to run from that memory as well. She wanted to get out of here, down the hill, far away. Scooting back, she scrambled to her knees.

Paden's hand clamped tight around her wrist. He pulled her down, but not before he'd put himself between her and the top of ridge, like a shield. "Hannah, calm down. I don't want to hurt you."

"Then let me go!"

He released her at the same moment she tried to jerk free. She fell on her backside. Then she toppled backward and rolled heels-over-head down the hill toward their horses. Hard. Fast. Unstoppable.

Behind her, rocks scraped and scattered. Footsteps pounded after her. Something brushed her cheek, soft as buckskin, diving over her. Then she slammed to a halt atop a muscular chest encased in a leather jacket. A grunt reverberated in her ear. Thickly corded arms enveloped her, holding her secure.

Paden's face, an inch beneath hers, was set in rigid lines. His chest rose and fell in time with hers as they both struggled to regain their breath. His gray eyes pierced her, sharp as steel, probing, questioning.

She squeezed her eyes shut.

His hold loosened. His arms cradled her as if she were made of glass. "Are you injured?"

"How was I supposed to know they'd follow us here?" she whispered.

"Hannah, you're not making sense. The Pawnee in the valley aren't following us. They didn't see us."

"No. The white trappers." She waited for the panic to overwhelm her again, but all she felt was Paden's solid form under her and his hands rubbing soothing circles across her back. How could a man so big, so tormented by a violent past, have such gentle hands?

"What white trappers? Are you running from them as well as that Osage man Dawson mentioned? Tell me so I can help."

"It's better if you don't know." *Better for me and for you.* The trappers were dead. Eagle Feather had seen to that. Paden had made war on Indians who killed whites. She didn't think she could bear it if he killed Eagle Feather. If Morning Star's last remaining blood relative died because of her, she'd be beyond all redemption. She'd deserve to burn in hell forever.

"Hannah." Paden voice had gone low and soothing. "If I'm going to have any chance of keeping you safe, you have to trust me."

She shook her head again. She couldn't trust the security she felt in his arms. "We should get back to the wagons." She pushed up on her elbows, preparing to scramble off him.

His body stiffened beneath her, muscles flexing, rippling. His barely restrained strength made her tense as well. What could she say to make him understand that leaving this hillside was their best option?

"Every mile we travel west is a mile closer to safety." She shimmied sideways, intent on sliding off him.

A groan rumbled deep in his chest. "Hannah. Stop squirming." His eyes had darkened the deep gray of ash over banked coals. The heat from his eyes was already aflame in his flesh. His body scorched her where her thigh slid over the bulge at his groin.

She froze but her gaze searched his face. When he wasn't scowling, he was a very handsome man. His high cheekbones and dark hair seemed as familiar as his scent of sweet sage. Suddenly she didn't want to go anywhere. Lying atop him, a strong sense of rightness pushed aside her doubts.

Tell me you feel the same, that I have a home in your arms. She watched his lips, breathless for his answer. *Don't push me away. Don't say—*

"This is wrong."

Wrong. The word stabbed her like a thorn, making her flinch. A shudder ripped through him in response. Then he set her carefully on the ground beside him. As soon as his hands released her, he spun to sit cross-legged with his back to her. "Coming here was a mistake," he growled.

"You're right. I shouldn't be here." But she didn't mean on this hillside or even on the wagon train. She couldn't be with him. And wishing otherwise would only lead to heartache.

"You haven't touched your supper, Hannah." Gabe's young voice was pitched high with concern. "Are you all right?"

Slouching against his saddle on the ground, Paden stared over the campfire at Hannah. Her gaze remained fixed on her dinner plate. General Sherwood sat to his right, studying a map of the trail. Virgil and Alejandro sat to his left, exchanging hurried glances. The two scouts must've informed

Gabe about their ride out to the valley, since Hannah
hadn't uttered a word since their return. Now, they
all sat around their camp finishing the evening meal,
and Gabe had asked the question Paden dreaded the
answer to.

How badly had he hurt Hannah when he'd jerked
her to the ground? How badly had he offended her
when his bloody erection had made it obvious that
he wanted to do more than keep her safe?

Hellfire and brimstone. The cat, or rather the
beast, was out of the bag now. A beast that
continued burning inside him, desperate to hold her
again.

Virgil rose and stretched awkwardly. "I'm beat.
I'd best be off. I wanna sneak in a little shuteye
before my turn on night watch."

Alejandro stood as well. "I think I might go visit
Miss Riley."

Paden grimaced, remembering the insufferable
Mr. Riley and the man's insistence on bringing up
his past. But others had it worse. The challenge of
having Riley for a father must be a heavy burden for
his daughter.

"The pretty redhead?" Virgil slapped Alejandro
on the back. "The one you mentioned helping
yesterday? Have you warmed to her father as well?
Or is he still a horse's ass?"

"He remains the same." A blush stained
Alejandro's face. "But she is not like her father."

Hannah's gaze remained on the untouched dinner
plate balanced on her lap. She needed to eat. When
he'd pulled her to the ground, her wrist had felt as
fragile as a china teacup in his hand. But the curve of
her breast and hips pressed snug against him
conjured only one word. Perfection.

Virgil's chuckle wrenched him from his
daydream of touching all of Hannah. "What does

Riley say about you visiting his daughter?"

"He would not approve…if he knew," Alejandro muttered. "But he leaves her on her own too much, and she could use a friend."

"A friend?" Virgil shook his finger at Alejandro. "Love can sneak up on a man. Don't you try denying it."

"I have only known her a day."

Virgil heaved a sigh. "Young fools never listen to good advice. Well, you'd better get going. There's only so much visiting you can do in one evening. Time's a-wasting."

Paden watched the two men leave. Love was for fools. It didn't last. It couldn't. It either faded slowly or died violently. In his case, both had happened. And all he had left was a hole in his soul that would never heal.

"Hannah?" Gabe's voice had risen to a squeak.

She wasn't looking at her plate anymore. She was staring back the way the wagons had come, but also slightly toward the north and the valley.

"Before you joined us—" A frown pinched Gabe's brow as he glanced from Hannah to where she stared and back to her again. "What was your life like with the Indians?"

Her gaze jerked 'round, flying to Gabe before just as swiftly dropping to her plate. "I was happy for many years."

Disbelief made Paden's thoughts spin. How could she have been happy?

Gabe's frown deepened. "Then why leave them?"

"I was told to go."

Paden hadn't expected her to say that either. She sounded like she hadn't wanted to leave.

Gabe's eyes, wide and searching, resembled an owl's. "Do you…want to return to them?"

Paden sat upright. *Return to them?* The

possibility hadn't even crossed his mind. He didn't like the thought one bit. He couldn't protect her if she left him. Left the wagon train, he corrected. He needed to gain her trust.

He'd been angry when she'd feared he'd harm the Indians in the valley. Although, considering his background, it was a logical assumption. Anyone else would have thought the same. But he didn't care what anyone else thought. He cared what *she* thought. Why did it matter so much what this wisp of a woman believed?

She lifted her hand to stare at her palm again. This time he made out a dark oval with lines radiating out of it. She glanced up and their gazes locked. She quickly looked away, tugging her cuffs down over her hands and fidgeting with the frayed edges. Another puzzling habit he'd observed her do many times.

"Those people in the valley weren't from my tribe." Her voice was flat. "Even if they were, there's no place for me with them anymore." She carefully set her plate on the ground and walked away, heading across the center of the circled wagons with her arms wrapped around her waist.

Gabe stared after her. "I shouldn't have said anything. I didn't mean to pry." His Adam's apple bobbed. He jumped up and nearly tripped over his own feet as he stumbled after her. "I should apologize."

Sherwood raised his hand. "Give her some space."

Gabe nodded, but his furrowed brow contradicted his agreement as to whether that was the best decision. Finally, he heaved a huge sigh of resignation. "I'll go check on the wagons for the night." He shuffled off in the opposite direction Hannah had taken.

"And you..." Sherwood gave him a thorough appraisal, suggesting to Paden that he wasn't going to like what came next. "Sooner or later you'll have to start treating her like a scout. That means letting her ride out on her own, or with Alejandro or Virgil. People are beginning to talk. They're wondering why you took on a scout who doesn't scout. They're wondering if maybe you brought her along to warm your bedroll."

Outrage curled Paden's fingers into fists. "Tell me who's doing the talking."

"She's already seen as an outcast. Do you wish to add to that?" Sherwood stared at the fire. "Are you worried she's not up to the task of being a scout?"

Paden scoffed at the absurdity. "Absolutely not. She's a better scout than I could've ever hoped for. She's as good as Virgil or Alejandro." His shoulders slumped as his anger left him. "Hell, she's better."

"I thought so. She is a remarkable young woman." Sherwood reached over and clasped Paden's shoulder. "Son..." Paden's breath left him in a hiss. "I'll say this as many times as I have to. She's not Jeannie. A decade has past. Isn't it time you let Jeannie go? Time you forgave her and yourself?"

Silence filled the gap between them. Silence broken only by Paden's breathing. The rasping sound coming from him sounded like a dying animal.

"It wasn't your fault," Sherwood finally said. "You wouldn't listen to me then, but I hope you will now."

Paden tried to stand, but the general held him in a surprisingly strong grip.

"No. Hear me out. I was never happier than the day Jeannie chose you as her husband and made you my son in name, as well as in my heart. God graced me with two beautiful daughters, and I loved them both dearly. But Jeannie was always frail, and I worried she wouldn't be with us long. That's why I agreed to you marrying so young. But later I wondered if you only married to please me. Whatever the case, you need to let her go, son. You need to start living again."

"Living?" Paden eyed him tiredly. His life was a solitary one. He'd made it that way. He'd lived for his work, for his sawmill in Oregon, for the business he was building. How could something that once seemed so important suddenly feel so pointless?

Sherwood released his shoulder. "Now *you'd* better go after Hannah and make sure she's all right."

Paden's heart missed a beat. "She knows not to leave the wagons when it's getting dark." Despite his words, he was already on his feet. He glanced at the sky. Towering clouds rolled closer. "Or when there's a storm coming."

"With the look in her eyes when she left, I'd say she rather be out in a torrential downpour than stay near us tonight."

Paden's running strides couldn't take him fast enough in the direction he'd seen Hannah go. The gloom gathering outside the circle of wagons forced him to squint. He circled the perimeter of the camp, scanning the grass. When he spotted a trail, he dropped on one knee beside it with a prayer on his lips. Small moccasin-clad feet had bent, but hadn't crushed, the green blades.

He tracked her prints across the open plain until they brought him to a stand of trees. With a curse, he plunged into their leafy shadows. The distant light of the campfires vanished.

In the darkness, he had to rely on his other senses. The earth was uneven beneath his feet, requiring him to place each step with precision. He strained for some sight or sound that might alert him to Hannah's whereabouts, but the wind picked up and the trees swayed and creaked, their leaves rustling. Shadows played tricks on his eyes, appearing and disappearing as the clouds danced across what little light remained in the sky above.

He was forced to pause with increasing regularity until his progress dwindled to a crawl and his temper flared in frustration.

What if he'd lost her? He wasn't going back without her.

A tall granite outcrop blocked his path, and he veered to the right. Not much farther on, he came to a halt by a narrow stream. Had she crossed it?

Suddenly the hair on the back of his neck stood on end. He wasn't alone.

He froze, dead still, only his eyes scanning the forest around him. Something was out there. He heard a small sound. Then another. Like a whisper.

He would have missed her if not for the murmur of her breathing. She was sitting with her back against a tree trunk, her legs tucked up close to her chest. Her forehead rested on her knees, blocking out the world, making her oblivious to its dangers. He'd only meant to come out here and bring her back to safety, but at her carelessness, his anger boiled over.

"Hannah." Too late he realized he'd practically barked her name. He struggled for a gentler tone. "You need to come back to the wagons. You don't want to be out here alone."

She scrambled to her feet. "I do so." When he made no move to leave, she turned her back on him, as if banishing him from her sight would gain her wish.

He took a step toward her. "No. You don't. You may not want to be near me, but you don't want to be alone. You said you were happy with the Osage."

Spinning around, she glared at him. "And am I damned for that? Does it make me a savage as well?"

"No. I only mentioned it because I want to understand." *I want to learn how to make you happy.* He also wanted to drag her into his arms and kiss her senseless.

Even in the shelter of the trees, the wind had picked up enough to sweep her hair out behind her like a golden flag that needed to be captured. Had the white trappers she'd mentioned felt the same? Had they hurt her? The urge to protect her brought him closer.

"Wait." She raised her hands between them.

He strained to see the mark on her palm, but the night was too dark.

"Don't come any closer." She buried her face in her hands, muffling her voice. "I want you to go—"

He strode a step closer.

"—a—"

And then another.

"—way!"

He took the final step and they stood toe to toe. *Don't touch her,* he warned himself. But he couldn't stop himself from leaning in as far as he could to better inhale her scent. Fresh as a leaf, Sweet as a flower. He held on to that breath, then reluctantly let it go.

She must have felt it brush the top of her bowed head, because she raised her face to stare up at him. "You said this was wrong."

The darkness hid even the color of her eyes. He was blind, but he wasn't deaf. He finally recognized the hurt in her voice. It rang as clear as a warning bell in the fog. "What did I say was wrong?"

"Lying together on the hillside."

The night, the forest, the entire world faded. She wanted him as well? Every nerve in his body sparked and blood surged into his groin. He lowered his head to hers. Their lips brushed and her mouth opened. He deepened the kiss. So warm, so sweet, like a plum ripe with the heat of the sun. Heaven help him but he wanted to taste all of her.

A pinprick struck his shoulder, then another. Soon a barrage of pellets pummeled his back. He lifted his head. It was raining like the devil. Hannah edged closer to him. Was she trying to find cover in the lee of his tall frame?

Selfish bastard. He'd taken advantage of her in a storm, far from any shelter or safety. She laid her palm, the one with the mysterious mark, over his heart and leaned against him. The reverence she instilled into the simple act robbed him of coherent thought. Suddenly, a shiver racked her, shaking him as well. His coat was plastered against his spine like a cold dead weight. Hers must feel the same.

With a grimace, he grabbed her hand and pulled her through the trees, heading back the way he'd come. Her small hand held him tight as she followed him. He glanced back. She had her head lowered against the rain, trusting him to lead the way. A corner of his heart pinched at her faith. He needed to find her shelter. Quick. The rain had now turned to hail, each drop stabbing like a miniature dagger.

The rocky outcrop he'd been searching for loomed up in front of him. Skidding to a halt, he drew Hannah snug against the wall. At least it offered protection from one side. She immediately tucked herself under his hunched shoulders and once again pressed her palm to his heart. Sweet heaven, but he yearned to wrap his arms around her and never let go.

Lightning illuminated the darkness above.

Glancing up, he glimpsed a black crevice in the gray rock. Then all went dark again. The crack of thunder jolted him into action. He scooped Hannah up in his arms, lifted her high, set her on the ledge and—employing every ounce of his willpower—let her go.

Set free, she rolled onto her side, then flat on her belly to stare down at him. Not just a ledge then but a hole too, and deep enough to hold her height. Could it hold him as well?

Grasping the rock, he pulled himself up to look. It was too dark to see far, but it didn't matter how deep the hole was because it wasn't wide enough for him and Hannah to fit inside together. Outside the wind howled, continuing to beat the storm's anger against his swiftly numbing back. He probably had just enough feeling left in his fingers to lower himself to the ground.

She grabbed his hand, halting him. "Where are you going?"

"I'll have to wait outside until the storm breaks. There isn't room for both of us in here."

"Then we'll make room." She rolled onto her hip with her back turned to one wall of the hole. She'd created a space for him on the other side. She wanted him to lie down next to her as if they were sharing a bed?

With the rain soaking him to the skin, it was ironic that his mouth felt so dry. "Are you sure about this?"

She nodded. "Don't leave me."

CHAPTER 6

Paden's indecision made Hannah's heart thump wildly against her ribcage. Why was he hovering in the mouth of the cave? Why wouldn't he come inside with her? One of his hands released the ledge. Spirits Above, he really was going to abandon her to stay alone in this cave.

He reached up and grabbed hold of the low rock ceiling above him. His other hand followed. Hanging by his fingertips, he pulled his knees up to his chest and in one fluid motion inserted his body feet first into the empty space to lie on his side facing her. It happened as quickly as it took for her to inhale one astonished breath.

His strength made her once again feel small and weak. Like a moth that'd flown blindly into Grandfather Spider's web. Or a child who'd crawled under a bush bristling with razor-sharp thorns.

The ceiling pressed down, the walls in. The air went out of the cave, out of her lungs. She couldn't breathe. A shudder racked her body.

"You're freezing." The low rumble of Paden's voice reverberated off the walls.

It was true. Her teeth were chattering to prove it. She'd rather he believed her cold than weak. She couldn't show him her weakness again. Not twice in one day. The valley. Morning Star. Laughing Eyes. Hot tears of shame and remorse trickled from the corner of her eyes, down her cheeks to disappear in her cold, wet hair. Another tremor shook her.

"Give me your hands," Paden growled. "I'll warm them for you." His big, work-callused palms enveloped hers. He rubbed, chafing them gently, then lifted her hands to his mouth and blew his warm breath on her icy skin.

His breath tickled her palm, the one with her spider tattoo. The one she'd started turning to in her bleakest moments to gain strength. But Grandfather Spider and his message to be patient hadn't helped.

Paden pressed a kiss to her palm and held it there. Heat surged through her veins. On the hillside, he'd filled her with the same warmth. *This can't last,* a corner of her heart whispered. But she needed the immediate distraction from her surroundings. She craved his warmth, the strange feeling of rightness she felt in his presence, the strength she gained when she touched him.

No matter what came afterward, she needed that strength now.

This time, instead of pressing her hand to his heart, she drew his hand to her chest and laid his palm over her own heart, and the second tattoo hidden there.

He jerked in surprise and his hand slid down to her breast. She started in return, but neither of them pulled away. The only sound was the rasping of her breath in unison with his. She could breathe again. His fingers curled around the curve of her breast and his thumb slowly began to move. Through the wet wool of her coat, he traced circles, spiraling ever closer until his thumb rubbed her into a tight little bud.

With a groan, he lowered his head to hers. His

lips brushed her mouth, feathery soft before skimming across her cheek. He went dead still. Then he jerked his hand away from her. "Hannah, why are you crying?"

A gasp of denial burst from her mouth. Knowing it was too late to hide her tears from him, she still shoved both palms against his chest. Her arms arced outward as she pushed away from him. Pain sliced the back of her hand. She cried out. The cave. The ceiling. Paden's touch had given her what she wanted. She'd forgotten where she was.

Paden grabbed her wrist and yanked her hand safely away from the rocks. He cursed under his breath. "How bad is it?"

When she didn't answer, his fingers brushed the back of her hand. Her breath hissed through her teeth.

"You're bleeding!" He released her and unbuttoned his coat. Cloth rustled. Spirits Above, had he pulled his shirttail from his trousers? The ripping of cloth followed. Then his hand clamped around her wrist again. Holding her still, he wrapped a strip of cloth, slightly damp from the rain and very warm with the heat of his belly, around her hand.

When he was done, she tried to pull her hand free again. He held her arm between them, almost like a barrier. He also kept it low, near the floor of the cave and away from the ceiling.

"Hannah…" He heaved a sigh. "Pull all you like. I'm not letting go this time."

Dawson sat hunched under the narrow overhang of his makeshift tent, watching the rain pummel the wagon train and shroud its inhabitants from view. His two friends lay beside him, doing what they usually did when they had time to burn: one stroked his knife, the other slept.

The more bloodthirsty of the pair finally spoke over the other one's snores. "Now'd be a good time to get her."

Dawson yearned to do just that, to sneak up on the wagons undercover of the storm and snatch Callahan's squaw right out from under the arrogant bastard's nose. But what if the rain slowed their escape and Callahan found them before he was done breaking the wagon master's precious new scout?

He needed time to grind her spirit to dust. Doing so would crush Callahan as well. By all accounts, that was how the Texan had previously been brought low. The gossip about Callahan's murdered wife flickered thorough his mind. Dawson wouldn't kill his new woman, though. He'd leave her alive for Callahan to deal with. Then the pair would be forced to dwell on their downfall just like him.

He lifted his whiskey bottle to his lips and tried once more to drown the memory of competing against a woman and losing.

The snoring on the other side of the tent halted abruptly. His lethargic companion pushed up on his elbows and squinted at him with heavy-lidded eyes. "You still thinking 'bout going out in this pissin' downpour 'n stealing her for ransom?"

Dawson snorted. There'd be no ransom. But if the thought of receiving money kept the fool eager, then he wouldn't correct him. Instead, he downed another swig of whiskey. "We wait. I ain't done drinking."

The man arched one brow dubiously. "You look as full as tick."

"I plan to get even fuller. Tomorrow when the rain stops, we'll..." He waved his bottle at the wagons, casting about for the answer.

His blade-obsessed friend began throwing his

knife at the ground between his feet, retrieving it and casting it again. The routine never failed to make Dawson's blood race.

"Sooner or later," the man said, "he'll have to let her ride out alone. He can't always hover over her like he done today at that valley."

Dawson nodded. "When he lowers his guard, we'll take her."

Outside the cave, the night was hushed. The storm had passed. Paden had no reason to continue holding Hannah. He released her slowly, then forced himself to put even more distance between them. He swung out of their shelter and dropped to the ground. Hannah moved to follow but stopped when he reached up to help her down. She stared at the ledge beneath her knees.

If he didn't move, she couldn't ignore him. Half of him wanted to bullishly stay where he was, blocking her path until she spoke to him again. The other half wanted to climb back into the cave in the hopes that she'd put his hand on her again. Had she really done that? Or had he just grabbed her in his own mindless lust? Was that why she'd been crying?

His gaze fell to her bandaged hand. Anger made his blood pound. Anger aimed solely at himself. He'd wanted to protect her and instead he'd manhandled her and caused her injury. He raked his fingers through his wet hair.

"Hannah, listen, I never wanted to overstep the boundaries of our relationship. I let you join the wagon train under the impression that you'd be a scout. I shouldn't be taking liberties. I shouldn't have touched you." He was doing exactly what the gossips on the wagon train said he was doing. He was taking advantage of a woman who was alone and vulnerable. "That's the last thing I wanted to do with someone..." *Someone who's become special to me.* "With someone like you."

She flinched but kept her gaze fastened downward.

Hellfire, she looks like I struck her!

He searched for another way to reassure her. "I'd be a liar if I said I could control my body's reaction to you. But if it made you feel better, I could promise not to touch you again."

His flesh rebelled at the suggestion. So did his heart. It'd been a long time since he'd been this attracted to a woman. Damn, he wasn't sure if he'd ever been this smitten. He sure as hell wasn't certain how to proceed. He didn't want her to think that he was a heartless bastard.

Her gaze rose to meet his. The dark still hide the blue of her eyes, but it failed to conceal the glisten of her tears. He hadn't thought anyone could convey so much hurt in a single look, but somehow she succeeded.

Alejandro turned his horse east and urged the animal into a gallop, heading back toward the wagons. The warmth of the midday sun felt good on his chest. He missed the heat. The sun here wasn't as strong as in Texas or Mexico, but then again, it was still early in the season. He had to be patient. Every place was different, he reminded himself. And after the rainstorm last night, he was just glad to be dry again.

He'd been scouting the trail ahead of the wagons. Everything looked clear and trouble free. The only excitement had been a pair of sage hens flying out of the grass in front of his horse. But his hand had been fast and his aim true. The birds were now strung over his saddle horn. They would make a welcome feast. No pork and beans tonight.

His thoughts shifted to the end of the day when he could enjoy an hour relaxing by the scouts' campfire. But that wasn't where his thoughts stayed.

Miss Riley. Maybe he'd see her tonight. He'd intended to visit her last night, but Virgil's words had thrown him. Virgil and his talk about love.

He liked Miss Riley, but love? He loved women. He'd never loved one woman. He enjoyed flirting with them, being in their company. To him they were one of God's most intriguing creatures. Could a man love only one woman? He didn't know if such a thing was possible. It certainly hadn't happened to him.

So, instead of visiting Miss Riley last night, he'd wandered aimlessly, trying to sort through his conflicting emotions. Then the rain had struck, fast and hard, the hail forcing him to take shelter in the scouts' wagon. He'd spent most of the night thinking about Miss Riley, and his feelings weren't any clearer this morning.

Was she different? Or was he different because of her? The answer eluded him.

He needed to be patient, he reminded himself.

But Virgil's words kept running through his mind. *Love can sneak up on a man. Don't you try denying it.* Had he meant denying that love could come out of nowhere? Or had he meant that Alejandro shouldn't deny love from entering his heart? Damn Virgil and his interference.

He caught sight of the wagon train ahead. The settlers had stopped for the noon meal. Both human and beast were making the most of the break. Families sat together beside their wagons, eagerly munching on cold food rations. The rain made it too wet to build a fire.

Alejandro's gaze skimmed the line of white-crested wagons, searching—as had become his habit of late—until he saw the Riley wagon. A lone woman sat on a campstool, primly erect with flame-colored locks peeking from under her bonnet. Miss Riley's father liked the sound of his own voice, but he did not value his daughter as an audience. So, whenever he got the opportunity, he would abandon her to her own devices and seek out a willing listener at another wagon.

This was how Alejandro had first come to talk to her. He'd stopped to inquire about the absence of her father and ensure her wellbeing. It was not the reason he sought her out now. A powerful need to be near her gripped him.

Last night Virgil had also said, *Time's a wastin'*. Yes, why wait for tonight when he could talk to her now?

As he drew nearer, he noticed her shoulders and back weren't as straight as he first thought, and the corners of her mouth were turned down. But when she raised her head and saw him, a breathtaking smile lit her face. His heart skipped a beat. *Dios*, she was pretty. That she had smiled because she'd seen him made his heart race. He drew his horse to a halt beside her and dismounted.

"*Hola, señorita*. Is everything well with you?" He hoped the rush of words hadn't made him sound too eager.

"Very well, Mr. Ramirez. And you?" She spoke formally, as if she were discussing the weather with a maidenly aunt.

His elation evaporated like a rain drop on a hot skittle. "I am well."

"And the trail ahead?"

"*Si*, all is well there, too." He didn't know what else to say. He suddenly felt silly for seeking her out, for reacting to her smile like a lovesick schoolboy. He frowned at the ground.

"You look tired, Mr. Ramirez," she said in the same conversationally neutral tone. "We appreciate all the work you do for the wagon train. You're a very busy man, but you must remember to rest and take care of yourself."

If he looked tired, it was because he'd been awake all night thinking about her.

"I don't suppose you'd have time to...sit with me for awhile?" Her voice was different now, almost beseeching with equal parts hope and melancholy.

He lifted his gaze to meet hers. Her eyes were golden-brown, like warm honey. He stared at her, completely forgetting what she'd asked until her cheeks turned bright pink and she ducked her head.

A sudden euphoria brought him to one knee beside her. On impulse, he ran his finger down her nose. She looked up, eyes wide and uncertain, but she didn't pull away.

"Your nose is sunburned," he explained.

She covered her face with her hands. "I must look a fright."

He laughed, and she blushed even more. "I believe it would be impossible for you to look anything but lovely."

A frown marred her smooth brow. "You're teasing me."

"I have never been more serious in my admiration."

She dropped her clenched hands onto her lap. He took one of her small fists in his hand and slowly uncurled her fingers so her palm lay flat against his. Holding his breath, he waited for her to pull away, to rebuke him for his forwardness. But she did not. He stared at her pale, slender fingers, at the sharp contrast they made against his darker hand. Finally, he looked up.

"When I tease you, it is because I long for you to smile at me again."

Her lips parted as she drew in a startled breath. Then the corners of her mouth lifted ever so slightly, edging toward a smile.

"Rebecca! What're you doing?" a man hollered from behind him.

She jumped to her feet. Alejandro rose and turned to stand by her side.

Her father stomped toward them. Gone was the beaming man who'd fawned over Paden. Thomas Riley's glare was as hot as the blistering summer sun in the Rio Grande valley. Suddenly the Texas heat had lost its appeal.

"Haven't you got a lick of sense, girl?" Riley demanded, halting in front of his daughter.

"I was just asking Mr. Ramirez about the trail ahead."

"I forbid you to talk to him, to have anything to do with him."

"But Mr. Ramirez is a guardian of our wagons. He is hired to keep us safe. He—"

"He's a Mexican."

"Father!" she gasped.

Riley rounded on Alejandro and jabbed his finger at him. "You stay away from my daughter."

"Father, why must you say such things?" She looked from him to Alejandro and back again. Her smile was long gone. "I don't understand," she whispered.

Alejandro did. In Texas, many men similar to Thomas Riley had judged him. He had not cared until now.

Riley crossed his arms and delivered his verdict. "Yer not fit for the likes of my daughter."

Hannah rotated her wrist, frowning at the strip of homespun cotton wrapped around her hand. After helping settle the wagons for the evening, Paden had told General Sherwood that he needed to do something on the trail ahead and rode off. But part of him still clung to her. The hem of his shirt bound her wound, and the memory of last night held her thoughts. Her cheeks burned as she remembered what had happened in the cave. She shook her head, trying to expel the yearning from her body. It wouldn't go away.

She lowered her chin to her chest. Gazing down, she remembered the heat of his large hand on her breast, remembered his thumb teasing her. Her body responded again. It was as if he was still holding her, touching her, stroking her. Her skin tingled, while the rest of her thrummed with yearning.

She shook her head again. *He doesn't want me, not every part of me. So I shouldn't want him.*

She fidgeted with the edge of the bandage. It came loose and fell in a soft white puddle at her feet. The memories associated with it couldn't be as easily discarded. The cloth was a part of Paden. She scooped up the bandage and pressed it against her heart.

Her wound needed to be washed. So did the rest of her. There was a spring nearby. None of the women would go with her. Rebecca might, but she didn't want to get her in trouble again. She'd have to go alone.

Paden sat hunched by the scouts' campfire, scowling at his coffee cup. He'd just returned from racing up the trail so he could find an all-too-rare moment of seclusion and use his hand to ease his lust. He hadn't enjoyed it, and it hadn't helped much.

Now, every time he heard footsteps, he grew stiff and had to battle the urge to look up. He knew by their gait that the feet weren't Hannah's, but his craving to see her made it impossible to listen logically. Every waking minute had been the same since their encounter in the cave yesterday. Hell, if he were honest he'd acknowledge that he'd felt this way since he'd first seen her. He yearned to be near her.

Gabe's easy loping stride approached the fire. He sat down with a contented sigh.

Paden couldn't hold back any longer. "Where's Hannah?"

"At the spring, bathing." Gabe blushed. "Don't worry. We didn't let her go on her own."

Paden studied the settlers who'd long since returned to the wagons. They'd washed in shifts, first the women, then the men. "Which of the women went back with her?"

Gabe glared at the settlers. "None of them. They refused."

"What?" Paden snapped, sitting upright.

"She told us—me, Alejandro and Virgil—only a few minutes ago. But I knew before, because I overheard the women talking." His mouth pinched tight as if he'd bitten a lemon.

"Gabe," Paden said very slowly, trying to hold onto his patience, "tell me what you heard."

"They said that the dirt on Hannah was the kind that wouldn't wash off. They probably said worse to her face. But Hannah wouldn't tell us the details."

"Damn their sanctimonious hides," Paden hissed. Then he jumped to his feet. "Who's she with?"

"Alejandro and Virgil, of course."

Paden hand's tightened around his coffee cup.

"They're bathing with her?" His anger swelled until he felt ready to explode.

For the first time, Paden felt the weight of the young man's scowl. "Of course not," Gabe shot back. "They're keeping a watch out so she's not disturbed. Would you rather she was out there alone?"

Paden's mind spun. The women wouldn't bathe with her because— Hannah had to turn to Alejandro and Virgil because— General Sherwood's words, so very similar to his grandson's a moment ago, came back to him. *She's already seen as an outcast. Do you wish to add to that?*

He'd told himself that all he wanted was to protect Hannah. Now he knew he wanted more. She'd always be shunned by the majority of the white world. He couldn't change what others thought or did. He could only change what he did. He strode toward the spring.

Standing hidden beneath the limestone shelf projecting over the basin, Hannah let the cold water cascade over her naked body and shivered with delight. "This is heaven."

"Did you say something, miss?" Virgil called from above. "Is everything all right?"

Laughter tumbled from her lips as she tracked the trickling waterfall up to the ledge just out of reach above her. "Everything's wonderful."

Virgil's answering chuckle drifted down to her.

The rains had cleared and as the sun descended the rosy sky above the alcove was being overtaken by a deep magenta. Her smile faded. "It's getting late. I'm sorry I'm such a bother." She raised her voice as she sloshed the few steps through the pool to reach the bank where she'd left her clothing. She shivered again. "If it weren't for me, you could be back with the wagons, warming yourselves by the fire."

"Don't you worry 'bout us," Virgil replied without pause. "It's our pleasure helping you."

Alejandro's muffled voice floated over the ledge. "You should have told us about the women's refusal sooner. Who do they think they are anyway?"

A different chill invaded her as she remembered the women's harsh words and glares. Grabbing her blanket, she dried herself briskly. With the warmth came another memory. "Not all of them were unkind. Rebecca tried to defend me."

"She did?" Alejandro's voice held a note of surprise.

"Yes, but unfortunately her father came along. She got in trouble for helping me."

Alejandro muttered a string of Spanish words. Hannah's smile returned. One day she'd have to ask him to teach her his language.

The women's rejection had hurt, but she'd kept silent about it too long. She hadn't wanted the few friends she hoped she might be making to pity her. But when put to the test, they'd rallied around her. Just like Morning Star had, but then, Morning Star had found her in a much bleaker state than she was in now.

Usually she avoided her scars, kept them covered, tried not to touch them. Wrapping her blanket around her chest, she forced herself to look at them now. A dozen short ridges of puckered flesh marked her arms between her wrists and shoulders. She couldn't see her back, but she suspected similar scars were there as well. The thorns of the bramble bushes she'd crawled under had been sharp and painful, but the rejections heaped upon her by the pioneers, by Paden, had cut deeper.

Her gaze wandered to the fresh injury on the back of her hand. The wound wasn't deep and wouldn't leave a scar. But the rest of what happened in the cave might. Would the heat of Paden's touch be burned into her thoughts forever?

Stop thinking about him, she told herself.

She tried to focus on the beauty around her. Alcove Spring. When they'd arrived, Alejandro had read the name from a stone marker with carved letters. The waterfall, the product of snow runoff and a wet-weather creek, tumbled into a basin of polished river stones to join the waters of the spring, cold and pure as if instantly melted from ice.

Standing here surrounded by such a marvel of nature, the dust and grime of the trail and the condemning eyes of the pioneers seemed very far away. She tilted back her head and combed her fingers through the wet strands of her hair in an attempt to smooth the tangles. Stars peeked from the darkening indigo vault high above. She wished she could stay a little longer, but she should get dressed and leave so Virgil and Alejandro didn't have to sit in the growing darkness, twiddling their thumbs and playing nursemaid.

She sighed and called up to the ledge, "Thank you for staying with me, but we should get back. Gabe will wonder why we've been gone so long. I'm done. I'll be up in a moment."

"Don't rush," a deep voice drawled from above. "You won't see a spring as fine as this for a long time."

Surprise loosened her grip on her blanket. She scrambled to pull it snug around her again.

"Paden," Virgil said. "Didn't hear you come up. Everything all right with the wagons?"

"Just fine. You and Alejandro can head back now. I'll make sure Hannah returns safely."

Nerves taut, she strained to hear more in the silence that followed the scouts' retreating footsteps. Why was Paden here? He hadn't said anything to her since they'd returned from the cave. She knew she'd been foolhardy to leave the safety of the wagons that evening, but she'd never imagined he'd come after her with such tenderness and then passion. She'd expected disdain, not desire.

Worse was her reaction to him, her continued reaction, for she couldn't stop thinking about him...or his promise that despite everything that had passed between them, he should not touch her again. It was cruel to be given such a brief glimpse of a joy that could never be.

Something—a foot, maybe?—scraped the rock above her.

She groped in the growing darkness for her clothes. Where were they? They'd been here a moment ago. She pivoted in a circle, frantically searching the bank around her.

"Hannah?"

Her hands stalled in their quest, while her gaze shot up to the ledge above her. It remained empty, but Paden's voice had sounded closer than before.

She inhaled slowly, trying to calm her nerves. "I'm still here."

"I haven't seen the spring since last year. I'm coming down."

Coming down? Down here? With me? She opened her mouth to stop him, but at the same time her fingers brushed cloth. Dropping the blanket, she jerked her shirt over her head, letting it fall down to her hips. Far too big, the garment hung to her knees, her hands nearly disappearing beneath the sleeves.

Her fingers were fumbling with the laces at its neckline when river stones crunched behind her. She whirled around, her hair arcing behind her then catching up to slap wetly around her shoulders and chest. Water dripped, soaking the fabric, pressing it against her.

Paden stood beside her on the bank. "Heaven have mercy," he rasped. "Why didn't you tell me you weren't dressed?"

She curled her fingers into her cuffs, pulling her sleeves over her knuckles. "Why didn't you wait above?"

"You said you were done."

"I also said I'd be up in a moment."

His gaze dropped to her bare feet, then traveled up her legs. Heat flooded her face. She'd been so intent on hiding her scars she'd completely forgotten about the lack of clothing on her lower half.

"Where are your trousers?" he asked in a gruff voice.

"I was searching for them when you interrupted."

With a groan, his gaze skimmed the bank. He scrubbed his hand over the back of his neck. "Where did you last see them?"

She swayed toward him. Then drew back, making sure to keep her sleeves anchored over her hands. Why was it always like this? This desire to be near him?

His gaze snapped to hers. "Hannah, your trousers? Where are they? I need to get you clothed."

She gestured to the bank around them. "They're here somewhere."

Squatting on his heels, he began searching. A moment later, he rose with the garment in question in his grasp. He turned his back and he held her pants out behind him. With suddenly clumsy fingers, she donned the garment as quickly as she could.

"Ready?" he called over his shoulder. Impatience turned his voice gruff.

"Yes, you can turn around now."

His gaze ran the length of her, from her wet hair to her bare toes. He grunted. "Your feet must be ice cold." He hunkered down and searched the bank again.

This time she bent to help him.

"Found one," they both said in unison as they turned to face each other holding a moccasin.

He crouched beside her in the rising moonlight. Not even the shadows could dull his sharp perusal or the rising agitation in his entire frame. A muscle bunched in his jaw. "Hannah, what exactly did the women say to you?"

"Oh. You heard about that." Unable to hold his gaze, she stared at his hands. "Well, you'd probably know better than anyone what people might say about…someone who…someone like me."

His grip on her moccasin tightened. "A woman who lived with Indians? A woman who's now on her own?"

She nodded, not trusting herself to speak.

"Yes, I can imagine what they might say."

She cleared her throat, eager to change the subject. "They might also wonder why a scout doesn't go out and scout, like Alejandro and Virgil." She knew she was stretching, and "they" might be just her. Was Paden ever going to let her do the job she'd earned?

A frown pinched his brow. "What's this?" He gestured toward the skin above her heart, visible where her collar hung open.

She raised her hand to pull the fabric together. Midway to their destinations, their fingers brushed. With a start, she turned her palm to face him, fingers splayed wide.

His frown deepened. Grasping her hand, he pulled it toward him. "And this?"

"It's one of the symbols of my people."

He ran his thumb across her palm, sending a delicious shiver up her spine.

"A tattoo is a mark of honor among the Osage." She swallowed hard, trying to clear the huskiness in her voice. "A reward for bravery in warriors and their families."

"A spider is brave?" His brows arched as he traced with a slow precision the legs of the spider spanning her palm.

Her heartbeat had accelerated to a full-out gallop. "It's a mark of strength."

As if hearing its pounding, his gaze shifted to the web, the size of an apple, tattooed over her heart. "Something so small, so fragile?"

She couldn't help but smile. The act made it easier to speak. "That's what the Osage thought as well, back when the earth was young and they searched for a symbol to give them strength. But Grandfather Spider said, 'Look closer. While I spin the web that forms my life, I watch and I wait. I am patient. All things come to me when the time is right.'"

Still crouching beside her, his gaze probed hers with an unreadable expression. The heat of his hand enveloped hers, holding her carefully, tenderly. His thumb continued tracing circles over her palm. Last time, he'd done that to her breast before he'd kissed her.

She licked suddenly dry lips. "When I first joined the Osage, I yearned to belong. For years I begged Morning Star to give me a tattoo similar to hers and her children's. When she finally said I was ready, she gave me two because she said one day I might need double the strength."

She tried to pull her hand free of his, and he let her go.

"The web is here…" she pointed to her heart,

"…to remind me that strength comes from my home, my family. All of whom I hold in my heart. The spider is here…" she opened her hand, the palm once again facing him, "…to remind me of the strength in my body, strength that can be channeled through my hand either as an enemy…" she made a fist, the spider disappearing, "…or as a friend." She opened her hand and laid her palm over his heart.

He inhaled sharply, sending the hard muscles under her hand quivering.

"I'm sorry." She withdrew her touch.

He snatched her hand back and held it firmly in place. "That's why, in the cave, you took my hand and…held it to your heart?"

She nodded.

"And I—" He mumbled a curse. "Who is Morning Star?"

She blinked, startled by his shifting questions. "My mother, my Osage mother."

"She sounds like a wise woman."

"Yes, very wise and patient too." She smiled sadly. "She told me she was thinking of Grandfather Spider's words the day she found me. She knew he was guiding her, that I was waiting for her and that if she waited for me to come to her in return, then I would be the daughter of her heart."

"Why aren't you with her now?"

She tried to draw away again, but he held her fast, anchoring her to him. Beneath her hand laid undeniable strength, unrelenting. "The white trappers killed her."

Paden's heart kicked beneath her hand in response. "In the valley the old woman talked about, where we found the Pawnee?"

"She died there, along with her real daughter, Laughing Eyes." Shame made her eyes burn with tears. "I should have died instead of them."

His grip tightened. "Don't say that."

"I didn't belong with the Osage, and I don't belong here."

"That's not true."

"The people on this wagon train think it's true."

"They're wrong."

"Maybe, but maybe you regret hiring me as well. I'm a scout who isn't allowed to scout."

"It isn't safe." His voice turned gruff again. "You can't defend yourself against the men out there who prey on women."

"I can't hide forever, either."

"If you'd seen what the Comanche did to my wife—" He released her hand and stood.

She scrambled to her feet as well. Her heart hurt like it'd been pierced by an arrow. "That's what happened in San Antonio? Your wife was killed?"

"I can't talk to you about Jeannie." He turned his back to her, putting more distance between them.

She stepped around to stand in front of him again. Even though his head hung between his hunched shoulders, his turbulent smoky gaze met hers.

She lifted her hand, palm open and fingers wide. She tilted the spider up to his face. "You can. I'm stronger than you think...and so are you."

CHAPTER 7

The sun crept over the eastern horizon as the wagon train prepared to depart Alcove Spring. The settlers loaded their belongings and made last-minute repairs. Paden watched Hannah help Gabe get everyone ready. The men and women spoke only to Gabe. They either ignored Hannah or gawked at her rudely. She left a trail of whispering people in her wake.

Why hadn't he seen it before? Maybe because whenever he'd been near her, he'd been distracted by his feelings. Now everywhere he looked, he was aware of someone snubbing her. And Hannah? She pressed forward with a dogged determination.

He cursed himself for not paying attention sooner. Then he cursed himself again, because he didn't know what to do about it. All he knew was she looked sad. He wanted to change that. She'd been happy with the Osage. Why couldn't he make her happy?

Hannah and Gabe finished their rounds and returned to the scouts' wagon. They halted beside the general. Hannah kept her gaze lowered while the two men talked. She darted a glance in his direction, then went back to staring at the toes of her moccasins.

In contrast, a couple of wagons away, a group of women clustered in a circle, chattering briskly. One of them, a young woman with mousy-brown hair, gripped her throat with a fluttering hand. Her eyes were wide with excitement. The woman next to her couldn't seem to stop giggling and tossing her head to make her blond curls shake. The other one was older, sterner. Her arms were crossed over her ample form, her shoulder rigid.

All of them kept looking at Hannah. A flurry of conversation followed each glance.

"Move your wagons out, or you'll be left behind," Paden hollered.

They scattered like hens, hurrying back to their individual roosts. Hannah stared at him, eyes wide with uncertainty. He ground his teeth and glared in the direction the women had retreated. His scowl deepened when he spotted Thomas Riley waddling toward the scouts' wagon. The Texan's lowered gaze couldn't hide the disquiet marring his brow. The last time he'd seen Riley, he'd wanted to get as far away from the man as he could. This time he made a beeline for him, intent on intercepting him before he reached the scouts' wagon.

"Can I help you with something, Mr. Riley?" Paden planted himself in front of the man, forcing him to halt.

Riley lifted his head, frowning up at him for a split second. Then he blinked, and the same expression of awe as before rounded his eyes and arched his brows. "Of course you can! I was going to talk to General Sherwood, but speaking to you will be even better."

"What's on your mind?"

"Oh, it's something you've probably already acknowledged and intended to fix. I'm sure a man like you would see the error that has happened."

"Which is?"

"It's about that—that scout you took on at Fort Leavenworth." Riley thrust his finger in the direction where he'd last seen Hannah.

Paden couldn't stop his hands from clenching into fists. "What about her?"

Riley's brows rose even higher. "Well, surely you don't think it's wise to keep her on this wagon train."

"Why not? I hired her, didn't I?"

"But she…"

"She what?" Paden prompted.

Riley leaned forward and whispered, "I caught her talking to my daughter."

Paden snorted. "Talking isn't a crime." Although, he might have to rethink that, because he'd most certainly like to ban Riley from ever speaking another word.

"But she…"

"For Christ's sake, Riley, spit it out. You've got something to say. So say it. What did Hannah do?"

"She lived with the savages. She probably let their men touch her. And now she parades her shame in front of decent folk like it was *nothing*."

Paden nearly hit the man. The only thing that stopped him was the possibility that Hannah might be watching. He didn't want her to think he was a ruffian who couldn't control his temper.

"Those savages protected her." At least the women had. He sucked in a sharp breath, trying to rein in his anger at the unknown number of men, both white and Indian, who might have tried to hurt Hannah.

Her views on strength were an illusion. If a man had wanted to rape her, she wouldn't be able to stop him. Just like Jeannie hadn't been able to stop the Comanche. Even if Hannah had trusted one of the

Osage braves enough to accept his advances, she'd have given the man the power to harm her in a whole other way. Just like Paden's grandmother had done when she'd ignored her misgivings and accepted his grandfather's advances.

Could this be part of Hannah's reasons for fleeing the Osage man Dawson had seen near Fort Leavenworth?

He didn't want to contemplate any of those possibilities too closely, not when thinking about Hannah. Who was he to judge her anyway? That he or anyone else would judge her only added to his anger.

He turned his glare on Riley. "Keep your opinions to yourself. Whatever happened to Hannah, it's not her fault."

"But Captain Callahan. You of all men, you can't be serious."

"Hannah stays. She's done nothing wrong. And I'll warn you again—leave her alone. Don't spread any more foul gossip around the wagon train."

Riley's wide eyes narrowed. Then he stalked off as fast as he could with his awkward waddling gait.

Paden's gut rolled with unease. Riley wouldn't listen. The man was going to be trouble. Maybe he should throw someone off the train after all, that someone being Riley. That would solve the problem of Riley. It wouldn't solve the greater problem though. In fact, it would probably only add to it. Everyone would know he'd booted Riley because of Hannah. They'd blame her.

General Sherwood had said he shouldn't treat Hannah any differently than the other scouts. If he did, he'd make her more of an outcast.

He was a fool. He'd failed Jeannie, and still the hope that he could help Hannah had lodged in his heart. He'd failed again, and this time against a completely different enemy. He couldn't protect Hannah from the settlers, their narrow-mindedness and their gossip. At most, he'd given her a safe haven from her other troubles, but at what cost? He was forcing her to rub shoulders with bigots who treated her abominably every hour of the day.

Sherwood was right. He had to let Hannah go scouting. With her riding out ahead of the wagons, at least one good thing would happen. She'd be away from the settlers' spitefulness for part of the day. His heart rebelled against the decision. He didn't think he could bear it if she got hurt. That was another problem. He had to stop caring so much. That seemed as impossible an aim as changing the settlers' attitudes.

He was only certain of one thing now. Hannah was much stronger than him.

For the first time since joining the wagon train, Hannah was riding on her own. Ahead of her snaked the trail, scored with ruts from the wheels of those who'd gone before. Sparrows and gophers darted through the sagebrush, chirping and chattering to each other, secure in the knowledge that they were home and need not journey anywhere. She'd been relieved when Paden finally gave her the order to ride out alone, but now she felt as if something were missing.

How could this be? She'd spent the last two years on her own and now, after a week with these people, being alone was odd. What in the heavens was wrong with her?

One thing remained certain. All of these emotions paled in comparison to what she experienced whenever she was near Paden. Around him, she always ended up befuddled. As she had yesterday at the spring when he'd found her practically naked, or the night when the storm had forced them to seek shelter together in the cave, or the day she'd lain on top of him on the hillside.

He'd said he shouldn't have taken liberties, shouldn't have touched her. Was she so unappealing? So different from the woman he'd chosen as his wife?

Jeannie's death had fueled Paden's hatred for the Comanche. It wasn't a stretch to realize he might spurn Hannah because she'd lived with the Osage. The emigrants on the wagon train had. They couldn't understand how a white woman would willingly live with Indians. Neither could the white trappers. All of the whites wanted to save women like her from such a life, to return them to their own kind. But after they did, they decided their souls were beyond saving.

Women like her were tainted forever.

She'd never wanted to leave her tribe, but the whites had made it impossible for her to stay. If she could go back, she would. But she could only go forward. She was going to the Western Territories, to a land Gabe and Paden had called Oregon. No one would know her there. If she traveled far enough, could she make a future worthy of Morning Star's sacrifice?

"All this worry and uncertainty, I'm going to drive myself mad," she grumbled under her breath. But today something else was also bothering her. More than anything, she missed Paden's company.

She urged White Cloud into a gallop. The rhythm of his pounding hooves and flexing muscles flowed into her body, merging with her heartbeat until they became one. The prairie grass, thickening in the late May sunshine, rippled on either side of them like an emerald blanket in the gentle breeze. Faster and faster they went, until she was able to push aside everything except the rush of the wind in her ears and the blur of the earth flying by beneath her.

They swept over the crest of a hill, and suddenly were no longer alone. Smack in the middle of the wagon trail, where it crossed a muddy gully, sat a single wagon.

Cursing her impetuousness, she hauled White Cloud to a stop.

Two figures stood next to the wagon. Luckily their heads were bent, seemingly engrossed in their own troubles. They hadn't yet noticed her. She wished she could turn tail, but her job this morning was to ensure the trail was clear for the wagon train. That meant confronting and resolving whatever problems she found.

She rode closer.

The wagon tilted at a corner, where it was missing a wheel. Barrels and crates had been removed from the interior and lay scattered willy-nilly. On the grass sat a small boy with slumped shoulders, while a woman and an older boy of maybe twelve slipped around in the sticky clay, trying to prop the wagon up and reattach the wheel.

The older boy caught sight of her and froze. The woman straightened and, shading her eyes with a mucky hand, followed his gaze. Her hopeful posture vanished in a heartbeat. Hannah tensed as the woman scrambled to the front of the wagon. She pulled out a shotgun.

Before she could turn White Cloud and urge him to run, buckshot peppered the ground in front of them, making him rear.

"Stay where you are!" the woman's voice split the air. "Move and I'll blow you to Kingdom Come, you savage."

She berated herself for not fleeing sooner. Spirits

Above, she was ill equipped to deal with this. What did someone say in such a situation? Well, she'd better come up with something, or Paden would arrive and have a good deal to say.

Don't just sit here, she chastised herself. *Say something. Anything.*

"Sorry, ma'am, but you'll have to move yourself as there's a wagon train coming." She groaned and hung her head, wishing she'd kept silent. Obviously for some time this poor woman had been trying her best to do just that. She'd think Hannah was a complete simpleton.

The shotgun trained on her dipped. At least she had the woman's attention.

"My name's Hannah, and if you'll permit me to come closer, maybe we can have a proper discussion on the matter."

The woman's mouth sagged, as did the barrel of her shotgun. Then she gave her head a shake and her weapon rose to level on Hannah. "All right, come closer," she ordered in a no-nonsense voice, "but be warned, I'll fill you full of buckshot if you give me the slightest reason. Same goes for any friends of ill repute you might have hiding nearby."

Fair enough, Hannah thought. She'd be as careful too, if she was in this woman's position. She nudged White Cloud forward and soon realized the woman was older than she'd first assumed, probably in her fifties. Where were the children's parents? When she'd advanced as far as she dared, she stopped White Cloud and reached up to push her hat from her head, letting it fall to rest on her back, dangling by its chin strap.

"Well, I'll be," drawled the woman. "If that don't take the cake. I thought me and my grandsons must surely be the oddest sight within a hundred miles, but you're a stranger thing than us."

Hannah couldn't stop the smile that curved her lips. Even in her current predicament, the woman was able to rally her sense of humor and sum up the situation uniquely.

"Where are your…" Hannah paused, lost for the appropriate words. When she continued, her voice was edged with uncertainty. "Where are your traveling companions?"

The woman laughed and lowered her shotgun to her hip. "The good Christian congregation that made up my wagon train? Not a one of 'em bothered to stop and lend a hand when this bucket of wood got stuck."

"They left you here?"

"Even worse, no one returned to help when I failed to catch up by the next day."

"What about your wagon captain?" Hannah's thoughts returned to Paden. Surely he wouldn't leave anyone behind.

"Ha! Our captain, Mr. Finnegan, was a black-hearted soul and more'n likely welcomed the opportunity to rid himself of one more nuisance. Now, sadly I believe me and my grandsons have only made things worse with our efforts to free this contraption. It's sunk even lower than it was in the beginning."

Her eldest grandson stared at Hannah with enormous eyes. The younger boy shyly peered out from behind the protection of his grandmother and big brother.

Hannah smiled reassuringly at them. "My wagon train's not far behind me. If we can get you free of the mud, they can see to mending your wheel."

"If your wagons stop to give me aid, I'll be truly amazed. Don't have much faith in folks these days." The woman stowed her shotgun in the wagon, then settled her hands on her hips and took a long moment to assess Hannah. "I won't turn down any help that's offered though. Name's Miriam Jennings, and these are my grandsons, William and Charlie." She glanced over her shoulder at her wagon. "You got any ideas for freeing this thing?"

A few minutes later, they'd fashioned a makeshift harness out of spare rope and hooked White Cloud to Miriam's mules. With the animals pulling and the people pushing, they strained and heaved, slipped and slid, and with a lurch the wagon broke free and emerged from the gummy clay.

But there was still the matter of the wheel. Mending it was beyond Hannah's knowledge, and she was glad the general had convinced a blacksmith to travel with them.

She and the Jennings family sat on the grass across from the wagon, trying to regain their breath while shaking the clay from their feet and hands. Hannah was as muddy as them now.

Miriam chortled. "Well, I don't know if your wagon train will help us or not, but I thank you for all you've done so far." Raising her gaze from the mud staining her clothing, she studied Hannah. "On closer inspection, you look like an angel. I'm happy the good Lord chose to put you on this path."

Uncomfortable with the praise, Hannah rose to her feet. "I'll ride back and inform my wagon train you'll need the blacksmith. He should be able to fix your wheel, and then you can join our group. Or at least I hope you will. I know what it's like to be cast out. I wouldn't wish that fate on anyone."

Miriam stared at her, head tilted and one eyebrow raised.

Stop talking and get moving, Hannah told herself. She unhitched White Cloud and swung up into her saddle. The oldest boy, William, ran over to her. He chewed his lip before blurting out, "You're sure someone will come for us?"

The first words he'd spoken since her arrival.

"Yes, I'm sure."

Hunching his shoulders, he rammed his hands deep in his pockets. His gaze swept the land around them. Miles of endless prairieland stretched out as far as the eye could see. The only sound was the breeze rustling the grass. The boy sucked in a deep breath, but Hannah still saw the tremor that shook his body.

"How can you be so sure someone will come?" he asked, looking back at his family. So young, and already the boy felt the weight of the world on his shoulders.

"Because…" She waited until his gaze met hers again. "*I'm* coming back for you."

Nerves scraped raw, Dawson interrupted his pacing to kick dirt over the flames of his campfire. "We're leaving."

For once, his black-eyed friend's fingers weren't caressing the blade of his knife. He gripped the handle with a sudden intensity. "What happened?"

Hissing and spitting, the fire snuffed out. If only everything was so easy. He'd almost had her. That's what happened! He'd watched in glee as she'd ridden out alone. He'd followed at a distance, content to let his anticipation build. Then she'd raced ahead over a rise, and he'd lost sight of her and heard gunfire.

His second traveling companion moved to stand beside the first. "Yeah, tell us what's got you spooked, boss."

He wasn't about to tell them he'd been defeated again, that although he wasn't sure who'd been doing the shooting, he'd feared that Callahan had discovered him. So he'd turned tail and run. He stalked over to his saddle bags and began rifling through them. "I need a drink."

"The whiskey's gone, boss. You'll have to wait till we reach Fort Laramie."

"To hell with that," Dawson shot back, "and with creeping along behind a slow-as-molasses line of wagons. If we ride hard for Laramie, we can entertain ourselves properly while we wait for them to catch up."

His companions stared at him without blinking, then asked in turn…

"I'll get to use my knife at the fort?"

"We'll steal enough to live high on the hog?"

Dawson nodded. When both men hurried to pack the camp, his anxiety eased. Things weren't all grim. His friends' thirst for killing and thieving matched his for drinking. While they waited at Laramie and fed their individual appetites, he could craft a foolproof plan for Callahan and his bitch. He'd have his revenge at Fort Laramie.

CHAPTER 8

Alejandro paced next to the scouts' campfire, listening to Gabe regale Virgil with tales of Texas and the "good ol' days." As far as he was concerned, those days had not been that good. Then again, the last few days hadn't been that great either.

Why did it bother him now? In the past, he'd ignored the slurs about his Mexican heritage and the ones about his white ancestors as well. He'd left Mexico in search of the Texan who'd sired him and disappeared. He'd wandered all over Texas looking for the man. He'd never found him.

Instead, he'd found General Sherwood. The general sat nearby, smiling at Gabe's lighthearted chatter while saying very little. Sherwood was their cornerstone. He held them together with a quiet patience more powerful than any brawn Alejandro had witnessed. Praise the Saints that the general had a penchant for picking up strays.

Had Hannah wandered in a similar fashion until she'd found their wagon train? The settlers had no right treating her like they did. But Rebecca had defended Hannah. A deep relief filled him. It meant that when Rebecca had tried to contest her father's ill words against him as well, her actions had been genuine.

A voice as grating at the braying of a burro claimed his attention. Thomas Riley swaggered by with several men in his wake. Riley had his audience. What did his daughter have?

Alejandro rose to his feet. The Riley wagon wasn't far away and when he drew near, he saw Rebecca, once again alone by her wagon. She was preparing the evening meal. The meal was probably the only reason Riley would return to their wagon.

He frowned. Whenever he saw Rebecca, she was alone. He never saw her talking to any of the other women. But Hannah had said Rebecca had defended her against them.

Rebecca picked up a bucket and went around the far side of her wagon. He followed her. When she dumped the water in her bucket and turned, he stood directly in front of her. A gasp broke from her lips as she pressed her free hand to her throat. Just as quickly her hand dropped to her side.

"Mr. Ramirez, you startled me." A tentative smile lifted the corners of her lips.

They stood in the shadow of the wagon. Out of sight. Alone.

He stepped closer. "I wanted to thank you for trying to help Hannah."

Her gaze lowered. "The women had no call to treat her that way. And my father—" She grimaced. "He shouldn't have treated either of you so poorly. I'm sorry." She glanced up at him. "Can you tell Hannah I'm sorry for what my father said? Please? I can't talk to her. I wish I could, but I can't. If I did, and he saw... Well, I'd only make things worse."

Unease made his scalp prickle. "Rebecca, are you afraid of your father?"

"I'm afraid of what he'll say to Hannah, of what he'll coerce others into saying."

"What about your safety?"

Her brow puckered. "What do you mean?"

"Will you live under your *padre's* rule forever?"

"He's my father, my family. He's all I have." She pressed her lips tight.

"What about starting a family of your own?"

She blushed. "Father says there are several men on the wagon train he wants me to consider. Possible business partners once we reach the west."

Anger surged through him. "Business partners?"

"Isn't a marriage a type of partnership?"

"Yes, but one based on love, not money."

"I don't have anyone who loves me," she said, sounding lost and forlorn.

"You have me."

Her lips parted in surprise and her hand rose to shield her throat again.

He remembered all the women he'd flirted with, how easily the words had come then. Now when it was most important, his tongue felt like a lead weight. He could think of little to say that would persuade her of his worth as her partner.

Every morning Hannah rode ahead of the wagons, leading the pioneers steadily west along a trail unraveling before them like a never-ending ribbon. Paden had even started allowing her to take a turn on the nightly guard duty. She was truly a scout now.

The wagon train's newest family had settled in nicely. Miriam Jennings was a no-nonsense woman who handled her mule team and her grandsons with a firm but fair hand. To Hannah's surprise, Miriam took her under her wing as well and clucked over her like a sage hen.

With Miriam, Hannah found herself in a world without borders, without the boundaries Paden had mentioned when he'd rejected her by the cave. She swayed between wanting to spend time with the Jennings family and needing to be near the scouts' wagon and Paden.

The Great Plains affected her in a similar fashion. She was now adrift in the vast expanse between the east and west, the past and future. Travelers did not stay here long. The dream of a new life in the Western Territories kept them marching forward.

After shadowing the south bank of the Platte River for four hundred miles, where the only thing taller than the prairie grass was an occasional thicket of sycamores or willows, they reached the convergence of the great waterway's north and south forks. Hannah halted, along with everyone else, and stared in awe at the turbulent meeting of the waters. The current churned the river a frothy white and raised its voice to a rumbling roar.

Paden pulled his stallion to a skidding stop beside her and Gabe. "Keep moving upstream. Don't stop until you reach the bend where the rivers divide and the water calms." He rode up the line, calling for everyone to do the same.

With a snap of his reins, Gabe set the scouts' wagon in motion. "We need to follow the trail along the North Platte, which means crossing the southern branch."

Hannah eyed the raging river dubiously. They'd crossed several smaller waterways, but nothing like the one they now faced. When they reached the bend Paden had mentioned, they found him surveying the river with General Sherwood, Alejandro and Virgil mounted beside him.

"The river must be nearly a mile wide in the shallows," Alejandro remarked. "We shall be forever crossing there."

Virgil stroked his moustache. "These greenhorns'

grit would be sorely tested in the rougher narrows."

The general continued scanning the river. "We face difficulties no matter which course we choose to navigate."

"We'll cross there." Paden pointed toward the bend in river. "It's not as wide as some parts, but the current is slowest as the river turns. There's a lull before it picks up again. Each wagon should cross as fast as it can. The less time in the water, the less time for something to go wrong. Now's the moment for everyone to seriously consider lighting their loads."

Virgil snorted. "What? You're not a music lover? You think the piano should stay behind?"

Paden's shoulders stiffened. "I like music just fine. But I haven't heard any. So why haul a piano around if you're never gonna play it?"

Gabe gave one of familiar easygoing shrugs. "Maybe they're keeping it 'cause Granddad gave it to them."

Paden's breath hissed through his teeth. "Please tell me that's not Jeannie's—

"Gabe," the general interrupted. "Can you let them know it's time to leave my daughter's piano behind?"

Paden's wife had been the general's daughter? Hannah clasped her hand over her mouth to stifle her gasp of disbelief.

"Speak to the others as well," the general continued. "We don't want to jeopardize our futures by clinging to the past."

An uneasy silence stretched out as the scouts' wagon rattled off with Gabe at the helm.

"It appears I haven't let go of the past either," General Sherwood murmured. "But our futures lie across the river. So, my question is: what other measures might we take to speed our crossing?"

The conversation started again. Hannah didn't

join in. She stared at the river, plagued by a slew of additional questions. Was Jeannie the reason Paden had agreed to lead this wagon train? Was that why both he and the general had finally abandoned Texas? What unspeakable atrocity had the Comanche done to Jeannie in San Antonio to provoke such an outcome? Was it any wonder these two men wanted to leave the past behind?

The loss of a loved one, of two, had set Eagle Feather's heart against Hannah. He held the past tight. Could any of these men truly forget and move forward? Could she?

As her gaze wandered the river, several Indian riders appeared on the opposite bank. She stole a glance at Paden, praying his restraint would continue. The wagon train's few interactions with the Indians near Fort Leavenworth, and the Delaware by the valley, had been strained but peaceful. Guided by their expert riders, the sturdy Indian ponies made quick work of crossing the river and galloping up the bank toward Hannah's party.

In keeping with their usual routine, General Sherwood moved his mount forward to greet them. Hannah kept White Cloud close to the general's side.

The visitors were lean, hard-faced men dressed in tattered calico shirts with bands of the same colorful material tied around their foreheads. Their dark but dull hair, hacked off bluntly at their shoulders, framed restless eyes. Unease tightened her chest. They weren't white men, but they somehow reminded her of the militiamen from her youth.

She translated the general's words of welcome in Pawnee and then Sioux. The Indians stared at her in silence. She tried several other dialects, but they shook their heads. Raising their hands, they opted to communicate in the Plains Indian sign language, using an intricate combination of shapes and movements.

"They help travelers ferry their wagons across the river," she translated. "They say it will be easier if we accept. Only a small payment will be necessary." A frown pinched her brow. If these men had been helping emigrants, surely they would've picked up some English by now. So why were they refusing to speak a single word? In any language?

"We are best handling this on our own," the general replied. "Kindly let them know we do not require their services and they should be on their way."

But when Hannah did, the Indians signed that the whites must accept their assistance. They urged their mounts closer. One of them jostled her and White Cloud. They slid down the bank. The Indian pony and its rider slid with them, pushing them closer to the river.

Suddenly, the Indian rider jerked his horse to a halt. A pistol muzzle pressed against the man's temple. She twisted in her saddle to face the man holding the gun.

Paden sat with lethal stillness, his finger hovering on the trigger. "Tell them to leave, Hannah, or I put a bullet in his head."

Nobody said a word. Nobody moved. Sweat beaded the Indian's brow, his eyes round with terror.

Paden pressed his gun even harder against the man's temple. "Tell them. Now!"

Quickly she translated in sign language and every Indian dialect she knew. She glanced repeatedly at Paden, terrified the gun would go off at any moment. He looked ten times colder and harsher than the stranger she'd met that first day at Fort Leavenworth.

Making no sudden moves, the Indians backed

their ponies away. Then they urged them into the river, whipping and kicking until they reached the opposite side. When they did, they halted still as statues to stare back at them.

Paden kept his revolver trained on them the entire time. Finally, he lowered his weapon but didn't return it to its holster. "Hannah, stay with the general. Don't leave his side. Find Gabe and get the wagons organized. Double up the teams so eight pull each wagon. Alejandro and Virgil, come with me. I want to inspect the crossing." Without a backward glance, he headed toward the river.

The scouts followed him. Hannah twisted in her saddle to face General Sherwood.

He shook his head, halting any question she might have asked. "Let's find Gabe and get to work."

Ten minutes later, the first wagons entered the river. Fifteen minutes after that, the wagon reached the other side.

"This might take all day," Gabe observed.

"Might take two." The general squinted up at the midday sun, then scanned the opposite bank. Their Indian visitors had disappeared. "Today, time seems the least of our worries."

In between her duties on the riverbank, Hannah watched the crossings. All too often a nervous ox balked and refused to enter the water, or a stubborn mule took it into his head to turn back. The only solution was for Paden, Alejandro or Virgil to slip a lasso over the reluctant beast's head and pull it in the desired direction.

Maneuvering in the water quickly fatigued both horse and rider. Paden started dividing the work so the scouts could recuperate while the crossings continued without pause.

He was sitting on the bank with Virgil when

Hannah, having finally rallied her courage, left the general's side and approached him. The memory of his revolver jammed against the Indian's temple made her fidget with her coat cuffs. Even when she realized what she was doing, she didn't stop herself. She needed something to hide the shaking in her hands.

She'd finally witnessed a side of Paden that brought into sharp focus his violent past. He would've pulled the trigger if those men hadn't left.

He sat with his back to her. He'd removed his coat and shirt. The thick cords of his muscles, slick with sweat and river water, rippled in the afternoon sun. He probably hadn't required his gun earlier. He could've killed the man with his bare hands. Hands that had touched her with remarkable gentleness. He lifted one now to rub the back of his neck.

Heat started in her midsection and burned like wildfire through her veins. He didn't even need to touch her now to set her aflame.

As if sensing her presence, he turned. His unblinking gray gaze swept over her, making the heat in her body flare in her face as well. She fought the urge to bolt like a coward and forced her feet to take the final steps separating them.

"Hello, miss." Virgil tipped his hat in greeting.

Paden's gaze remained on her. "Didn't I tell you to stay close to the general?"

Virgil cleared his throat. "Well, I'd best get back to helping Alejandro. Daylight's burning, and those tenderfoots would take a week of Sundays to cross if left to their own devices." He strode away, heading in the direction of his horse, which grazed next to Paden's in the distance.

When Virgil was out of earshot, she swallowed her trepidation and voiced the question bedeviling her. "Why won't you let me help in the river? It's no different than scouting the trail ahead of the wagons."

Paden's gaze fixed on the opposite bank. "Those men made things different. You need to stay close to the general until we put some distance between us and them."

"About what happened—"

"If they'd left when asked, none of it would've happened. Hell, they should've been smart and never came close in the first place. You need to be on guard with men like them."

"You mean men who are Indians." Her reply came out sharper than she'd intended.

A muscle bunched in his jaw. "I mean men who for whatever reason decided to cut loose from their homes to ride as a pack. I'd draw my gun on a white man just as easily as an Indian if he tried to do what they just did."

The sudden ferocity in his tone made her shiver. Had she been so worried about Paden's reaction to the Indians that she'd missed something? "What did they try to do?"

"Distract us with some *loco* story about helping when all they wanted was you. They were herding you toward the river. I'm surprised they didn't draw their weapons before I did. You'd be easier to take if I were sprawled in the dirt with a bullet in *my* head."

Hannah gasped before the image of Paden lying bleeding on the ground morphed into a recollection of her father in a similar state. The memory turned crystal-sharp. The militiamen said they'd only wanted to talk to Papa as well. Then they'd shot him. They'd killed him because they wanted to take Mama! Her chest tightened and her vision tunneled. She laid her hand on White Cloud's shoulder to keep her upright.

A shadow fell over her, easing the overwhelming

brightness of her past. Her gaze traveled up a lofty expanse of naked male torso until she met Paden's gaze.

He retreated a stride. "You looked like your legs were about to give out."

"Not my legs but my lungs," she rasped. "I feel like I'm suffocating."

"Hannah..." Bracing his hands on his thighs, he leaned down until his eyes were at her level. "I'm not trying to smother you. I only want you to exercise more caution. You need to acknowledge the dangers around you. Those white trappers who killed your Osage mother and sister, they tried to take you as well, didn't they?"

She flinched. "You don't have to tell me I'm responsible for Morning Star and Laughing Eyes' deaths. I know that."

"That's not what I'm trying to say." He rubbed the frown that now furrowed his brow.

"If I didn't look like I do, if I didn't look like Mama, maybe they'd—"

"You can't change how you look. But those men could've acted differently. You're not at fault."

"How can you say that? I know you feel responsible for your wife's death."

Paden's hands dropped to his sides as he drew back and straightened to his full height. "That's different." His fingers curled into fists. "The Comanche killed Jeannie because of what I did, not what I looked like. They were angry when they learned I'd become a Ranger."

Hannah shook her head. "Why would they care?"

"I'd betrayed them."

"How?"

"They tried their best to make me one of their braves. I grew up in a Comanche village." Paden went very still, as if he'd uttered the unimaginable.

She gasped in disbelief. With that breath came his familiar scent of sweet sage. Understanding flooded her. He smelled like home because they'd shared a similar youth. He held on to his past as tightly she did.

"You're the first person I've ever told," he said.

"Why didn't you tell me sooner?"

"Because I wasn't happy with them." He stared at her with such intensity that she felt the words he'd left out—*like you were*.

His words, both spoken and silent, stung. But mostly she hurt from the pain she saw etched on his face. She struggled for a reply. "I'm sorry."

"Don't be. The first years were tolerable because I had Kaku."

She frowned. "Kaku? Is that a Comanche name?"

"It means 'Grandmother' in their language. Kaku looked after me. She was kind but also tough as buffalo hide. The old Delaware woman reminded me of her. The Comanche figured they could easily turn me into one of their braves, because I came to them young and Kaku was a good teacher."

"How old were you?"

"Kaku said I was three. She taught me everything, including things I wasn't supposed to know. She told me the story of my parents, that my father had been a Ranger. When Kaku died, my life felt unbearable, so I vowed to leave. I made things harder on myself by not being very good at it. That's when the Comanche jokingly started calling me *Boy Made of Smoke*, and I took to proving them right in earnest. When I was twelve, I ran just fast enough and far enough that they couldn't find me and drag me back."

Unease rolled Hannah's stomach into a hard knot. "Boy? Not Devil?"

His eyes went flat and dull as if he were once

again staring through her. "The switch came many years later after they caught up with me in San Antonio."

"No!" The word rang out, clear as a bell. It took Hannah a moment to realize she hadn't said it. The shout had come from the river, from Miriam's wagon, which was being pushed downstream by a sudden swell in the water. William hung out the back of the wagon, trying to reach Charlie, who flailed in the water struggling to stay afloat.

Paden sprinted for his horse, and Hannah leaped on White Cloud.

The wagon lurched to a stop, caught on a rock and nearly toppled over. The wagon had halted but Charlie had not. William dove into the water and swam after his brother. Miriam's cries increased. The current caught both boys and pulled them away from their wagon at a rapidly accelerating pace.

Hannah urged White Cloud full tilt down the bank. Behind her, Paden's order for her to stop reverberated in her ears. She asked White Cloud to go faster. They had to reach the boys before they hit narrows. White Cloud was a strong swimmer, but no one would be safe in those churning rapids.

She used the current to help propel them toward the boys, who now clung together as one. Fear and the frigid water made her fumble as she tied the end of her rope around her saddle horn. As they drew near the boys, she gathered her strength. She might only have one chance. *Please don't let me miss,* she prayed.

Holding her breath, she cast her lasso. It dropped around the boys. She pulled it snug and urged White Cloud toward the nearest shore. He obeyed wholeheartedly.

The line attaching them to the boys snapped tight and jerked them away from their goal. The boys were caught in the narrows. Soon White Cloud would be too. The current buffeted her. A wave splashed her face. She choked, coughed, couldn't breathe.

Had she reached the boys only to perish with them?

Paden's lungs burned as he sprinted for his horse. Why hadn't he kept Cholla close, rather than letting him graze so far away? Behind him, Miriam's cries ricocheted like gunfire between the banks. Hannah would be in the river with them now. The thought made him run faster.

Without breaking stride, he jerked free the rope tethering Cholla's halter to a stake in the ground and jumped on him bareback. He urged him into a flat-out run toward the river. What he saw there made his heart seize with dread. The Jennings boys were being tossed about by the chop in the narrows. Attached to them by a line, Hannah and her horse were being dragged into the same rough water.

Cholla hit the river and swam after them. But the distance separating them was greater than the distance between Hannah and the rapids. He urged Cholla to go faster.

The current spun Hannah's mount around and propelled them toward the opposite shore. For a brief moment, horse and rider drifted in an eddy near the bank. Then the current caught them and began tugging them downstream again. But not before White Cloud found his footing on the riverbed. He surged toward the bank and broke free of the water with William and Charlie in tow.

Hannah hauled the boys to shore, then slid from her saddle and drew them into her arms. They collapsed together in a heap on the sand. White

Cloud stood beside them, head low, sides heaving. All safe. Out of danger.

Paden's eyes clearly saw all of this, but the rest of him wouldn't listen. Every fiber of his being demanded he finish crossing at breakneck speed in order to determine firsthand if she was all right. But he wasn't certain he could control himself if he went anywhere near her right now. Would he shake her or kiss her? Whatever he chose, it wouldn't be wise to do it in front of the entire wagon train.

Letting Cholla decide their pace and path, he tried to distract himself by scanning the river for hazards like rocks or floating debris between him and Hannah. When yelling erupted again, his gaze flew back to her.

A man was dragging her away from the boys. His multicolored shirt flashed like a brigand's flag, as did the white rump of the familiar appaloosa that stood waiting. One of the Indians who'd failed to steal Hannah earlier was making a second attempt.

Rage and fear sank their claws into his heart. His shouts were lost in the rising din as he once again urged Cholla straight for Hannah.

She kicked and twisted, breaking free of her abductor several times. Each time she was recaptured with increasing roughness. The Indian lashed out and backhanded her across the face. Her knees buckled. Her abductor threw her belly down onto his horse and jumped up behind her.

A howl like a wounded wolf rose in Paden's throat. He begged Cholla to swim faster. Try as he might, his trusted stallion couldn't do the impossible. They weren't going to reach Hannah in time. He was going to lose her.

CHAPTER 9

Lying with her head and heels dangling on either side of the horse struggling up the riverbank, Hannah fought the weight on her back. The Indian's arm held her prisoner as surely as the jaw of a steel trap. Her head throbbed and her vision spun from the blow he'd dealt her. Even though her strength had all but vanished, she kept fighting.

Her captor grunted a laugh. "You are too weak. You cannot escape. I shall not be denied the reward for delivering you to him."

Disbelief stole the air from her lungs. Her abductor had spoken in Osage.

"He described you perfectly," the Indian continued in a begrudging grumble. "Your eyes are as blue as the sky, your hair as light as the sun, your spirit as determined as the eagle for which he is named."

Eagle Feather had sent him? An icy dread weighed her down as well. How close was he? A day's ride? An hour? A minute? If she didn't get off this horse, she'd find out. They'd almost crested the riverbank. When they did, the horse would find its footing and be able to run, far away from the wagon train and Paden.

The Indian's grip loosened, growing lax with his

impending success. She threw all of her weight against him, using surprise and the angle of the incline to topple him off his mount. They hit the ground together. Hard. He came up snarling and struck her another blow. White light exploded behind her eyes. All of the fight went out of her. Once again, he threw her onto his horse and sprang up behind her.

The mount's muscles coiled to leap forward. Instead, it whinnied shrilly and reared, unseating her and her captor again. He released her, trying to halt his mount which shied away, heading up the riverbank. Hope flared in her heart and gave her the strength to raise her head. In a blur, she glimpsed William and Charlie hurling rocks at the Indian.

Surprise was on their side. Her abductor had no idea how many people were attacking him. Like a coward, he started running. When he glanced back and realized his assailants were only children, he halted. Face contorted with contempt, he drew a tomahawk from his belt and came back at them.

A new terror enveloped her. Two boys were no match for an Indian in his prime. Though they'd fought valiantly, William and Charlie had only succeeded in endangering themselves as well.

The clatter of hooves striking river rocks brought the Indian up short. Crouching low, he swung to face the noise. His dark skin turned pale, then he pivoted and sprinted after his horse. The boys hurried him along with a bombardment of stones and unceasing shouts.

A pair of booted feet hit the sand beside her. Strong arms lifted her against a solid chest and a wildly pounding heart. "Sweet heaven," Paden said. "I almost didn't reach you in time. What if he'd taken you and—?" His arms tightened around her.

Safe in his embrace, her fear evaporated. She

opened her mouth to assure him she was fine. Nothing came out. She tried to draw in a deep breath. A spasm of pain in her side made her immediately regret the attempt.

Paden gently brushed her hair back from her face. "What's wrong?"

"Is she all right, Mr. Callahan?" William and Charlie huddled beside them, sodden and shivering.

"My ribs are just a bit tender," she whispered.

"He hit you there as well?" Paden's words burst out in a roar.

"Probably bruised them when I fell from the horse. It's nothing. Once I catch my breath—" Another twinge halted her. She focused on taking shallow breaths to keep the pain at bay. "Before I get up…can I lie here…without moving…for a moment?"

"All three of you need to get out of your wet clothes. Your lips are turning blue." His words sounded muffled and far away.

A chill, as sudden and frigid as an avalanche, enveloped her. The sun had dipped behind the western horizon, taking its meager warmth with it.

Splashing sounded nearby. Paden's arms tightened around her, then relaxed.

"Alejandro, can you deliver the boys to Miriam as soon as she's ashore? Virgil, I need you to take care of our horses. Rub them down and give them an extra ration of feed." With each word, Paden's tone turned increasingly authoritative. "Gabe, run ahead and lay out as many blankets as you can in the back of one my wagons. Then lend a hand settling the wagons. Double the men on night watch. We're done crossing for the day."

Without a backward glance, Paden carried her up the bank. He passed several wagons, including the scouts'.

"Our wagon's...back there," Hannah mumbled.

He grunted but didn't stop until he'd stood behind one of his supply wagons. "You need privacy, and this is the best I can give you." Stepping up on the tailgate, he lifted her inside and laid her on a pile blankets. Then he closed the rear flap snug behind him. Under the pale canopy of canvas, the light was dim and fading fast. Paden moved just as quickly. After removing her moccasin, he reached for her belt.

"What are you doing?" She tried to intercept him. Heavy as lead weights, her arms barely lifted before falling to her sides, limp and trembling.

His large hands engulfed hers as he raised her hands to his lips. "You can't remain in these wet clothes. You'll catch a fever."

Just like in the cave, the warmth of his breath permeated her icy shell. But this time, only for a brief moment. Her shivering wouldn't stop.

"Hannah..." He pressed a kiss to each of her palms before lingering on her spider tattoo. "For once, let me be your strength."

Her thoughts turned sluggish, like a thick fog drifting aimlessly.

Only his direct gaze held her secure. "Do you trust me?"

Her resistance vanished. She nodded. His gaze never left hers as he worked by touch to undress her in the dwindling light. The muscles along his jaw tightened. So did his lips, forming a white line across his tanned face. With each article of clothing, his face became more rigid, his hands slower, more clumsy. She yearned to reach up and wipe the strain from his brow.

His movements became swift again. He covered her with several wool blankets, then peeled off his buckskin coat and pulled his shirt over his head. Her trembling invaded the pit of her stomach and sent it fluttering. She squeezed her eyes shut. A boot fell with a thud, followed by another. A wet plop warned her he'd tossed his trousers aside.

Abruptly her blankets lifted. A wave of cold air hit her. Her eyes popped open. Paden's naked form descended in a blur of solid muscles to stretch out beside her. Before she could say anything, he lay plastered against her from head to heel. His eyes, inches from hers, flashed a mercurial gray. His heat flooded into her, easing her tremors.

Instinctively she pressed closer. A sigh spilled from her lips. Her eyelids were suddenly very heavy. She couldn't keep them open. She imagined she felt his lips brush soft as a butterfly's wings against the top of her head.

"Heaven have mercy on my soul," a voice muttered from very far away. "You're going to be the end of me."

Hannah jerked awake in the back of the supply wagon. A quick glance confirmed she was alone…and naked with only blankets wrapped around her. Heat scorched her face. Spirits Above, why had she allowed Paden to undress her? To lie next to her? And how could she have fallen asleep with him just as naked against her?

Because…she'd felt safe. Safer than she'd ever felt before.

She sat up, groaning, her ribs and jaw complaining at the swift movement. At least they didn't hurt as much as when she'd last been awake. A nagging ache persisted, though. Not unlike the guilt.

Her spare set of clothes lay folded neatly beside her. Had Paden put them there? The gesture warmed her in a different way, a stronger way. After she dressed, she spent several futile minutes trying to finger comb her hair into some semblance of order. Why was she delaying? She couldn't remain hidden away in this cocoon forever. Inhaling a deep breath, she poked her head out the back flap.

The sun was high overhead, well past midday. She sighed then straightened her backbone. *No more stalling*, she told herself and headed for the river.

The last emigrants had made good progress crossing the river. Only four wagons remained. One was in the water behind Paden and Cholla. He'd secured a rope around the lead ox's neck, the other end attached to his saddle horn. Man and horse parted the waters, guiding the wagon in their wake. Paden's muscles flexed as he worked to keep the oxen moving forward. Not long ago that strength had lain next to her. Legs weak, she sat down with a thump on the riverbank.

A small but solid form crashed into her back, making her wince. Little arms wrapped around her, while a tousled blond head burrowed against her shoulder.

Ignoring her discomfort, she smiled. "Good morning, Charlie."

The boy laughed a child's carefree giggle and hugged her tighter. "It's afternoon, Hannah. You've slept the day away."

Careful not to move too quickly, she reached up with one arm and embraced him in return. "So it seems."

Footsteps approached from behind her, then Miriam and William sat on either side of her.

"Thank you, Hannah." Miriam pulled Hannah's other hand into her lap and clasped it between hers.

Below them, the wagon rumbled up the riverbank. The crack of the driver's reins, the creaking of the wagon bed and its cargo rattling made further conversation impossible. Paden freed his lasso from the ox's head and pulled his lathered stallion to a halt beside their little group. The wagon continued clattering up the bank, leaving them in silence.

Paden tugged the brim of his hat. "Mrs. Jennings."

"Mr. Callahan." She dipped her head in return. "Thank you for rescuing my boys and our Hannah."

"My pleasure, ma'am." His gaze slid to Hannah. "Shouldn't you be resting?"

"I've slept all night and morning."

"What of your injuries?"

"I feel fine." She swallowed around the lump in her throat. "Thank you for yesterday."

The gray of his eyes sharpened to silver steel, boring into her.

She hastened to add, "For coming after me, for saving me."

"As I said, it was my pleasure."

Paden lay in his bedroll on the cold, hard ground. The campfire next to him had long since burned out. An almost full moon hung in the indigo sky, its waning light casting shadows across the camp and illuminating the wagons' canvas tops with a pale-blue glow.

Everyone was asleep. Everyone except him and Hannah.

His gaze tracked her blond head as she headed out for her turn on night watch. Before she disappeared into the gloom, he rose and followed her. When she stopped, choosing a dip on the riverbank for her post, he settled into the tall grass close by with his back to the moon.

Every night during her guard duty, he'd sat silent, motionless, keeping watch over her as she watched the wagons. Then he'd return to the camp minutes before her, so she'd never know he'd been near.

Each time it became more and more difficult to keep his distance.

Tonight it was a hundred times harder. He'd held her naked in his arms. Had fallen asleep for a few brief hours and woken with her slim limbs intertwined with his. It had taken all of his willpower to hold her like that and not act on his desires. When he'd undressed her, the light in the wagon had been dim and he'd refused to look at her body, sparing himself the exquisite torture of drinking in every glorious detail of her.

Now he wished he hadn't been so chivalrous. A certain part of his anatomy had been in a constant state of arousal today, even while riding in the chill river water.

Now Hannah was near again. And they were alone.

His blood pumped thick and hot through his veins, his flesh straining against his breeches. Burning with need, his body would not let him sit idle any longer. He rose and moved along the riverbank toward Hannah.

Hannah scanned the Platte River, admiring how the moon made its cascading rapids glow white and its swirling eddies shimmer. The gentle rumbling of the river soothed her, while the earthiness of the damp soil grounded her. Tomorrow they would leave the southern branch and continue along the northern one, heading ever westward. And when they reached the trail's end, she'd have to leave Paden. Each day brought her closer to that unhappy, unalterable outcome.

A prickle of unease skittered up her spine. Even though she'd neither seen nor heard anything, she sensed something approaching. She lifted her rifle and waited.

Paden strode through the moonlight toward the hollow she was using to conceal herself. His breath came hard and fast, as if he'd sprinted from the camp.

"Did you see something out there?" she whispered. "Are the wagons and livestock all right?"

He crouched down, balancing on his heels beside her.

"What's wrong?" Worry made her voice catch on the last word.

"I want you." His reply came out gravelly, as if it were a monumental effort to speak.

She blinked. She couldn't have heard him right.

His fingertips skimmed her jaw, tracing the bruise her Indian abductor had dealt her. "Does it hurt?" he asked, his eyes hungry, devouring.

Her breath caught in her throat. "A little."

Cradling her chin in his palm, he ran his thumb over her parted lips. She set her rifle aside, leaned into his hand and closed her eyes.

His fingers slid deep into her hair and, cradling her head, pulled her close. His mouth slanted across hers. She clutched his coat and held on.

A groan escaped him as he eased her onto her back. With jerky movements, he tugged the hem of her shirt free from her trousers, his hand sliding up and underneath. The instant his fingers touched her skin, he slowed his movements, as if wanting to savor the journey. She sucked in a breath in anticipation as his large, callused hand slid higher.

Until he cupped her breast and this time ran the pad of his thumb over her bare nipple. She shuddered and arched her back, trying to get even closer to him. She expected his thumb to continue the magic it'd created in the cave during the storm. Instead, his tongue found her, licking and teasing until her flesh was taut and firm. An ache formed low in her body, making her shift restlessly against him.

He released her, and a moan of protest escaped her lips. He pulled her shirt over her head and tossed it aside. Pale moonlight illuminated his face, as she was sure it did to her skin as well. His gaze, smoky with desire, roamed over her, his hands following in their wake to stop on her arms. His eyes flared wide.

She followed his gaze to the scars on her skin. Her stomach dropped.

A snarl twisted his lips as he jerked her close. She gasped at the sudden change in him. His narrowed gaze raced up her arms to her shoulders. Turning her, he ran his hands down her back, where she knew he'd find more marred flesh.

"These cuts?" he rasped. "Who did this to you?"

"I did them to myself. I—"

He spun her to face him. Gave her a shake. "Don't protect them. If they cut you—"

She gasped, disbelief stabbing her heart. "No one cut me."

"The Osage did this to you."

This time her gasp was one of outrage. "They'd never do such a thing!"

"I've seen cuts like these before, mutilation wounds. Some tribes inflict them on their captives and their dead, so their enemy's soul is weakened. So they can't rise to their spiritual resting place, their heaven."

"The Osage do not—"

"You'd protect them even after they did this?"

"I told you, they didn't do this. These cuts

happened before I met them."

With a roar like a bear rising to rip open a trespasser's throat, he jumped to his feet. Where was he going?

Wherever it was, she reached to stop him. "Wait. Listen to me."

He shook off her hand. "No, I can't bear to hear you make any excuses for them. How can you be like the others? After living with them for too long, they were broken, damaged."

She shrank back.

The anger drained from his face, and he reached for her this time.

She shoved his hands away, grabbed her shirt and jerked it back on. On trembling legs, she rose to face him. "No, *you* are the one like the others. Like the white trappers who tried to take me from Morning Star and Laughing Eyes. Do you honestly think after what I told you about those women that they'd cut me? Or that they'd allow anyone else to do so? You are no better than the men who killed them!"

She fled up the riverbank. Fell to her knees. Scrambled up blindly and ran on, ignoring her tears.

Paden's voice shouting her name echoed in her ears, but so did his previous words. *Broken, damaged.* He'd warned her to be wary of men. She should've taken his advice. She should've been more wary of him.

CHAPTER 10

Sitting at Miriam's camp, Hannah stared at her breakfast plate, her appetite non-existent, her mind numb.

How could Paden believe that Morning Star and Laughing Eyes could hurt her? How could he say she was *broken and damaged* from living with the Osage? They who had taught her to ride and shoot and speak their language. They who had seen beauty and strength in all of the Great Spirit's creatures. They who had opened their arms to a scared, bramble-cut nine-year-old.

She couldn't forgive him for this. Even though she now better understood his hatred of Indians, his need to avoid anything that reminded him of his unhappy youth living with the Comanche or their role in his wife's death.

He hadn't dismissed her at first sight. He hadn't lashed out physically with the anger that simmered inside him. Instead, he'd used words, raining them down on her like arrows. And only after he'd lulled her into a false peace, making her drop her guard and let him in. Now it was too late. He was lodged deep in her thoughts and her heart.

She lifted her fork, pushed around her food.

"Hannah, who is Eagle Feather?"

Her fork hit the ground with a thud, her plate nearly following.

Charlie sat next to her, munching on a biscuit. He gazed up at her with his innocent young face, awaiting her answer. "The Indian who tried to take you, he said he'd be rewarded for bringing you to someone. You said Eagle Feather."

"Charles Jennings!" Miriam waved her wooden spoon at her grandson. "Don't be pestering Hannah with your endless questions, young man. Let her have some privacy."

Charlie hung his head.

"It's all right, Miriam. Charlie has a right to know who he was fighting. After all, I wouldn't be here if it wasn't for him and William."

The boy's face lit up, his little body straightening with pride.

"The man who tried to take me was a stranger, but the one he mentioned, Eagle Feather…was my brother."

Charlie's eyes turned as round as her plate.

"When I was young, about your age in fact, the mother and father who gave me life were killed by the whites. But I lived. The Osage found me and took me in."

"B-but Indians are evil." His vehement response filled her heart with sadness.

"If that's true, then so am I."

His brow knitted as he mulled over her words. Then he asked, "Why is your brother looking for you? Has your mother sent him to bring you home?"

"No, I can't go back. When Morning Star adopted me, she had one daughter, Laughing Eyes, and one son, Eagle Feather. Laughing Eyes loved me as a sister, but Eagle Feather always held back a part of himself. He treated me with the respect befitting a member of his family, but no more than that. Then

Morning Star and Laughing Eyes were killed." She drew in a deep breath, steeling herself to utter the horrible truth, the truth that haunted her. "They died because of me, and for that I was rightfully cast out."

Charlie shook his head.

"It's true. And it's the reason why Eagle Feather still searches for me. You see, the last time I saw him he was very angry and he…made me a promise. He vowed that if he ever laid eyes on me again, he'd kill me. I've been hiding ever since."

"Hannah!" Miriam was on her feet. "Have you told General Sherwood and Mr. Callahan?"

Charlie jumped to his feet too. "Yes! Mr. Callahan can help you. He's a famous war hero, a soldier who—" An uncertain frown wrinkled his brow.

Hannah nodded. "Mr. Callahan was a soldier who killed Indians." She released a weary sigh of defeat. "And I'm a white woman who lived with the Osage, was one of them heart and soul. Mr. Callahan would view my relationship with my brother harshly. It's better if he doesn't know any more about me or Eagle Feather."

After last night, Hannah was never more certain of anything. How could she enlist help against Eagle Feather without igniting Paden's anger? And disgust? Would he even listen? He hadn't when she'd tried to explain about her scars. He'd believed what he wanted.

Where Paden was concerned, the most she could hope for would be to find a way for them to exist together on this wagon train, to get by, to reach the end of the trail without constantly stirring up the past.

Her past reminded him too much of his own: his youth with the Comanche, their role in his wife's death, his war against them. She brought his buried rage to the surface. How quickly the man who'd saved her from her abductor at the river—who'd held her so gently, cared for her so diligently so she wouldn't fall ill—had vanished. Or maybe this angry, hurtful side was his true self. His gentle side was the illusion.

"But what will you do?" Miriam asked.

"I don't know." Hannah smiled sadly. "I joined this wagon train hoping I could find a place far away, a place where I wouldn't have to hide anymore. I'm starting to fear that such a place doesn't exist."

After crossing the Platte River, Paden pushed the settlers to travel faster. The southern branch disappeared in their dust. He couldn't outrun the hurt he'd seen in Hannah's eyes though. She'd suffered injuries, and he'd made her feel worse about the ordeal. That she'd survived should've been all that mattered.

Many others hadn't been as lucky. Scores of graves lined the trailside, their rounded humps dotting the earth. While Paden's thoughts were filled with Hannah, only one word was on the settlers' lips.

Cholera.

When questioned about the sickness, Paden told them the disease was common on this leg of the trail. He didn't tell them that its onset was sudden, that the mortality rate high, that it attacked the old and young, the strong and weak. There was no use dwelling on those harsh truths. Instead he said that respite could be found by reaching the higher altitudes of the Laramie Hills.

So the settlers quickened their pace, their gazes fixed on the horizon in hopes of catching a glimpse of Fort Laramie—gateway to the hills and salvation.

By the sixth day, the heat and dust, combined with their grim surroundings, were making both man and beast irritable. The settlers grumbled, wishing for anything to break the monotony of their march. One step at a time, hour after hour, day after day. Paden had only one wish. He wished he could take back the harsh words he'd said to Hannah.

A cloud of dust rose on the trail ahead, growing larger, coming closer. With his hand on his revolver, Paden galloped to the head of the wagon train and strained to see through the haze.

A dozen shaggy Indian ponies pulling travois came into view. They plodded along without riders or handlers. Their heads bobbed low to the ground as they pushed forward with a single-mindedness that made Paden's throat dry from witnessing their thirst. Strapped to the travois that each animal pulled were long bundles wrapped in deerskins stained with unusual markings.

Paden raised his hand in warning for the wagon train to halt. His gesture caused the lead Indian pony to shy sideways before settling into a track parallel to the wagons. The other ponies followed blindly, allowing the curious settlers ample time to peruse their cargo as they trudged down the line.

Little Charlie Jennings was the first to voice the horrible truth Paden didn't want to accept. "They're pulling bodies."

"Cholera," Miriam whispered, tugging Charlie closer on her wagon seat. "Must've struck 'em fast and killed the folks transporting their deceased as well. Now these poor beasts plod along with a will of their own."

They were heading for the river. They wouldn't make it that far.

"Keep moving as well," Paden ordered.

The settlers obeyed with renewed vigor. As soon as the procession of Indian dead disappeared behind them, Paden galloped up the trail. He craved a moment alone. When he saw the familiar marker, he brought Cholla to a halt and stared at the words carved in stone below him.

Loving wife, devoted daughter.
Peace in heaven, if not on earth.
1822 – 1843

It was a good grave, for one out here on the trail. A split field rock stood as a headstone, rough and weathered on one side, smooth with neatly engraved script on the other. It hadn't changed much in the three years since he'd first seen it, probably looked the same as the day it was made. Most travelers hastily scratched out a shallow hole, rolled in a body and tossed a few shovelfuls of dirt on top. The scavengers thanked them for it later.

This grave was different. Someone had taken considerable time to pay their last respects in a place where time could be ill afforded. This woman had more than likely died of cholera, and that grim specter would've dogged the steps of everyone in her party. Not as tangible as the procession of Indian dead they'd just seen, but still felt.

Guilt and remorse sunk their talons deep into Paden's conscious, making him squirm in his saddle. Even during those final years in Texas, he'd never visited Jeannie's grave. He'd been too busy killing those responsible for putting her in the ground. But this grave… He'd been drawn to stop by it on his first trip, and the second, and now here he was a third time. The *last* journey, he vowed.

When he'd first arrived in Oregon, he'd lost himself in clearing his plot of land in the forest and building his cabin. It hadn't taken him long to see the need for a logging mill and build one as well. If he wanted his mill to flourish, he needed to stay near it. He'd never ride this way again. He'd never see this grave, just like he'd never see Jeannie's.

He'd always worried that Jeannie, with her frail constitution, would contract some fatal illness like cholera. So his guilt had hit doubly hard when she was taken by the very people he'd been hired to combat. He was a Texas Ranger who hadn't even been able to save his own wife.

Hannah's scars reminded him of all that Jeannie had suffered due to his failings.

Behind him, the first wagon rattled up the rutted trail. The man driving it bounced on his seat, suffering the bone-jarring experience in silence.

His wife had wisely opted to walk beside their wagon. She carried a toddler strapped to her chest with sack-cloth, and a little girl of maybe six years stepped in double-time by her side. Though trail-worn with chapped skin and threadbare clothing, the woman's stride was robust, and her hand holding her daughter's swung in a jaunty arc. The pair tackled the trail together.

Hannah would make a fine mother. The way she hovered over the Jennings boys left him no doubt. She was fierce and steadfastly determined. Patient too. Like the spider on her hand.

The wagon with its family drew even with him.

"When we get to California, can I have a puppy?" the girl asked, craning her tiny head to peer up at her mother.

"Aye, but we'll have to wait awhile, until we get settled. There's plenty of time. We've all the time in the world."

All the time in the world...

To this family, time was something to look

forward to. To him it was an enemy. He fought against it, struggled through it, wished the years ahead had already passed and he was on the other side of them. Wishing his life away.

As the rest of the wagons rolled by, he nodded absently to those who called out greetings. Near the rear of the column, the scouts' wagon appeared, Gabe driving, Hannah riding her pinto next to him. When they neared him, they stopped talking.

"Everything all right, Gabe?" he asked.

"Yes sir, just fine."

Paden's gaze flicked to Hannah. "Will you stop a moment? I have something on my mind I hope I might discuss with you."

She pulled her horse off the trail and stared at the horizon. They sat in silence as the final wagons clattered past. Her gaze strayed to the grave beside him, and she arched a questioning brow.

He groped for something to say. "She died too young," he finally commented, inclining his head toward the headstone.

"A woman? How young?" Her forehead puckered as she peered closer at the inscription. "One day I would like to learn to read," she said wistfully. "The Osage have no need for the white man's letters. I can't quite remember, but I think I was learning them when—" Her lips pressed into a grim line. "Well, that was a long time ago."

"How old were you?"

"Nine."

He felt a pinch in the corner of his heart and he suddenly wanted to know everything, could no longer take the easy way out by letting the past sleep. He cleared his raw throat and forced the words out. "You wanted to tell me something the other night, but I wouldn't let you. I'm sorry."

Her blue-eyed gaze darted to him, wary.

"You have every right to say no...but will you tell me now?"

Her gaze dropped to the grave. She was silent for such a long moment he feared she wouldn't answer. "A bramble patch is an excellent hiding place, but the thorns are very unforgiving. My mother made me hide under them after a band of militiamen shot my father and set fire to our cabin."

The old rage that had driven him as a Ranger to exact vengeance raced through his veins. Men like the ones she'd described didn't deserve to live. He struggled to keep his anger out of his voice. "Your first mother?"

"Yes...though I can't remember her name or my father's. I can't even remember their faces." She straightened her spine, sitting taller in her saddle. "But I recall her telling me something about the letters. They're familiar, like old friends."

Her gaze slid to the faded ridge of white on the back of her wrist. The scar was half concealed by the cuff of her coat. She tugged her sleeve down, hiding from him. So many times he'd seen the action and never understood. The weight of his regrets bowed his back.

"Morning Star put medicine on my cuts," she continued in a low voice, "and they healed as well as could be expected, but I knew the scars would never go away completely. I can't see all of them..." Her gaze traveled up her arm till she reached her shoulder. "Are there many?" She asked the question matter-of-factly, but then she blushed. Was she remembering him seeing her naked? Remembering him getting her that way?

"I'm deeply sorry for being rough with you that night, for losing my temper."

"They are ugly scars."

"No. They aren't."

"You said differently before." Her voice was hoarse but determined. "According to you, I'm broken."

"I shouldn't have said that." She was as strong as she was beautiful, not only in body but in spirit. He'd never believed something more deeply. He felt it in his bones. God, he wanted her more than anything else. And not just in his bedroll, but in his life as well. The realization hit him like a punch in the heart, taking all the fortitude out of him with one blow.

"The thought of someone hurting you..." he whispered. What if someone tried to hurt her again, and he couldn't stop them? The prospect chilled him to the core.

"I'm stronger than Jeannie," she said.

He no longer doubted her. He only doubted himself. He longed to tell her everything, to unburden his guilt and sorrow, but the words still wouldn't form. He couldn't give her false hope that he would ever be trustworthy again. He should dash all their hopes against the nearest rock and bury the fragments deep. He steeled himself for what he must do.

"I loved my wife, and the Comanche did more than take her life. They made her suffer as a warning to me, and because of that I—I will never love anyone again." The half-lie clawed at him. But which part was the lie? Was it the fact that instead of "will never" he should've said "should never"? Or that his feelings for Hannah were more intense than any love he'd ever felt for Jeannie?

His feelings for Hannah were fervent, explosive, all-consuming. They unnerved him so much he refused to analyze them any closer. All that mattered was that whatever they were, he couldn't burden Hannah with them.

Nor could he face her. He reined Cholla away and galloped after the wagons.

CHAPTER 11

"Well, I don't care what you say it's called, William." Charlie's tone was stubborn.

They'd been climbing the rock single-file for a good quarter hour and, although Hannah couldn't see William's face, she could picture him pursing his lips in his typical big-brother fashion. Despite her gloomy mood, a faint smile curved her own mouth as she realized she was starting to know the dispositions of both boys quite well.

"I ain't never seen no courthouse," Charlie continued, "so I'm a-callin' it the Tower of Babel, after that story Gran read us out of the Bible, 'cause that's what it reminds me of."

The wagon train had made its midday halt next to Courthouse Rock—the Tower of Babel, as Charlie had coined it—and many of their group were exploring its strange wonders. The rock had sprung out of the surrounding plains in four tiers, topped by a triangular peak. A miniature version, called Chimney Rock, stood off to one side, like a small but attentive sibling.

She leaned sideways to peer around the two boys. But all she saw was Charlie in the lead and William tucked between them. "How far to the top?" she asked.

"I think we've gone far enough," William grumbled under his breath.

"Don't be such a spoilsport." Charlie's step quickened. "We just passed the halfway point."

"Only halfway?" William groaned.

Hannah bit her lip to suppress her chuckle.

"What if we slip and fall?" William paused to peer down the way they'd come. He gulped, turned a pasty shade of green and raised his gaze forward again.

"Don't let him turn tail, no matter what, Hannah. You heard Gran say this outing would be good for him."

"If it's so good for a person, why didn't she come with us?"

"'Cause she needs her rest. And besides, we got Hannah to watch over us now."

Her heart squeezed tight. The boys were including her in their family. After 550 miles and eighteen days on the trail, Hannah realized her traveling companions were a jumble of contradictions.

Miriam and her grandsons had accepted her without question. Miriam hadn't batted an eyelash when the boys had begged Hannah to come with them, as if it was the most natural thing in the world. And here she was, climbing a rock hundreds of feet high with William and Charlie, like their long-lost sister. Since the first hour of their meeting, the three Jennings had never seemed to doubt her.

Others, like the women who'd snubbed her at Alcove Spring, openly expressed their aversion every chance they got. Thomas Riley worshipped Paden's skills as a Ranger but always favored her with a haughty eyebrow or a sneer.

Then there was Paden... His actions had opened a new and entirely astonishing world for her. How he'd sheltered her in the cave during the storm. How he'd tended to her in the back of his supply wagon. How he'd first touched her on the riverbank under the moonlight. That wasn't contempt. It wasn't love either. Yesterday, he'd told her as much. He'd never love again.

So what did he feel for her? He'd called her broken and damaged, said he was sorry. Her stomach dropped. He'd apologized for uttering those words, but he hadn't said he didn't believe them. Could he really think such a horrible thing? Her confusion snaked around itself and spiraled on and on.

He was as bewildering as the landscape they traveled through.

The Jennings boys were tickled to have this adventure and leave behind the dreary repetitiveness of marching the trail. Their never-ending banter kept her going. When they reached the top, their chatter stopped, and so did she. Up ahead, someone shouted that they'd found a fossil, and the boys sprinted away to take a look.

Hannah was content to sit and wait for their return. She passed the time by studying the view. Not far to the west stood another rock of equal grandeur and uniqueness, a long, thin spire growing out of its mounded base. It was as if each formation was trying to outdo the other, each wanting to delight and amaze its visitors more than its predecessor.

Lost in her thoughts, she started when Alejandro sat down beside her. Lines bracketed the corners of his eyes now as well as his mouth. Deep grooves that hadn't been there when she'd first met him.

Worry pinched her brow. "Are you well, Alejandro?"

His gaze met hers then skittered across the vista

around them. He gave a halfhearted laugh. "*Si*, of course. I—" His eyes narrowed to slits.

Rebecca Riley stood a score of yards away, surrounded by a swarm of men who pointed this way and that while spouting endless quotes on the geological formations. She nodded politely and smiled at each man in turn, but her body was stiff as she tried to keep her distance.

So, Alejandro was truly and hopelessly smitten with Thomas Riley's daughter. But love didn't seem to be agreeing with him.

"Did something happen between you and Rebecca?" Hannah asked.

A slash of a smile twisted his lips. "Apparently I am beneath her."

"Alejandro! How can you say such a thing?"

"I only repeat that which I have been told."

"By…Rebecca?"

"No."

"Her father said this?"

"*Si*, he does not believe a Mexican is good enough for his daughter. In his opinion, I am the equal to a renegade Comanche."

She opened her mouth to defend him, but he barrelled on.

"It counts little that I fought in the same battles as Callahan. No, that does not tally at all in his books."

Her gaze darted from Alejandro to Rebecca then back again. Taking a deep breath, she lowered her head and muttered, "Mr. Riley, he— Well, he's—" She clamped her lips tight in anger. "He's a horse's ass."

Alejandro's head snapped around and his jaw fell open. Then a smile twitched his mouth. "Those were my words, back at Fort Leavenworth, on the first day we met." His grin spread from ear to ear.

"Well, you were right," she mumbled.

Laughter burst out of him and soon he was doubled over, wiping away tears of merriment. "Thank—you—Hannah." He gasped for breath, his eyes twinkling like the old Alejandro. "Thank you for reminding me."

Her laughter tumbled out to join his. "You're welcome. And don't worry, I'll keep reminding you. Now get over there and save poor Rebecca from those men."

Alejandro strode across the sandstone vault of Courthouse Rock toward heaven, toward an angel. *Dios*, she was breathtaking, standing in the sun with her glorious red hair and golden eyes. Rebecca Riley held him spellbound. She made his chest ache. But she wasn't merely beautiful on the outside. She had a kind heart, too.

He scowled. Too kind. She was trying hard to be pleasant to the men surrounding her, which couldn't have been easy as they were a rowdy bunch, full of foolish banter—and getting more impudent by the second. As he drew near, one of them grasped Rebecca's elbow and pulled her away from the others. Alejandro broke into a run.

Rebecca twisted her arm, to no avail. "Release me!"

The man did, but he didn't retreat. Instead, he leaned over her with a scowl. "Shh. Why you yelling?" he growled. "I just wanna go for a walk with you." He dropped his voice to a whisper. "Alone."

The other men exchanged nervous glances. Their lighthearted rivalry and quest to impress Rebecca had disappeared. Alejandro positioned himself behind the group, making sure her most persistent suitor was within easy striking distance.

Rubbing her arm, she swung back to face the view. "I'd prefer to stay here." Her voice was quiet but firm.

The man took a step toward her, but he didn't touch her this time. "No, you'd prefer to come with me."

"I think I know my own mind, sir. I'm just here for the view."

"Your father said you'd be nice to me."

Rebecca frowned. "He did not."

He gave her a disgruntled look. "He told me to come over tonight. That you'd cook me supper."

Her brows rose as she cast a sideways glance at him. "Visitors in need of food are welcome at my father's wagon."

"This is different," he shot back. "Yer father and I agreed to buy land next to each other. We have a special arrangement. We shook on it. We'll be combining our resources and living together. All of us."

Rebecca spun to face the man, her guarded countenance collapsing into a look of utter disbelief. "I'm not living with you. We aren't married."

"We will be, just as soon as we reach the coast and Sutter's Fort."

Her face turned white as sand in the Tularosa Basin. "This entire conversation is preposterous. I can't be your wife, because— I'm already married." She looked down at her feet and then added in a rush, "It was a secret wedding."

"Your father never said anything."

"Secret weddings are usually secret from fathers," Rebecca retorted.

Her reply made her suitor's mouth drop. "We'll see about that," he muttered and stalked off.

The other men cast her uncertain glances. Then they departed as well, leaving Alejandro and

Rebecca alone.

She caught sight of him for the first time and blushed. "I thought you were sitting with Hannah."

"I was."

"Did you hear…?"

"I did."

"Oh. Well. I wanted them to leave and I guess I got a little carried away."

He grinned at her. "I don't know. I kind of liked the idea of a secret wedding."

Her shoulders slumped and she groaned. He moved to stand beside her, and together they faced the wide-open expanse stretching as far as the eye could see around Courthouse Rock.

"This is going to get you in trouble with your *padre*, isn't it?"

"It'll be better than having to deal with those men, especially one who thinks I'll marry him without him first *asking* me. I have no idea what came over him, or the others for that matter. I can't figure out why they all wanted to talk to me."

"I know why. You're too pretty."

Her mouth dropped open and she turned to face him.

"But your nose is still sunburned."

She stared at him for a moment then laughed. "It's the fault of my red hair. I hate it."

"There is nothing about you that I could hate. *Estás el amor de mi corazón.*"

"*Amor?*" she said tentatively.

"Love. Not just any love, though," he said with conviction. "I said you are the love of my heart."

She inhaled sharply. "We hardly know each other."

"I know enough."

A sad smile curved her lips. "You're teasing me again."

"I'm not. Not now." Suddenly he knew what he must do, knew what he wanted to do. There wasn't a doubt in his body. He reached out and took her hand in his. "I'm asking you. Will you marry me? And make your secret wedding a real one?"

He was in heaven. Dawson stood in Fort Laramie's trading store, his mouth watering in anticipation. Things were looking up. Laramie had no shortage of whiskey or folks eager to sell it. He grumbled as he handed over his money, gained from loot stolen only this morning and bartered for greenbacks. His surliness was all for show. When he picked up the crate of bottles and left the store, a grin twitched his lips.

He'd always been happiest in the far reaches of the frontier. He understood the people who populated it. He liked their roughness, their simple ways and their lack of rules. Life had been sweet until he'd met Callahan and the uppity Ranger had upset his apple cart.

His smile disappeared along with the confidence he'd mustered since arriving at Laramie. Callahan had no call to want him off his wagon train or to demean him by replacing him with a woman. Dawson couldn't escape the memory of that disgrace. Time and distance hadn't helped.

He'd been a coward to abandon his pursuit. He wouldn't run again. Callahan and his squaw wouldn't pass Laramie without feeling his revenge.

As he crossed the fort's parade ground, his friends fell into step on either side of him.

This morning they'd robbed a pair of army stiffs they'd encountered ten miles outside the fort, where the army had sent the men to cut wood. When the soldiers saw they weren't Indians, they'd lowered their weapons and welcomed them, eager to talk.

The fools had deserved to die, and his friend had finally had a chance to put his blade to good use. Signs of Sioux riders in the vicinity had provided the inspiration. With the soldiers' scalps lifted, the army would never think to suspect Dawson and his comrades.

The men's belongings had bought him an entire case of red-eye. He had everything he needed while he waited for Callahan and his squaw to arrive. Unfortunately, his friend was once again caressing his knife and staring a little too intently at the army barracks. This morning's killings had only increased his bloodlust.

"We need to lay low for a while," he warned. "Keep yer knife sheathed until Callahan 'n his bitch arrive."

"They'd better get here soon. I've been dreaming about slitting your wagon master's throat."

"Jesus Christ!" Alarm made him shout. He scanned the parade ground, hoping he hadn't drawn too much attention. "We're not killing him, or her," he said in a low voice. "I want them to live so they can suffer indefinitely. I need this."

The man stared at him with bottomless black eyes and clutched his knife as if it were all he had, or ever would have. "I have needs as well."

Dawson's love for Fort Laramie and the frontier dropped a notch. If he wanted his revenge to go as planned, he'd have to keep a close watch over his volatile friend. That would mean limiting his drinking while encouraging his friend's.

"Drown your needs in this." He pulled a bottle from his crate and tossed it to the man. When the man released his knife and snatched the bottle out of the air, he breathed easier.

"Don't forget about me," his other friend whined.

He didn't catch his bottle as neatly as the other man. He almost dropped it in the dirt.

Dawson gritted his teeth. Heaven was a complicated place. It could so easily transform into hell. He clenched his hands, trying to hold onto his restraint, and failed. He reached for his own bottle.

Two days outside Fort Laramie, Paden halted the wagon train in the cooling shadow of Scott's Bluff, a rocky cliff so high that it appeared to touch the sky. Tomorrow they'd leave the plains behind, push through the narrow gap of Mitchell Pass and be rewarded with their first glimpse of the Rocky Mountain foothills. The pioneers were abuzz with excitement at reaching this important milestone.

Paden was not.

Once again Hannah hadn't returned to the scouts' wagon for the evening meal. He tried to oust her from his thoughts by listening to the conversation between General Sherwood, Gabe and Virgil. Scott's Bluff being another source of geological wonder and tall tales, the three men seated across from him were engrossed in a spirited debate about what really happened to Hiram Scott, the fur trader whom these formations were named after.

"Some believe he was abandoned by his companions after falling ill," Sherwood remarked.

Virgil studied the coffee beans roasting on his skillet. "Could just as well have been ambushed by the Sioux."

Gabe shrugged. "Maybe he got chewed up by a cantankerous grizzly bear?"

The two older men laughed, and Gabe's cheeks turned red.

Sherwood clasped his grandson's shoulder. "Anything's possible." His gaze slid to Paden. They stared at each other in silence for a moment, and Paden realized the general was reminding him of his words when he first met Hannah. Sherwood sighed and turned back to Gabe. "The only thing agreed upon is that Scott's skeleton was found alone among these rocks, contorted in agony."

Paden commiserated with Scott. Dying alone would be a cruel fate. Solitude had lost the appeal it once held. His gaze skimmed the circle of wagons. When he didn't see Hannah, he went back to glaring at the scouts' campfire.

The crackling flames gave him no comfort, no joy, not even any warmth. He was no better than the irritable bear Gabe had mentioned. Why couldn't he be happy? Or even content? Why did he only feel this simmering anger? This never-ending restlessness?

If Hannah wasn't at their camp, where was she? More importantly, who was she with? He snorted, knowing the likely answer—with Miriam Jennings and her boys. He liked the Jennings family, but he didn't like Hannah spending more and more time with them to the point where he never saw her. But he had only himself to blame, seeing as he'd been the one to push her away.

Another burr had lodged under his blanket, though. Alejandro had yet to join their camp. What if the smooth-spoken Mexican was with Hannah?

Two days ago at Courthouse Rock, he'd spied them chatting about some topic so interesting that she'd made Alejandro break out in peals of laughter. But he'd later seen Alejandro with Riley's daughter. Paden's scowl deepened. The man was too much of a charmer for his liking. Back in Texas, he had all the ladies flocking around him with his easy words and smooth manners.

By comparison, Paden felt like an outcast from

the backwoods. One look at his sharp, brooding features, and the ladies had steered well clear of him. No one besides the general knew he'd grown up with the Comanche, but…could others sense it?

Only one thing was certain. He was tired of sitting here waiting for a glimpse of Hannah. He rose to his feet. A stroll by the Jennings' camp was in order. He just wanted to see Hannah and reassure himself that she was safe. He'd keep his distance. He wouldn't say anything. And above all, he wouldn't lose his temper.

As he searched for Miriam's wagon, children streamed past him, chasing each other and leaving laughter bubbling in their wake. Their mother cut short their game with a shout that supper was ready. They raced back to her side. She filled plates and passed them to her husband, who set aside his corncob pipe and handed them out to their brood. Then they all sat together to eat while speculating about the trail ahead.

Paden's restlessness grew, quickening his strides. Even when he'd been married, he'd never enjoyed this family life. He'd been too busy being a Ranger, protecting others' families.

Thomas Riley's grating voice, raised in conversation with another man, reached him. Paden lowered his head and walked even faster. He didn't want to be distracted by Riley right now. He wanted to find Hannah. As far as he was concerned, Riley was a jabbering fool who enjoyed the sound of his own voice too much. As soon as he'd passed the pair of men, he slowed down and breathed a little easier.

Behind him, Riley's words faded to a murmur. "I knew having a female as a scout would be asking for trouble."

Paden's footsteps ground to a halt.

"Don't know why Captain Callahan allowed it,"

Riley continued.

The other man grunted his agreement. "He ain't so bang-up after all."

"Now see here," Riley burst out. "The captain's a war hero."

"That was years ago. Could be living in the frontier has whittled away his good judgment."

"Well, I admit he's made some questionable selections for scouts in a bean-eater 'n a half-breed girl." Riley spoke slowly as if the words pained him.

The other man laughed. "She ain't no half-breed, not with her blond hair 'n blue eyes."

"She lived with heathens. She's a fallen woman." Riley's tone had turned clipped and decisive, and full of condemnation. "She goes off alone with men from this wagon train."

Rage whipped Paden around. He bore down, unnoticed on Riley.

"You should be happy," Riley's friend said, "that the Mexican's with her instead of your daughter. Solves one problem at least."

"If it stops him sniffing around my girl, I'm glad of it. Still sets a bad example, them going off together alone. As we speak, they're probably—" Riley glanced up as Paden's shadow fell over him. The fat toad gulped and forced an uncertain smile to his lips. "Captain Callahan, it's a pleasure to see you."

"Oh, believe me, the pleasure's all mine," Paden snarled before his fist connected with Riley's face.

"This place is even more remarkable than Courthouse Rock." Hannah craned her neck and used one hand to shade her eyes so she could study the cliff-tops high above them.

"Are we hunting or sightseeing?" Alejandro's

voiced teased from beside her.

She grinned sheepishly. "You got me there. All right, we're hunting."

"*Bueno*, because we haven't much light left, and I've picked up a deer trail."

Together they followed the tracks down a long gulch whose stone walls pressed closer with every step they took. Now it was Alejandro's turn to stop and lift his gaze to the craggy bluff above them. A red-tailed hawk soared on the thermals, also searching for its next meal. Alejandro tracked the bird until it disappeared, then continued staring at the sky.

"Are we hunting or daydreaming?" Hannah asked, biting her lip to keep from smiling.

He chuckled. "Hmm, I guess we're doing a bit of everything this evening." He paused and when he spoke again, the laughing lilt was gone from his voice. "I talked to Rebecca and..." He scrubbed a hand over the back of his neck.

"You've spoken to her since that day at Courthouse Rock? When you first told me you had strong feelings for her?"

"We haven't had a chance to speak to each other very often, but when we have it's been... Well, the last time we..." His gaze dropped to his boots.

"Something changed?" Hannah prompted.

He shrugged one shoulder.

Unease tightened her chest, making it hard to speak. "What— What did Rebecca say?"

Alejandro's dark-eyed gaze rose to meet hers. "She didn't say anything."

"I thought you said—"

He held up his hands. "It's not so much what Rebecca said that's got me in a whirl. It's what *I* said and what I feel." He squared his shoulders. "*Ella es el amor de mi corazón.*" His lips pressed into a determined line. "I told her I love her. That I want to marry her."

Hannah inhaled sharply. "And Rebecca said yes?" She hoped with all her heart that this was the case.

Alejandro smiled back.

She bounded the few steps separating them and flung her arms around his neck. "I'm so happy for you! This is wonderful news."

He staggered under the exuberance of her embrace, then chuckled. "*Si*, it is good news, but now we have to deal with her *padre* and that's not going to be easy."

"But as long as there's love," she replied, "there's hope."

"Didn't I say not to touch her?" The question was sharp as the crack of a whip slicing the air over her and Alejandro's heads.

She leaped away from him, and he from her.

Paden advanced on them with swift strides. His face was hard, his eyes narrowed, but he wasn't looking at her. His gaze skewered Alejandro and when he spoke again, his voice was low and grinding. "Shouldn't you be getting back to the wagons?"

Alejandro stepped closer to her.

Lightning quick, Paden closed the remaining distance between the two men. His chest came up hard against Alejandro's, knocking the slighter man backward. "What part of this conversation don't you understand?"

Hannah's heart contracted with dismay. She pushed her way between the two men and, standing with her back to Alejandro, faced Paden with both palms raised.

Paden stared at Hannah's hands, at her spider tattoo, raised against him in defense of another man. Hellfire, what had he done? Had he pushed her away, only for her to fall into Alejandro's arms? He'd thought the man was sweet on Rebecca. Was Riley correct in assessing a shift in Alejandro's affections? Did Hannah return them?

He sought the answer in the one place he knew to look.

Hannah's eyes were wide with concern. But she didn't meet his gaze. Instead, she stared at his fist, still raised toward Alejandro. "What happened to your poor hand?" she whispered.

His knuckles were scraped and bloodied from hitting Riley. He crossed his arms so he could hide them and fixed his gaze on Alejandro. "I want to know your intentions toward Hannah."

"His intentions?" Her voice rose with disbelief. "We're friends. It's good to have a friend. You should try it sometime." She winced. Even now, when he was behaving abominably, she worried about hurting his feelings. "We were talking about—" She glanced over her shoulder at Alejandro. "Do you want him to know? He might be able to help."

Paden's gut lurched. She'd said she and Alejandro were only friends, but whatever they'd been discussing sounded weighty. "What's going on?"

Alejandro glared at him with an almost defiant look. "Miss Riley and I plan to be wed."

Paden's stomach dropped back into place. *Praise heaven.* He hadn't lost Hannah to another man. Then he frowned, unsure if he should believe his luck. "Didn't think you were the marrying sort. What happened?"

"I fell in love." Alejandro cocked one eyebrow. "Unlike others, I decided to embrace the situation like a rational man."

Paden ignored the barb. "So you need—" his gaze slid to Hannah, "—a friend to aid you in circumnavigating Miss Riley's father?"

"Unfortunately that must be part of the plan," Alejandro's muttered. "A very significant part."

"Will you help?" Hannah asked.

If he didn't, she would. She'd launch herself headfirst into this new danger, alone. "Fort Laramie has a chapel. Preacher's open-minded. Marries whites, natives, anyone who asks. Rather marry folks than have them live in sin." He slanted a hard look at Alejandro. "Why Miss Riley?"

A frown wrinkled Alejandro's brow. "What do you mean?"

"No offense, but she's probably better off hitched to someone else. She won't have it easy with her father if she's hitched to you. So why marry her?"

"Because I love her." Alejandro's reply was swift. "Others want her for more selfish reasons."

"Isn't putting your needs above hers selfish?" Paden shot back.

"I intend to spend my life making her happy."

"Happiness is an elusive target."

"It's the only target worth pursuing."

"What if you fail?"

"What if I succeed?"

"What if you get her killed?"

Alejandro drew in a deep breath, halting their rapid-fire exchange. "Do you honestly think anyone else would expend more effort protecting Hannah than you would?"

Paden flinched. He stole a glance at Hannah. Once again, she stared at him with wide eyes, this time full of hope.

He glared at Alejandro. "We're not talking about me."

Alejandro contemplated him with his damned annoying eyebrow raised again. "Our situations are not that different."

"Fine." He strove to soften his churlish tone. "I'll help you. Let me know when you're going to Laramie's chapel. I'll make sure Riley remains with the wagon train."

A huge smile brightened Hannah's face, filling him with a sudden euphoria. But her next words cut his happiness off at the knees. "I'll go with Alejandro and Rebecca to the chapel."

"Hell no, you won't. Laramie's too dangerous."

Hannah's expression fell, making his mood plummet even further.

"I could ask Virgil and the general to accompany us," Alejandro offered. "We'd keep both ladies safe."

"The fort's off limits to Hannah. That's not open to negotiation."

"Why can Rebecca go and I can't?" Hannah raised her chin. "I made out fine in Fort Leavenworth."

Paden blew out a breath, trying to hold onto his patience and not growl like a surly bear. "Laramie's worse than Leavenworth."

"Why?" Hannah's unblinking regard challenged him.

He removed his hat and slapped it against his thigh, trying to shake some of the dust free. There was no shaking Hannah's questions though. He'd have to tell her, but how much? He jammed his hat back on his head. "I am, unfortunately, acquainted with the present colonel of Fort Laramie. His contempt for natives is only rivaled by his disgust for those who chose, or have chosen, to associate with them."

"You know him from our Texas days?"

Alejandro asked.

Paden nodded.

Alejandro remained silent. They knew the same people from Texas. Alejandro was probably rifling through a list of likely candidates.

"The name you're searching for is Jim Weston."

Alejandro spat out a particularly colorful curse in Spanish.

Paden agreed wholeheartedly. Weston would be to blame for the trigger-finger mentality rumored to be present in Fort Laramie's soldiers. An attitude reserved for natives.

"Well," Alejandro said with a resigned sigh. "At least we are no longer under Weston's command. You should try to stir clear of him as well. You won't get along out here any better than you did in Texas."

"Because you lived with—" Hannah's gaze dropped and a flush brightened her cheeks.

So, she saw the wisdom in keeping his secret about growing up with the Comanche. Now was the time to tell her another secret, this one only a handful of people knew.

"Weston has many reasons to despise me. Jeannie's the one Alejandro is referring to now. Weston wanted to marry her."

"Oh." Hannah's simple reply raked his conscience. Why couldn't he tell her something positive for once?

Alejandro broke the heavy silence that had stifled the conversation "Jeannie turned Weston down. She knew he was more enamored with being the son of a general than her husband. Weston wouldn't have made her happy."

"She'd still have been better off with him." Pushing aside his old regrets, Paden concentrated on preventing a new one. He leaned forward to stare directly into Hannah's eyes. "Do you now agree that you shouldn't go inside Fort Laramie?"

Her breathing grew fast and shallow.

His gaze dipped to the fluttering pulse at the base of her throat. He was frightening her. He drew back.

She reached out as if to stop him, then let her hand fall to her side. "I agree." Her voice sounded wooden with disappointment or sadness, or both. "But I'll never agree that you were responsible for Jeannie's death."

Her steadfast determination to defend him robbed him of speech, which was good. There was no sense arguing the point. Not when he had what he wanted. Or did he? Too many things had gone wrong in the past for him to relax completely. "Do I have your word that you won't go inside the fort, that you'll avoid Weston at all costs?"

Hannah nodded. "You do."

Alejandro was nodding as well and staring at Hannah with worried eyes. Good. Finally someone else shared his fears. Alejandro would help him, and he'd help Alejandro. Alejandro would marry Rebecca, and he'd figure out what to do about Hannah after he got her safely past Fort Laramie.

CHAPTER 12

"Gone?" Paden's throat closed up. He struggled to breathe, to think. How could Hannah have disappeared so quickly? They'd arrived at Fort Laramie less than an hour ago. "Where the hell is she?"

"I'm sorry, sir. I don't know." Gabe's gaze dropped, unable to hold Paden's.

Miriam shot Paden a look full of reproach, while her grandsons hovered beside her, gaping at him. "When did you last see her?" she asked Gabe in a gentle voice.

"She helped me set up our camp," he replied, "like she always does when we halt for the night."

Paden scanned the wagons. Instead of forming their usual circle, they were scattered about the field surrounding Fort Laramie. The fort had imbued the settlers with a false sense of security. The tall walls of the fortress standing sentinel above him filled him only with foreboding.

Had someone forced her to go inside? One of Weston's soldiers? Weston himself? "I'll rip him limb from limb."

Miriam planted her hands on her hips and glowered at him. "Growling in such a fashion isn't constructive, Mr. Callahan. Your temper won't help us find Hannah."

Paden matched her scowl before acknowledging that she was right. He counted to ten while trying to harness his anger and fear. "Gabe," he said slowly. "What did Hannah say when you last saw her?"

Gabe's gaze remained lowered. "She didn't say anything, which was odd. She seemed preoccupied and kept glancing at the fort."

She wouldn't have gone inside freely. She'd given her word. He knew her well enough to know she wouldn't break it. He rubbed the ache building between his brows, trying to erase the annoying twinge so he could better focus. It didn't work.

"I hope Eagle Feather hasn't got her." Charlie's softly spoken words transformed Paden's discomfort into a stabbing pain.

He dropped his hand and spun to face the boy.

Miriam wrapped her arm around her grandson and held him tight. "Not another word, Charlie."

"Who's Eagle Feather?" Paden demanded.

The nervous shuffling of feet was his only answer.

"Is he the Osage brave who talked to Dawson?" His tone sounded lethal even to his own ears.

"We don't know anyone named Dawson," Miriam replied. "And as far as the rest... Well, I'm sorry, Mr. Callahan, but we shouldn't be repeating something Hannah told us in confidence. I advised her to tell you, but seeing as you don't get along too well with the natives, and with her believing you don't think much of her either for having lived with them, she said no." Miriam gaze lowered in a similar fashion to Gabe's. Even the unflappable Miriam was now unable to look at him.

The frustration swelling in his chest made him feel like he'd explode.

Charlie met his gaze without blinking. "I know

you wouldn't hurt Hannah. Not after you saved her."

Disbelief made him draw back his head. "Who said I'd do such a thing?"

"Everyone on the wagon train says you've killed dozens of Indians. Hannah says she's more native than white, 'cause she grew up with them. She also said Eagle Feather promised to kill her. But I can't believe that. Not if he's her—"

"Charlie, that's enough." Miriam's reprimand cut off her grandson.

Kill her? Paden's stomach dropped, threatening to drop him as well. The ground seemed to sway under his feet. If this Indian named Eagle Feather had Hannah, he wouldn't take her inside the fort. He'd take her far away from it, and him. He scanned the horizon.

A lone wagon sat near the fort, separate from all the others. Behind the white canopy, the setting sun threw its blazing brightness into his eyes, making him squint to see more. One of the horses beside the wagon seemed familiar. Brown head. White back. Hannah's pinto.

He vaulted onto Cholla and urged him into a gallop. When they rounded the wagon, his heart was in his throat and his hand was on his revolver.

Hannah sat beside a man and woman he'd never seen before. He pulled Cholla to a skidding halt. Her gaze met his with a jerk. She hastily shook her head and pressed the tip of her finger to her lips. The tension left his body in a whoosh. She was safe.

The man beside Hannah stared at him with tired eyes set deep in a haggard face. The woman hadn't even acknowledged his arrival.

"Hannah, why did you leave the wagon train?" He cast a second glance over the woman beside her.

With skin as pale as ice and dark hair sticking out around her face like a storm cloud, she looked like a banshee come to earth on the rough end of a squall. Her eyes, two dark smudges in her wan face, gazed straight ahead, locked in an unblinking stare. But it was her incessant rocking and how she clutched a tattered bundle to her chest that made the skin along his shoulders itch.

His gaze swung back to Hannah, but she'd already returned her attention to the woman. Seeking answers, he looked to the man who continued watching Paden with the same air of hopelessness.

"Your daughter wouldn't want you to give up on your dream to reach the Western Territories," Hannah said in a low, soothing voice. "Your husband was just saying how happy she'd been on your journey."

As soon as Hannah began speaking, the rigid set of the husband's face softened and he leaned closer to the two women. His wife nodded but kept rocking.

"My mother told me the greatest disservice we can do a loved one is not honor them. She believed we must keep their memories and dreams alive."

The woman stopped moving. She didn't look at Hannah, but she now leaned toward Hannah like her husband did. Paden could feel the hope radiating from the couple.

"How will your daughter be remembered if you remain here and fade into the earth, forgotten?" Although Hannah had continued speaking in the same reassuring voice, her question filled him with a sudden unease.

He scanned the couple's wagon and campsite as he tried to make sense of the situation. In growing confusion, he continued searching until he saw a shovel and a shallow hole. A grave. A small one.

His gaze snapped back to the bundle clutched in the woman's arms. A little foot dangled from beneath the blanket, gray and limp. The child had been dead awhile. The couple's grief was so strong it rendered Paden immobile.

But Hannah's calmness also held him captive. She seemed to bind the couple together, as if without her they'd shatter. A crazy notion, because she couldn't have been with them very long.

"If you die here as well," she continued, "no one will know what a beautiful girl your daughter was. How precious and special. If you don't fulfill your shared dream to reach the West, she will not be honored. Who will you tell her story to? It's the way of things. To honor your loved ones with tales of their lives so they won't be forgotten, so they will live on."

The woman closed her eyes as she turned to face Hannah. When she opened them, they glistened with tears...but her brow lifted in a hopeful arc.

Hannah gestured for the woman's husband to take the child. Instantly his wife and hugged the bundle closer.

Hannah placed her hand on the woman's shoulder. "It's all right to let go," she said, using the same gentle voice. "You must be strong for your daughter."

The woman's head twitched in a jerky nod, and this time she allowed her husband to take the child. Relief softened his features when he gained his daughter's body.

Hannah clasped the woman's hands in hers and stood. "Come with me," she urged. "My friend, Miriam, is nearby. You can tell her all about your daughter, and she'll be the first to keep your little girl's memory alive."

She helped the woman to her feet and guided her away. The woman clung to Hannah as if her life depended on it. Paden waited until they were out of sight before picking up the shovel. He didn't want to ruin the peace Hannah had given the woman.

When the last scoop of earth had been placed on the grave, the father knelt beside it with his hat in his hands. "I couldn't get Sarah to let go. I stopped trying when she said she'd hate me forever if I put our daughter in a ground." He scrubbed at the tears on his cheeks. "When I told our wagon train we wouldn't be continuing on with them, they seemed relieved to leave the sight of our grieving behind. I didn't try to stop them. I'd given up as well." He stared in the direction Hannah and his wife had departed. "Then *she* came along," he whispered in voice filled with wonder.

"She has that way about her. She arrives out of nowhere and then you can't remember what your life was like before she came." He finally accepted that his life would never be the same. Sometimes things happened to a man, and he had no way of fighting them. He didn't want to fight anymore.

The admission drained the tension out of him like water from a dam. Then he stiffened again. The biggest fight of his life was about to begin, and the outcome was more precious than anything he'd known before.

Hannah had convinced him, like she'd convinced the grieving couple, to give life a second chance. But he only wanted his second chance if Hannah was in it.

Hannah poured coffee into two mugs, handed one to Miriam and pressed the other into the cold hands of the grieving mother seated beside her. As soon as they'd arrived, she'd drawn Miriam aside and told her of the woman's loss. Miriam had immediately taken charge, coaxing their visitor to sit by the fire and wrapping a blanket around her thin shoulders.

Relief flooded Hannah, followed quickly by fatigue. Getting the woman this far had taken all her strength.

Miriam patted her hand before addressing their guest. "My name's Miriam. What's yours, honey?"

"Sarah." The reply was as hushed as the embers sighing in the fire.

"Well, you've arrived just in time for supper. Do you like dumplings and stew?"

Sarah's head bobbed in the barest of nods. "My daughter did as well. Her name was Hope."

Hannah's heart missed a beat. *Hope.* All her words of wisdom dried up. She didn't know what to say.

Miriam reply came swiftly though. "That's a right pretty name. I had a daughter once too. My pride and joy, left me those two young'uns over there." She gestured to William and Charlie, brushing down the mules.

Hannah's gaze flew to Miriam. Her friend's expression was as tranquil as if she were discussing the weather or the last mile of trail they'd covered. She'd never talked about the boys' parents before, and Hannah hadn't asked. She hadn't wanted to pry. Until now, she hadn't known whether Miriam had born a son or a daughter.

Sarah's vacant stare receded, allowing the green of her eyes to shine through. "Your daughter...died?"

"Sadly, yes."

Paden arrived with Sarah's husband by his side. His gunmetal gaze immediately found her, fortifying her with a reassuring warmth. For all her confident words while trying to coax Sarah away from her daughter's body, she'd been scared until Paden had charged up on Cholla. She hadn't been sure she'd be able to reach Sarah and convince her to go on living. But Paden's presence had once again made her feel stronger.

"I'm glad you're still here." The intensity in his gaze made her heart race, as did his words. He tipped his hat to Miriam. "This is Sarah's husband, Nathaniel."

"Most folks just call me Nate." He stared longingly at his wife, while Sarah's attention was now fixed on her hands clasped in her lap. Her mug lay on the ground, unnoticed, coffee seeping into the dirt.

"Will you join us, Nate?" Miriam asked. "Supper's ready, and I'd appreciate the company. Can get a mite lonesome on the trail."

Nate gave an awkward nod, then took a seat next to his wife. After the briefest hesitation, and without looking at her, he reached over and covered her hands with one of his. He sat ramrod straight. When Sarah's fingers finally untwined to wrap around his instead, the starch went out of him along with a heavy sigh.

Blinking damp eyes, Hannah turned away and ended up staring up at Paden. When had he moved to stand directly in front of her, only an arm's length away?

"I require a word with you. In private." His quiet tone filled her with anxiety.

She couldn't move, couldn't speak.

Crouching to her level, he pitched his voice even lower. "It's about Eagle Feather."

Alarm shot through her, launching her to her feet. Paden rose with her.

Had he seen her brother? Had Eagle Feather finally found her?

Sarah and Nate gaped at her, their own fears temporarily forgotten. Miriam stared as well, looking concerned but also guilty. Then she ducked her head, grabbed a plate and began spooning out her stew.

Hannah released a shaky breath. Eagle Feather wasn't here. Paden only knew about him because Miriam had told him.

Paden opened his mouth to speak again. He wasn't going to stop until he got his conversation. Sarah and Nate shouldn't hear this. They had enough worries. She turned and walked away from the campfire.

Paden's footsteps came close behind her. As soon as they were out of earshot, he said, "Who is he?"

She forced herself to stop and meet this gaze. Then she forced herself to stand her ground. "You look angry."

He rubbed his brow. "Not angry. Concerned. There's a difference."

Unfortunately, his concern only increased hers. He looked ready to do battle. "He's my brother," she blurted.

He blinked only once before saying, "He's Morning Star's son."

"Her last remaining family," she added in a rush. "No harm must come to him. This is the only way I can repay her for all she sacrificed to keep me safe. It doesn't matter that he vowed to—" She shook her head unable to say the words to Paden. "That was long ago." And hopefully far away. She tried to force a conviction into her voice that she didn't feel. "Every mile I travel west makes him less of a concern."

"If he promised to kill you, then he'll always be a concern to me. I'd go to my own grave before I let him get within even a foot of you."

Her eyes closed convulsively against the image of a gravestone bearing Paden's name. She'd never seen anyone more capable, more determined, than him…except for maybe Eagle Feather. The two men would be evenly matched. In such battles, both opponents usually ended up seriously injured, if not dead. She couldn't let that happen.

She backed away, wanting to put distance between Paden and Eagle Feather now as well.

Paden reached out to stop her. She wrapped her arms around her waist to prevent herself from taking his hand and instead scanned the horizon. A deep indigo had slipped down from the heavens to shroud the earth. It was too dark to go anywhere tonight.

"If we leave in the morning and keep moving," she said, "we'll stay ahead of him."

"There's a wedding in the morning."

Guilt bowed her head. How could she have forgotten Alejandro and Rebecca's joyous day?

"And I agreed to keep an eye on Riley," Paden continued. "Distract him if necessary. Then Sherwood and I need to visit Laramie's trading post and gather news of the trail ahead. We'll be here one day. That's it."

So much could happen in a day. Worry kept her head lowered. "What can I do to help?"

Paden's callused fingertips brushed her jaw. A gasp of pleasure, and panic, parted her lips. Every muscle in her body tensed with hope. *Please don't stop. Please don't pull away.*

With a slow deliberation that held her in thrall, Paden lifted her chin until she met his gaze. Then he slid his fingers deep into her hair and drew her close. He stopped short of their bodies touching, but his heat still curled around her like an embrace. He held her like that for a long time, only his eyes moving, searching her face as if all his answers lay there.

"We'll talk more when we're clear of Fort Laramie." A smile tugged his lips, then vanished.

"Until then, you can help by remembering your promise. Stay away from the fort and if you see Weston, walk the other way."

CHAPTER 13

Long rows of barracks stretched out on either side of Alejandro as he strode down Fort Laramie's main thoroughfare. Ahead lay a parade ground full of soldiers assembling for morning duties. On the other side sat a narrow clapboard building with a steeple atop its roof and a cross above its door.

He'd walk through the doors of hell to wed the woman beside him. Bright red curls had come loose from the knot at the nape of Rebecca's neck. The wind whipped the strands against her cheek, making him want to reach over and tuck them behind her ear.

Every man they passed stared at her with hungry eyes. Their fingers were probably itching to touch her as well.

He kept his hands on the pistols strapped to his hips, and the men kept their distance.

And Rebecca? She kept a proper distance from him as well, making sure not even their elbows brushed. "Is the chapel much farther?" she asked.

His brow tightened with worry. Rebecca hadn't raised her gaze from the path two strides in front of them since they'd entered the fort.

"It's not far," he replied.

When she didn't answer, his anxiety moved to

his chest, making even breathing difficult. "Are you having second thoughts?"

"No, of course not." She released a small sigh. "I'm worried what my father will do."

"You said you weren't afraid of him. Has that changed?"

"He's not a bad man. He's just suffered too many disappointments. I'm all he's got."

Riley didn't deserve his daughter's loyalty, but he admired her for wanting to give it to him.

"Maybe with time he'll grow to accept our marriage," she murmured.

Alejandro didn't answer. Even if heaven and hell and the cavernous gulf between the two locations froze over, Riley wouldn't accept him as a son-in-law.

They reached the edge of the parade ground and stopped on the same stride. After a heavy silence, they spoke at the same time as well.

"Can we wait until—?"

"You don't have to—" His fingers clenched his pistol like they were lifelines. It didn't help. He could feel his dreams being washed away. All that remained was the memory of her suitors at Courthouse Rock. "Do you wish to wait until we reach California so you can find someone better there? Someone up to your father's standards?"

Her gasp tore at his conscience. She had every right to change her mind without him pestering her with useless questions.

"How can you think I'd want someone else?" she said. "You're the one I want, the only one I've ever wanted. I just need time to convince my father."

Her words filled him with hope and despair, a combination that made his gut churn. He spun away from her and strode back along the street leading out of the fort. Rebecca raced after him, her breathing ragged as she tried to keep up with him. He slowed his pace but kept his face averted not wanting her to glimpse his anguish.

"I'll speak to my father. The next fort with a chaplain can't be too far away."

"We'll reach Fort Bridger in a few weeks. It doesn't matter, though. Your *padre* will never approve of me."

"We don't know that for certain."

He was done sugarcoating things for her. "I know." His voice was a mere rasp, a dry husk of withered hopes. He sounded as old and tired as he felt.

In comparison, Rebecca's tone was as full of life as a spring bud. "Maybe Hannah and Mr. Callahan will join us when we reach the next chapel."

"Why would they?"

"To get married."

He felt his jaw sag. He managed to keep walking, but he lost his battle not to look at her.

She held her chin high with conviction. "I've seen how he looks at her and how she looks at him."

"It matters little. He cannot let go of his past or his hate."

"He can if he's fallen in love with her." Her voice rang with absolute certainty.

He shook his head. "It will not do him any good." In that area, he and Paden were similar.

They left the fort, and Alejandro was glad to escape its walls. The urge to run from this conversation with Rebecca overwhelmed him. He'd been *loco* to believe she would marry him. Every muscle in his body begged him to jump on his horse and ride south as fast as he could.

"Love is stronger than hate. Love will find a way."

Rebecca's words reminded him of Hannah's: *As*

long as there's love, there's hope. He'd left his hope inside Laramie. He forced his love into a deep corner of his heart and concentrated on the wagon train still camped on the cropped grassland outside the fort. Now there was only duty.

He steeled himself to return to his, and for what he must say next. He must accept that Rebecca was better off without him. He halted and gestured toward the wagons. "From here, you had best go forward on your own."

Her determined expression faltered. "Only until we reach the next fort."

Nothing would change when they did. He didn't voice his opinion. Instead, he steeled himself for her departure. When she finally walked away, all of his happiness went with her.

❧ ❧ ❧

"Wonder what they'll be wanting?" Miriam asked, raising her hands from her mending to shade her eyes against the afternoon sun.

Sarah mimicked the movement. Both women gazed in the direction of Fort Laramie's gates. They didn't blink. They didn't move. They just stared.

Hannah craned her neck to see who'd captured their attention so intently. Half-dozen mounted men had galloped out of the fort and were heading for the closest of the wagons sprawled haphazardly around the fort.

"Cavalry," Miriam announced. "Looking for General Sherwood and Mr. Callahan, no doubt." She went back to her sewing. "They'll learn soon enough that they're inside the fort, gathering news of the trail ahead. Then they'll go back inside."

"Oh dear," Sarah whispered. Her wild hair had been cajoled into a tidy plait that hung down her back, but inside she was still as jumpy as a cricket.

"I hope everything's all right."

Hannah shared the same hope, but a niggling worry kept her attention fixed on the soldiers. "Paden said he knew Laramie's colonel in Texas. They didn't get along."

Several of the emigrants talking to the soldiers pointed in the direction of Miriam's wagon. A jolt of alarm brought Hannah to her feet.

Just as quickly, Miriam was standing between her and the soldiers, blocking her view as well as theirs. "What else did Mr. Callahan say?"

"He made me promise that I'd avoid the man."

Miriam grasped Hannah's elbow and started walking. "Stay in my shadow. When we get to my wagon, hide in the back. I'll pretend I'm retrieving something and return to the fire. If we're lucky, they won't see you. They're still a good distance away. But not for long. Hurry."

Hannah obeyed. Through the crack between the wagon bed and its canopy, she watched Miriam retrace her footsteps to Sarah's side. Then the pounding of hooves claimed her attention.

The soldiers projected an image of grandeur as they rode in tight formation toward Miriam's camp. Their dark blue jackets, studded with brass buttons, contrasted sharply against Miriam and Sarah's travel-worn, much-patched clothing. When the men reined their mounts to a halt, dust billowed under their hooves, coiling around her friends' feet like a snare.

Hannah's stomach rolled into a tight knot of dread.

At the forefront of the soldiers sat a fair-haired man with impeccable posture. A pair of mirrored silver eagles glinted in the sunlight, one on each shoulder. Some might have deemed his stature and bearing handsome. Hannah did not. He stared down his nose at her friends, silent and scornful, and also superior.

Finally he said, "I'm searching for the scout who lived with the savages, the one who's rumored to speak several of their languages, including Sioux."

A roaring in her ears drowned out any response Miriam and Sarah might have uttered. How had the soldiers learned about her so quickly?

"Answer Colonel Weston when he speaks!" One of the soldiers kneed his horse toward her friends.

Sarah leaped back. Pots and plates clattered to the ground, where they lay waiting to trip Sarah and cast her under foot. Miriam inserted herself between Sarah and the soldiers. Miriam would protect the woman, but who'd protect Miriam?

Hannah couldn't keep her promise to Paden. She couldn't walk the other way or hide. She spun toward the back of the wagon, preparing to jump out.

"Halt." Weston's command froze both his subordinate and Hannah. The colonel had raised his hand in a restraining gesture, or maybe a warning one. "There's no need for violence," he said in a smooth voice. "I've merely come to secure the services of a translator for my prisoners. They've vital information I must extract before their transported east. The Sioux killed two of my men on a woodcutting duty. Learning the location of the rest of these murderous barbarians will save countless lives."

Miriam and Sarah remained silent. Hannah turned back to her peephole.

Weston's focus had settled on Miriam. "Madam, I'm certain you do not wish to see anyone hurt, whether they be a stranger or—" his gaze swept meaningfully over Sarah, "—a friend."

Trembling with fear, Sarah appeared on the verge

of collapsing. Miriam's coiled stiffness suggested she was a heartbeat away from laying into the colonel with her blistering temper.

Hannah couldn't let her friends be harmed. Weston had come for her, and her alone. She scrambled out of the wagon. "I'm the scout you want."

Everyone spun to face her.

Weston's eyes widened with disbelief. "You can't be. Callahan wouldn't accept a woman as his scout." He shook his head. "Tell me where the real scout is, the one who can translate the heathen's gibberish."

"Where are your prisoners?" she asked, first in English, then in Sioux.

Weston's gaze sharpened with an unsettling intensity. "Inside my fort." He glanced at Miriam and Sarah before addressing her again. "I assume you wish for me to escort you there without further delay?"

Colonel Weston led Hannah to a squat structure of stone in the heart of Fort Laramie.

When they entered, the stifling interior filled her with nausea. Her skin turned clammy. Breathing became a monumental effort. Inside this dim hole, the wide-open plains with their clear blue sky vanished like a dream. She might as well have returned to the cave in the storm. But Paden wasn't with her. She was with a man he'd vehemently warned her to stay away from.

She was also with three bloodied and bruised Sioux prisoners.

Despite their injuries and bleak surroundings, the men sat with unbowed backs. They stared wooden-faced at Weston, but when they saw her they rose to their feet, their shackles clattering around their ankles and wrists. The stockade seemed to shrink even further. Three pillars of lean but solid muscle stood before her. Curiosity flickered in their dark eyes.

Weston remained behind her, preventing her retreat. His tone held nothing but contempt. "Ask them where the others are, the ones who escaped when I found their camp, the ones who helped them slaughter my men."

The Osage had roamed great distances while trading with the Sioux in the north and other Plains tribes in the south. Suddenly those days seemed like a dream as well. Now she struggled to recall the Sioux language, translating haltingly.

The tallest of the braves answered. "We know nothing of his men. We did not kill them."

She relayed his response to Weston, who swore and glared at the men with a growing fury vibrating inside him. "They lie. Ask them where they planned to meet next." His voice dropped to a barely comprehendible snarl. "I must find all of them and eradicate their kind from this country. They are thieves and murderers, every last man, woman and child."

Horror clawed at her heart. "You were with your families when the colonel attacked your camp?" she asked the Sioux.

The prisoners shook their heads. "Our young and old, our women, stay far away from the fort. We travel as a small band of hunters."

Hannah recalled Paden's words about men cutting loose from their families to ride as a pack. Were these men hunters as they claimed, or a war party?

"Where are the rest of them?" Weston's voice had regained full force.

The braves' brows arched with scorn. Without waiting for her translation, the tallest spoke again. "Even if we knew the answer to the question he keeps barking like a rabid dog, we would not tell him. Our people no longer stay in one place long. Better to move constantly than make it easy for our white enemies to spill one more drop of Sioux blood."

After she translated, Weston pivoted to glare at the nearest wall and grumble more caustic comments. Hannah's gaze locked with longing on the door behind him.

"Too late we understand the white man's true nature." The Sioux's words, hushed with sorrow, dragged her attention back to him. "He destroys everything in his path. He is a plague upon the land. His only love is for himself." The man cocked his head and contemplated her. "But we concede that occasionally someone different is born to the whites. Someone who has lived among us. Someone with a past as unique as her eyes."

Her eyes? Had Eagle Feather told them about her? Her chest constricted, then just as quickly relaxed. He was merely making assumptions based on the familiarity of her clothing and her knowledge of his language. That was all.

His dark gaze held hers. "Are you not the one the Osage call Blue Sky?"

She lurched back. If he knew her name, he knew Eagle Feather.

All three of the Sioux leaned even closer, bearing down on her in the gloom of the cell. She gulped for air. The walls pressed closer along with the men. She spun and raced for the door.

Weston stepped sideways to block her escape. "What did they say?"

"Nothing!"

"What're you hiding? They told you something important enough to make you run."

"They repeat that they know nothing of the whereabouts of the men you want."

Weston's face twisted with fury. "Now you're lying as well." He grabbed her throat and lifted her to his eye level. "Tell me."

She clawed his hand and kicked, frantically trying to reach the floor. Her toes brushed the dirt. The pressure on her throat eased. Blessed air filled her lungs but only for a second. Weston lifted her higher. She flailed in every direction. Stars danced behind her eyes.

Weston's gaze shifted to something behind her. He smiled and released her with a shove that laid her out flat on the ground. Her throat burned with every rasping breath she gulped.

"We'll see what you say after you're forced to endure these savages' company alone. A few minutes with them will loosen your tongue. But I won't return right away. I want to listen to you scream."

He pivoted on his heel and marched out. The door slammed behind him. A key grated in the lock. Then only the harsh scrape of her breath, and the muted voices of the three men crouching to form a circle around her, remained.

The tallest Sioux leaned over her, surveying her from head to toe and back again. His gaze locked with hers. "Do not move," he commanded and reached out to touch her.

Despite his warning, she raised her hand to halt him.

He snared her wrist easily while at the same time the fingers of his other hand brushed her throat. Pain lanced her raw, bruised flesh. She swallowed jerkily, only adding to the hurt. Too late, her own fingers curled into a fist as she fought to escape and failed.

"The white chief has a black heart. He is also a fool. He glimpses one truth but hasn't the vision to know where to look next." The Sioux's gaze lowered, along with his hand, skimming downward. "We are all hiding something." His fingers crossed the hollow at the base of her throat and parted the collar of her shirt.

Weston paced outside the stockade in the glaring sun. Sweat beaded his neck, trickling down his spine and plastering his freshly laundered uniform against his back. His posting at Fort Laramie wasn't yielding the results he desired. Today was the pinnacle of his disappointments. The fact that he couldn't bend a mere slip of a woman to his will made his pulse pound in his head.

Damn her. Damn Fort Laramie's rules. Damn these godless heathens most of all.

He glared at his two men guarding the prison door. Then he jerked his watch from his pocket and glared at it as well. He'd delayed the transport convoy as long as he could. It'd leave within the hour. The Sioux prisoners would have to be on it. He couldn't stop their departure. He could only strive to pry the information he wanted out of them faster.

Leaving a white woman alone with the savages had been cruel. They'd use her harshly. He shouldn't care, but he did. He wanted to watch them abuse her, but he'd have to settle for listening. His heart beat faster as he anticipated hearing Callahan's infuriatingly stubborn woman brought down a notch.

She had to be his. Why else would he have allowed such a woman on his wagon train?

An image of Callahan's wife rose in his mind. He hadn't thought of her in ages. What was her name?

Damned if he could remember. But he remembered raping her in retaliation for rejecting him for her father's lapdog, the general's favorite, his surrogate son.

He'd still shown her kindness. He'd killed her before he'd mutilated her body. He nodded with satisfaction, recalling how he'd staged the scene of Comanche rape and torture, then spread the rumors of Indian savagery and how swiftly his countrymen had believed his story.

Callahan had been among them. He'd embarked on a one-man mission to track down every Comanche brave he could and slaughter them. Each kill had put Weston one stride closer to his quest for Indian annihilation. Only one insignificant woman had to die in exchange. The ends justified the means. If given the chance, the Comanche would've done everything he'd done to Callahan's wife. All Indians abused their captives.

The stockade was deathly quiet. What was taking those heathen bucks so long? Why wasn't Callahan's new woman screaming?

A pounding, mixed with a cacophony of shouts, graced his ears. Sadly, the hullabaloo wasn't coming from the prison. A rider on a big bay thundered across the parade ground toward him. His soldiers scurried to avoid being trampled, then expressed their outrage by hurling insults at Paden Callahan's back.

Satisfaction lifted Weston's dark mood. Once again he'd taken something that belonged to Callahan, just as Callahan had stolen Sherwood's daughter from him. A scout wasn't as good as a general's daughter, but he'd take whatever was in his grasp.

Callahan was out of this saddle before his mount had even stopped. He planted himself directly in front of Weston. "Where is she?" he yelled.

Weston forced himself not to retreat. Only his many years with the army allowed him to succeed, that and a flicker of astonishment. Could Captain Callahan, the soulless hero of Texas, the Devil made of Smoke, actually have feelings for the woman now in Weston's hands? Maybe this scout was worth as much as a general's daughter.

A smile curved his lips. "What? No hello for an old friend?"

"I'm not here to listen to you flap your gums. I'm here to get Hannah."

"What if I decide to keep her?"

"Tell me where she is." Callahan's voice had dropped to a hiss.

The fact that Callahan hadn't acknowledged his threat irked him. "Must I remind you that you are under my jurisdiction? I still hold the power. I could have you cut down where you stand." He laughed. "Besides, your lady friend came with me willingly. I think she prefers my company over yours."

"She only went with you after you bullied two women. Have you threatened her as well? If you've even laid a finger on her, you'll pay dearly."

Behind Weston came the dry scrape of shuffling feet.

Callahan's glare raked the two soldiers guarding the stockade before pinning him again. "You locked her up?" His bellow made Weston's ears ring.

He drew himself up, trying to look down on Callahan. The useless attempt pricked his pride. "She stopped translating and wouldn't answer my questions. She forced me to leave her inside with them."

Callahan's eyes flared wide in an expression that in any other man Weston would've interpreted as fear. Then they narrowed to slits. "*Them?*"

The single word pierced him like a bayonet to the belly. He couldn't remember Callahan ever being so enraged, and he'd seen him plenty furious after his wife's death. Callahan was close enough to break his neck. He'd watched Callahan kill a man in that very way. It'd happened fast. He'd be dead before his soldiers could raise their Remingtons.

All his plans for Callahan's new woman would die with him.

"Calm down," he rasped. He wasted valuable seconds clearing his throat before he could continue. "She's fine." At least he now fervently hoped so.

Callahan's fists opened and closed in convulsive bursts. "Open that door."

He'd never been a praying man, but a silent plea now reverberated in his head. *Lord, don't let those bucks be the animals I assumed. Or at least let them be slow about their business.*

Either way, someone was going to die very soon. His training took over and a battle plan formed in his head. He tossed the stockade keys to Callahan. "Why don't you open the door yourself?" Better to be behind the devil than between him and a heathen when all hell broke loose. If it did, he could shoot Callahan in the back.

Hannah's lungs seized beneath the Sioux's hand, paralyzing her with dizziness and fear.

His fingers traced her skin, then withdrew to pry open the fist he held captive in his other hand. "A spider—" his gaze slid from her palm back to the markings over her heart he'd just outlined, "—and a web." He nodded solemnly. "I have seen these symbols before. The first time was long ago at a gathering of the tribes to celebrate the Sun Dance. Your eyes are not the only window to your past."

Her heart raced with a sudden hope. "If you remember that peaceful summer, have mercy. Let me go."

His hold on her remained solid. "Many moons have passed since then. Why did you leave the Osage?"

She forced herself not to shrink from him like a coward. Instead, she raised her chin and sealed her lips.

A smile tugged the corners of his mouth, then vanished. "You dislike our questions as much as those of the white chief who left us together in this hole. But the legend of Grandfather Spider is imprinted on your skin, while your own story has also become a source of much discussion."

Despite her determination not to speak, she asked, "What is being said?" Her voice sounded reedy and hardly comprehendible to her own ears.

"Two summers ago, you walked toward the horizon and disappeared in the blue depths of the Great Spirit's embrace. I wondered if you'd returned to your rightful home. But another, bearing tattoos like yours, told me differently."

The urge to flee made her tremble uncontrollably. The only one still alive who bore a similar web upon his chest was Eagle Feather.

"He said you must be found and returned to him. We have smoked as brothers, but he never joins our hunts. He is consumed by his own quest."

An awful certainty stole over her. "You've seen him recently."

"Just before our capture, but this time he didn't ask if we'd seen you. He said his journey was almost over. Everything he needed was within his grasp." The Sioux brave stared at her wrist imprisoned in his hand, then he released her. "He told us he'd discovered you with the whites and he'd take you from them soon."

A murderous rage, primed to explode and rip apart the first man he saw, propelled Paden through the stockade door.

He forced himself to slow down, to think. Hannah had to be alive. He couldn't allow himself to believe otherwise. But if she'd been abused, he must free her quickly and spend every day of his life trying to erase that horror from her memories. That wouldn't stop him from coming back to the fort in the dead of night and slitting the throat of every man responsible for hurting her. Weston included.

Relief nearly dropped him to his knees. Hannah sat untouched but surrounded by three bloodied and bruised Indians bearing shackles on their wrists and ankles.

Damn Weston to hell and back. He'd locked her in with men he'd treated like animals. She appeared unharmed. She also looked incredibly fragile sitting so close to warriors who glared at him as if they'd strangle him with their chains if he took one step closer.

He strode straight toward Hannah.

She met him halfway, keeping him out of the Sioux's reach. Her raised palms told him she was probably more worried about keeping them out of his. Then her slender hand found his like it was made to be there. He fought the urge to wrap his arms around her and hold her tight. He needed to keep at least one hand free. Weston still hovered close behind him, mostly likely with his revolver pointed at his back.

"We're leaving," he said.

Behind him came the whisper of steel against leather, a revolver returning to its holster.

Weston marched up beside him. "Not until she tells me what they said." The colonel's glare was on his prisoners and his hands were on his hips.

He'd forgotten who the real threat was in this cramped hellhole. Paden's hand itched to knock him out cold and leave him in the jail in Hannah's place.

"She can't tell you what she doesn't know," he replied from between clenched teeth.

Weston snorted. "She knows...something. She translated freely at first, then they jabbered on about that *something* and she clammed up tight."

Paden glanced at Hannah. She immediately lowered her gaze. She wasn't going to tell him what the Sioux had said with Weston nearby. Hell, she might not tell him even when they were alone.

"Colonel Weston?" one of the guards called from the doorway. "Leader of the transport convoy's outside. Says he can't wait any longer."

"Fine." Weston spat out the word. "Take them."

Paden backed Hannah up until she was between him and the nearest wall. The two guards entered, prodded the Sioux to their feet with their rifle barrels, then herded them out the door. Keeping a firm grip on Hannah's hand, Paden moved to follow.

Weston jumped to block their way. "Not so fast. She stays until she tells me what those savages said."

Hannah's grip on his hand tightened.

"I won't let you force her to do anything she doesn't want to do."

"Guard," Weston yelled over his shoulder. One of the privates returning, Remington raised and cocked. Weston retreated until he stood behind the man. "Do you have anything else to say?"

"I'm not leaving her here alone."

A smirk contorted Weston's face. "Fine." This time he uttered the word approvingly, and he continued retreating. The guard did the same. As door swung closed with the men on the other side, Weston continued, "I don't mind locking you both in for the night. It'll give everyone time to ponder their options. Or in your cases, your complete lack of them."

The light from the doorway disappeared, casting the cell in shadows. A key turned in the lock. Then silence. Paden tested the door. It wouldn't budge. He circled the enclosure. The bars on the single window, more air hole than anything else, were solid.

He wasn't getting Hannah out of here tonight. They were staying. All night. Alone. Together.

He stole a glance at her. She shivered and hugged her arms around her waist. He had no means to comfort her. He couldn't even offer her his coat. With the warmer weather during the daytime, he'd taken to leaving it in his wagon.

Leaning against the wall, he sunk to the ground and stretched his legs out in front of him. A weary sigh escaped him. "It's going to be a long night. Might as well make yourself comfortable." When Hannah remained rooted in place, he gestured to the ground beside him. "Come sit beside me. I want to be between you and any unexpected visitors."

Her gaze darted to the door, and he felt like a bastard for bringing up that very unsettling possibility. But his words did the trick. She finally moved toward him.

He stared at the door as she occupied the space he'd left for her between him and the back wall. "Try to sleep. I'll make sure no one disturbs you." He crossed his arms, struggling to ensure that someone wasn't him. He blew out another breath. It was going to be a *very* long night.

His eyes might've been focused on the door, but

all of his other senses were locked on Hannah. The rustle of her clothing as she shifted, attempting to get comfortable. The faint warmth of her breath as she settled on a position facing him. The scent of her hair and her skin as time passed and the room continued to grow colder and darker.

"Paden?" It was the first word she'd spoken since he'd found her in this prison. He gloried in the hushed sound of his name spilling from her lips like a lover's sigh.

"Yes?"

When she didn't respond, he turned toward her. She lay on her side facing him with her arms clasping her knees tight against her chest. He couldn't see much more in the descending gloom but he saw the tremors rocking her.

With a will of its own, his hand reached out to reassure her. He halted. His worries, never far from his thoughts, had returned full force. "Hannah," he said as gently as he could, "you can tell me if those men hurt you."

"They didn't." Her pale hair shimmered in the dark as she shook her head.

He was suddenly reminded of being in another cramped hole with her. The cave in the storm. She'd been crying then, and he hadn't known it until he'd touched her. With the guide of the ghostly arc of her hair, his hand found her cheek. He exhaled in relief. Her skin was cold but dry.

He couldn't stop himself. His hand slid down the curve of her determined little chin. She flinched as if in pain.

He froze. "What's wrong?"

"Weston— He— You'll probably see the bruises in the morning."

Disbelief, then fury tore through him. "He struck you in the face?"

Her head moved under his palm, telling him no again. She guided his hand lower so it covered her throat. The trust in that gesture humbled him. Then the reality of where his hand lay gutted him. Weston had tried to choke his answers out of her. And she still hadn't told him.

"What did the Sioux say that was so important you couldn't tell Weston?"

She swallowed roughly under his hand. He was scaring her again. Very carefully, he traced his fingertips over her shoulder and down her arm in search of her hand. His muscles tensed with the urge to touch all of her. He'd be damned though if he'd do that after the hell she'd just been through.

Lifting her hand, he pressed her palm against his heart. "You're safe now."

"No, I'm not. The Sioux told me they'd spoken to Eagle Feather. He knows I'm on the wagon train."

He swore softly. "Seems both of our pasts are catching up with us today."

"I'm sorry I got you into this mess," she said in rush. "With both Weston and Eagle Feather."

"None of this is your fault."

"Eagle Feather mustn't find me on the wagon train. I won't let anyone else be hurt because of me."

"We'll be leaving in the morning. We'll put as much distance as we can between us and him."

"But what if—" A shudder ran up her arm to vibrate in his chest.

His gut clenched. She was rocking with a force that reminded him of Sarah's anguish.

"What if something happens tonight and we can't get out?" she asked.

He lay down facing her. "Shh." Her hair was soft under his hand. "Nothing's going to happen."

"I don't like small spaces." Uncurling her body, she shimmied closer to him.

His breath lodged in his chest with her increasing nearness. "Why not?"

She went rigid. "It's a fear from long ago. A child's fear."

"You can still tell me."

She sucked in a breath, then blurted, "When one is trapped, something bad usually happens. To you or the ones you love."

He gave in to the urge that had gripped him since he'd first entered the cell. He gathered her in his arms. The tension drained from her, one delicate muscle, one slender-boned limb at a time.

"Try to sleep," he whispered against the top of her head. "Tomorrow will come quicker if you do."

Her cheek brushed his chest as she nodded, then her arms looped around his chest and held onto him as well. Every inch of him swelled with an intense need. The longing in his heart was almost unbearable. All he wanted lay in his embrace. Could she feel the same? She'd finally shared some of her fears with him. She was beginning to trust him.

He'd be damned if he broke that faith now. This might very well be the longest night of his life.

CHAPTER 14

Hannah opened her eyes and saw...nothing. She blinked. The darkness remained, but so did the scent of sweet sage. Just beyond circled whiffs of dank earth and stone, above her, all around her, threatening to stifle her. She waited for the fear to come. It didn't. She felt only contentment.

Paden's strong arms held her against his long, warm frame. Was this what heaven felt like? Guilt pricked her conscience. Heaven for her. Certainly not for him. If she didn't know the Sioux's language, if they hadn't known Eagle Feather, she wouldn't be in this cell and neither would Paden.

A draft skimmed her back, making her shiver. Paden pulled her closer.

Was he awake? She lifted her head from the pillow of his bicep to peer into the darkness above her.

His lips brushed hers. Her eyes flared wide, then fluttered closed. When she sighed with pleasure, he deepened the kiss. His hand slid down her spine to cup her bottom and pull her against him. She arched her back, wanting to get even closer.

He broke the kiss. His breath came in puffs, hot and quick against her cheek. "I'm not making love to you in the dark and the dirt." He was so close she not only heard but felt the grind of his teeth. "So lie still and go back to sleep."

His hair tickled her nose. She nuzzled closer so she could better inhale his scent.

"Hannah," he growled. "Lie still."

She heaved a sigh. She was close, but she wanted to be closer still.

"I can't even see your lips and they still tempt me." He turned her in his arms until her back faced his chest with a hand's-breadth of frigid air between them.

She wiggled back to lean against him.

"Hellfire," he muttered as his hands opened and closed on the curve of her waist. "Every inch of you is tempting beyond belief." He reached around her to gather her hands in his and then snorted. "The only safe spot on you tonight are your fingers, and only because they're cold as icicles." He rubbed her hands, warming them as he'd done in the cave.

For several moments he applied himself to that task. Then he asked very softly, "Why won't you tell me about Eagle Feather?"

Her contentment slipped a notch. "It's the only way to repay Morning Star."

"You said this before. I still don't understand."

"I must do everything I can to ensure her son remains alive." The words slipped out before she could stop them.

"Her son doesn't deserve to live if he wants to harm you," he shot back.

"What if his reasons are the same as yours for killing your enemy?"

His hands stilled on hers. "We're not the same, and you're no one's enemy."

"I brought heartbreak to his family."

"How can he hold you responsible for their deaths?"

A fierce yearning rose inside her. More than anything she wanted to tell him, to finally stop hiding in all ways. Could she share her part in the story and still keep Eagle Feather's secret?

She selected her words carefully. "The white trappers said they'd come to trade for furs. When they saw me, they demanded to trade for me instead. They said no white woman would willingly wish to stay with Indians. They wouldn't listen when I told them otherwise. If I hadn't looked like I do, they would have left my tribe in peace."

"Eagle Feather can't blame you for that. He should've protected you and his family."

"He couldn't be everywhere. The trappers waited until only the women were in the valley."

Paden pulled her closer. "I'm sorry I made you go back there."

"You didn't know. I didn't tell you."

For a long moment they were both silent. Even more than the strength of Paden's embrace, it was his calmness that gave her the courage to continue.

"The women fled, all except Morning Star and Laughing Eyes. I begged them to go as well. But Morning Star had never run from anything. One of the trappers shot her. She fell, but she wasn't dead. So he aimed his rifle at her again. Laughing Eyes put herself between them. Only when I did the same did he stop. I told him I'd go with him. He laughed and said, 'Of course you will.' Laughing Eyes cried out behind me. When I turned, the second man held a knife to her throat. The blade—" It flashed as bright in her memories as the cell was dark. She hid her face against Paden's hands.

"You don't have to say anymore." Paden's voice rasped in her ear, mirroring how painful it had become for her to speak.

Even in the dark, the urge to continue hiding was

overpowering. She forced herself to raise her head and say the words. "Less than an arm's length. That's all that separated us, and I still couldn't save her. Her blood was hot on my face as I watched the life drain from her eyes." Something cracked inside Hannah. Her voice or her heart, she didn't know. The pain of the past bit deep then faded, leaving her hollow. "She had the most joyful eyes I've ever seen. Until her death, she'd never seen the violence that follows me like a shadow."

"Did your brother kill those men in the valley?" Paden's voice had never sounded more like a growl, like a pack of wolves clamored to leap out of him.

When she stiffened, Paden did the same and his embrace turned from haven to cage.

"They tied my wrist," she replied, "and took me with them."

"Tell me your brother came after you." His voice had gone hoarse with what sounded like both hope and dread. "Tell me that he didn't leave you with those men."

"This is the part I'm afraid to share with you."

"So help me God!" he roared. "If I ever see your brother, I'll rip out his heart for not coming after you and killing those men."

Disbelief made her blink. "But they were white. You made war on Indians who killed white men."

"Not if those white men had hearts as black as the pit of hell. Not if they murdered two women. Not if they raped you."

"They died before they had the chance."

Paden slumped against her. The anger she'd felt vibrating in him, the fury holding him prisoner as solidly as the stone walls around them, was suddenly gone. "Then there is a God," he said. "Besides Him, who do I have to thank?"

"Eagle Feather. And White Cloud too. They

caught up with us that night. White Cloud has an uncanny ability to find me even in the dark. He led Eagle Feather to me."

"And the men?" Paden prompted.

"Eagle Feather gave them a relatively quick death."

"He's a kinder man than I would've been."

"I've never known him to be kind, but he allowed the trappers to draw first blood. They gave him a scar from his left eye down to his jaw but nothing more. When we got back to the village, Morning Star was dead."

"He still shouldn't have blamed you."

"I blamed myself. I didn't argue when he cast me out. He told me to run fast and far, because if he found me he'd kill me as well." She released a deep breath. "I'm so very tired of running. Did it bring you any peace?"

"What?"

"Killing those who destroyed what you loved."

Once more Paden went rigid against her. "No. So don't even think of offering yourself as a martyr to your brother's blade. If you see him, you run." He huffed out a breath as if everything were settled and went back to warming her hands with his. "The only thing that helped me was distance. I needed to get as far away from Texas and its memories as possible."

The outlines of Paden's massive arms on either side of her were now visible. So were the pale arcs of his broad hands covering hers. She was struck again by how gentle his were for a man of his size and past. Just like on the hillside by the valley, she was in no hurry to leave this cell. Not if it meant leaving Paden's embrace. She couldn't stop the sun from rising and the world outside from parting them though.

The thought of never seeing him again made her

entire body hurt. Surely others had felt the same way. "You must have family in Texas who miss you."

"After I left the Comanche, I learned that my father's people did not want me."

Anger swept away her melancholy. How could they not want him? She searched for a way to soften their rejection. "Maybe too much time had passed. I'm sorry your family couldn't find you when the Comanche first took you from them."

"The Comanche didn't take me away from anyone. General Sherwood and Kaku were the only ones who ever accepted me unconditionally." His voice had thickened with emotion. Not with anger, but a profound sorrow. Why hadn't he included his wife?

Before she could voice her query in a way that wouldn't add to his hurt, he asked a question of his own. "Do you remember what I told you about Kaku?"

"She was the Comanche grandmother who raised you. She told you about your parents."

"She also told me that my father had a friend who was a fellow Ranger. If I ever needed help, I was to go to him. His name was Augustus Sherwood. Finding the general was the closest I ever came to having a family of my own."

"Sounds like you had Kaku as well. Sometimes it only takes two to make a family."

Paden inhaled sharply. "What if I asked you to be my family?"

Hope, bright and dazzling, blazed in her heart.

"I can give you a home in Oregon. My cabin's waiting, and a logging company I intend to grow and improve." His tone was earnest but also rushed, as if he didn't quite believe the worth of his words so he had to keep talking. "I want to try a new water-powered sawmill I heard about and ship lumber to China and Australia. I can provide for you. I can keep you safe. When we leave Fort Laramie, we'll need to move fast and put as much distance between us and your brother as we can. But at the next fort, at Fort Bridger, we could—"

On the other side of the cell, metal grated against metal. They scrambled to their feet as the door swung open with a groan. The sound echoed in her heart. It mirrored her regret at having to leave Paden's embrace. Paden didn't go far though. He stood between her and the man silhouetted in the doorway with only the faint light of pre-dawn framing his head and shoulders.

The man lit a lantern and raised it to survey them. The light revealed him as much as them. Fair hair framed a haughty brow and hard eyes. A face as unwelcome as it was now familiar.

"Well." Colonel Weston arched a condescending brow. "It appears the white squaw survived, and maybe even thrived on, being locked in a cell first with a band of depraved bucks and then a lonely wagon master. Or at least that's what Fort Laramie shall soon be gossiping about."

Hannah's gasp mixed with Paden's curse.

Weston laughed. "One more night, and imagine what your wagon train will be saying?" The colonel's brow arched even higher. "Will they accept your return? Their wagon master? Certainly. But his whore? Unlikely. Why not give me what I want so I can release you and spare you the disgrace?"

Paden widened his stance, holding his arms loose by his side, preparing for battle. "The only thing I'll give you is a cracked skull."

Hannah's stomach felt heavy as stone. How many people would believe Weston's accusations?

When would she stop adding to Paden's woes?

Voices sounded outside, raised in discord.

Paden cocked his head to one side, listening. "I wondered how long you'd be able to keep Sherwood and Miriam away. Will you lock them in this cell with us?"

"If I could, I would," Weston shot back. Turning in the doorway, he gestured to someone unseen outside. "Ladies. General," he called out with forced pleasantness. "Come see for yourself how your wagon master and scout have fared."

Hannah struggled to breathe. Weston meant to bring them inside? They'd see just how small a space she and Paden had shared overnight. What if Weston started making rude comments again?

Paden glanced over his shoulder at her. Worry creased his brow. "Hannah, we've done nothing wrong."

Miriam and Sarah hurried into the cell, halting any reply she might have said. General Sherwood followed close behind them. The women's worried gazes went straight to Hannah, while the general faced Weston with an expression she couldn't decipher.

"As you can see," Weston drawled, "they survived their night together."

"A night that should never have happened." The general's words made Hannah cringe with remorse.

She should've tried harder to keep Paden out of her troubles.

"You had no reason to hold them," General Sherwood's gaze remained on Weston. "You still have none. So I assume you will be releasing them into our care, immediately?" His manner and voice were civil, but Hannah now recognized his formality was caused by dislike. It was the same tone he'd used when she'd first heard him speak to Dawson.

"Fort Laramie regrets the suffering you endured during your stay." Weston's gaze raked her before he gestured to the door. "I release you into your friends' care with the hope that they protect you better than Captain Callahan did last night."

Miriam swept by Paden and wrapped her arm around Hannah's shoulder. "Lord in merciful heaven. Are you all right, honey?" Her voice overflowed with motherly concern.

Hannah hung her head. "Nothing happened."

"Well, thank the Lord for that." Miriam released a lengthy sigh, then glared at Weston. "When that despicable lout forced you to go with him, Sarah and I were beside ourselves with worry."

Sarah rushed forward and grasped her hand. "Are you certain you are well? I cannot believe he locked you all night in a place such as this." With huge eyes, she surveyed the cell and shuddered. "Good thing Mr. Callahan was with you. I would've died of fright being shut up all night in here alone. Did you have to sleep on the floor together?"

Weston's laughter made Hannah flinch.

Miriam gave her a reassuring squeeze. "What's done is done." She cast a sideways glance at Paden. "What comes next is all that matters."

Paden watched Miriam and Sarah guide Hannah out the prison door. Regret made his gut roll. He hadn't considered how others would view his night alone with Hannah. He hadn't considered how Weston might contort the truth in a final bid to get what he wanted. He'd been too concerned with finding Hannah and keeping her safe.

He'd talk to her tonight when the wagons halted to make camp. Right now he had to get her as far away as possible from Weston, and Eagle Feather too.

Ducking his head, he squeezed through the small door. When he straightened, he came face to face with a soldier, followed by more soldiers dragging three men toward the stockade. Even though the new prisoners reeked of whiskey and hung limply from captors' grasps with bent heads, they seemed coherent enough to sense an opportunity in their sudden stop. All three bolted upright, brandishing their fists and yelling.

The ladies pulled Hannah to one side to avoid being hit. Sherwood installed himself between them and the chaos. Weston stood at a distance, arms crossed, his smirk having returned.

The most spirited drunk lurched about like a bleary-eyed bear coming out of hibernation. His antics threatened to trample the general and his charges. Paden seized the man by the back of his collar. His captive lashed out with a series of punches. Paden evaded him easily. The man didn't escape the foot Paden hooked around his ankles. He fell. Paden let him go.

All three of the men now lay in the dirt, heads bent and mumbling unintelligently.

Paden's gaze sought Hannah. Miriam and Sarah still held on to her, but it now appeared as if she were the one supporting them. He wasn't sure how much more excitement he could handle either. They needed to get the hell out of here. He made a beeline for her.

"You—You—bastard," a befuddled voice whined behind him. "You knocked out my tooth!"

Hannah's gaze locked on the man. Paden halted, recognizing the voice as well. Steeling himself, he faced its owner and found the familiar face flushed from drink.

Dawson gaped up at him, blinking rapidly to

maintain his focus. "Callahan," he finally said. "You've ruined everything again."

Unease rippled through Paden. "You're a long way from Leavenworth. Why are you here?"

Their old scout pressed his lips tight.

Weston's shadow fell over Dawson. His tone, sharp as broken glass, cut the silence. "How do you know each other?"

Dawson lowered his chin and his voice. "None of yer stiff-rumped army-ass' business. This is between me 'n him 'n—" He suddenly straightened and searched the faces around him. When his gaze found Hannah, it stuck. "Yer always there to see me laid low. I vow you'll pay for this as well."

Paden moved to stand between him and Hannah, shielding her from the scout's glare. "I'll see you in hell first, Dawson."

The soldiers hoisted Dawson up by his arms and dragged him toward the stockade.

"And I'll gladly meet you there, just as soon as I can." Dawson's laughter vibrated with as much menace as his words. "That's another promise you can count on."

Gaze locked on Fort Laramie's gates, Alejandro released a relieved breath when he finally glimpsed General Sherwood stride out with Hannah beside him. Miriam and Sarah hovered close to her other side. Paden stalked a pace behind all four, repeatedly glancing over his shoulder as if he'd like to go back and throttle someone inside.

Alejandro tossed his belongings in the back of the scouts' wagon, saddled his horse and jumped astride.

Paden surged past him toward his own horse. "Get everyone moving. We're leaving."

Alejandro turned to Hannah. She met his gaze briefly, then began helping Gabe load their camp supplies.

"Alejandro!" Paden sat close by, mounted on his stallion. He heaved a sigh and his scowl vanished. "Hannah's unharmed. But she'll only remain that way if we put as much distance between us and Laramie as we can. Right now I need everyone, including you and her, to focus on one thing. We need to get this wagon train rolling."

Receiving an explanation from Paden left Alejandro speechless. He could only nod and lift his reins to comply.

"Wait." The word sounded as if it'd been torn from Paden. "There's something more that I need from you."

Alejandro's surprise made him mute. Paden never asked anyone for help.

Paden leaned closer and lowered his voice. "I need your help keeping a lookout for an Indian with a scar like this." He traced his finger from his left eye to his chin. "Don't kill him. But don't let him anywhere near Hannah either."

Alejandro managed another nod before Paden galloped off. Then he rode in the opposite direction, stopping at each wagon to spread the call to load up and move out. When he reached the Riley wagon, he repeated the same order then paused. Thomas Riley ignored him, distracted by harnessing a reluctant ox. Alejandro's gaze met Rebecca's over the beast's back. When she remained silent, he rode on.

Moments later, Rebecca's voice whispering his name brought him up short. The sound hadn't come from behind where he'd last seen her though. It'd come from a wagon on his left.

Peering around the tailgate, Rebecca gestured for him to come closer. When he did and they were hidden from her father's view, she reached up to grasp his hand. "Is Hannah all right?"

Her simple touch made his blood race in his veins. "Although everyone has been saying otherwise, Paden assured me Hannah was unharmed and she appeared that way. I knew General Sherwood would not allow Weston to detain them for long." He strove to ease her troubled expression. "And with Miriam and Sarah by the general's side, how could he fail?"

"Thank heavens they succeeded. It was very brave of those women to accompany the general to the prison." The melancholy note in her voice made him frown.

"You are brave as well," he insisted.

She shook her head. "Hannah is truly blessed to have earned such friends."

"They would help you as well. They would help both of us."

"My father says I'm unworthy." She tried to pull away from him, but he laid his other hand over hers. Her fingers were cold and stiff between his. Inside she'd already let go of him.

There was only one thing he could give her now. It wasn't his love, although she would always have that as well.

"Rebecca, listen. Your father tries to dictate your future by filling your head with falsehoods. Just as Weston and others on this wagon train try to make us believe their assumptions about Hannah and Paden. They strive to divide us, make us feel as if we are alone. You must trust that others will help you. But even if they do not, know this. I will always lend you my aid. No matter what you choose, even if your decision is to wed another."

They stood together, saying nothing, while the world swept by. Men and women tossed supplies into wagons. Children rounded up unwilling livestock. Oxen and mules resisted without success the familiar but unwelcome harness. As far as Alejandro was concerned, whenever he was near Rebecca, nothing else mattered. There was only him and her.

"You'd let me marry someone else to make me happy?" she asked in a hushed voice.

The sadness inside him spiked. "Very reluctantly."

Her lips twitched as if she tried to suppress a smile. "It'd be foolish to wed someone else if you're just going to continue hanging around and annoying my father."

He blinked in surprise, then lifted her hand and pressed a kiss to her knuckles. "You are not a foolish woman. You are the woman I wish to kneel before and woo with grand words. But time is scarce. So, I shall ask you plainly. Rebecca Riley, are you going to marry me?"

"I am." Her fingers squeezed his with a sudden urgency as her gaze darted to the fort then the settlers still hastily packing their wagons. "There isn't time to visit the chapel again, is there? What if I've ruined our one chance to wed?"

"The next fort is not far." The lie was necessary, Alejandro told himself. He didn't want her to fret. Not when he was anxious enough for both of them. Even traveling as fast as they could, Fort Bridger— with both its chapel and its refuge from their enemies—was days away.

Over the flickering light of the fire she'd just coaxed to life, Hannah watched Paden stride toward her. The temperature had dropped with the sun, so she wasn't surprised to see he'd donned his buckskin jacket or that he held his rifle in both hands, at the ready.

She glanced at her own rifle lying by her feet, then at Alejandro and Virgil behind her. Armed as well, the two scouts scanned the wall of twilight outside the circled wagons. Paden had instructed them to watch over her while he, the general and Gabe fortified their defenses.

They were safe. At least for the night. But come morning? Why did she continue putting everyone in danger—these men, Miriam and her grandsons, Rebecca, Sarah and Nate, the entire wagon train?

She glanced at White Cloud, a handful of strides away, tied to the back of the scouts' wagon with Cholla beside him. She'd unsaddled both horses and settled them for the night. She should be jumping on White Cloud right now and leaving. Why wasn't she? Because she was tired and craved the light and warmth the campfire would bring. Most of all, she couldn't make herself ride away from Paden.

After leaving Fort Laramie, they'd covered twice as many miles as normal and halted only minutes ago. They'd forced the march longer than usual. The dark was descending fast. So was Paden.

When he reached her, he pulled the kindling from her hands and tossed it aside. "Don't even think about running." He drew her away from the firelight and into the shadow next to the scouts' wagon. "You're staying with me so I can keep you safe."

Alejandro and Virgil kept their attention fixed on the world beyond the wagons as Paden towered over her. Rifle still in hand, he planted both hands on the canvas on either side of her head and leaned even closer, blocking everything until she saw only him.

Thankful for the wagon's support behind her back, she fought the sudden tightness in her throat and forced herself to speak. "I cannot stay here. It's not safe for the wagon train."

"It's not safe for you either. Even a blind man could find you following the ruts the wagon wheels have gouged into the earth over the years." His jaw tightened. "And a half-blind man could've seen you standing like a bloody bright bull's-eye back there in the firelight. Your brother could be hiding in the dark, waiting for an opportunity to shoot you from a distance.

She stiffened. "Eagle Feather may be many things, but I've never known him to be a coward."

"Anger can turn a man into what you'd least expect."

"If he wanted to end my life in this way, I'd be dead. He's seen me here already."

"Come morning, no one will see you here again."

She released a weary breath. She must accept this. "I'll leave."

"*We* will leave."

"But you're needed here. They need you to guide the settlers west."

"I've discussed it with Sherwood. He agrees there's no other way to protect you. We leave in the morning. *Together*."

She wasn't sure what to say. How could one feel worried and excited about something at the same time? Peering up at him, she ended up saying the first thing that came to mind. "And tonight? Will we stand this close till morning? It's rather intimate." Heat crept up her neck.

His hand, the one that wasn't holding his rifle, slid down the canvas to caress her hair like the gentlest of breezes. The heat inside her flared as if fed by a gale force wind.

He curled a lock of her hair around his finger, forming a bridge between them with the delicate strands. "Thank you for reminding me there's another reason for drawing you near. I won't forget again." The hint of a smile curved his lips.

Spirits Above. She wanted to stand like this forever.

"My first thought," he continued, "was simply to insert myself between you and the firelight and a sniper's bullet."

"Paden!" She shoved his chest. The wall of muscle wouldn't budge. She pushed harder. "I won't have you putting yourself in danger to protect me. Please move!"

He complied but only to lean into her touch, inch by inch, until the smallest gap separated them. "I'm not going anywhere." His lips brushed her forehead. "We need to finish our conversation from the stockade. We need to acknowledge Weston's foul words. You know what people will say if we arrive at Fort Bridger alone together."

"I no longer care." She removed the final distance between them, pressing against the hot, hard length of him.

He sucked in a ragged breath. Surprise then hunger flared in his eyes before his lids lowered, half shuttered to hide their silver intensity. "You care. Far too much."

"I only care what—" She sealed her lips against the truth, against the desperate longing that voicing such an admission would reveal. She cared too much about what he thought. "It's only the good opinion of a certain few that matters."

A groan rumbled from his chest into her, making her tremble with need but also with apprehension. What if he pulled away? What if he set her at a distance again?

Instead, he thrust his fingers deep into her hair and grasped the back of her neck. His hold was gentle though, allowing her every opportunity to slip free. "And there is the complication. Your friends' respect means a great deal to you. I saw your reaction when they learned exactly how we'd spent our night together."

An undeniable sadness swept over her. She bowed her head, tucking herself under his chin, sliding her palm between them in search of his heart. The pounding she found there was startling. His heart thundered at a pace that matched hers. Now was not the time to show him her sorrow or her worries.

"I may never see Miriam and Sarah again," she said softly, trying to sound at peace with the possibility, trying to sound strong. "I must accept this as well."

Arms, thick and sturdy as oak limbs, folded around her, bringing her even closer. "You won't be alone." His tone was firm. "I'll protect you in every way. I'll give you my strength, my home, my name. At Fort Bridger, there's another chapel."

A shot cracked the air. Paden slammed forward. His weight pinned her against the wagon, hard and heavy. Just as quickly, he lurched back, spinning with his rifle raised so he could sight down the barrel. As he did, she'd glimpsed the return of his familiar scowl. Or was it a grimace of pain?

More shots rang out. This time they came from the other side of the wagon circle. The bellowing of oxen and braying of mules filled her ears, while the beasts' hooves raised enough dust to shroud the night sky. The settlers' shouts soon joined in.

"We're under attack!"

"They're trying to steal the livestock!"

Blurred shapes swept by, running in every direction. The livestock couldn't escape the circle of wagons, but they could trample everyone inside. Alejandro and Virgil disappeared into the dust, racing to help.

Paden stood dead still in front of her, once again placing himself between her and danger. "Don't move," he growled over his shoulder.

She hadn't realized she had. She froze, obeying the intensity in his command.

"It's a diversion. Eagle Feather's here." His breathing was ragged, and he held his shoulder at an odd angle.

She reached up to touch him. Her hand came away wet and sticky. "The first shot hit you!"

"Thank God. And thank every other divine being known to man that the bullet's still in me and didn't pass through into you. Where's your rifle?"

"By the fire."

Without turning, he handed her his rifle and drew his revolver from its holster. "Stay here, out of the light and the mayhem. You could as easily get trampled as shot tonight." He sprinted the short distance to their campfire.

Raising his rifle, she searched for weapons pointed in his direction. He scooped up her rifle and turned. Two strides from her, a hand reached around him from behind. A flash of silver arced between them, then settled against Paden's neck. He halted with her rifle and his revolver held by his sides, a knife against his throat.

Soulless night-black eyes stared at her over Paden's shoulder. "Drop your gun."

She hadn't realized she was pointing it directly at the man's face.

"Don't listen to him, Hannah. Shoot him."

"Drop your gun," the man repeated, "or I open his throat."

Terror surged up inside her like a shriek. Paden was going to die just like Laughing Eyes.

"Hannah," Paden whispered very softly. "Don't

think. Just pull the trigger."

"I can't. He might slip and—" An image of Paden's life blood flowing like a scarlet river down his chest and his steely-eyed gaze going dull as lead hit her like a fist to the heart. She would do anything other than see that. She threw the rifle on the ground. "I'm sorry."

"Don't be. Long before this, I should've shown you how to handle a knife attack." Despite his words, he released his weapons and raised his palms in surrender. "But I never wanted you to see a blade in my hand. Now you will."

"I doubt that." Their assailant's hand was steady, keeping the knife firm against Paden's throat. "I'd like to kill you while she watches, to see your death reflected in her eyes."

"No!" Someone shouted the word before she could. A barrel-chested man stood beside her.

Disbelief weakened Hannah's knees, making her sway. How had Dawson escaped from Laramie's stockade so quickly? How had he escaped at all?

"No," Dawson repeated. "I told you they'd both suffer more if they lived. We stick to my plan."

"You're as addle-headed as your plan," Paden said. "Only fools with more *cojones* than common sense use a long blade this close." Lightning fast, he grabbed his captor's wrist and jerked down, pinning the knife flat against his chest. Then he slammed back his head.

Bone cracked. Blood blossomed from his attacker's nose. The man stumbled back. Still holding the knife immobile against his chest, Paden pivoted in a crouch and slipped under his opponent's arm. Then he rose up, twisting that arm as he did. The man howled in pain.

"Stop him!" The demand seemed to come from both Dawson and his crony. It ricocheted between the pair. Then it launched Dawson toward the fray.

Hannah jumped on his back. He grunted but didn't stop. Her grip on his ample girth slipped. She let herself fall. As she did, she made sure she tangled her foot around his, just like she'd seen Paden do at Fort Laramie. They hit the ground together. Luckily Dawson landed beneath her. Planting her elbow between his shoulder blades, she raised her head in search of Paden.

Paden still gripped his attacker's arm, but his attention was fixed on her. Another man sprang from the shadows. Fear iced her veins. The man's pistol was aimed at Paden's back.

"Behind you," she tried to scream. Her warning came out no better than a raven's squawk.

But Paden was already spinning to follow her gaze. As he did, he twisted his first assailant's wrist enough to make the man finally release his knife. Paden caught the blade and threw it, all in one motion. The man hurtling toward him dropped his gun in favor of clutching the knife now protruding from his chest. When he collapsed on the ground, he didn't move.

The opponent still in Paden's grasp snatched the man's dropped revolver and pistol-whipped Paden across the side of the head. Both of them went down together.

She scrambled off Dawson on her hands and knees. "Paden!" Just short of reaching him, a bruising hand caught her and flipped her over on her back.

Dawson's broad silhouette reared up between her and the night sky. Because of him, Paden was hurt. Maybe dying. Fury exploded inside her. She slammed her heel into Dawson's gut. He grunted, his fingers biting deeper into her arm. The rage that contorted his face promised even greater retribution.

She kicked again. This time she aimed lower.

"You—bitch." Dawson's words dissolved into a whimper. Clutching his groin, he toppled sideways and curled up in a ball.

Hannah gained Paden's side. As gently as she could, she turned his face toward her. His scalp was as slick with blood as his shoulder. "Paden," she whispered.

His eyes remained closed. Her lungs seized, leaving her gasping for air.

Behind her, someone breathed just as raggedly. Coming closer. As she turned, an object on the ground bumped her knee, skittering away. Paden's revolver. Still within reach.

An unyielding weight came down on her outstretched hand. A boot ground her fingers into the dirt. She cried out in pain. Dawson's friend crouched over her hand. He reached across to snare her other hand. A coarse band of rope slipped over her wrist. Fear jolted through her. She tried to kick him. Propelled by fury. Consumed by desperation. He wanted to kill Paden. She had to stop him from finishing the job.

He shoved her onto her belly. His weight fell on the back of her knees like a toppled tree, holding her prisoner while he bound her wrists and then her ankles.

"Is she tied up tight?" Dawson rasped from a distance.

"Like a bird trussed 'n ready for the carving."

Hesitant footsteps shuffled closer. "Why must she make everything so frickin' difficult? She nearly unmanned me. I can barely walk."

"You're better off than others," came the dry reply. "Frank didn't have a chance. The knife hit him square in the heart. A helluva throw."

"How's the bastard who threw it?"

"Still breathing."

Hannah went limp with relief.

"I still think I should fix that."

No, she begged silently. *Please. Please. No.* This couldn't be happening. She shouldn't have let this happen.

Dawson huffed out a breath. "A quick death's too easy. He needs to worry about what we'll do to her. Then he needs to see her after we've done ten times worse than he could've imagined. Let's go."

His accomplice tossed her over his shoulder and carried her into the dark.

Dawson hobbled beside them with a gait that became smoother with each step. He touched his groin gingerly. When he didn't wince, his gaze swung around to clash with hers. "Feeling's returning to my prick. It's twitching to make you pay for nearly snapping it in half."

"You know Paden won't rest until he kills you." Despite her faith in Paden's strength, her heart was racing fast enough to make even speaking a challenge.

Dawson shook his head. "He won't find us. Not in the dark. And by morning me 'n my friend will be long gone."

"You can't run far enough to escape him."

"Leaving has its drawbacks." A smile twisted his lips. "I'll miss seeing Callahan's reaction when he discovers exactly what I've done to you. But that's thinking too far ahead." He rubbed his crotch again, grinned even wider and lengthened his stride. "You 'n I have all night, and I'm eager to get started."

CHAPTER 15

"Leave it!" Paden bellowed. "I don't have time for this." His shoulder burned and his head throbbed. Overhead, the inky sky lurched, making the stars spin. He fell to his knees.

"The bullet needs to come out." Sherwood's hands were on his shoulders, one supporting him, the other pressing a cloth to his wound.

"The hell it does. Not when Hannah's gone." He surged to his feet, casting off Sherwood's hold, only to collapse on his ass.

"Dawson and his friends might not have split your skull wide open," Sherwood muttered, "but you could still have a concussion. You need time to clear your thinking. And I need time to get the bullet out. Gabe, Alejandro, Virgil, hold him down while I fetch my field kit."

Many hands pushed him flat on the ground. He struggled to break free.

Alejandro leaned over him, his knee pinning Paden's good shoulder. "Lie still, *amigo*. No one can see their tracks in the dark. Unfortunately, you will have to wait until morning to go after her."

He was right. Paden went limp. He'd lost Hannah. He'd let her down. He couldn't hold back the avalanche of fear threatening to suffocate him.

"My fault," he mumbled. "This is entirely my fault."

"Just bad luck," Gabe countered from his post across Paden's legs.

Paden squeezed shut his eyes. The lad was so very like his grandfather, always trying to make others feel better. There'd be no dodging this failure though. It stabbed deep into his soul.

Virgil grunted. "It's a hell of thing, first running into Dawson at Fort Laramie, then Weston releasing him so quickly."

The truth made Paden's gut clench. "No luck in that. Only one reason for Dawson being this far west. He was following us. And Weston released him so he could catch us."

Weston shared Dawson's hatred for Paden. Hannah would suffer for his sins. His eyes burned. He kept them closed, holding in the useless tears. Footsteps approached. Halted beside him. That'd be Sherwood, returning with his field kit.

Alejandro whistled low in his throat. "Been a while since I saw those."

Paden didn't need to open his eyes to see the forceps Sherwood would hold. The old man had dug enough bullets out of his men after a skirmish had gone south. "Hurry up," he growled.

Sherwood smelled of lye soap. He always washed before he started. Familiar hands carefully pushed aside Paden's jacket and shirt, baring his shoulder. Paden gritted his teeth. He knew what came next.

"Do you want a swig before I start?" Sherwood voice was steady. He'd done this routine too many times to count.

"I'm not getting drunk. I'm going after—" Paden's breath hissed through his teeth as the whisky hit his wound. Funny how something so wet could burn like a firebrand.

"You were saying something, son?"

"I was saying to hurry. Dark or not, I'm going after Hannah. So dig this goddamn bullet out and let me up."

"Thought as much." The forceps started their probing.

He kept his eyes shut and concentrated on how it'd felt to hold Hannah in the dark in Laramie's stockade. He didn't want the memory to be the only thing he ever had to hold on to.

"*Eres un idiota,*" Alejandro muttered. "So like you to want to race after three banditos, alone and injured. Too many times in Texas I watched you do something just as *loco.*" He drew in a deep breath. "This time I will go with you."

"Me too," Virgil and Gabe chimed in together.

Their offers humbled Paden, held him down more strongly than their hands. Hannah had true friends on this wagon train. He couldn't let them be killed because of his failures.

Sherwood's forceps retreated. "All done," he pronounced after tying the ends of a bandage around Paden's shoulder.

When he opened his eyes and sat up, he discovered that the stars hadn't stopped their blasted spinning. He was thankful for the hands that helped him climb to his feet. "I can't let you come with me. With me gone, the wagon train will need you more than ever."

The men followed him to where Cholla and White Cloud remained tethered to the scouts' wagon. Luckily, during all the shooting and fighting, neither horse had broken free. Hannah's pinto was still doing his darnedest to change that, however. He halted and whinnied shrilly when he saw Paden.

Paden shared the horse's anguish. They both wanted Hannah back. He patted White Cloud's shoulder. "Easy, boy. I'll find her."

"How?" Gabe asked.

"It won't take long for Dawson to feel cocky enough to stop running and make a camp. They'll light a fire. I'll ride in an ever-widening circle until I see that light." Fear ripped through him, threatening to lay him out on the ground again. As soon as they stopped and lit that fire, Dawson would continue with his revenge.

White Cloud whinnied again and jerked on his tether.

"He misses Hannah," Gabe murmured. "He keeps pulling in the direction I saw them ride off."

A memory sparked inside Paden. It was better than the light of any campfire. Hannah had told him that when she'd been taken by the trappers, Eagle Feather had found them at night. She'd said White Cloud had led him to her. Right now, White Cloud wanted to go in only one direction.

Paden turned to face Sherwood. Alejandro, Virgil and Gabe stood close behind the general. A grim resignation etched each of their faces. He clasped the old man's shoulder.

The general stiffened under the unexpected gesture, then sagged once more. "We'll wait as long as it takes."

"You won't, because you know that if I don't return by tomorrow's sunset, there'll be nothing to wait for." He hauled himself onto Cholla's bare back, ignored the pain in his shoulder and reached down to untie White Cloud. He'd barely gotten the lead looped around his saddle horn before the horse started pulling him and Cholla away from the wagon train.

He'd ridden Cholla many times at night. Like all horses, Cholla could maneuver over terrain too dark for human eyes. He could also pick up dangers via hearing and smell. What Cholla had never done was help him track a quarry. But White Cloud was searching for something much more important than an enemy. He was looking for the woman they both loved.

He loved her. He knew that without a doubt now.

It'd take a miracle for White Cloud to find her with so much distance already between them. It'd be an even greater miracle for them to find Hannah before Dawson unleashed his rage on her. A rage strong enough to have fueled their old scout's pursuit all the way from Fort Leavenworth.

Paden hung his hopes on a miracle and followed White Cloud into the dark.

The hard earth slapped Hannah, jarring her awake and straight back into her nightmare. Dawson's barrel-chested bulk loomed over her in the dark, laughing, standing beside a horse. He'd dragged her from its back and dumped her like a sack of feed at his feet.

When she'd last opened her eyes, they'd been traveling fast. But for how long, she didn't know. A blissful unconsciousness had claimed her. She willed the oblivion to return but it wouldn't. Worry for Paden hounded her. He'd been shot and hit on the head. Was he conscious now? Was he even alive? She fought to contain her rising panic.

Dawson pulled a bottle from his saddlebag and downed a generous swig. His hand returned to his crotch, this time sliding beneath his trousers. Rubbing hard, he raised the bottle to his lips in a rhythm just as desperate. She couldn't help but shrink from him.

His breathing became faster than the pace of his hand or his drinking. "Damned darkness," he muttered. "It ain't as good when I can't see you." Suddenly he halted and stalked off, yelling for his friend. "Help me build a fire!"

She drew her knees tight against her chest. Every muscle in her body contracted with fear, begged to flee. The thick rope around her ankles and wrists denied her. She struggled to break free. She only succeeded in making the cord bite deeper into her flesh. But the pain helped. It reminded her that she was still alive. That she still had a chance to stay that way.

She had to escape. She had to get back to Paden. She struggled harder.

A fire flickered to life nearby. Then Dawson stood over her again. He grabbed her feet and dragged her into the circle of light. His friend moved to stand beside him.

"Still got your knife?" Dawson asked without taking his gaze off her.

"Of course."

She forgot how to breathe.

Dawson took another pull on his bottle. "Cut the ropes on her legs. Leave her hands tied."

His cohort did as instructed. Pins and needles pricked Hannah's flesh. She bit her lip to stifle her groan. The man still crouched by her side concerned her more.

His soulless eyes, black as the pit of hell, never left her. He grasped her trouser's waistband. A silent cry for help shrieked in her brain. She kicked clumsily, fighting him as well as the numbness in her body.

"Wait your turn," Dawson snarled.

The man paused with his hands fisted in her clothing. "How do I know I'll get a turn?"

"You'll get several. But you ain't gettin' the first." Dawson held out his whiskey. "Have a drink."

His friend released her and took the bottle. He paused with it halfway to his lips. "I still get to use my knife?"

"Save it for the end. You don't want her passin' out during your turn."

"She won't. I'll make sure of that."

They shared the whiskey, staring down at her, hashing out who'd do what and when. Crude innuendos, mixed with blatant descriptions, brought into glaring focus the details of her ruin. Her dread turned to horror.

The ghost of another nightmare whispered around her. She realized that every time she'd seen Dawson, he'd merely been surly from the bitter end of overindulgence. Not drunk. She was about to discover the difference. She was about to learn what would've happened to her mother if the renegade militiamen had succeeded in extracting her from their cabin.

She couldn't hold back a sob born of equal parts loss and desperation. She was never going to see Paden again.

Dawson drained the dregs of his bottle, tossed it aside and squatted beside her. He jerked her up by her shirtfront until her face was a hairsbreadth from his. "Where is your precious wagon master now?" Waves of his sickly, sour breath hit her, choked her.

Don't react, she begged herself. If she showed her fear, he'd feed on it like a wolf. Trouble was, she was beyond fear. Sheer terror was devouring her from the inside.

Dawson's eyes glowed in the firelight, reflecting the flames of her hell. "When I'm done with you, Callahan won't want you anywhere near his damned wagon train." He licked his lips, breathing fast again. "He won't even be able to look at you. You'll remind him too much of his dead wife."

His words wrenched a gasp of disbelief from the bottom of her lungs.

Dawson laughed with glee. "I see he mentioned her. Did he tell you exactly how 'n where she was cut? No? Don't worry, you'll find out tonight."

Fury rose inside her. Fury that Dawson would use Paden's past to hurt him. "No, I won't," she shot back. "You can hurt me in a hundred different ways, but not *exactly* like Jeannie. You don't know what happened. You've never been to Texas. You weren't in San Antonio when she was killed."

"Jeannie? Was that her name? Weston had forgotten that detail. But he told me the rest." Dawson leaned closer to whisper near her ear, "All of it. How he raped her 'n cut her. My friend is lookin' forward to carvin' that same story on your flesh."

"You're lying. Weston didn't kill Jeannie, the Comanche did."

"Is that so? When I'm finished, I've been instructed to use my blade here." His fingers brushed her throat. "Just like Weston did to Callahan's wife."

No... It couldn't be. All those years that tortured Paden. They'd been for nothing. He'd pursued the wrong enemy. "Weston's a dead man."

"If I do as told and slit your throat at the end, Callahan will never know of Weston's involvement. That's Weston's hope, at least. That's why he practically threw me out of his jail—to do what he's afraid to do. Kept going on 'bout some fairytale with a devil made of smoke."

"Weston's using you. If you do what he asks, you'll be the dead man."

Dawson puffed out his chest. "I ain't afraid, 'n I ain't being used. This is my revenge. That's why I'm ignoring Weston and letting you live so you can tell the mighty Callahan *exactly* how he was bested not once, but twice."

The truth would destroy Paden. He'd plunge straight back into his old life, into a darkness where only vengeance mattered. "He won't stop until you're both dead." She squeezed shut her eyes, trying to block out that possibility.

"He'll never find me. But you—" He shoved her hard against the dirt, so hard her teeth clacked and she tasted blood. "He'll find you. Or what's left of you." He fumbled with his belt. Then his weight fell on her.

She fought to breathe. Struggled to buck him off. Couldn't even arch her back.

"All yer wiggling—" he laughed, panting rough and ragged against her neck, "—only makes this sweeter." Her clothing ripped. A knee thrust between hers. Then another, shoving her legs wide.

Her heart slammed against her ribcage in a final bid to escape. Dawson must have sensed her terror because he paused, lifting up on one elbow to stare down at her. A terrible smile spread across his face.

She lurched up. Her head slammed forward. For a fleeting second only Dawson's eyes filled her vision, wide with shock, with disbelief. Then her forehead hit his face. Bone crushed something softer. A howl erupted, full of painful incredulity. Blood gushed from Dawson's nose, over a mouth now parted in a silent scream.

"You bitch," he finally gasped.

A low whistle came from nearby. "You really have no luck with her."

Dawson staggered to his feet. "I'm gonna slice 'er to ribbons." He turned to his friend. "Yer knife. Give it to me!"

Hannah scrambled back on her butt and heels.

"To hell with that." The other man clamped his hand over the knife strapped to his belt. "I ain't had my turn, 'n you agreed that *I* get to cut her."

Dawson leaped at him with a roar. Hannah struggled against the rope binding her wrists, her gaze locked on the two men grappling for the blade. Her bonds defied her, tight as ever. Dawson finally gained possession of the knife. With a snarl of victory, he spun to face her again, arm raised to strike.

A dark shadow sprang between them. The silhouette of a man. A large one. He snared Dawson's arm and twisted, parting knife from hand. Then he grabbed Dawson's neck and wrenched even harder, this time parting breath from body, life from flesh. Dawson went limp as a rag doll as his eyes rolled back in his head. An unnatural stillness bore him to the ground.

"*Jesus Christ!*" his friend hissed, fumbling for his revolver.

Gunfire boomed. Multiple shots left her ears ringing. Dawson's friend dropped beside him. Two empty husks. Their reaper fell near them as well, first on his knees with a groan, then onto his side with a mighty thud. Paden's deep voice whispering her name filled the silence.

Shock and joy and dread hit her in rapid succession.

Blood soaked Paden's shirt. His? Or the men he'd just killed? Most likely both. Hopefully more of theirs than his. He had to live. He couldn't have survived the attack at the wagon camp only to die out here in the dark.

She reached for him, couldn't. She'd forgotten her hands were still bound. On trembling legs, she staggered to her feet, only to topple to her knees. She ended up crawling to where Dawson had dropped the knife. His eyes were still open, staring sightlessly up at the black sky.

Her stomach heaved. Too much death. Paden couldn't die as well. Not here. Not ever. Averting her face, she forced herself to concentrate on freeing her hands. She needed to save Paden. He needed her to be strong for him.

Her numb fingers kept dropping the knife. Her frustration swelled, making her even clumsier. She drew in a long breath then balanced the knife between her wrists, found her mark and began sawing. She was taking too long.

She glanced to where Paden had fallen. Where he now lay as silent as the two men he'd dispatched to hell. All in order to save her. She hacked madly, ignoring the blade when it nicked her flesh. Her bonds loosened. She sawed faster.

Her heart gave a joyful leap when the rope finally gave way. She scrambled to Paden's side and touched his cheek. Cold. He'd never been cold before.

His eyes fluttered open then held hers. "Are they dead?" he asked hoarsely.

She nodded, unable to speak.

"That's all that matters, then." He blinked, once, twice, his eyes drifting closed.

"No!" Her throat constricted and she fought to speak. "There's a great deal more that matters."

His eyes snapped open again, and he scanned her face with every drop of his old intensity. "Hannah…" Her name rumbled from a place deep inside him, a place heavy with fatigue. "This isn't your fault. I've cheated death so many times that this was inevitable."

"That's not true! I'm going to get you back to the wagons. I won't fail you."

"You never could."

"You're going to live."

The hint of a smile curved his lips. "I already

have. The moment you rode into Fort Leavenworth, I started living again. You gave me a second chance, an opportunity to do something with my life. Something good. I nearly botched it up, but you're alive. Nothing else matters." He released a sigh, a deep breath full of acceptance. Then he slumped dead still.

"Paden!" She pressed her cheek to his. Tears flooded her eyes and spilled onto his face. She brushed them away, first with her hands, then with her lips. His skin was so cold, too cold. More tears fell, an endless torrent of regrets and sorrow.

She pressed her lips to his and felt the smallest puff of warm there. He still breathed! She raised her head with a cry of happiness, turning her gaze to the heavens. *Thank you.*

Then she studied the stars and found her bearings there. When she decided which direction she must head, she bowed her head to Paden's again. "Be strong," she whispered against his lips, demanding and pleading with her whole body and soul. "One last time. Hold on. Don't—die." Her voice cracked on the last word, but she held back her tears as a grim determination filled her.

She'd rather kill herself trying to save him than live without him.

The sun beat down harsh and merciless, leaving Hannah slumped over White Cloud's withers. Lifting her head, she swallowed in a throat dry as sand. The empty plains swayed and spun, nearly toppling her off her perch. Threading her fingers through White Cloud's mane, she locked her grip. Then she glanced over her shoulder to check Cholla's progress.

The same as a minute ago. The same as each

proceeding hour. Enough hours to drain the day and one woman and two horses. Paden's usually spirited stallion plodded behind White Cloud, head hung low, pulling his master on a travois Hannah had cobbled together from saplings.

Paden hadn't uttered a sound since she'd searched him for more bullet wounds. Fortunately, she'd found only the first. But it wouldn't stop bleeding. So, once again, she'd had to turn to the blade Dawson had promised to use on her. She'd heated it in the campfire until it glowed red. Then she'd pressed it to Paden's wound.

She'd hurt him terribly. She'd also bought him time. "Hold on," she mumbled. "Just a little longer."

More than anything, they needed to move faster. That they were moving at all was a stroke of luck. All day, they'd marched forward, and she'd been able to keep her anxiety at bay. Now as the sun started its descent, her fear returned full force.

During Dawson's getaway, she'd hung facedown across his saddle. She'd lost her sense of direction, had only reclaimed it using the stars and then the sun. Now, before the light disappeared, she had to find the tracks gouged into the earth by the wagon wheels. Without them she could only continue heading in the general direction of west. Finding the wagons that way would be akin to finding a single blade of grass in a meadow.

She had to return Paden to the wagon train as quickly as possible. An unconscious man and a half-spent woman would be easily overcome by any predator on the prowl. By either the animal or human variety.

By a man driven by revenge and reported to be nearby.

If Eagle Feather found her, she wouldn't be able to help Paden. The prospect of making it this far, only to fail him, sent a suffocating tightness coiling around her chest. She swayed in her saddle.

Panic jerked her upright, made her sit taller in her saddle. The position improved her view for a fleeting moment. To her left, lay a narrow band of crisscrossed ground. She turned White Cloud and Cholla to follow the wagon trail, trembling with the realization that she'd almost ridden by without noticing it. She stared at the ruts as if they were a lifeline and urged the horses toward an ever-darkening horizon. Minutes later, the sun left her to the night's embrace.

She could no longer see the trail.

She swayed again. This time she let herself fall. She landed hard on her knees and barely felt the pain. The dark was everywhere now. Somewhere behind her, strapped to a travois, Paden lay unseen but still depending on her.

Exhaustion bowed her head, brought her chin to rest upon her collarbone as she blindly tied White Cloud's reins around one wrist and Cholla's around the other. Then she drew in a deep breath and used its release to help propel herself up onto her feet.

For an all-too-real moment she grappled with the likelihood that she wouldn't be able to remain standing. But she did. She put one foot in front of the other, searching for the ruts with the soles of her moccasins.

When she felt them, she kept moving, concentrating only on keeping them beneath her feet. It was the only way to follow them...and they were her and Paden's only hope.

CHAPTER 16

A soothing rhythm of creaking wood and jingling harness lulled Hannah while at the same time rousing her. Her body felt heavy, as did her eyes. She should open them. She had to stay awake. Confusion tightened her brow. Wasn't there something important she was meant to be doing?

Voices teased her, rising, overlapping, fading. A song hummed softly. A child's carefree laugh. Calls of encouragement for beasts to keep moving.

She was lying in the back of a rolling wagon. She opened her eyes with a jerk. The canvas arching overhead glowed bright from the sun on the other side. She'd survived the night. But had Paden? Fear trapped the air in her lungs.

"One morning, I'd like to watch you wake up with a smile on your lips. Even better, I'd like to be the one who's put it there."

She gasped in surprise and then sheer joy when she rolled to find Paden stretched out on his back next to her. Her happiness faded. Paden's eyes were open, but their usual steely sharpness had been replaced by a murky gray.

She scanned the rest of him. He wore only trousers and bandages. White bandages with no blood. That was a good sign, wasn't it? She laid her palm over his forehead. Last night he'd been distressingly cold. Now he was alarmingly hot. "How do you feel?"

It was his turn to frown as his gaze moved to her hand. "I'd feel much better if I had the power to reach your hand."

A sudden shyness, made her draw back. "You should try to sleep."

His lips pressed into an obstinate line. "I'm not closing my eyes till your hand is in mine."

She gently placed her hand over his, only to have his fingers clasp hers almost convulsively before going slack again.

"Stay with me." The need in his words and the weakness in his grip left her stunned. She'd never seen him anything but a pillar of unending strength.

"Rest," she said, "and you'll soon feel better."

"I already do," he replied on a sigh and let his eyes drift closed. "If I'm touching you, then I won't have to open my eyes to know if you're gone, if I need to get up and find you. I haven't forgotten that Eagle Feather's nearby. Neither should you." His voice turned hushed, almost as if he were talking to himself. "I'm going to do a much better job of keeping you safe this time."

"So am I," she whispered back. Having someone to hold on to after all her years of struggling alone empowered her. But her feelings went beyond a mere boost in strength. She came alive whenever Paden was near. And when he wasn't, she felt as if a piece of her was missing.

She'd left her safe but solitary hiding place, searching for a new beginning far from her past, from the regrets that haunted her. All this time she'd been focused on a destination, believing she'd find her redemption when she finally arrived there. Now she realized *where* she was didn't matter. A place wouldn't make her feel safe and strong, make her feel whole again.

A person could. Paden could. But first he had to live.

"Hannah…" Paden's voice was hoarse and hesitant. She'd never heard him sound so lost. His eyes remained closed. What thoughts tormented him in his sleep?

She pressed a damp cloth against his brow and continued whispering endless words of comfort close to his ear. "We're safe. You need only rest while I tend to your fever. There's nothing more to do."

They lay together in the back of the same supply wagon where after her ordeal at the river, Paden had healed her with his warmth. They were alone again.

Respectability be damned. She wasn't leaving his side.

He'd asked her to stay with him, and she would. She wouldn't fail him completely. He'd saved her too many times. Why couldn't she save him in return? Why wouldn't his fever break?

He kept lurching in and out of consciousness, jerking awake to scowl at the wagon's canopy above them. His gaze searching, his entire body tense with his quest before slumping back into oblivion with a groan of defeat. What internal demons filled him with such unrest?

How many more demons would she saddle him with if she revealed what Dawson had told her about Weston? He'd seek vengeance. He'd ride straight back to Fort Laramie to kill the man. He'd either die in the attempt or succeed and be on the run from the army for the murder of one of their colonels.

He'd be safer if she didn't tell him. He'd have a

chance at life. But how could she live with such a secret between them? She had no answers to her questions. Paden had to survive his injuries before she could even concentrate on them for longer than a minute.

She marked his lack of improvement by the sun filling their wagon with light as they rolled forward, consigning them to the shadows when they halted. She ignored everything outside their cradle of wood and canvas. The world had faded to a distant murmur, intruding only when General Sherwood or Miriam checked in on them morning, midday and night. Three days had passed, and still Paden was no better.

He mumbled her name again. The gravelly uncertainty tore at her heart and conscience. He needed her to help him. But what more could she do?

Miriam's lantern poked through the wagon's back flap followed by her head. "He any better?"

She shook her head. "He's so gaunt."

Miriam heaved a sigh. "He's got muscle to spare, so my bets are on him pulling through. You, on the other hand." She shook her finger at Hannah. "You were too thin when I met you. Now..." She tsked and blew out a worried breath. "You'll be the one meeting your maker if you don't get some rest. You can't continue this way."

Neither could Paden. "I can't relax until I know he's all right." She rechecked his bandages, then brushed a stubborn lock of inky hair from his forehead and returned the damp cloth to its post. "I've never seen him so still. And his eyes...they frighten me." She released a strangled laugh. "What I wouldn't give for one of his sharp-eyed looks right now."

Miriam heaved another sigh. "I'll see you in the

morning."

Hannah nodded but she didn't watch Miriam leave. Instead, she tucked the blankets closer around her and Paden, preparing for another sleepless night.

Hannah woke with a start. Darkness cloaked the inside of the wagon. How long had she been asleep? The only illumination came from the moonlight spilling through a narrow gap in the flap at the rear of the wagon. Had Miriam accidently left it open when she'd departed? Had the general looked in on them later? Was someone else out there?

Careful not to make a sound, she eased away from Paden, from the whisper of his even breathing, and crawled toward the light. Without touching the canvas, she peered outside. Silent and empty as far as she could see. Which wasn't far at all. Not with only a crack to squint through and only moonlight to aid her.

"Hannah." Behind her, Paden's voice was louder, more urgent than before.

She hastened back to his side. He hadn't moved, except to prop himself up on his elbows so he could track her with an intensity that made her stomach dance with butterflies. She touched his brow. His skin, although hot, didn't burn like before. His fever had broken.

She released a sigh of relief. "Everything's going to be all right."

"Not if you leave me." He sounded like a child facing the loss of his most cherished possession. "What can I do to convince you to stay with me? To make you *want* to stay?"

"Stop worrying. Go back to sleep. That's what you can do. I'm not going anywhere."

He shook his head. "You were staring outside

very intently. Too intently."

She mimicked his headshake. "I wasn't thinking of leaving."

"Don't try to spare my feelings. They're not worth a plug nickel. I'm not good or kind or anything worthy of your concern. And for that I'm sorry. With you, I want to do better, be better. But I also want—" he reached for her, stopped just short of touching her, "—*more*."

The yearning in the single word held her captive. She couldn't move. The silence that descended trapped the air in her lungs as well, making her lightheaded with her own longing.

"How much more?" she whispered.

His fingertips brushed her cheek. "I want to lie with you."

Disappointment pinched her heart. He could sleep with any woman. How long did physical desire last? Not long enough for what she truly craved. Him by her side forever. For a brief moment, she'd hoped he felt the same way. But only love could create that kind of bond. Why couldn't she accept what he'd told her? He'd never love again.

"I've be lying beside you in this wagon for days." She lay down on her side, facing him in the spot she'd occupied since first waking beside him. "Here I am again. Just as requested. Will you sleep now?"

He followed her down, with his body and his gaze, never once taking his eyes off her. How was it possible for eyes the color of steel to grow even sharper?

"You pretend to misunderstand," he said in a gruff voice that was strangely gentle as well, "in order to hide from me. The distance between us feels like a thousand miles when my one wish is to be as close as a man and woman can be."

His words mesmerized her. Or maybe she only

heard what she wanted to hear. She'd be a fool to—
She leaned forward until her chest brushed his.

His breath hissed between his teeth.

"Your wound's not yet healed." She drew back.
"We cannot do this." For so many reasons.

His arm snaked around her waist. With surprising
strength, he pulled her on top of him.

"Paden, you're going to hurt yourself." She
braced her arms between them, sliding her hands
down and away from his wound. The blanket
accidently fell to his trousers. Under her palms, the
naked planes of his abdomen shuddered and
contracted, hard as polished stone.

A gasp parted her lips. "Now I've hurt you."

"No." He gripped her waist, bunching her shirt
between his fingers, kneading the flesh beneath.
"Not in the way you think, at least. Even if you had,
it'd be worth it if I'd found the key to making you
want to stay with me."

But he wouldn't stay with her in return. Not if
she told him that Weston had killed Jeannie. And if
she said nothing and he found out later? She'd lose
him as well. She'd most likely lose him no matter
what she did. Too much had happened in the last
few days not to realize that they might not have even
tomorrow together.

She could accept that she'd never have his love,
but to lose him entirely? This new deprivation that
could arrive at any time left her desolate. It made her
want to cling to this night and him, and never let go.

His hands, work-roughened yet so very gentle,
stole under her shirt to settle on her back just above
her trousers. Skin against skin. Deliciously hot.
Wickedly sinful. He stroked the length of her spine,
long fingers massaging her taut muscles. Soothing
and exciting her at the same time. Distracting her.
Making her melt against him.

Her head unerringly found the perfect resting spot on his good shoulder, while her fingers worried the edge of his bandage. She wanted to touch more of him, but the bandage stopped her, reminded her that he was still injured. "I wouldn't dream of deserting you while you were unwell."

His heavenly caresses stopped. "See? You only agree to be with me until I'm healed. But you must stay because—" He rolled her beneath him.

She gasped with shock, and he immediately went still, braced on his elbows above her.

A low growl vibrated in his throat. "I put you in danger. I put you on this wagon train. I put you on a path where every ruffian roaming the frontier could find you." He dropped his head. His breath puffed out, hot and ragged, against her neck. "Dawson nearly killed you because of me."

"Shh." She stroked his hair, wanting to banish his demons. "None of that's your fault."

"I even allowed you to compete against Dawson at Leavenworth. I should've taken you in my arms instead. Like I wanted to do from the first moment I saw you."

The revelation made her hand go still.

"You were wise to keep your distance." His stubble scraped her neck, teased her in the most divine way possible as he pressed closer. "Even then, I wanted to do this."

"Paden, we—" The heat of his mouth against her throat stole her words. She struggled for air. "You're injured. We cannot—" His teeth nipped her, sending a delicious shiver along her veins. She couldn't stop her moan as his lips and his teeth and, *dear Lord*, his tongue kept moving, distracting her with desire. "We shouldn't…"

"We should," he said. "We should do this every day and every night. I should spend every minute I have convincing you that this is good. That I am worthy."

She already knew that. But he didn't. And she might have little time left to prove it to him. They might only have tonight…if she was strong enough to take it.

"How can I make you want me as much as I want you?" His fingers curled around the collar of her shirt, tugging it down to expose her shoulders to his searching mouth. His lips skimmed the line of her collarbone before continuing their descent.

She shivered as her desire grew, concentrating in a knot low in her body. "I'm filled with want."

"Tell me. Tell me what you want, and I'll give it to you." The heat of his mouth paused on the swell of her breast. "Do you want me to kiss you here?"

"*Yes.*" Was that her voice? So husky? So breathless? She was drowning in waves of desire, of need and longing. The feeling unnerved her, left her trembling. Because she craved so much…*more*. She wanted him, body and soul. "I think I want…too much."

"There's no such thing. Whatever you want is perfect. You are perfect." He explored the hills and hollows of one breast before he claimed the peak that ached for him and drew her inside his mouth.

A thunderbolt of pleasure hit her, making his name fly from her lips, making her writhe against him. The blanket stopped her. It'd slipped even lower, become tangled around her legs. She couldn't move. She couldn't get close enough. She groaned her disappointment.

His mouth retreated but didn't go far. He hovered above her, over the place where she was wet and tingling from his attention. "What's wrong?"

"There's too much cloth between us."

He raised his head to stare directly into her eyes.

He didn't move, didn't speak.

"Please say something. What are you thinking?" Her voice sounded small and weak in the silence.

"That I agree with you."

A flurry of rustling followed his words. Cloth being tugged free and tossed away. The blanket was gone...and his trousers as well. For a moment, she felt only shock. Then the long, naked length of him eased down to hover over her. Heat rolled off him in waves to singe her through the thin barrier of her clothing.

He stared at her with an unreadable expression, waiting for what, she did not know.

But she knew what she wanted. "Touch me."

His palm settled, large and heavy, on her hipbone and paused again as if seeking permission. A memory skimmed like the gentlest of breezes around her mind, an echo of his words. *Tell me. Tell me what you want, and I'll give it to you.*

Love me. Stay with me forever. Those joys were beyond their reach. *Stop torturing yourself and him.*

She released a shuddery breath. "I want you to touch me everywhere."

His hand slid down in a tortuously slow caress, over her hip, her leg to the back of her knee. He paused again.

Whatever he wanted, she wanted it to. "Yes. A hundred times, yes."

He drew her leg up and around his waist while at the same time settling his weight onto her. As he did, the hot brand of him slid along her inner thigh to nestle unerringly against her most intimate place. His mouth descended as well. He swallowed her moan. His tongue stroked hers, creating a tempo that she matched with her hips.

And it still wasn't enough.

She pulled her mouth free. "Paden, I need— I

want—*more*."

His fingers knotted in her shirt, pulling it up, pausing just under her breasts. "Do you want this gone?"

"Yes."

Her shirt vanished over her head and into a dark corner of the wagon.

"You're certain I can touch you…everywhere?"

"Yes," she replied even quicker than before. Finally he was going to remove her trousers and join that mysterious part of himself with her, the long, thick shaft that lay between her legs.

Without taking his gaze off hers, he reached down. His fingers brushed the back of her hand and very slowly slid up her arm. Confusion knotted her brow. What was he doing? Why was he touching something as uninspiring as her arm?

Then it came to her. He was touching her scars. Disbelief made her stiffen.

His hand immediately retreated.

The loss of his touch filled her with sadness. How could she have forgotten about her scars, about his reaction to them? Not long ago, her scars had been a shadow constantly hounding her thoughts. Tonight she hadn't thought about them once. But he had.

"What I said before." He cleared his throat. "There aren't enough words to tell you how sorry I am for the way I treated you that night by the river. It's a hurt I can never undo."

He was wrong. Once again she just had to show him. "I know a way."

"How?" The word was barely a whisper. He didn't believe her.

She swallowed the urge to say no more, to hide from him. "With your lips and your tongue. I think your kisses have the power to heal anything."

He immediately lifted her hand to his mouth. He kissed every scar, slowly and reverently, driving her wild as he inched up her arm. Then he claimed her other hand and did the same.

"You are the light in my dark," he whispered when he'd finished and turned her bones to liquid in the process. "You are everything to me. I never want to hurt you again, but in order to touch you everywhere, I will have to—" He cupped her cheeks between his palms so he could stare deep into her eyes.

Her heart missed a beat.

"Hannah, I won't lie to you. This first time, it will hurt."

She nodded, trying to appear knowledgeable about the subject. She had, after all, grown up around horses and wild animals. She'd seen them mate. "It's to be expected. You are bigger than me. And you feel even larger against me, down there." Heat burned her cheeks.

"My size complicates matters."

"Will it hurt every time?"

"God, no. But this first time…if it hurts too much…tell me, and I will stop."

She shook her head. "I can't turn back."

"You can." His tone had turned fierce. "Never, *ever* feel that when we're together you don't have a choice."

The urgency in his voice made her breath hitch in her throat.

"Hell, I'm scaring you. We're stopping. There'll be other nights."

There might not be. And she wanted this night. She wanted the man she loved. She bit her lip to halt those impetuous declarations.

Paden had warned her he could never love again. Not after what had happened to Jeannie. How much worse would he feel if he learned he'd never avenged Jeannie in the slightest? That he'd let her real killer go unpunished, let the man manipulate him into pursuing the wrong foe?

"I can feel you retreating." His lips took hers in an all-too-brief kiss that spoke of endings. "It's settled. We wait." He pushed himself up on his elbows again.

She kept him from going any farther with arm looped around his neck.

"What's wrong?" he asked.

I love you. That was what was wrong. Saying the words would only be another burden to him. That wasn't the same as showing him though. She released him and reached for her trousers instead.

A frown creased his brow. "What're you doing?"

"Undressing."

"Hannah." He said her name on a sigh, tense with worry.

She longing for him to say her name in a completely different manner. "I've made my choice."

He stared at her without blinking, making her fingers fumble with her task.

"Are you going to help me?" she asked.

He rolled to his side, taking her with him and drawing off her trousers in one swift tug. This time when he kissed her it was with a fierce urgency that showed her how much he'd been holding back. Was it really possible he might hurt her?

"You've gone stiff as a board," he said, breaking the kiss and allowing her to breathe again, but not without effort. "You're thinking too much. I can help you with that as well." His fingers skimmed down her belly.

Breathing became increasingly difficult again. He couldn't be thinking of touching her—?

Pleasure rocked her, making her gasp and arch against his hand.

The growl at the back of his throat was filled with male satisfaction. "You're already wet. Wet for me. Let's see if I can make you even more so." He traced his fingertips over her, searching until he found the spot that ached the most for him. "Do you want me to touch you here?"

"Yes." Her whisper was urgent, filled with a desperate yearning for more.

He rewarded her with a short, quick stroke that left her quivering. Then he gave her more. So much more. She surrendered herself to the heaven of his fingers. Her desire coiled tight, poised to spring beneath his fingers. When her breath came in harsh little pants, he suddenly stopped. Before she could protest, the tip of his finger slid inside her.

She moaned and arched her hips, trying to take him deeper.

He denied her, withdrawing his finger slowly. Then he pressed inside her again and repeated the dance. Slow retreat. Quicker thrust. Until his finger was fully inside her and she was still begging him for more.

But what version of more, she didn't know.

"Shall I kiss you here as well?" he asked.

She went very still. She couldn't have heard him right. He couldn't mean to put his mouth...there. But he was already moving down, his shoulders already gently nudging her thighs wider to allow his mouth to settle between them. All while his finger kept stroking her from within.

His tongue flicked the tight little bud that his fingers had previously teased to a state of such exquisite tightness. She grew even tighter. His mouth and fingers worked together until she was overcome with a rapture she'd never dreamed possible, until she pressed against him in uncontrollable abandon. She cried out as a burst of ecstasy exploded inside her with an intensity that seemed to shatter her into pieces.

Instantly, his arms wrapped around her to catch her and hold her secure against his chest. Next to her ear, his heart pounded, loud and fast.

"I've got you," he murmured, his lips brushing her hair.

For a long moment, he simply held her. The only sound beside his heartbeat was the gradual slowing of their breathing.

As soon as she had the strength, she lifted her head to stare at him. Above her, his face was cast in shadows, reminding her that this man, so complex and passionate about everything, was still a great mystery to her.

"I never imagined that it would be like that. That you would use your hands and your mouth to... That it would feel so..."

"How do you feel?"

"Amazing." But a single word wasn't enough. She wasn't sure that a thousand words could describe how he'd made her feel, how he continued to make her feel. "Can the same thing happen for you?"

"Yes, if I'm inside you." The hard maleness of him twitched against her, as eager as his voice. His fingers curled around her shoulder and stroked down to her elbow and back again. "Or if you put your hand around me."

"Oh," she said as an image of her doing just that filled her thoughts. She felt her eyes grow even rounder with this new wonder. She yearned to give him the pleasure he'd given her with his hands and his— "Could I use my mouth as well?"

He swore, soft and low. "You most definitely

can." The trembling in his muscles, always so strong and steady, surprised her. He vibrated with a need he held in check. He held himself back, waiting for her to tell him what came next, what she wanted to come next.

"Then we should do one or the other. Or both." Heat scorched her entire body at her bold words. "I want you to feel what I feel, this gift. Does it happen every time for a man and a woman?"

"Not for the woman and not in such an all-consuming way for the man. I'm humbled that you'd open yourself to me so completely, without the fear of me hurting you. That's the true gift. That you trust me."

She flinched. Trust could only be maintained with honesty. Lies would crush whatever affection he might be developing for her. Better that than send him hurtling down a path filled only with hate and death.

He stared at her with an intensity that made her want to run. She hadn't felt this way in a long time.

His brow lowered. "I'm pushing you away again."

"Not you, the past."

"You sense it," he said so softly he might have been talking to himself. "My lie, the dark truth I've never shared with anyone. Hannah…I haven't been honest with you about my past, about the Comanche."

She blinked. He already knew that it was Weston who'd killed Jeannie, and not the Comanche?

"I should've known that you'd be the one to guess, having lived with Indians as well."

She opened her mouth to tell him she hadn't guessed, that she'd been told.

He continued speaking, before she could. "I'm a callous bastard to ask you to bind yourself to me without knowing who I am, without knowing the truth. I have to tell you everything before we go any further. No more secrets, no more lies. The Comanche didn't—" He swallowed hard. "They…"

"They didn't hurt Jeannie," she said.

He drew back his head in surprise. "Of course they hurt Jeannie. But they didn't steal me away from my family. They were my family."

Bewilderment crept over her, cold as the north wind. All of his warmth had disappeared. He'd let go of her so he could roll onto his back. Close enough to reach out and comfort, but clearly not wanting her. He'd closed his eyes, blocking her out. He didn't even want the sight of her.

"This is the truth I hid from you," he said in a voice so hoarse it sounded as if his confession were being ripped out of him. "Kaku was my grandmother. In spirit and in blood. I'm part Comanche. I killed my own people."

Not only was he a cold-blooded murderer, he was a fool. He'd been a hairsbreadth from making Hannah his and he decided now was the time to be honest with her, to reveal a secret he'd never told anyone?

Maybe he was still ill. He might no longer burn with a fever hot enough to make him want to crawl out of his skin, but he smoldered with something much more enduring. He couldn't imagine his passion for Hannah ever fading. He kept his eyes shut, trying to forget the sounds she'd made as he'd brought her release. Her throaty little gasps had pushed him to the edge of his own, to the brink of thrusting himself deep inside her. The memory nearly drove him to the same action now.

Instead, he shoved his fingers in his hair. He

refused to behave like his grandfather. He'd rather burn in hell, and on earth, than be anything like that bastard. A ghost he'd never met. A man he never wanted to meet. If he did, he'd be tempted to kill again.

And as much as he wanted Hannah tonight, he needed something more. He needed her in his life tomorrow and every day that followed.

And Hannah? What did she need? Certainly not a quick toss in the back of a wagon, followed by a morning full of uncertainty. She needed commitment and stability, marriage and a family. He wanted to give her all of that. Give her children—his children, but with her compassionate blue eyes. Not his cold gray ones born from a lie.

The silence filling the wagon made him tense. Could Hannah have climbed out without him hearing? Had she finally left him?

He bolted upright, gaze ricocheting around the cramped interior of the wagon.

Hannah still lay on her side next to him, watching him with wide eyes, frozen like a doe in the sights of a hunter. She didn't stay that way for long.

Scrambling to her knees, she snatched the nearest thing, the blanket, and clutched it under her chin, shielding her body from his gaze and his hands. It'd be a cold day in hell before she let him touch her again.

She had yet to run though. An ember of hope sparked inside him. She continued staring at him as if waiting for him to do something, to say something. After all he'd done, she was still strong enough to face him. He owed her the truth…even if it destroyed his last hope for keeping her by his side.

"After Jeannie's death, the Comanche braves I killed—" He hauled in a rough breath and forced himself to continue. "I remembered several of them from Kaku's village, from *my* village. Though most had only been boys when I last saw them."

She nodded slowly. "You remembered them because when you were young, they were cruel to you."

He stiffened. How had she known?

Her fingers worried the wool blanket in her grasp. "You told me you weren't happy growing up with the Comanche."

"I was a child of mixed blood, a hellion with a trigger-finger temper. The other boys taunted me for that very reason. I was easy to anger. When Kaku learned what they were saying, she told me she would empower me with the truth. What she told me didn't make me feel strong. It made me feel even angrier. I hated my Comanche blood, but her confession made me hate my white blood even more, the blood of my grandfather."

"What did he do?"

"When he met Kaku, he pressured her to run away with him. She worried that their different worlds would tear them apart. He vowed he'd use all of his strength to keep her with him. He said everything he could to make her trust him enough to sleep with him. Then he left."

"She never saw him again?" Hannah's eyes glittered with compassion for a woman she'd never met. Her kindness stole the air from his lungs.

Not everyone in Kaku's tribe had forgiven her for almost abandoning them. If Hannah had lived in his village all those years ago, she'd have befriended Kaku and defended him. Just as she'd done with Miriam and her grandsons.

"He left her pregnant and without a husband?" The disbelief in Hannah's whisper tore at his conscience.

He couldn't sleep with her without first giving

her the security of marriage. "He never came back, and she still tried to defend him. She said he'd had no choice. He was this legendary warrior in a faraway army, a huge man with gray eyes. I hate that I look like him, that I allowed myself to become him."

"You might look similar," Hannah shot back, her spine straight as an arrow, "but you are nothing like him."

Her defense humbled him. If she ever fell in love, she'd do so with nothing held back. What he wouldn't give to be that man. He fixed his gaze on the canopy of the wagon before she could see his longing.

She released a wistful sigh that stabbed his conscience even more. "Kaku was blessed with the gift of your mother and you."

He snorted. "I was no gift. I was a reminder of everything she'd lost. Too many times she'd stare at me with the unfocused look of someone longing for another place and time. I despised my grandfather for that. Even after all those years, he had the power to make her miss him."

"The last time I saw my mother." Hannah's voice was so hushed he strained to hear her. "She stared at my face as if she'd never see it again. My memories are faded now...but I think we had the same eyes. Was that true for you and your mother?"

He shrugged one shoulder. "Kaku said we did."

"I thought as much. When she looked at you, she was remembering her daughter. She missed your mother, not your grandfather."

He couldn't stop his gaze from snapping back to her. "That's not possible." He scrubbed one hand over the back of his neck in frustration. It was very possible and more likely than what he'd assumed. "Why didn't I see that?"

"You were young, and you never really knew your parents. You were caught between two worlds. Like me."

"And still I only made things harder for you. I wouldn't blame you if regretted every moment you were forced to spend with me."

"You didn't force me!"

"I won't follow in my grandfather's footsteps."

"We haven't—" Her cheeks turned pink. "I'm not pregnant."

"Neither are you untouched. Marriages have become necessary for less."

She drew back. "You'd bind yourself to someone you could never…?"

"Never?" he prompted.

Shaking her head, she pulled the blanket over her legs and hugged them to her chest.

Paden exhaled a lengthy breath. The only "never" where she was concerned was that he'd never to be able to let her go. *I can't go anywhere without you.* "I have to marry you. There's no other choice."

She blinked, startled. Then she blinked again and her lashes came away wet. "But you said I'd always have a choice."

Hellfire, he was a bigger fool than he could've ever thought. He hadn't asked her to marry him. Dread constricted his throat. What if she said no? His heart pounded, anticipating her refusal. He practically growled his request in order to get it out. "Will you marry me?"

She glanced toward the rear of the wagon. "Our pasts will tear us apart. Eagle Feather is still out there, and Jeannie's killer."

"I won't leave you alone like I did with Jeannie. I'll be near if Eagle Feather tries anything. I'm not leaving you."

Her eyes closed almost convulsively. "But you're

not done avenging Jeannie."

"Some say I've killed enough men to avenge her a hundred times." *All that I care about is here in this wagon.* "My old life is over."

"The past is full of shadows." Her breathing had turned increasingly fast.

"I'm not hiding anything else. I've told you everything."

"But I haven't." The pulse at the base of her neck pounded at a frantic pace. "I hold a secret that would put you back on a path of vengeance and get you killed. When I was with Dawson, he—" Her gaze darted, wide-eyed and frightened, around the wagon.

"You're safe now." He reached out to reassure her.

She scuttled back, evading him. The blanket she clutched as a shield lowered as her palm dropped to her heart. The top of the spider web, a talisman given to her by a people who hadn't been able to protect her either, was stark against her pale body. Dark bruises marred her skin. Were they from lying belly-down over Dawson's saddle when he'd abducted her?

His breath hissed through his teeth. Dear God, had Dawson—? His mind balked at the thought. Mere moments ago, she'd opened herself to him. Welcoming and trusting. She wouldn't have done so if she'd been violated. Would she?

He'd thought he'd stopped Dawson in time. But he hadn't asked her what had happened before he'd found her. Instead of using his first moments of coherent thought to comfort her, he'd given in to his own lust.

"Hannah," he said very softly, trying not to frighten her further, "did Dawson rape you?"

"No! But he told me that Weston—" She slumped sideways against the wagon, turning away from him to lean her forehead against the canvas.

He'd thought he'd kissed all of her, but he hadn't. He'd reached the scars on her arms but not the ones facing him now, the ones on her back. The urge to press his lips to her wounds, to soothe her hurt and her fears, overwhelmed him. But he feared he'd only make things worse if he didn't understand her fully.

"Hannah, tell me what's wrong."

"I don't want you to go back to Laramie."

Nothing important remained at the fort. There was only Weston and his meddling. The truth slapped him hard, jarring his teeth together. "Weston released Dawson so he could chase after us. Yes, I'd like to return and throttle him for allowing Dawson to hurt you, but I won't. I'm only going forward."

"The past is too strong. It'll drag you back to hell." She raised her chin. "I won't be the one to send you there to die." She kept her profile to him, her expression distant, guarded.

His heart seized. He remembered that look. It was the one she'd used when she'd first joined them at Leavenworth, then during the competition with Dawson, and with him. He hadn't seen it in a long time. She was hiding from him again, pushing him away. He was continually the fool while she was wise—wise to fear he'd leave her, because right now part of him wanted to race back to Fort Laramie and discover what lay there.

But he wasn't going to because a bigger part of him, one that he'd long thought lost, held him here. He loved Hannah with all of his heart.

"Hannah, I need to tell you something."

"A moment ago, you said you'd told me everything." Her voice was heavy with fatigue, with suspicion.

He'd had so much to say that he'd left out the

most important thing. If he told her he loved her now, she wouldn't believe him.

CHAPTER 17

Alejandro strode as fast as he could through the shadows cast by the wagons while still keeping his tread silent and his gaze vigilant. He'd finally finished his turn on guard duty. Now he could honor his promise.

On the other side of the circled wagons, firelight flickered and sputtered. Most of the campfires had burned down to embers. Less than a handful of the settlers remained awake. The rest had retired for the evening, leaving the stragglers to gossip in murmurs. One of them was Thomas Riley. Tonight, Riley's penchant for long-winded conversation was a boon.

Alejandro halted beside the Riley wagon and waited.

The night wind blew hot against his face and made the grass rustle. Beneath his boots, fissures had cracked the ground. It hadn't rained in days. Another absence disturbed him more deeply. He hadn't seen Rebecca since she'd spoken to him at daybreak.

She'd said, "Meet me tonight. At my wagon. After everyone's asleep."

Being separated for even a day now made his heart feel as parched as the earth.

He stared at the back of her wagon, unwilling to

blink. A silent prayer moved his lips as he beseeched heaven to open the wagon's flap and let Rebecca climb out. Only when he saw her again and ensured she was well, could he relax.

Hannah's abduction had rattled him. Thank Jesus, Paden had found her in time. He couldn't even think about what might have happened. What if someone similar to Dawson took Rebecca and he couldn't reach her in time? His chest constricted. He didn't want to think about that possibility either.

Luckily Hannah had survived her ordeal, and Paden had as well. But now something else was wrong. There was a strained silence whenever the pair was together. More so now than ever.

In contrast to their discord, both Alejandro and Rebecca were now in tune. They'd agreed to let nothing, including prejudice and misplaced loyalty, keep them apart. Soon they would be husband and wife. They only had to wait until they reached Fort Bridger.

Still, they needed to be careful. They had to keep their meetings secret, and their plans as well. He wanted to tell Hannah everything, but he feared he'd only add to her worry. She looked dead tired these days. She wouldn't tell him what kept her awake, but he knew it had to be something to do with Paden.

The wagon canopy shifted, rippling in the flickering firelight. His heart thundered with hope. Rebecca pushed the flap apart and jumped to the ground. She clutched the tailgate of her wagon, her back to the campfires as she scanned the darkness.

"I am here, *mi amor*," he called out softly.

She spun toward the sound of his voice. A smile of pure joy lit her face. He pulled her into the shadows and his arms. Holding her loosely, he marveled when she snuggled closer until she lay nestled against his chest.

"I was afraid you wouldn't be here." Her words were muffled against his shoulder.

"How can you think such a thing? I shall always be here for you."

"I know you will…if you can." She lifted her head and stared up into his face. "But I keep having nightmares where a river of fire chases the wagon train."

He pressed a kiss to her forehead. "Together we are too strong to let even the flames of hell hurt us."

She sighed, then nodded and rested her head on his chest again. He laid his cheek against hair, loving how the locks felt soft as silk against his skin, wishing he could hold her like this all night.

The whisper of footsteps scraped the earth nearby, followed by breathless giggling.

Rebecca couldn't be seen with him. He needed to disappear. He drew back, gathering his strength to leap into the shadows and leave her.

Two young women sprinted around the back of Rebecca's wagon before he could. The girls skidded to a halt, facing them. They each clutched a flannel blanket around their shoulders, their nightgowns glowing ghostly pale over their bare feet. They hadn't taken the time to dress for their moonlight excursion and their eyes were wide, not with surprise but with glee.

"I told you I heard voices." The intruder with mousy-brown hair raised a fluttering hand to her throat.

Her friend nodded briskly, making her blond curls bounce. "How shocking to have stumbled upon a lovers' tryst."

Anger ripped through Alejandro. "You should have stayed inside your wagons."

The blonde stared hard at Rebecca. "You mean

Rebecca should have. She's in trouble now."

"Don't do this," Rebecca said, taking a step toward the girls.

Their tittering laughter was strident in the hushed night air.

"We're telling your father." The mousy one's voice had gone high-pitched with excitement.

The other girl nodded. "How awkward this will be for both of you."

"It'll be a helluva lot more awkward for you." Paden stood with arms crossed beside the wagon. "Tell Riley, tell anyone, and I'll throw the pair of you off this wagon train."

Both girls blanched and retreated several steps.

The blonde was the first to recover. She lifted her chin and jabbed her finger at Alejandro and Rebecca. "You mean them, of course. We haven't done anything wrong."

"That remains to be seen," Paden drawled. "Utter one word about tonight, and you'll be standing by the trailside, watching the wagons roll away. I suspect you won't be alone for long. Some drifters or renegades will find you and take you in hand."

The girls' faces went as white as chalk.

"Why are you still standing here?" Paden asked. "Get your meddling asses back to your families."

The girls bolted like spooked antelopes, leaving Alejandro to gape at Paden in astonishment.

Rebecca moved toward Paden. "Thank you, Captain Callahan."

Alejandro grabbed her hand, halting her, wanting to shield her from Paden's harsh rebuke whenever anyone called him captain.

"You're welcome," Paden replied gruffly, then pivoted to leave.

"Wait," Rebecca called out, not bothering to lower her voice.

Paden turned slowly to face them. His eyes held a bleakness Alejandro recalled from Texas.

He strode forward to stand shoulder to shoulder with Rebecca in front of Paden. "What's wrong?"

"Why are you and Hannah at odds again?" Rebecca asked.

Paden flushed a deep red and let his gaze drop to the ground. "She won't marry me."

"Dios," Alejandro swore softly. Rebecca was right. Paden loved Hannah.

"She won't marry you yet," Rebecca corrected.

Paden's head jerked up. Hope flickered in his eyes. "You think I should ask her again?"

"No." Rebecca's fingers tightened around his. "Alejandro and I are getting married in Fort Bridger. If you truly love Hannah, then I suggest you spend all of your time between here and the fort doing everything you can to *show* her that she should marry you there as well."

Hemmed in on either side by walls of tall green pines, Hannah sat beside Miriam's wagon and stared at the path rising before her. The trees' fresh scent, warmed by the midday sun, was pleasant. So was her friend's chatter about how to prepare biscuits. But her many worries wouldn't let her relax.

Miriam paused then heaved a sigh. "You look ready to keel over. Have you been getting any sleep?"

"Some." Not wanting Miriam to read the lie in her eyes, she kept her gaze on the wagons lined up in the trench cut into the pale sandstone. An ever-deepening channel eroded by the constant flow of settlers climbing steadily toward the Black Hills. Wagon after wagon, year after year. Hannah's many regrets cut her just as deeply. Evading Miriam's question joined the weight on her shoulders. So did her feelings for Paden.

She straightened her spine. She wouldn't allow their time together to become one of her regrets. No matter what happened, she'd always hold dear the night where she'd felt his love, even if she never heard the word on his lips. The memory of that night might sit heavy on her conscience, but she would never cast it aside. Not now. Not ever.

Not like how the settlers around her, and the ones who'd come before, had finally abandoned mementos they'd previously clutched tight. The trailside was littered with possessions, somber and stark against the pale earth. It was either leave them behind or watch the mules and oxen perish from exhaustion under their weight. Then the settlers would have to travel by foot and lose everything, including their lives, if they failed to cross the high mountain passes before winter.

The image of Jeannie's piano sitting all alone back by the Platte River rose in her mind. What right did Hannah have to keep the truth about his wife's death from Paden? Was it enough that she loved him? That she'd give her own life to keep him safe and sound?

And he looked very sound now. After a week, no one would guess from his outside appearance that he'd come close to dying. If she told him the truth, he'd rally his still-mending body and race straight back to hell, back to Fort Laramie and Weston. This time he'd destroy himself completely in the pursuit of revenge.

"I've come to collect you." Paden's deep voice rumbled close behind her.

A delicious shiver rocked her. She went rigid, trying to contain her reaction.

Miriam's gaze darted from a point above

Hannah's head down to her face. "Go on," she urged softly. "You two need to talk more than you need to listen to me prattle on about biscuit making."

Hannah rose and faced him. He'd halted just far enough away to remain out of reach. A mountain of muscle and strength, he still towered over her. The same as when she'd first seen him in Leavenworth. But he looked different now as well.

She devoured the sight of him as if she was starving and he was a feast. Under his hat, the breeze teased his dark hair, making her ache to sooth their unruly waves. The dark color had been familiar, and so had his scent of sweet sage. Why hadn't she guessed that Comanche blood flowed in his veins and not just on his hands?

Why hadn't she pushed herself to understand his past better?

Because he always distracted her with the present. Now was no different. His eyes claimed her attention. Eyes he said he hated. Today, the steely-eyed gaze studying her made her heart race with one emotion.

She loved his eyes. She loved all of him.

And what did he feel? The way he was scowling suggested anger. Her stomach knotted.

He glanced over his shoulder, glaring down the line of wagons in the direction he'd come. "We have another Indian visitor." His frown deepened but his tone held no emotion when he said, "I won't lie. I thought about putting a bullet in this one's head as well."

Miriam's gasp echoed Hannah's.

His gaze swung back to her. "But I find myself...reluctant to harm him." He huffed out a breath. "He might leave me no choice though. He's *loco* enough to eat the devil with the horns on. Rode straight up the path behind the scouts' wagon and announced that he knew Eagle Feather."

She shook her head in disbelief.

"He said he had a message for you."

Her hand jumped to her throat as if the message were a knife.

"You don't have to speak with him." Miriam's voice was sharp with concern.

Paden nodded. "His message might do more harm than good."

"Or it might do the opposite." She forced her hand down, resigning herself to whatever waited for her at the tail end of the wagon train. Her palm settled over her heart and her tattoo of home and family. She'd do what she must. She'd do it for Morning Star and Laughing Eyes.

But Paden remained standing between her and their visitor.

"I can't run from this." Before her feet could betray her and do just that, she climbed onto the bank so she could walk past Paden and down the line of wagons.

He immediately jumped up and fell into step beside her. "Are you…"

She couldn't help but glance at him.

A worried expression had replaced his scowl. "Are you well?"

"I'm fine." She hoped the tremor in her voice hadn't betrayed her.

"You look tired." He cleared his throat. "After our night in my wagon, I wondered if you might be having second thoughts."

"I'm fine," she repeated, forcing a smile to her lips. Could he tell she was lying?

"Happy to hear it."

She struggled to remain silent and failed. "Second thoughts about what?"

"My offer of—" Ducking his head, he scrubbed

his hand over the back of his neck as if he wanted to take back his words.

She didn't want him to take them back. Her heart ached to accept his offer of marriage. But how could she build a life with him while still holding on to her lie?

"I hope you'll tell me if you aren't fine," he said. He was changing the subject.

Her steps dragged. She hated lying to him. "I haven't been sleeping very well."

"I know." Dark circles underscored his eyes. He hadn't been sleeping either. He'd been too busy watching over her, protecting her.

Guilt made her shoulders droop.

"You forget that Eagle Feather's still out there." His gaze searched her face. "Even now when you're only moments away from receiving a message from him, you seem distracted by something else."

Distracted by you. Always you.

"There are things I need to show you," he said.

"Show me?"

"How much I've changed. How much I care for you."

Her heart raced with joy, then faltered. Care wasn't the same as love.

The last wagon came into view, the scouts' wagon with Alejandro and Paden's mounts tied behind it. She squinted to focus beyond the wagon, where Alejandro and Gabe stood a dozen paces farther down the trail, facing a raven-haired man holding the reins of his own horse.

"We'll talk more later." Paden lengthened his stride to walk ahead of her. He'd put himself between her and their visitor, protecting her again. Not just a visitor. Eagle Feather's messenger. What would he tell her?

When they'd passed the scouts' wagon, Paden

jumped down into the channel. She caught sight of the brave standing on the other side of Alejandro and Gabe. He towered over the two men. His buckskin shirt stretched across broad shoulders.

Paden grabbed her by the waist and swung her down behind him, blocking her view again.

Their visitor had rivaled Paden's size and strength. The only man she'd known who could do that was—

Paden moved to her side. Ahead of them, Alejandro and Gabe remained rooted in place, still facing their visitor. The brave stared over their heads at her. A scar, now white and puckered with age, slashed down from his left eye to the corner of his jaw.

Her lungs refused to work. The vivid recollection of the last time she'd seen that scar, dripping scarlet, filled her mind, along with its owner's cries for vengeance. Eagle Feather's expression remained impassive, while Hannah gaped at him in silent horror.

Two long years had passed, but now they were reunited. She wished they could've been closer. He was her only link to Morning Star and Laughing Eyes, to a life she'd cherished and missed so very dearly.

Tears blurred her eyes. All she wanted was to pretend that horrible day had never happened. She wanted to embrace Morning Star's only living relative. And him? He'd probably meet her open arms with a knife.

Paden took an abrupt stride forward as if sensing her impulse, as if knowing he must protect her from not only their visitor but herself. "You have a message from Eagle Feather," he said. "If it's anything worth hearing, why didn't he deliver it himself? Why are you here instead?"

A new fear gripped Hannah. In Laramie's stockade, she'd told Paden about Eagle Feather's scar. What if he realized this messenger was Eagle Feather?

Spirits Above! Both men were warriors. Angry ones. There'd be a fight. Neither man would back down. One would be killed. In her heart, Eagle Feather was still her brother. She couldn't bear to see him killed, while the mere prospect of someone harming Paden in any way made her go cold with dread.

Eagle Feather's gaze hadn't left her since she'd arrived.

"Go away," she choked out. "I no longer want to hear this message."

"But I do," Paden said swiftly. "I want to hear his answer to my question as well. Why are you here?"

Her brother's gaze remained fixed on her. "For Blue Sky."

Hannah flinched. He meant to take her right now? With three men standing between them? She didn't want to see Alejandro or Gabe hurt either.

"Her name is Hannah," Paden's voice was thick with possession.

Eagle Feather's gaze finally shifted to him. "To the Osage she is, and will always be, Blue Sky. Her life belongs to them."

"Like hell it does." Paden's hands moved to his revolvers.

"No!" Hannah reached out to stop him.

He shoved his half-drawn pistols back into their holsters. He didn't let go of them though.

"You would shoot a mere messenger?" Eagle Feather's tone was full of scorn.

"I'm trying not to, but maybe it's no use. So, I'll give you a message for Eagle Feather. Leave Hannah alone or else. Can you deliver that message, or should I go straight to the 'or else' part?"

She reached for him again, then changed her mind and swung to face Eagle Feather. "Don't say any more. Please go."

Eagle Feather's gaze remained locked on Paden.

"She stays with me," Paden said firmly. "Why don't you deliver that message as well?"

Eagle Feather's gaze narrowed, but he didn't move. "The white man is arrogant. He thinks everything belongs to him. He takes what he wants, by force if necessary. He believes it is his right." His disapproving gaze shifted to Hannah. "Blue Sky knows this, the same way that all Osage know. She should remember her past. Has she forgotten it was the whites who murdered both of her families?"

"Not a day passes that I don't think of them." She drew in a breath for courage. "And the man who was my brother."

Eagle Feather's scowl deepened. He mounted his horse and stared at a point over her head. "This is Eagle Feather's message. He was wrong to banish Blue Sky. He will return her to her tribe where she will accept Osage justice." His attention swung to Paden. "And no one will stop him." He reined his horse around and galloped away.

Shock numbed Hannah. He'd left. He'd left her unscathed. He'd left without a scratch on himself either.

Paden's gaze followed her brother's retreating back. "Alejandro—"

"I'm on it." Alejandro sprinted for his horse and leaped astride. "He won't turn back on the sly and catch us unaware." With a kick of his heels, he chased after Eagle Feather.

"What can I do?" Gabe asked.

The general answered for Paden. "You can get the wagons moving, while I stay here and cover our rear in case our visitor decides to return. An unlikely possibility with Alejandro on his tail, but still…"

Hannah's heart seized with worry for Alejandro.

"We cannot wait for Virgil to get back from scouting the trail ahead," the general added. "We leave immediately."

Gabe scrambled up the bank.

"Wait," Paden called after him. "When you reach Miriam's wagon, tell her Hannah and I will join her shortly. I don't want Hannah left alone for a minute. She stays out of sight in the back of Miriam's wagon, while we form our guard around her."

"Yes, sir." Gabe saluted him then sprinted off.

Paden turned to the general. He opened his mouth to say something then clamped it shut.

The general laid his palm on Paden's shoulder. "We'll all help keep her safe, son."

Paden nodded and then his big hands clasped her waist again and lifted her easily onto the bank. When he released her, she almost cried out with loss. Before she could, he vaulted up beside her and his hand claimed hers, strong and certain. He pulled her toward Miriam's wagon.

Hannah glanced over her shoulder at the trail behind them. The general stood alone. No sight of Eagle Feather or Alejandro. *Please stay safe, Alejandro.*

"What did you make of our visitor?" Paden asked.

The impulse to protect Eagle Feather, to lie about his proximity, stuck in her throat. Eagle Feather had chosen to put himself in danger. But he was gone now. He was safe. So was everyone else, for the moment. But she couldn't withhold the truth and jeopardize their continued safety. "Our visitor was Eagle Feather."

"I know."

Her lips parted with surprise. What had she said or done to make him realize the truth? She tensed in anticipation of his anger, his disappointment.

He kept walking.

She swallowed, her mouth dry as sand. "I'm sorry I didn't tell you who he was when I first recognized him."

Paden snorted. "I'm not. If you had, he might not have left so quietly."

"You call that quietly?"

"I imagine that was quiet for him. He's a hot head."

"I should've warned you it was him." She heaved a sigh, unsure how but feeling she should've tried.

"You warned me days ago." Paden turned his profile to her and gestured to his cheek. "You told me about his scar."

"You knew it was him when you came to get me?" But he hadn't put a bullet in Eagle Feather's head like he'd said he wanted to do. She glanced over her shoulder, down the trail where her brother had made his escape. Except he hadn't escaped. "Why did you let him go?"

"Because it's what you wanted. You want to pay back Morning Star, and so do I. She saved you, so I saved her son. I gave him a fair warning and a second chance. If he returns, I—" A muscle bunched in his jaw. When he spoke again, it was through gritted teeth. "I don't know what I'll do."

She jerked free of his grasp, forcing him to halt with her. "I can't let you hurt him."

He flexed his fingers as if he battled the urge to take hold of her again. Instead, he crossed his arms over his chest. "This is out of your control, Hannah."

"But he's Morning Star's son. He's my brother." Her voice cracked on the last word and her gaze plummeted to the ground. "He *was* my brother."

Strong arms immediately came around her and cradled her to his chest. "Stop torturing yourself," he whispered against her hair. "You can't save him. Only he can do that."

"But I can't let him die just to save myself."

Paden's muscles went rigid around her, but when he spoke his voice was gentle. "I don't agree. All I'll agree to is this… I won't go after him right now. I won't hunt him down and kill him. If he comes back, things will be different."

Her head spun. She couldn't figure out how to save both Paden and Eagle Feather. "I need to lie down."

He pressed a quick kiss to the top of her head. "I'll keep watch while you sleep."

"You need to check on Alejandro."

"I'm not leaving your side."

"What if Alejandro gets hurt because of me?"

His arms tightened around her. "Promise me you'll stay with Miriam, where I can find you."

"I promise." With heavy feet, she followed him back to Miriam's wagon. When they arrived, Miriam had her shotgun in her hand and Gabe by her side.

"I need the two of you to watch Hannah, while I find Alejandro and make sure Hannah's brother has left."

"Her brother?" Miriam spun to face her. "Eagle Feather was here?"

"He's gone." She watched Paden leave as well, his long stride taking him swiftly away from her. When she couldn't see him anymore, her shoulders sagged with fatigue.

"You look awfully pale," Miriam said. "You'd better lie down before you fall down."

She stared after Paden. What if he didn't come back?

Miriam nudged her toward her wagon. "Lie down

while Gabe stands guard and I finish packing my camp. I'll join you in a minute."

She trudged the few paces to the wagon. Setting her toe on the tailgate, she hoisted herself up to climb inside.

"If you need us," Gabe called after her, "just holler."

Hannah ducked her head to slip through the canvas flap. It fell closed behind her, blocking out the sunshine. When she lifted her head, she came face to face with a man with long raven hair. He wasn't Eagle Feather. She opened her mouth to scream.

His palm came down hard over her mouth. Then his knife flashed as he raised it between them. She jerked back.

He shoved her sideways, pinning her against the side of the wagon opposite from Miriam and Gabe. "Fight me," he growled in Sioux, keeping his voice low, "and I'll kill the woman and youth. Then I'll come back for you." He traced the tip of his blade over her cheek just below her eye. "And hand you their eyes."

She went dead still.

He drew back his knife as if to strike, and she forgot to breathe. The knife slashed down and ripped a hole in the canvas beside her, in the side farthest from Miriam and Gabe.

Without a sound, he slipped through the gap, pulling her with him onto the bank and into the pines. Faster than she could draw breath, the wagon train, her home for the last month and a half, had vanished.

The Indian raised his knife again. The tip pricked the side of her throat as he shoved her ahead of him through the trees. Her throat constricted. She couldn't breathe. Focusing on the thick green branches above her, she tried to force down her panic. She wanted to live. She wanted Paden. Her heart cried out for him, for all she was about to lose.

She must escape. Were they far enough from the wagons for her to get away without the fear of him turning back and hurting Miriam and Gabe? The forest was hushed. They were alone, far away from anyone. She steeled herself to break free.

Eagle Feather stepped out of the trees to stand directly in front of her. "You've done well," he said softly in Sioux. He didn't look at her. His gaze was fixed on her abductor. "But you should leave now. The forest is too quiet. We are already being tracked."

"I don't hear anyone." Her abductor's hold tightened on her collar.

"And you won't," Eagle Feather replied. "Not until it is too late."

She was abruptly shoved forward into Eagle's Feather's grasp. Pulling her by her arm, he forced her to run beside him. They ran until her lungs ached. Then Eagle Feather's foot took her legs out from under her and she crashed to her knees. He crouched over her, his hand on the back of her neck, keeping her down. He went perfectly still. Waiting.

Around them the forest was unearthly quiet. Not even a bird sang or a leaf rustled. Behind them came the click of a gun being cocked.

Eagle Feather lurched up, dragging her to her feet and turning. He slammed to a stop as if he'd hit something hard. He stiffened, his whole body tensing, preparing to fight.

"Let her go...slowly." The words, low and guttural, sounded more like the snarl of an animal than anything human. "Don't make me do something I'll regret," Paden added.

Muffled voices echoed behind them. Running

footsteps crashed through the trees.

"Thank Jesus you found them." Breathing hard, Alejandro came into her line of vision, his pistol trained on Eagle Feather.

Gabe was close behind him, followed by General Sherwood. "This is my fault," the young man burst out. "I never thought he'd be fast enough to circle back 'n wait for her in Miriam's wagon."

"He didn't," Paden said. "I found his accomplice's tracks and followed them to Miriam's wagon, then into the forest. The body of the snake might have gotten away. But the head won't."

Alejandro, Gabe and the general fanned out in a half-circle in front of her, their weapons fixed on Eagle Feather. The only person she couldn't see was Paden. She felt his presence, though, knew he was there by the way Eagle Feather held his body as well. All of his attention concentrated on the single threat behind him rather the multiple ones in front of him.

Eagle Feather's grip on the back of her neck tightened.

"To hell with this," Paden growled, the words chasing up her spine like the claws of a mountain cat.

The crack of a pistol butt striking flesh and bone sounded close to her ear. Eagle Feather slammed against her. His fingers bit into her neck before he lost all rigidity and fell to the ground with a thump. His big body lay tangled at her feet, the hard lines of his face softened. He looked young again, at peace, all anger drained away.

Was he dead?

She reached for him. Paden jerked her back. All of Eagle Feather's anger was in him now, fierce and hard.

Gabe bent to inspect Eagle Feather. "He's still

breathing."

She could breathe again as well.

"What do we do with him?" Gabe asked.

"We tie him up," General Sherwood replied, "and deliver him to the authorities at Fort Bridger."

Hannah went rigid with disbelief and dread. She'd seen what Weston had done to his Sioux prisoners at Fort Laramie. If Eagle Feather reached Fort Bridger, they'd chain him and beat him, then transport him east to a prison from which he'd never escape.

"You know," Alejandro said very slowly, "that they will most likely hang him."

"No!" Hannah finally spun to face Paden.

His expression was hard, unalterable. "I gave him a chance. He's sealed his own fate. He chose death."

CHAPTER 18

Rifle in hand, Hannah crept along the perimeter of the circled wagons, concentrating on placing one moccasin-clad foot silently in front of the other. Every nerve in her body felt close to snapping, begging her to move faster. Now wasn't the time for haste. It wasn't the time to dilly-dally either.

She'd never get another opportunity like this.

Crouching on her heels, she peered under the wagon in front of her. On the other side, Eagle Feather sat with his back to her, leaning against the wheel, his arms and legs tied. General Sherwood, Gabe and Virgil were out of sight, asleep by the scouts' wagon. Alejandro was patrolling the wagons, currently on the side farthest from her. But it was Paden who'd unknowingly made her goal obtainable.

He'd finally broken his self-imposed watch over her brother. Something he hadn't done during any of the nights since Eagle Feather had been captured. Not when the cover of darkness would be the most opportune time for her brother to escape.

Before Paden had mounted Cholla and disappeared into the night, she'd listened to him question the two remaining guards as to whether they could handle the watch for an hour without him.

He'd told the guards he had his doubts. Riley and his friend, the one who'd pestered Rebecca back at Courthouse Rock, bragged they could handle a dozen hours.

After he'd left, she'd waited several minutes. Enough time for him to put some distance between him and the wagons. She couldn't wait any longer. He'd told the guards he'd be gone an hour. Dawn's return was only an hour away as well. This was her one chance.

And still she hesitated.

Threatening to shoot her fellow travelers in order to gain Eagle Feather's freedom would cast her into uncertain waters. She'd also have to threaten to shoot Eagle Feather if he attacked her or wouldn't come with her. None of which she was certain she could do.

Laughter and mumbled snatches of conversation sounded on the other side of the wagon. "Bloody heathen deserves— only good Indian's a— wish I could see them string him up."

Her stomach rolled with dread. She couldn't let him be hanged. But she also couldn't stop images of that all-too-likely outcome from increasing her fear. Eagle Feather surrounded by the inescapably high walls of a fort as he stood beaten but unbowed before a crowd of jeering whites. Morning Star's son fighting the noose as it was forced over his head and tight around his neck. Hannah's brother dying while she did nothing.

Her chances of saving both him and herself were slim. It didn't matter. She had no other choice. Tightening her grip on her rifle, she rose to accept the path before her.

A hand clamped over her mouth while an arm snared her waist, lifting her off the ground and up against a rock wall. Or a man. A very strong man.

Panic hit her like a bolt of lightning.

Just as swiftly she went limp. The scent surrounding her was a familiar one. Sweet sage.

Paden carried her away from the wagons. As soon as they were hidden in the dark, he returned her feet to the ground and spun her to face him. But he kept hold of her waist the entire time as if worried she might flee.

"You know you're *loco*, don't you?" he said in a low voice as he bent to her eye level. "You realize how much trouble you'd be in right now if someone other than me caught you trying to free him?"

She hugged her rifle to her chest, worrying he'd take it from her, worrying he'd take the only chance she had of saving Eagle Feather. She also made sure to keep the barrel pointed well away from him. "I won't let him be hanged."

He grunted then said, "I suspected as much."

"Eagle Feather's not all bad. There's good inside him still. Like you, he's worth saving. He's worth lo—" She pressed her lips tight. Spirits Above, now was not the time to blurt out her love for him.

Paden released a long, slow breath. "If you say he's worth it, then he is."

Her lips flew open in surprise.

"But I'll never trust him. I only trust you." He leaned closer. "I still think you're too forgiving though. And you always try to tackle too much on your own. Next time, I hope you'll come to me before you do something as crazy as what we're about to attempt."

She felt her lips part even wider. "You're not going to stop me?"

"No." He slanted a glare at the wagon between them and Eagle Feather and the two settlers guarding him. "I'm going to help you free a man who looks at you with only hate in his eyes. A man who'll never change."

"He might." Reaching up, she pressed her hand to Paden's cheek.

His startled gaze swung back to hers.

"Sometimes it takes the good ones longer to let go of the past," she added.

He stood unmoving under her touch, his eyes full of questions.

She lowered her hand. A groan, full of frustration, rumbled inside Paden. She fought the urge to touch him again, to soothe him. Instead, she clasped her rifle with both hands. "What do we do about the guards?"

Paden's palms glided slowly up her sides, pulling her toward him as they did. Then he lifted her high against his chest and kissed her with nothing held back. He kissed her until she thought only of his mouth's wicked possession. He stole her reasoning and her breath. She gladly let him have them, along with her heart.

Just as quickly as he'd lifted her, he set her down and drew his revolver from its holster on his hip. "It's unfortunate that those guards will wake to splitting headaches. Still, one of them is Riley. So it's not completely unfortunate."

A moment later, they stood, unseen and unheard, behind the two guards. The men were too busy discussing more ways their prisoner might suffer upon reaching Fort Bridger. The steel of Paden's pistol flashed as the butt struck the back of each man's skull in quick succession. She breathed easier after their vile conversation ended.

When they turned to face Eagle Feather, she fought to breathe at all. He'd scrambled to his knees, his eyes flashing like obsidian daggers, promising them a real fight, challenging them to an all-out war.

Paden didn't hesitate. He surged forward to

accept. Eagle Feather managed to gain his feet before Paden barreled into him. He knocked her brother flat on his back in the dirt and pinned him there with one knee, and all his weight, on his chest.

"Be careful." Hannah tried to keep her voice as low as possible as she kneeled beside them. "Try not to hurt him."

"I think I'm being lenient, considering." Paden holstered his revolver and held his arm between her and Eagle Feather. "Better keep your distance."

"Untie me, coward," Eagle Feather snarled, struggling to twist free of his bounds and throw Paden off. "Fight me with honor."

"We're making too much noise." Hannah scanned the wagons around them. They remained silent. No faces peered out of them. "We need to make him disappear."

Paden grabbed the rope binding Eagle Feather's ankles. "Lead the way."

As soon as she did, he dragged her brother feet first away from the wagons and followed her into the night. She headed for where she'd hidden White Cloud and Eagle Feather's pony before coming to free him. When she reached the horses, she halted in shock. A third horse stood tethered beside them. Cholla lifted his head and nickered softly in greeting.

"How did you know I'd hidden the horses here?" she asked.

"I didn't." Paden dropped Eagle Feather's feet and drew her out of striking range. "I just knew you were somewhere outside the wagons' perimeter."

Even through the wool of her coat, the heat of his hand cupping her elbow made her skin tingle. "You must have the ears of an owl."

"He is the lowest of curs." Eagle Feather rolled into a sitting position and glared at them. "You insult the owl with your comparison."

Paden returned his glare. "Well, heaven forbid that a bird was insulted. Or a horse." His gaze swung back to her and softened. "Cholla heard you. When I let him have his head in the forest, I hoped he'd lead me to you. Instead, he came here. So I went back on foot for you."

Dismay coiled around her heart. "You left the guards to find me? What if they guess the truth and hold you accountable for Eagle Feather's disappearance?"

Paden shrugged. "They'll do more than guess when I fail to return at dawn. I hope you haven't left anything important with the wagons. After this, there's no going back."

"But you have to go back! The wagon train needs your protection."

"You need me more. Hellfire, *I* need you more. After we release him and leave, we—"

"You're letting me go?" Eagle Feather's tone was sharp with disbelief. "You won't fight me?"

Paden pulled her closer and lowered his voice. "It pains me that you're giving up the life you just started to rebuild, that you'll have to hide again. I wish I could tell you it'd be easy eluding your brother, but it won't. He's like me, a hunter."

She closed her eyes for a moment, considering his words. "Then I must be the opposite. I must be even more like Grandfather Spider."

"You're too much like him already. *You are patient. You watch and you wait.* But have you forgotten the part about *all things coming to you*?" Paden jabbed his finger at Eagle Feather but his gaze never left her. "I don't want him coming one step closer to you."

"He quotes our legends?" Eagle Feather asked in a hushed voice. "He has no right. He's not one of us."

Paden continued staring at her. "I have the right of my Comanche grandmother. Kaku's blood is the best part of me."

A sudden euphoria lifted her spirits and her hand. She paused with her spider tattoo tilted toward him. Then very deliberately, she laid her palm against his chest. "You have her heart."

Eagle Feather spat out a string of words in rapid-fire Osage, snuffing out Hannah's happiness like gust of wind.

She spun to face him. "No! Do not say that."

"Say what?" Paden demanded.

She forced herself to repeat the dire declaration. "He says he'd rather be killed than saved by us. Death is preferable to being in our debt."

Eagle Feather became the recipient of one of Paden's sharp appraisals. "It's hard to believe he's Morning Star's son."

Eagle Feather flinched. "You know nothing about my mother."

"I know that Hannah's more like the woman she described than you are. She's sacrificing her future to save yours. Does that sound familiar?"

Eagle Feather's breath hissed through his teeth.

"I also know this," Paden continued. "Of the three of us, Hannah's life is the only one worth saving tonight."

Eagle Feather's gaze narrowed on Paden. "Untie me."

"Why?" Paden folded his arms. "So we can fight and you can die?"

"So I can leave and you—" his gaze flicked to Hannah before turning in the direction he'd been dragged through the trees, "—can return to your precious wagons. I will not spend another minute in your debt. You saved my life, so I will return you to yours."

Hannah's heart raced with joy. She didn't think she'd made a sound, but Eagle Feather's gaze swung back to her.

"But only for one week. I won't come after you during that time. This I vow on my mother's memory." A frown lowered his brow as if he were already vexed by his new pledge. "I will use this time to consider the path ahead."

"And if our *paths* should cross before the week is over?" Paden asked.

"You would be unwise to let that happen. Even now I regret my decision. One week is too long. I have never been patient like Grandfather Spider." He huffed out a breath. "Which is unfortunate for Blue Sky, because from the day she chose to run into my mother's arms, our contrary spirits have been linked. One cannot go forward without the other. Together we will live, or together we will die."

Keeping his expression neutral, Paden met the questioning eyes of the settlers assembled before him. Hannah stood off to one side with General Sherwood, Gabe, Alejandro and Virgil forming a protective circle around her. She hadn't looked at him since the wagon train had woken to a blood-red sunrise and the news of an escaped prisoner.

Crossing his arms, he propped his hip against the wheel Eagle Feather had leaned on only an hour ago. "Well, he's gone and there's no time to chase after him."

Sticking to the basic facts was always best. Not that he needed to say any more. Although shocked, the settlers had accepted the story he'd laid out for them. The prisoner had been spirited away by his friends, who'd snuck up and clobbered the guards on the head. They were all lucky to be alive.

Eagle Feather and himself included, he reflected. He had a growing respect for the patience Hannah found in her legend about Grandfather Spider. If he hadn't found the patience to resist Eagle Feather's desire to fight, they wouldn't have gained his promise of a week without persecution. He'd gladly embrace anything that made Hannah safer.

"But you can't let them get away with this!" Riley wailed from his position slumped against the other wagon wheel, where he gingerly probed the wound on his head. "Those heathens tried to kill me." He must've hit an especially tender spot, because he screwed up his face tight as a preacher's collar on the Sabbath. "Only by the grace of God did I survive. I demand justice."

"You sound more interested in settling a score than losing a prisoner," Paden observed dryly.

Riley's gaze snapped up to meet his. "That's absurd," he mumbled. "I'm merely thinking of the other innocent souls those savages will hurt. Besides, you're a Texas Ranger. It's your job to track down criminals."

Paden ground his teeth. "I *was* a Ranger. I'm not anymore. The only thing I signed on for was guiding this wagon train west."

"He's right," Sherwood said. "I asked him to help with the wagons. Not with personal grievances."

Riley's mouth opened and closed as if he were struggling for air and an answer. "This—this is an outrage. I will file a complaint with the authorities in Fort Bridger."

Paden raised his brow. "Will you tell them you were responsible for guarding the prisoner when he escaped? That you assured me you could handle such a duty, even when I expressed my doubts? It'll all have to go in the report."

Riley went very still. "You've fallen out of my favor, Callahan. You're no better than—" his gaze darted around and landed on Alejandro, "—that Mexican."

Paden dipped his head. "Much obliged for the compliment."

Surprise widened Alejandro's eyes. Then he smiled and released a quiet chuckle.

Virgil wasn't so restrained. He let out a loud hoot.

"Don't you dare laugh at me," Riley cried. "You!" He jabbed his finger at Alejandro. "You will never get my permission to court my daughter." His expression turned smug. "Now who's laughing?"

"Enough." Paden shoved away from the wagon so he could crouch directly in front of Riley.

Riley shrank back.

"Listen well," Paden said. "Because I don't know how many more times I can say this before I—" *Think of Grandfather Spider*, he urged, struggling to hold on to his patience. He blew out a breath. "Either button your lip or leave this wagon train."

"If anyone should leave, it's her." Riley gestured wildly over Paden's shoulder at Hannah. "She's the reason the savage was here in the first place."

Hannah finally looked at him, with eyes so dark they resembled bruises on her pale face, while everyone else turned to stare at her.

"She's the reason he'll come back." Riley lurched to his feet. "He'll murder us all to get to her." He scrambled away as if Eagle Feather might descend on them that very instant.

The crowd received him with outstretched arms, welcoming him into their protective mass. Riley made sure he came to rest at their forefront, in a place of leadership.

The settlers' voices grew louder and louder.

"We aren't safe while she's here."

"She should leave."

"We should make her leave."

"Cast her out."

"Right now!"

Led by Riley, the crowd surged toward Hannah. Sherwood, Gabe, Alejandro and Virgil moved to stop them. But Paden was already standing between her and the settlers.

"If she goes, I go," he said.

From behind him came Sherwood's quiet voice. "You should both go."

Shock leeched the strength from his limbs, making him sway as he turned to stare at the one man who'd always supported him. Until now.

Sherwood shook his head. "I should never have asked you to accompany us all the way to California. It isn't your home. When our journey ends, yours would be starting again. North by ship along the coast, or backtracking down the trail to the Oregon branch. Why not take that trail when we first reach it?"

If they pushed hard, they could be there before the week ended. The Oregon branch came just after Fort Bridger. He knew that section of the trail well. Eagle Feather didn't. He and Hannah could move faster after they left the wagons. Hellfire, he could fly along that trail with a rider as agile as Hannah by his side.

Sherwood stood waiting, his silver-haired head tilted, his face wrinkled with both old and new lines. When had the general aged so much? Guilt pressed down on him. Sherwood wasn't abandoning him. He was giving Paden a chance to abandon him.

"It doesn't sit well with me—" he swallowed hard, his mouth dry as ash, "—leaving you alone."

In an all-too-familiar gesture, Sherwood clasped

Gabe's shoulder. "I'm not alone." He canted his head toward Hannah, who watched them with wide eyes. "And now that you aren't either, I can rest easy about letting you go." He released Gabe. "Shall we help Paden let go of us, son?"

"I'll miss you both." An unusual solemnity had deepened the young man's voice. He'd aged as well. Then he suddenly grinned like the boy who'd eagerly rattled on to Hannah at Fort Leavenworth. "Maybe you'll both visit us in California. One day. When our lives are simpler."

Paden nodded. Sherwood and Gabe strode forward to stand by his side and face the unruly mob.

"This is my proposal…" Sherwood's gaze swept over the settlers. "Hannah and Paden shall remain with us until Fort Bridger. Once there, he hands the reins over to a new wagon master. I'm confident my grandson will do an excellent job."

Gabe's lips parted in surprise then just as quickly pressed into a determined line. "I will call on everything I've learned from my very excellent teachers."

A fleeting smile touched the old man's lips before his gaze turned back to the crowd and his expression hardened. "But if you cannot see the wisdom in my offer, then Gabe and I are of no use to you either. We will leave with Paden and Hannah. Right now."

A chorus of shocked gasps and shouted nos rippled through the crowd.

Sherwood glanced over his shoulder at Virgil and Alejandro. "The scouts would, of course, be immediately released from their duties. It would be their choice to stay with the wagon train or come with us."

The settlers' objections turned louder.

Virgil snorted. "I'd be a fool to remain here. I'd go with you."

Alejandro's gaze was locked on one person in the crowd. Rebecca.

"I have to stay," he said.

"No, you don't," Rebecca shot back, making Alejandro flinch. "Not if I left as well."

"Rebecca!" her father roared. "Don't make me reprimand you again."

"I cannot make you do anything, Father. You do it all on your own. And this time you've gone too far." She raised her chin. "If you cannot accept the general's wisdom after all he's done for us, then I will not follow you."

"Fine. Good riddance to the lot of you." Riley spun to face the settlers. "We don't need them. I'll lead you."

"You?" Miriam scoffed. "A man who couldn't protect one prisoner for one night is going to guide me safely down a trail he's never seen? Staying with you would be suicide. I'm leaving."

Nate and Sarah nodded in unison. "We'll go as well."

The crowd dissolved into a chaos of wailing and ranting. "We're all going to die," was the common refrain.

Paden scrubbed his hand over his jaw in frustration. Maybe the settlers deserved to take their chances without them. Nevertheless, the possibility of their demise as a result of his actions plagued his conscience. He opened his mouth to speak.

Riley beat him to it. "You'll die quickest when that heathen rallies his forces and attacks this wagon train to get to her again."

"He won't attack." Paden sealed his lips. He needed to stick to his rule of sharing only the basic facts.

"You can't know that for sure," Riley replied.

"No, he can't. But I do." Hannah pressed her palm with the spider tattoo against her heart. "I was raised in the same village as the man who tried to take me. He is my brother. Before he left, he promised me a one-week reprieve. He is a man who keeps his promises. And so will I." She drew in a deep breath. "I vow to leave the wagon train at Fort Bridger. When I do, you'll never see me or my brother again."

"Do you accept her promise and my proposal?" Sherwood asked.

Except for Riley and his friend, the crowd nodded as one.

"I'm gonna miss you, honey." Miriam stepped around Paden to wrap Hannah in her embrace. Her grandsons did the same. As did Sarah and even Nate.

"You could still come with us," Hannah whispered.

Miriam pulled back, dragging her grandsons and Sarah and Nate with her. She shook her head and swiped the tears from her cheeks. "We'd only slow you down. We'd get you killed."

Hannah's shoulders slumped and her gaze plummeted to the ground.

Eagle Feather had allowed her to return to the wagon train and her friends, only to have the settlers make it impossible for her to stay with them. In a single moment, Eagle Feather had shown Hannah more compassion than the settlers had shown her in months. Paden's arms ached to hold her, to reassure her that she wasn't alone.

Hannah's gaze rose to meet his. She stared at him with eyes so sad and full of loss that his concern left him shaking.

He had until Fort Bridger to earn her trust so completely she'd race up the trail to Oregon with no question. If she hesitated, Eagle Feather might catch them and kill her. He needed to bind her to him body and soul. Marriage couldn't give him that kind of commitment. Only love could. Hannah might never love him as much as he loved her, but he had less than a week to make her love him enough to ensure she stayed alive.

That evening, after the last wagon pulled into the protective circle, Hannah decided she couldn't go another mile without telling Paden about Weston. If Eagle Feather had succeeded in killing her, the truth would've died with her. Just as it had with Jeannie. If Paden and Weston's paths ever crossed again, Paden wouldn't know the extent of the evil he faced.

Fear would've made her squander her one chance to strengthen Paden. How could she weaken him when he'd done the opposite for her? If she loved him, she had to tell him and let him do what was best. For him. Not for her.

And she must tell him before Fort Bridger and Eagle Feather's return.

So why wasn't she searching him out right now and doing just that? Why did she still hesitate? Maybe if she wasn't feeling so bedraggled… All day long, they'd ridden in the hot sun and the dust kicked up from the wagons and animals. She needed a bath. Then she could face Paden.

They'd made camp near a small river hidden by a thicket of leafy green cottonwoods. A place she didn't want to go alone. Not with the memory of Eagle Feather dragging her through the trees still fresh in her mind.

All around her, the pioneers were busy with their evening routines: tending livestock, mending wagons, making suppers. Alejandro strode across the center of the circled wagons and halted mid-stride when he saw Rebecca lugging an armful of firewood toward her wagon. He didn't pause long. He went straight to her and took the burden from her arms.

They talked quickly, smiling all the while. But after Alejandro deposited the wood by her wagon, their movements turned hesitant, then awkward. They glanced around as if searching for a reason to stay together. Their smiles faded. Alejandro tugged the brim of his hat, and Rebecca answered his farewell with a nod. Then he resumed his course for the scouts' wagon. His downcast gaze suggested that was the last thing he wanted to do.

When he finally glanced up and saw Hannah watching him, his smile returned, albeit a smaller one than he'd given Rebecca. Hannah smiled back. Alejandro was the perfect person to help her. He'd already assisted her in a similar fashion.

"*Buenas tardes*. I hope all is well with you, Hannah."

"I'm well except for one thing."

His brows lifted questioningly.

"I could be cleaner."

He laughed and ran his gaze over his own dust-covered clothing. "We could all be cleaner."

She gestured toward the trees. "I'd like to go to the river."

A frown chased away his smile.

"Yes, I know. It's too dangerous to go alone," she added before he could say the same. "But we can do what we did at Alcove Spring. You stand in the trees nearest the river. And I'll chatter on like a magpie so you'll know I'm all right."

"You're that set on a bath?"

She paused then said, "I want to talk to Paden, but not before I bathe."

Alejandro's eyebrows shot up. "Ah, then you are indeed set on going to the river. And I know better than to argue with a woman when her mind is set on anything."

Laughter bubbled from her lips as she ran to the back of the wagon to fetch her bar of soap and spare clothing. They'd crossed to the trees when a shout stopped them. Paden strode toward them at a brisk pace, a scowl on his face.

"This does not bode well," Alejandro said under his breath.

"Maybe he—" She groaned. Who was she trying to fool?

Paden halted in front of them and crossed his arms. "I hope your reason for leaving the wagons is a good one."

"Hannah wanted to bathe at the river," Alejandro blurted. "*And*—" he paused to stress the word, "—she acknowledged the wisdom of having someone stand guard."

Paden watched her very closely. "Why didn't you ask me?"

"She could not," Alejandro replied, before she could. "You are the reason she wanted to bathe."

The shreds of her composure went up in flames, leaving her burning with mortification. "Of all the things you could've said, you tell him that?" She lowered her voice to a whisper. "That was between me and you."

Alejandro shrugged. "Now I have made it between Paden and you, as it should be. You said you wished to speak with him."

Laughter made them both spin to face Paden. He wiped one hand across his eyes and shook his head. Then he finally looked at her and smiled. And kept smiling. Amazement left her speechless.

"I'll accompany her to the river, Alejandro. You

have your own woman to watch over."

"Aye-aye, Captain." Alejandro gave him a mock salute and headed back to the wagons at brisk pace.

Paden stared at her for a long moment. His smile stayed on his lips. "You wanted to talk with me?"

"I do." The words shot from her lips, breathless and much too eager.

Paden removed the distance between them. His smile had vanished. The intensity of his gaze made her heart pound.

"But first you wanted to bathe." He slipped by her without touching her.

Biting her lip to stifle her disappointment, she turned so her gaze could follow him.

He continued striding toward the trees. "We can talk while you bathe." When she didn't follow, he halted. But he didn't look back. Instead he stared at the trees, the line of his shoulders tense. "The choice is, as always, yours. Do you want to return to the wagons or come with me?"

The answer was easy. She moved to his side. "I want to be with you."

Hannah's reply reverberated in Paden's mind. *I want to be with you.* She hadn't said *I want to come with you.* He clung to the difference of a single word and stared at the river when all he wanted to do was stare at Hannah. She stood close beside him. So close he felt the heat of her skin, smelled the wind's freshness in her hair.

She wouldn't stand that close if she didn't want to be with him. He was afraid to look at her and find out he was wrong.

I want to be with you. She'd also said she wanted a bath before she talked to him.

Now was the time to show her that she could

trust him, that she could share the secret she'd mentioned that night in his wagon, that he wouldn't leave her like she feared. He had to be patient and let her talk. After she did, then he could ask her again to— "Will you marry me, Hannah?" He pinched the bridge of his nose. Hellfire, he had no patience at all. Grandfather Spider would be disgusted.

"Nothing would make me happier than being your wife."

A surge of elation whipped him around to face her. His happiness froze in his veins. Hannah clutched her soap and clothing to her chest in a white-knuckled grip. She also kept her gaze downcast, refusing to look at him.

"You don't look very happy."

"We still need to talk."

Suddenly, talking was the last thing he wanted to do.

He retreated one step, then another. "You said you want to bathe first. I'll stand guard while you do." He turned his back to her. His gaze immediately traveled up the cottonwoods, thick with leaves, to halt on the sky above.

Before he'd met Hannah, he'd never looked to the sky other than to determine the weather or the time of day. Now he looked at it because it reminded him of Hannah's eyes, or at least a paler version.

Today was no different. Even though the sky above was a vibrant cerulean, his reaction was the same. The blue failed to match the richness of Hannah's eyes. She held his whole world, his future, in her eyes. If he saw happiness there, he'd be happy as well.

She'd said she wanted to be with him and that nothing would make her happier than being his wife. But she also wouldn't look at him.

Behind him, the whisper of cloth sliding over

skin snared his attention. Then water swished, filling his mind with images of it lapping around Hannah's bare feet, rising up her knees and higher. Her breath hissed softly as the chilly water reached more sensitive parts.

She was cold. His hands itched to warm her.

Water splashed. He strained to hear more. The splash came again. Had she dove underwater so she could wet her hair, then lather it with soap? His fingers moved restlessly as he imagined how her hair would feel in the water. Its length would lie sleek against her skull, flowing down her back to spread out in the water, floating soft as silk, slick as—

He gritted his teeth and counted to fifty. Then he lost count when he heard another splash, followed by a soft, breathless sigh. Not as breathless though as when he'd made her wet with his fingers. He clenched his hands and tried to hang on to his patience.

After what felt like an eternity, she said in a hushed voice, "I'm done."

He steeled himself not to turn and look at her as she came out of the water. Another eternity followed. This one filled only with silence. Why didn't he hear her getting out and donning her clothing?

Alarm prickled the skin across his shoulders. What if she was gone? He spun to scan the river.

Hannah stood on the bank directly in front of him. Wet and naked. Her blue eyes glittered like the sky after a rainstorm. "I wish I could return to that night in your wagon. If I could, I wouldn't turn my back and hide. I'd face you, even if you left me."

The need to reassure her overwhelmed him. He bent his head and claimed her mouth, putting all his love and his hopes into his kiss. She was wrong. He wouldn't leave her. He also wouldn't spend another moment letting the few times he had alone with her slip through his fingers.

He wanted to feel the silk of her hair floating in the water.

He swept her up in his arms and carried her into the river. Cradling her head in his palm, he tipped her until her hair flowed around her just as he'd imagined. He trailed his fingers through its weight, savoring the feel. Silk failed to describe its softness. It was a hundred times lusher than he'd imagined. So was her wet skin. Holding her with one arm, he explored every inch of the sleek form floating before him.

Until she pushed herself out of the water to clutch him, arms around his neck, legs around his waist. Pressing her cheek against his, she whispered, "Don't let go."

He didn't plan to. "You're safe. I've got you."

"I want to be closer. I want that closeness you talked about in your wagon."

Shock made him flinch…and harden until his wet trousers became unbearably tight. Hannah continued to have the ability to make even the temperature of a river irrelevant.

Her slender arms tightened around him. "Don't push me away."

"If we were married, things would be different."

"Why isn't my word that I'll marry you enough?"

He pondered her question. Yes, why wasn't it? If Hannah said she'd do something, she did it. And he sure as hell wasn't going to change his mind about marrying her. So why couldn't he fulfill her request?

He lowered one hand below the water and opened the fall of his trousers. The head of his erection unerringly found the notch between her legs and stayed there, eager to slide home.

Instead, he ran his hand up his shaft to stroke one

finger inside her. Then two. Her breathing quickened. Delicate little pants brushing his ear. Her cheek rubbed his as she began to move as well. Silk against stone. When her hips matched the rhythm of his hand, he guided her onto him. He pressed up slowly, wanting to savor every second as she took him in. Until her exquisite tightness halted him.

"Why have we stopped?" She squirmed in his arms, flexing around him but still not taking him in any further.

He stiffened against a wave of raw lust. "I'm sorry."

"Why?"

"That I can't be gentle." His desire surged again, thrusting him forward. He buried himself inside her to the hilt.

Her cry of pain stabbed him even deeper.

"I'm sorry," he repeated.

"I'm not." She released a tremulous sigh and went limp in his arms, trusting him to keep her above water.

He cradled her close as the river rippled around them and away. Its wet embrace did nothing to dampen his still raging need.

"No matter what happens," she said, "I'll never be sorry you were the first."

His hold on her tightened possessively. "And the last. We're getting married, remember? Very soon. In Fort Bridger."

"I remember. The future's never far from my thoughts."

The worry in her voice made him frown. "You're thinking too much. I can help you with that again." He lifted her until she held only the tip of him. Then he guided her down and filled her again.

Her eyes widened. The light dancing in their exquisite blue held him in thrall.

"It's torture to feel you leave me." Wonder softened her voice to the sigh of a summer breeze. "Still, it makes your return so much…sweeter."

"It can be even sweeter. Let me show you." He eased into her in a rhythm that made her eyes flare even wider. Eyes that urged him on, growing brighter, until they glowed almost incandescent. The desire to give her even more pleasure made him search out the tight little bud between her legs.

She pressed hard against the pad of his thumb and his hand matched the pace of his hips. He reached a fevered pitch, a heaven full of blinding bliss. He didn't stop. Not until she cried out and clenched around him, arching her back to somehow draw him even deeper.

Nothing remained between them. He wanted the feeling to last forever. He fought for control. He struggled to hold back.

She wouldn't let him. She drew forth his own release a second after he'd given her hers.

He came, hard and fast with a force that bowed his head against her. But it didn't end there. His surrender ripped through him again and again, making his entire body shudder…while Hannah cradled his head against her breast, holding him safe.

They held each for a long time, until she shivered. He immediately raised his head. The sun was slipping below the horizon. The air around them had grown chill, making the water feel even colder. He carried her to the riverbank and forced himself to set her down, to release her so he could help her dress.

He adjusted his trousers, covering himself as well. "We'd better get back to the wagons."

"But we didn't get to talk." The light in her eyes disappeared, filling him with the urge to run from whatever she had to say.

"We're getting married in Fort Bridger, that's all that matters." He took several strides toward the trees. "Come back to the wagons with me."

She didn't move. He couldn't go if she wouldn't follow.

"By then it might be too late." Her voice was heavy with sadness. "I won't take this secret to my grave. The Comanche weren't the ones who killed Jeannie."

Her declaration turned his blood to ice, made him colder than he'd ever been in his life. All this time, she'd wanted to talk to him about the Comanche and Jeannie? "If they didn't kill her, who did?"

"Weston."

"That's not possible." His stomach lurched. It was very possible, just as possible as the Comanche killing her. Weston had always believed Jeannie was his. But she'd chosen to marry him instead. Weston would've wanted to punish her for that. Punish him as well. That was the truth. His insides burned with another horrible truth. "I killed men for a sin they didn't commit."

"Everyone believed it was the Comanche."

"But I'm not everyone." He hid his face in his hands. "I knew them. Why didn't I question the story?"

"You were consumed by grief. The woman you loved had been killed."

Jeannie hadn't just been killed. She'd been violated and mutilated. Rage ripped through him. "I'll tear out Weston's black heart." He spun to face the east, as if he could reach across the miles, all the way back to Fort Laramie, and do just that.

"When will you leave?" Hannah's whispered words sounded like gunshots.

Immediately. Never. He needed to make Weston pay. He needed to keep Hannah safe. Hate and love.

They pulled him in opposite directions.

If he got her to Fort Bridger, she'd be safe inside its walls. She'd also be alone with strangers when the wagon train departed with her friends. Was he actually contemplating leaving Hannah as well? He couldn't. He could if he came back for her.

She wouldn't be there when he did. A fort's walls might protect her from some dangers, but they'd make her vulnerable to others. The confinement would smother her. She'd run. Just as she'd wanted to run from Fort Leavenworth the day he'd first met her. She'd have been better off if she'd run from him.

CHAPTER 19

Surrounded by land covered in bone-dry grass, Hannah couldn't stop glancing over her shoulder to watch the giant mass of Independence Rock, an almost perfectly rounded dome of gray granite, grow smaller as the wagons rolled west at a brisk pace. The rising wind whipped up a cloud of dust, obscuring the rock. If only everything behind them could vanish so swiftly.

With under a week to reach Fort Bridger, the weather had turned uncooperative. Dark clouds shrouded the usually sunny midday sky. Then a flash of lightning illuminated the trail ahead. Hannah longed for a similar clarity within herself, if only for a moment.

Had she done the right thing, telling Paden about Weston? Or had she caused more damage than good? He hadn't left her to seek out Weston. Not yet, at least.

Did she have a place by Paden's side, or was any hope of a future with him an illusion? Would she have been better off bowing to Eagle Feather's decree that her life belonged to the Osage?

As if conjured by her doubts, a band of raven-haired figures came out of another dust cloud on her left. Hannah's breath stalled in her throat until she saw the small forms with them. A war party wouldn't include children.

Both the settlers and the Indians spared each other the briefest of glances. Only Paden changed course and turned Cholla to gallop along the wagons toward her. But he couldn't protect her from a storm like this.

All they could do was keep clear of the trees and higher elevations to reduce the risk of being struck by lightning. That was the only reason they and the Indians shared the same strip of tinder-dry grassland crackling beneath their feet and the wagon wheels.

Hannah watched the lightning streak across the sky behind Paden's rapidly approaching silhouette. The corresponding rumbles of thunder followed with increasing speed and volume, until the flash and boom were only seconds apart.

The storm was too close. Paden wasn't close enough. He reined Cholla to an abrupt halt. The mules and oxen had spooked and verged off the path, blocking him from reaching her.

The next bolt struck the ground between the settlers and the Indians. The earth shook. Sparks flew. Flames shot up in their wake. Then a scorching ribbon of red rushed toward them. The Indians on one side of the blaze, the wagon train on the other.

Terror made the animals stampede. Riders and drivers clung to their perches doing their best to avoid trampling the people fleeing on foot. Hannah swung White Cloud around to help William and Charlie jump in the back of Miriam's wagon. She'd barely succeeded when White Cloud leaped sideways.

A team of mules swept by so close her fingertips brushed their sides.

A familiar hand, large and strong, snared her arm and pulled her upright in her saddle. "Get going!"

Paden yelled over the rising roar of the fire.

Hannah's gaze followed the finger he pointed westward. Instead of a single-file line flowing down the trail, the settlers now surged like a rogue wave toward the horizon. The wind gusted in her face, shifting directions. She glanced over her shoulder to confirm what she hoped.

The fire now burned in the opposite direction of the fleeing wagon train.

Unfortunately the shift had separated two children from their band. Indian men and women ran up and down the wall of flames, searching for a way to break through and rescue their children. Thick flames and billowing black smoke thwarted them at every turn.

Hannah twisted in her saddle to face Paden. "We have to help them."

"I'll get them." Paden pinned her with a sharp look. "You stay here." He kicked his heels to Cholla's flanks and raced away.

White Cloud didn't require any urging. He caught up with Cholla's tail as Paden guided the stallion through a gap in the fire. Heat singed her skin when White Cloud darted through the hole after them. She glanced back. The opening had disappeared.

White Cloud skidded to a halt.

Paden's hand once again grasped her arm. "What're you doing?" he yelled above the flames now crackling on all sides of them. "You were supposed to wait for me."

"I didn't want you to have to do this alone."

Paden stared at her without blinking. Then he urged Cholla even closer to White Cloud. His hand shot up to capture the back of her neck and pull her close for an all-too-brief kiss. When it ended, he drew back just far enough to stare into her eyes. "We will continue discussing this as soon as we're back with the wagons."

He swung Cholla toward the children.

The girl cried out and the boy, not much older than Hannah had been when her mother had saved her from their burning cabin, pushed the girl behind him.

"Keep away!" he shouted, pulling a knife from his belt and raising it between him and Paden.

She moved White Cloud to put herself between Paden and the blade.

"Get back," Paden growled. "He's scared enough to actually hurt you."

"He spoke in Osage. I can reason with him."

Paden scanned the flames drawing closer and finally nodded.

She leaned down toward boy. "We don't want to stay here a moment longer and neither do you," she said in Osage. "Come with us. Quick."

Hope and trepidation warred on the boy's smoke-blackened face. The girl stared over his shoulder with white-rimmed eyes stark against her equally sooty skin. Then she doubled over in a fit of coughing. The children had been in the fire far too long. They wouldn't last much longer.

She held out her hand to boy. "Pass up your sister, then jump on the back of my horse."

The boy did not move. She tried to smile reassuringly but feared her expression probably appeared more like a grimace. "I won't make you ride with him." She canted her head in Paden's direction. "So it's either me or the flames."

The boy blinked, then sheathed his knife and lifted his sister up to Hannah. When she finally sat on Hannah's lap, her tiny arms latched around Hannah's waist with surprising strength. So did the boy's when Hannah swung him up behind her. Their combined grips made it hard to breathe.

She looked up to find Paden close beside her. A worried look pinched his face.

"Lead the way." Her words came out rough as river stones grinding underfoot. They scraped her already sore throat raw.

Paden shook his head. "From this point forward, we ride as one. You hold on to the children. I'll hold on to you." Leaning across the narrow gap separating them, he grasped White Cloud's rein, then turned both horses together so he could scan the flames.

Hannah's skin prickled from the heat. Then the heat diminished.

"There," she called out, ignoring the pain she caused her throat. "Do you feel it?"

"Yes." Paden urged both horses toward the cooler temperature. They galloped side by side down a corridor of tall flames. They rode until either of them felt or saw a break in the fire. If Paden detected it first, he turned her with his hand on White Cloud's rein. If she did, she maneuvered White Cloud with the pressure of her knees, and Paden moved Cholla to follow.

They turned many times, darting through narrow gaps or jumping over low-burning patches. They even doubled back once.

They rode together until White Cloud stumbled and almost fell. Paden didn't have time to release his grip on her rein. Hannah cried out as he was jerked from his saddle to tumble to the ground in front of both horses. They instinctively veered in opposite directions to avoid stepping on him. A hole opened ahead of White Cloud, and he jumped through.

A blessed coolness washed over Hannah. She was free of the fire. She spun White Cloud around in search of Paden while at the same time trying to liberate herself from the children's grasp. As soon as she did, she could go back for Paden.

Through the hole she'd just come through, she glimpsed him already on his feet, then leaping astride Cholla and urging him toward her. Her heat raced with them. In another second, Paden would be through the hole and by her side.

With a whistling howl, the wind shifted. The fire roared in response, flames shooting up, scorching her flesh. White Cloud shied back. Cholla skidded to a halt. The hole disappeared. A solid wall of fire stood between her and Paden.

Her cry of disbelief was drowned out by a cacophony of yelling. A group of mounted Indians charged toward her. They wanted their children. Muscles trembling with fatigue and fear, she once more tried to peel the tiny arms from her waist. This time the children obliged, releasing her and jumping to the ground. Their haste nearly made her tumble after them. Slumped over her saddle horn, she watched them run toward their loved ones.

She cast a hopeful glance at the fire, but the flames remained solid. Paden was somewhere on the other side. The wind might turn at any moment. It'd done it before. It could do it again. She'd be ready. She wasn't leaving. A gap in the fire here would be her quickest path back to Paden.

All around her, the air was hot and thick with ash. Any coolness here had been an illusion.

Breathing heavily, she glanced around to check the children's progress. They'd reached the riders and been scooped up behind two of them. The Indians hadn't left though. They'd halted their mounts in a row facing her. They might not have formed a circle around her, but they still reminded her of the men who'd found her after her cabin had burned and her parents had died.

Their silence was familiar. So was their lack of expression and movement.

She went still as well. She wasn't going anywhere without Paden. The wind would shift. The hole would open again. She just had to wait a little longer.

The smoke and the heat stung her eyes. So did her tears. She tried to blink them back and failed. She refused to raise her hand and wipe them away. The Indians would see her weakness.

One of the riders broke away from the others and galloped toward her. His familiar size made her go numb with disbelief. When Eagle Feather's horse halted beside White Cloud, her tears flowed in earnest, her sobs choking her.

"Go away. My week isn't up."

His expression remained blank betraying none of his emotions. "You can't stay here."

"I'm not leaving without him."

Eagle Feather's expression suddenly shifted. Gone was the unemotional brave who'd first visited the wagon train or the conflicted man who'd retreated after promising her a one-week reprieve. Her brother was as livid as the day he'd banished her.

She lurched back, pulling her reins to urge White Cloud back as well.

His hand seized her wrist, halting her. "You would race into the fire to escape me?"

"I would run into hell itself to save Paden."

"You're a fool, Blue Sky. He's most likely dead."

"He isn't. And I'll never leave him."

"Then I must make you leave. I won't let you stay in this smoke and kill yourself."

"You promised me one week," she repeated.

"I'm reverting to my original promise. I'm taking

you back to the Osage."

Anguish sucked the strength from her, drained her almost to the bone. Before that happened, she gathered the dregs of her willpower and glanced one last time at the fire behind her. The wind hadn't shifted. The wall remained. She'd lost Paden.

Eagle Feather dragged her unresisting form off White Cloud and onto his horse. Mercifully, her world turned black. Without Paden, she didn't want to know what came next.

The pouring rain beat down on Paden as he rode Cholla as fast as he dared back toward where he'd last seen the wagon train. That he'd had to temporarily abandon his vigil over Hannah didn't sit well with him. He'd only done so in order to make his plan to save her a reality. And he'd only left when Eagle Feather was least likely to take her anywhere—in the dead of the night and in a torrential downpour.

Guilt pummeled him, along with the rain. He should've reached Hannah before her brother had, but the prairie fire had blocked him. It hadn't prevented him from following Eagle Feather as he carried off Hannah's unconscious form. Once clear of the fire, the stream of Osage men, women and children between him and Hannah had stopped him from racing in and saving her again. All he could do was follow at a distance and try to ensure none of the Osage saw him.

When the rain started to fall and doused the fire, he'd hunkered down and watched the Osage band make camp. He watched Eagle Feather put Hannah in a tepee and then come out to stand guard. The blasted brave hadn't budged. Not even when the heavens opened up and it started raining like the flood.

At least the rain had given him time to come up with a plan to save Hannah and hopefully leave the Osage unscathed.

He couldn't hurt women and children, and for Hannah's sake he'd decided against trying to sneak up behind her brother and bash him over the head liked he'd done to Riley. The chances of pulling off such a maneuver with someone as observant as Eagle Feather were slim. Being forced to turn his gun on her brother and shoot him made his stomach roll.

Unfortunately, his worry for Hannah wasn't allowing him to think straight. He'd only come up with a single plan for saving her. He might not survive such a hare-brained idea. It wouldn't matter if Hannah was already dead. His heart missed a beat. He'd gladly die in the Osage village as well.

Through sheets of rain, he finally glimpsed the pale canvas backs of the wagons. He headed for his supply wagons, ignoring the guards who aimed their rifles at him. Luckily, they lowered their weapons when they finally recognized him and began shouting that he'd returned.

Before Cholla had even come to a halt, he'd jumped onto his wagon to untie the canvas.

General Sherwood climbed up beside him. "Did you find Hannah, son?"

"It's raining like the devil," Gabe yelled, appearing on his other side. "Shouldn't the canvas stay on the wagon?"

When he didn't answer, the two men exchanged a look over his head and then started helping him remove the canvas. It came off quicker than he'd hoped—thanks to their help and Alejandro and Virgil, who'd been untying the other side.

"I need some paint," he hollered over his

shoulder as he rolled up the canvas and started strapping it behind Cholla's saddle.

"I'll see if Miriam has any," Gabe yelled back.

Alejandro offered to check with Rebecca, while Virgil said he'd go to Sarah and Nate. All three men disappeared into the rain, leaving Paden alone with Sherwood.

"Whatever you're planning to do, son, I'm coming with you. I won't let you lose Hannah like you lost Jeannie."

Paden's hands froze on the last tie of the canvas. Jeannie. Overwhelmed by the revelation of her real killer's identity, he hadn't thought to tell Sherwood the truth about his daughter's death. Now, just like Hannah, he realized he couldn't let the truth die with him. And die it would if he rode back to the Osage village and failed to save Hannah.

Weston couldn't be allowed the opportunity to kill again. Sherwood more than anyone had the right to know the extent of the colonel's evil. Paden hesitated. He loved the old man too much not to shy away from hurting him. The truth would wound Sherwood as deeply as it had wounded Paden.

This is how hard it must've been for Hannah to tell you. The thought of her strength gave him just enough power to turn and face Sherwood, and tell him who'd really killed his daughter.

CHAPTER 20

Hannah's eyelids fluttered. She opened her eyes to darkness and her mind to memories. The fire— the children— Eagle Feather— Paden— Fear swamped her, contracting every nerve. She tried to lurch upright, to escape. A gasp of pain burst from her lips, making her throat burn and throb. Her entire body hurt as well.

She lay very still, only moving her eyes as she searched the darkness. Where was she?

Above her, she made out the long lines of lodge poles bound together with raw hide, then lower down the faint seams on the wall circling her. She knew the sight well. Every morning after Morning Star had adopted her, she'd woken up in a tepee. Every morning until Eagle Feather had vowed revenge and forced her to flee the Osage.

She'd survived the fire, only to become Eagle Feather's captive again. He'd kept his part of the bargain. He hadn't looked for her. But she hadn't kept hers. She hadn't made sure their paths didn't cross. Her fate was sealed, but what of Paden's? A new fear gripped her. Had he survived the fire? If he had, had he then battled Eagle Feather? Was he dead?

She squeezed shut her eyes, trying to hold back

her grief. It didn't work. Tears streamed down her cheeks while her chest constricted. With a will of its own, her hand sprang up to press against her pounding heart.

Grandfather Spider, she prayed, *more than ever I need your wisdom, your patience. Give me strength.*

The tepee was silent around her, but she suddenly heard Morning Star's voice—in her heart, where she held her memories tight as well. Her mother's voice was firm. *You have seen too much for one so young, but you must not be afraid to open your eyes and see what comes next. Open your eyes, Blue Sky. Open your eyes.*

She obeyed.

Many webs were painted on the hides lining the walls. Grandfather Spider was there as well. She inched her way into a sitting position so she could see him better. The hides were closer than she'd first thought, which meant she was in a traveling tepee, the smallest version of her tribe's nomadic homes. They were traveling fast and light. They'd only camp here a day or two.

The air smelled of rain, felt damp with it. With the grass fire doused and the ashes turned to mud, her tracks and Eagle Feather's would be obliterated.

White Cloud was somewhere outside this tepee. He'd have followed her. Even if he hadn't, Eagle Feather would never leave a sound horse behind. Especially one who could lead someone to Hannah like he'd done when he'd led Eagle Feather to her and the white trappers. White Cloud couldn't help Paden find her this time.

The wagon train was miles away by now. The settlers would happily leave her behind, and Paden wouldn't be able to find her. No tracks to follow. No White Cloud to help him. No hope.

Very soon she'd be dead. Nothing had changed

in Eagle Feather's heart. He'd been livid when he'd taken her. And now…nothing stood in the way of him fulfilling his desire for revenge.

Maybe it was for the best. She was tired of running, of living in constant fear, always looking over her shoulder. She couldn't do it without Paden by her side. The time had come to face her future. She rose and crossed to the small hide that formed the tepee's door. Pushing it aside, she stepped through and froze.

Only a handful of steps away, a woman with shining raven-black hair kneeled over a rock, grinding dried meat into pemmican. Two small girls hovered on either side of her. Smiles curved their lips as they eagerly helped add berries and fat before packing the mixture into rawhide bags. A short distance from the trio, a gangly youth frowned at a Juneberry shoot in his grasp. He pulled and twisted the supple branch against a sandstone, intent on straightening a twig into an arrow so he could become a warrior.

The scene released a flood of memories. The many peaceful days spent with Morning Star's family. The joy of belonging and having a purpose. *Open your eyes.* She couldn't find her future if she dwelled in the past, whether it held good memories or bad.

She let the tepee flap fall behind her. It closed with a soft whoosh.

The family lifted their heads as one and turned to stare at her. Just as quickly they glanced away and went back to what they'd been doing. Too swiftly for her to read their expressions. Their silence spoke loudly though. They weren't calling for Eagle Feather. He wanted her to come to him on her own.

She lifted her chin and concentrated on doing just that. She didn't have to go far. When she rounded the tepee, she found him talking to several men. None of them noticed her. She seized the gift of being able to examine him without him glaring at her.

If possible, he'd grown even stronger in the two years since she'd last seen him. Unlike when he'd visited the wagon train, his chest was now bare. The familiar spider web tattoo still graced his torso, but today it was eclipsed by the massive expanse of his hard, broad-shoulder chest. The undefeatable warrior, he held himself with the bearing of a chief.

But when she looked closer, she saw the haggard lines marking his once-smooth face. Dark circles underscored eyes shadowed even further by a lowered brow, and his shoulders were stooped slightly as if he suffered under the weight of a great burden.

Hannah's heart hurt for him. He'd loved his mother and sister, only to have them taken from him violently. She hadn't thought she'd made a sound, but he suddenly turned to look at her, revealing the long scar that marred the other side of his face.

She couldn't stop herself from recoiling. For too long she'd lived in fear of him, remembering only his raging anger and his screams for vengeance.

His hand shot up, but not in a fist. He held out his palm, as if to halt her retreat. Unlike her, he'd never wanted a tattoo on his hand, and he hadn't had one when he'd visited the wagon train.

He had one now. An oval with eight lines radiating outward. A spider. Just like hers.

Suddenly, his hand clenched into the fist she'd feared. Her gaze darted up to his face. He wasn't looking at her but at something behind her, and his face was once more twisted with rage.

She spun to search the camp behind her. A horse wound its way through the tepees, heading toward her. A horse guided by no rider. A horse pulling a travois bearing a long form wrapped in painted deerskins identical to those of the Indian procession decimated by cholera. Disbelief and dread held her immobile.

The Osage must have witnessed something similar, because their screams filled the air— frightened cries speaking of disease and death. They fled.

Hannah remained rooted to the ground. She could only gape at the apparition coming toward her. Toward her like he knew her. She frowned. The horse seemed familiar. Sleek and healthy. Proud and strong. A big bay stallion. Cholla!

Where was Paden? That couldn't be him strapped on the travois behind? She'd only seen him yesterday. He'd been stuck in the fire. He hadn't been sick with cholera.

She sprinted toward his horse. Heart hammering, she fell to her knees beside the travois and stared at the form lying still as death, wrapped in canvas that usually covered a wagon. It couldn't conceal the breadth of the man's shoulders or his long length.

"Paden," she whispered, "you can't be dead."

The body abruptly surged upright, sending the canvas flying. Her shriek was stifled as arms as sturdy as tree trunks pulled her against a hard chest. She leaned into the familiar strength held in check and turned her cheek, searching for his heartbeat. Only after she found the strong, steady beat could she summon her own strength to speak. "I thought you'd died."

"Even if I had, I'd still find a way to crawl up from Hades to save you." Grasping her shoulders, he held her at arm's length so he could run his gaze over her. "If he hurt you— If anyone on this tribe hurt you—"

"Paden, no."

He rose up onto his knees.

Desperate to halt him, she grasped his face between her palms. Eyes as hard and gray as the revolver strapped to his hip met hers. "Paden, this isn't your tribe."

He climbed to his feet, pulling her up with him. "I don't care who they are. You aren't staying here."

A blood-chilling war cry split the air. Eagle Feather raced straight toward Paden, his knife in his hand, raised and ready to strike. Paden jumped back, shoving her behind him and drawing his revolver.

Eagle Feather switched his blade from one hand to the other as he circled them in a low crouch. "Unhand her, white dog."

Paden kept his body between her and her brother. "You'll have to kill me before I'll let you anywhere near her."

Her need to protect them both propelled her forward. "I'm not going to let either of you die." She tried to step between them. Paden's arm halted her.

Eagle Feather's gaze shifted from Paden to her. "Speak the truth, Blue Sky. Tell me why this man from the wagons has played this trick. There is no sickness. There is only him. A white man full of deceit."

Paden snorted a laugh. "Here's a truth for you. There's Indian blood in my veins."

Eagle Feather's gaze raked Paden, then narrowed. "What tribe?"

"Comanche."

Her brother looked to her again.

That he sought her confirmation, held her in startled disbelief. Finally, she remembered to nod. "He speaks the truth."

"Here's another," Paden said. "I came here to save her from her coward of a brother."

Eagle Feather went dead still with his gaze locked on her. "I will not harm you, Blue Sky." He sheathed his blade and beckoned her with both hands. "Come away from this man. You are not safe with him."

Her disbelief swelled to incredulity.

"Now who's the trickster?" Paden asked. "You promised her one week."

Eagle Feather stepped closer to Paden, ignoring the gun in his hand. "You let her chase after you into the fire. You put her in danger. You weren't there to carry her to safety when she wouldn't leave. I saved her."

"You stole her." Paden shoved his revolver back into its holster and took a step toward Eagle Feather as well.

Hannah laid a restraining hand on Paden's arm. She didn't want him any closer to her brother. He didn't move, but she felt the anger vibrating in his muscles.

"You came here and tried to steal her back." Her brother's next stride put him within striking distance.

"I'm here because you vowed to kill her," Paden shot back.

Eagle Feather sucked in a ragged breath. "I was the strongest warrior of my tribe, yet I could not keep my family safe. I have been searching for Blue Sky with anger in my heart for many, many moons. It was good that my journey was long, because now I can see that I wrongly blamed her."

She hadn't thought her astonishment could grow, but it did. "What changed your mind?"

He smiled at her sadly. "You are more like our mother and sister than I will ever be, always ignoring your own safety to aid others. You could have been killed when you rescued those children or helped me escape from your wagon train." He raised his palm toward her, the one with the new spider tattoo. His voice turned solemn when he said, "I give you a new vow. Blue Sky, you are my family. You are one of the Osage, now and forever."

She could only stare at him, stunned.

"Hannah," Paden said her name very softly, as if it might be the last time he ever got to say it.

The thought sent a shiver of apprehension through her.

"You once told me you wanted to return to the Osage. Is that still true?"

Once it had been all she'd wanted, but now she wanted Paden more. But he might be leaving her. A suffocating tightness gripped her chest. He still hadn't told her if he was returning to Fort Laramie and Weston. "I don't know anymore," she replied truthfully, forcing the words out.

"Are you afraid to speak freely in front of him?" Eagle Feather's raised hand had clenched into a fist, hiding his spider tattoo.

"No," she said on a gasp. "Of course not."

"This white man who is not white confuses me. I see my anger reflected in his eyes. But he risked his life when he believed I would hurt you. There is a fragment of your selflessness in him as well. How can a man be all of these things? I do not trust him. He is the wolf in disguise."

Hannah opened her mouth to defend Paden, but Eagle Feather continued speaking before she could. "I would make sure you are safe and free to do what is best for you, and you alone. Ask, and I will make him leave." His hand returned to the hilt of his knife. "Ask, and I will kill him."

Paden's hands curled into fists, driven not by the

urge to fight but the urge to stop one. He didn't want
to hurt Eagle Feather. Hell, if he fought her brother
he'd probably do a lot more than hurt him. Then
he'd have hurt Hannah as well.

Her time with the wagon train and him had been
anything but easy. He'd done little to make things
easier. He'd only be making her suffer more if she
stayed with him.

Now Eagle Feather was saying Hannah could
return to her old life. Hadn't she said if given the
choice, she'd never have left her tribe in the first
place? Now she said she didn't know what she
wanted. He wanted what was best for Hannah.
Although still uncertain he could trust Eagle Feather,
he knew she'd be better off with the Osage than with
the whites. She'd also be better off without him.

Every muscle in his body rebelled against the
notion of letting her go. But he had to go back to
Fort Laramie. Weston needed to pay for what he'd
done to Jeannie. He also needed to be prevented
from ever committing such an atrocity again.

He could drag Hannah back into a life of
uncertainty, or he could walk away and give her the
peace she'd been searching for. She deserved to be
happy; he wanted to make her happy. Walking away
from her would hurt like hell, but Eagle Feather and
the Osage would keep her safer than he ever could.

That was another truth.

He took a step toward Eagle Feather, but
Hannah's hold on his arm halted him. He covered
her hand with his. "You don't have to worry."

She pulled away and folded her arms across her
chest, as he'd often done when he'd wanted to avoid
someone. She shook her head, looking like she
might never stop.

In one swift motion he caught her face between
his palms. Staring down into her blue eyes, he

marveled again at the depth of her beauty. The pain of losing her was never going to go away.

"You don't have to worry," he repeated. "Everything will be all right." His gaze rose over her head to lock on Eagle Feather. "Your brother and I are going to have a long talk."

"Talk?" she blurted. "You mean fight."

"I mean talk. I've changed more than you can know, all because of you. It's time I put aside my selfishness and repaid you."

Hannah paced, her attention fixed on the spot where Eagle Feather and Paden sat conversing. Paden had insisted that they talk alone, but Hannah had been equally adamant that she wasn't going anywhere. She was desperately worried the two men would fight and hurt each other. She needed to be there to stop that from happening.

So they'd agreed on a compromise. The two men would have their talk, but she'd stay close by, just in case.

Her steps shortened and she turned her body, and her full attention, to the conversation. She couldn't hear what they said, but she could see their expressions. They looked so different, yet so similar. One Indian. One white and Indian. Both so proud and determined. She didn't know whose scowl was the darkest as they argued.

More than once they turned away from each other, shoulders hunched and arms folded, and brooded in stony silence. But they never resorted to violence. One or the other would turn back and break the stalemate.

Then something amazing began to happen. Their scowls lifted, their voices calmed, and their bodies relaxed. Soon they were immersed in a real conversation, each man keenly considering what the other said.

Eagle Feather's eyes became wider and wider, until his gaze swung to Hannah. The shock in his eyes made her gasp. Then he turned back to Paden and, shaking his head, began talking and gesturing rapidly.

Paden's lips tightened and he rose to his feet. Eagle Feather restrained him with a hand on his shoulder.

Then the true miracle came. Paden held out his hand...and Eagle Feather took it. Clasping hands, they stared at each other in silence for a long moment before they turned and walked as one toward her.

When they halted in front of her, she was trembling. Eagle Feather stood aside, arms folded, staring straight ahead.

Paden swept up both her hands and held them gently in his larger ones. He smiled sadly down at her.

"What's going on?" she asked.

He cleared his throat. "I was just hashing out a few things with your brother."

"You can talk to Eagle Feather, but you can't talk to me? What *things*?"

"You." He regarded her intently. "You know you'll be safer staying with the Osage. That's what we were discussing."

Her mouth dropped open. "You'd leave me here?"

"They can keep you safe. I only want what's best for you." He lifted her hand and pressed his lips to her palm, his warm breath blowing over her tattoo, seeping into her flesh.

She pulled free of his warmth, and a great heaviness descended upon her heart. "You're going after Weston. That's what you think is best."

He touched her hair, trailing his fingers lightly down the length, making her ache for so much more. Then he walked away without looking back. She knew because she watched him until he disappeared forever from her sight.

CHAPTER 21

Alejandro held Rebecca close and stroked her back, inhaling the sweet scent of her hair. They lay together in his bedroll, their arms and legs entwined.

The wagons were fifty yards away. Far enough to give them privacy while still close enough for protection if they needed to make a quick return. Overhead the sky was a blanket of midnight blue, twinkling with a thousand dots of light.

In the darkness, Alejandro couldn't see anything other than the muted white of Rebecca's face. Even her hair was shrouded, the vibrant red hidden from his gaze. It didn't matter. The color of her hair, the curve of her lips, the shape of her chin, they were all burned into his subconscious and his heart.

"I still can't believe Captain Callahan left her with them," Rebecca said in a hushed voice.

"He said Hannah was safer with them, with Eagle Feather. He said it was what she had yearned for from the beginning. She wanted to return to the Osage."

"But how could he let her go?" she asked, her voice thick with restrained tears.

He kissed her forehead, trying to comfort her. "I don't know."

"This journey to the West, it felt so long in the

beginning. The trail stretched forever in front of us. It didn't seem real that one day it would end, that we would all part ways. Now it's different. Hannah's gone. And I hardly got to speak to her. I was afraid of what my father would do if I did."

"Shh. It's not your fault. None of us could have guessed she'd be gone so soon."

"Do you think we'll ever see her again?"

Alejandro didn't know. He still couldn't believe Paden had risked his life to save Hannah, had succeeded against all odds, had been able to bring her back—and instead he'd left her with the Osage. He tightened his arms around Rebecca, and she held him tighter in return.

"All I know is that I can never let you go now, Rebecca."

"Fort Bridger," she said firmly.

"We shall be there tomorrow," he replied.

She pulled back to peer up into his face. "It's too late for Hannah and Paden."

He released a deep sigh of resignation. "But not for us."

"Then let's make a plan. For you, for me, for us in Fort Bridger," she said, her voice growing stronger with each word, "and for all our days after."

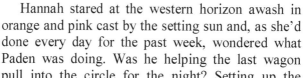

Hannah stared at the western horizon awash in orange and pink cast by the setting sun and, as she'd done every day for the past week, wondered what Paden was doing. Was he helping the last wagon pull into the circle for the night? Setting up the scouts' camp with Gabe? Discussing the trail ahead with the general? Or had he already left them, like he'd left her?

She looked to the east. Murky shadows lay there. By now, Paden could be halfway back to Fort

Laramie and Weston. Maybe he was already there. Her chest grew tight with worry.

Below her solitary perch on a slope brimming with purple wildflowers sat the Osage village. She closed her eyes, inhaled a deep breath and tried to focus on the comforting sounds of her new home that wasn't really new at all. The rhythmic thunk of firewood being chopped. The grinding of corn being crushed into meal. The wallop of robes being beaten free of dust.

Like Paden had slapped his hat on his trousers to shake lose the trail dust.

Once again, she tried to push aside her thoughts of Paden, and the nagging doubts and regrets of the last two months, to let this moment, this one place and time, bring her peace.

It wasn't working.

Releasing a sigh, she opened her eyes. She'd lived for so long with the dream of returning to her Osage family that she hadn't stopped to consider how this world had changed. The Great Spirit had reopened a door, and she'd allowed herself to be thrust through it. Her tribe had welcomed her back, accepting her as if she'd never been gone. But Morning Star and Laughing Eyes would never return.

Living with the Osage now, she felt their absence more strongly than ever. Paden's absence cut her even more keenly. He'd left her, and he hadn't loved her enough to tell her he'd return for her if he could.

She needed to forget. If her memories faded, the ache in her heart would, if not disappear, at least retreat and become bearable. The pain in her heart spiked. What if there came a time when her recollections of Paden—his dark scowls, his probing gaze, the way he said her name—became so eroded that she struggled to remember? Like her fading memories of her birth parents and soon Morning Star and Laughing Eyes.

She'd never forget completely. She'd recall just enough to remind her of those she'd held dear and lost. Paden, out there in some distant land, not dead but beyond her reach all the same.

Why? Why couldn't things be different?

The soft swish of someone striding through the grass claimed her attention. Eagle Feather walked up the slope toward her. Strong and determined but also more relaxed than she'd ever seen him. The line of his shoulders spoke of a man coming to terms with the world and himself.

Between dwelling on Paden and staring at the horizon, another occurrence had been happening regularly since she'd left the wagon train. Eagle Feather always found time to speak with her about the same topic. Her happiness. He was finally acting like her big brother.

Today, she decided, she'd repay him by greeting him with a real smile. She put her whole heart into the effort.

Eagle Feather frowned in return. "It pleases me to see you smiling again, Blue Sky. But a moment ago you looked sad. I hope you never hide your feelings just to put my mind at ease. What are you thinking?"

She struggled to keep smiling. "That I'm thankful my wish to rejoin the Osage has been granted."

"Is that all you wish for?"

She couldn't stop herself from glancing at the horizon.

"Your life no longer belongs with the Osage," Eagle Feather said softly.

She ducked her head, wanting to hide from this truth. "But the Osage are my family."

"A new family is waiting for you out there." He

gestured west. "You'll never be happy without that man, will you?"

"No." The simple reply, straight from her soul, melted her resistance. She raised her gaze to meet his.

Eagle Feather stared at her in silence, waiting for her to say more. He'd changed just as much as she had. She realized he'd support whatever choice she made.

"I'm going after him." Now that she'd said it aloud, her worries returned.

"Why did you choose to stay with us and not him?" Eagle Feather asked.

"He gave me no choice. He left me so he could revenge his dead wife. Her killer's in Fort Laramie."

A frown marred Eagle Feather's brow. "His future sounds precarious. I cannot believe I'm going to say this…if you love him, go after him and never let him go again."

"I don't know if I can."

"Why?"

She racked her brain and, finding every answer inside her lacking, spread her hands wide and said the simple truth. "I might have to watch him die."

"If you stay here, he might die alone."

A heavy sense of defeat kept Paden in his saddle as Cholla halted in the shadow of Fort Bridger. There was no need to go inside, to find a preacher, to look forward to the future. Hannah was gone.

The wagons disregarded the call to form a protective circle in favor of stopping wherever they wanted. Just like they'd done at Fort Laramie. They'd forgotten their fears of an Indian raid. When it suited them, the settlers had short memories.

He didn't. He'd promised the wagon train he'd

get them to Fort Bridger before leaving them in General Sherwood and Gabe's capable hands. It didn't matter that his promise had been made when Hannah had been by his side, with the hope she'd be there forever.

He'd completed one journey. Now another must begin. A lonely ride back to Laramie to finish what Weston had started a decade ago in San Antonio. But first he must say farewell to those responsible for giving him as much time as he'd had with Hannah.

He found them all together. General Sherwood, Gabe, Virgil, Alejandro, Miriam, her grandsons, Sarah, Nate and even Rebecca stood in their own circle, talking. When they saw him approaching, they went silent.

Shaking hands with each of them, he thanked them for the friendship they'd shown Hannah. As if by common accord, the general and he were left alone to say their goodbyes.

He clasped Sherwood's hand. "Thank you for insisting that Hannah come with us. I'm sorry I let the past distort my judgment that first day in Leavenworth." *And every other day.* The revelation about Weston and the Comanche had him questioning all of his decisions.

The old man's grip tightened. Then he pulled Paden into an equally strong embrace. "It is I who owe you an apology. Your father was a dear friend, and I failed him and you. I should have tried harder to find you after he and your mother died."

Shock made Paden stiffen. Had the old man been tormented by regrets as deep-rooted as his?

Sherwood exhaled a weary breath and drew back. "I'm sorry."

"I'm not." Paden finally returned the general's embrace. "My grandmother needed me. It was right that I was with her during her final years."

A long moment passed before they released each other.

"I'm glad you were with me during mine as well." Deep lines etched Sherwood's face. He'd aged considerably during the days since Paden had confided in him before riding into the Osage camp to rescue Hannah.

The knowledge that Weston had killed Jeannie was a burden he shouldn't have shared. "I'm the one who failed you," he said.

The general raised his chin. A determined look replaced the weary lines on his face. "I've lived my life. You on the other hand have yet to even start yours. I want you to seize your chance for happiness." His expression turned even more resolute. "In Oregon with Hannah."

Every night Paden dreamed of that possibility. And every morning he tried to bury his hopes in a far corner of his heart in an attempt to ignore them. "Not while Weston still needs to pay for what he did to Jeannie. If he doesn't, he'll continue destroying more lives."

"Agreed. But you won't be the one to make him pay. I will."

Paden jerked back, his entire body rebelling against putting the old man in danger, of losing him forever. He cast around for a way to dissuade him. His gaze halted on the settlers setting up their camps. "What about the wagon train?"

"That's what we were discussing when you arrived. Gabe will make sure everyone reaches California. If I can join him there, I will. But right now my future lies in Laramie."

"I can't let you do this."

"You can. What would you do if you and Hannah had children?"

Wave upon wave of protectiveness swept through Paden with a force that left him shaking.

Sherwood laid a steadying hand on his shoulder. "Let me be the father who not only brings his daughter's killer to justice but also saves his son." Sherwood released him with a push. "Now get going." He canted his head toward the east. "Go back and find Hannah."

CHAPTER 22

Paden slowed Cholla to a walk, giving them both time to catch their breath. A sad lack of patience had driven him to push hard. *No matter how quickly you want to reach your destination,* he reminded himself, *winding Cholla will only hinder your progress.*

He had a long search ahead of him.

The last time he'd seen Hannah was a week ago. Eagle Feather's tribe would have moved many times since. Their trail would've long since disappeared, and they'd be avoiding white people like the pox. The only souls with a clue to their whereabouts would be other Indians who sure as hell wouldn't be interested in telling him anything.

He wasn't going to let anything stand in his way though. He was riding east along the trail to the place where he'd last seen her. He'd start his search there.

General Sherwood had given him the gift of a life unfettered by the past. He wasn't going to squander that gift. He wasn't going to live his life without Hannah. He doubted if he even could.

He swore as Cholla's ears twitched back for the tenth time in as many minutes. Then the usually sensible, well-trained horse stopped, swinging his head around toward the trail behind them. He reined

Cholla back to face the east and thumped his heels against the horse's belly. Cholla hardly seemed to notice. He had a gut like an iron drum. Finally, he slowly started moving forward but kept one ear cocked.

Something or someone was following them.

Accepting the inevitable, Paden doubled back on his tracks and concealed himself in a knot of cedars. Drawing his revolver, he waited. Minutes ticked by. Through the thick foliage of his hiding place, he caught a glimpse of a rider. Half-hidden but still identifiable as human. He wasn't dealing with a bear or other wild animal.

His anger grew. He didn't have time for this. He had to find Hannah, and anyone who slowed him down would incur his wrath. He'd give the bastard a damned good scare and send him running.

He bit down a laugh. A good scare?

Previously, he would've done a lot more than that, especially if the man had been Indian. He couldn't tell if his pursuer was or not, but it didn't matter. The idea of shooting anyone left a sour taste in his mouth, like he'd swallowed vinegar.

A lucky break for the person following him. Whoever he was, he had Hannah to thank. He was lucky he hadn't met Paden a few months ago. He kept his revolver drawn though. He wasn't a fool.

Every bird singing, every tree creaking in the wind sounded as loud as a gunshot. The birds went suddenly quiet. Paden tensed as the hazy silhouette of the rider pulled to a stop and turned as if searching the forest. To hell with waiting.

Hannah urged White Cloud down the trail, heading east toward Fort Laramie at a fast clip. She studied the fresh tracks in front of her. One shod set of hooves. Not an Indian pony then. She glanced over her shoulder at her own tracks. The ones ahead had sunk deeper into the earth than White Cloud's. The rider ahead was heavy. Most likely, a man. A large one.

She spun to face forward. Shafts of sunlight peeked through the thick trees. Dust drifted in the beams, descending lazily to where it'd been kicked up. The man between her and Laramie wasn't far ahead now. Her frustration built as she pondered the quickest route around him.

A whippoorwill's plaintive song cascaded through the treetops and stopped mid-call. She jerked White Cloud to a halt. All that remained was the branches creaking in the sighing breeze. The scent of decaying leaves assailed her nose. Had the rider taken to the bush and disturbed the undergrowth?

She scanned the surrounding forest, and found nothing.

Her caution wavered along with her restraint. She couldn't wait. Paden was probably already at Fort Laramie. She had to reach him before he confronted Weston alone. She urged White Cloud forward.

On her right, the trees parted with a deafening crash. A big horse leaped out like a blast of buckshot. The rider jumped from the mount and hurtled toward her. She dug her knee into White Cloud's side, just like she'd done to avoid Dawson during the horserace at Leavenworth.

Her assailant fell hard on the earth beside White Cloud. She yanked her rifle from its scabbard and aimed it at the man who'd rolled to his feet in a half crouch, his pistol pointed in the air. A familiar dark-haired man stared at her with gunmetal gray eyes wide with disbelief.

She holstered her weapon as did Paden.

"What are you doing here?" she asked.

He plucked her from her saddle and set her on the ground in front of him. A rush of tears blurred her vision and made her sway toward him.

With hands that shook, he thrust his fingers deep in her hair and pulled her even closer. He paused before he gently tilted her face up to his. "I didn't mean to frighten you."

She swiped her tears away with the back of her hand. "I was more angry than frightened."

He stared at her with an intensity that made her breath hitch. "*Sweet heaven,* how I've missed you. Your bravery, your strength, your eyes—blue as the sky and a hundred times more precious to me."

She blinked wet lashes, loving how he gazed at her as if she were his whole world, as if he loved her. But he didn't. His heart had room for one thing. Revenge.

"I can't believe I found you," he said. "Or rather that you found me."

"I gave up everything to look for you, while you search only for Weston." The words came out sharp and spiteful. Being angry wouldn't help. She bowed her head.

"The only person I was looking for was you."

Her head snapped up with jerk. "Me?" She searched his face.

His eyes were free of shadows. The corners of his lips kicked up, framed by lines that suddenly lifted his mouth into a wide grin. Not a trace of his infamous scowl remained. She couldn't help but smile in return.

He folded her into his embrace. "To have you in my arms again—" His muscles tensed, and he drew back enough to look at her again. "Why aren't you with Eagle Feather and your tribe? Has something happened to them?"

"No, they're all right. They're wonderful. But after you left, Eagle Feather asked me if he'd made another mistake. He wondered why I'd agreed to stay with him and the Osage, and not with you. He told me—" Her tears returned, clogging her throat. She swallowed them and forced herself to continue. "He told me that if I loved you, I should go after you and never let you go again." A blush burned her face and, despite her determination, her gaze plummeted again.

"Hannah...look at me." His deliberate pause after saying her name, murmuring it in his deep and much-adored voice, brought to mind how he'd asked her to look at him that first day on the trail. That day, as they'd watched the settlers ready themselves to leave Fort Leavenworth, they'd sat side by side. But a world of misunderstandings and regrets had separated them.

Now he stood in front of her, holding her, waiting for something.

She raised her gaze to meet his.

His eyes glowed like molten steel, enveloping her in their heat until every drop of doubt melted within her. "I hope one day I can do something as wonderful for your brother as he has done for me. Will you come home with me to Oregon?"

Her hand rose to his chest. Paden's heart beat strong and certain against her spider tattoo. "My home is here."

His large palm covered hers and, pressing her hand snug against his chest, he drew her toward their horses. "Then I guess you'll have no objection to riding by my side to Fort Bridger and finally marrying me."

EPILOGUE

The following year…
Oregon—Spring 1851

The Spirits Above had blessed her. So had the God of her white parents. Hannah gazed at the spider on her palm, then pressed the tattoo over the one above her heart. *Thank you, Grandfather Spider. Thank you, Morning Star and Laughing Eyes and Eagle Feather and General Sherwood, too.*

She stood in the doorway of her new home and smiled with contentment. The cabin had been built with care. It had helped its creator keep her warm over the winter. Formed from the trees that once stood in the clearing surrounding, she liked to imagine that each log had a story and personality all of its own. The house had an upstairs bedroom and a ground floor kitchen with a table long enough to seat all her friends.

Right now, Miriam and Sarah sat at the table, rolling balls of sourdough in shortening and reminiscing about how, not so long ago, Miriam had tried to teach Hannah how to make biscuits. Hannah's concerns that the two women might regret abandoning their dreams of a life in California had proven unfounded.

Sarah smoothed a hand over her rounded belly. When she glanced up and caught Hannah watching her, she smiled and mouthed the words, *Thank you.*

Hannah tipped her head in acknowledgement and mouthed the same words right back at her and Miriam. Laughing, she slipped out the cabin door and down the path leading to the mill.

Nate was showing William and Charlie how to strip a pine tree and shape it into a log to build a home for him and Sarah. Charlie was too small to try it himself, but William gave it a go and beamed with pride when he mastered each step of the process. Hannah added her praise to Nate's before continuing down the hill.

Her steps quickened when she glimpsed a familiar redheaded woman perched by the water's edge on a stack of recently hewn logs. Miss Riley, now Mrs. Ramirez, had become a close friend.

Hannah never tired of hearing the story of how, a day after the California-bound emigrants had said their goodbyes to those who'd decided they were Oregon-bound, Alejandro had stolen Rebecca away from her overbearing father and spirited her up the Oregon branch to join them. Mrs. Ramirez referred to it as "the happiest day of my life."

The only friends missing from their little group were General Sherwood, Gabe and Virgil. The general may have placed himself in mortal danger by returning to Fort Laramie, but she held onto her hope that one day she'd see all three men again—if not in Oregon, then in California.

She climbed up beside Rebecca to sit on the topmost log. Her friend grinned at her and pointed, without being asked, toward the jetty forty yards downriver.

Paden stood there, as imposing as ever, talking to Alejandro. They were probably discussing the latest lumber shipment they planned to send to China.

As if Paden sensed her watching him, he lifted his dark head and his gaze scanned the riverbank until he found what he was looking for. Even at a distance, his metal-gray eyes warmed her straight through and his lips curved into the smile he wore often these days.

Her cheeks turned hot and her heart beat faster. She doubted that would ever change.

What had changed was there would be no more wandering, no more searching. She'd found her own little corner of Heaven.

The End

AUTHOR NOTE

Between Heaven and Hell was my first novel, so you can imagine how honored I was when it won the Romance Writers of America® Golden Heart® award for historical romance in 2010. I hope you enjoyed reading Paden and Hannah's story as much as I enjoyed writing it.

Authors appreciate hearing that readers liked their stories. Other readers appreciate hearing about stories they might find interesting. If you enjoyed this story, please consider writing a review.

Amazon
www.amazon.com/author/jacquinelson

Goodreads
www.goodreads.com/jacquinelson

For updates on my new releases, contests and events, please sign up for my newsletter at
www.JacquiNelson.com
I'd be delighted if you'd like to join my street team and help spread the word about my writing. Visit my website to find out more.

OTHER BOOKS BY JACQUI NELSON

Adella's Enemy
(a novella in *Passion's Prize* anthology)

www.amazon.com/dp/B00EE1UW5E

***Passion's Prize* anthology**

www.amazon.com/dp/B00EDSCZK8

Between Love and Lies

Coming in autumn 2014

Turn the page to read my bio and excerpts from
Adella's Enemy and
Between Love and Lies.

ABOUT THE AUTHOR

Jacqui Nelson writes historical romantic adventures set in the American West and Victorian London. Her love for the Old West came from watching classic Western movies while growing up on a cattle farm. Her passion for Victorian London wasn't far behind and only increased when she worked in England and explored the nooks and crannies of London on her weekends. She now lives on the west coast of Canada where she works in a bookstore. She is a RWA® Golden Heart® winner and three-time finalist.

Contact Jacqui at...
www.JacquiNelson.com
www.facebook.com/JacquiNelsonBooks
www.twitter.com/Jacqui_Nelson

ADELLA'S ENEMY – EXCERPT

*Can the pursuit of an old enemy
lead to a new love?*

Emporia, Kansas—March 1870

"It's one of the Joy Men." The declaration came
from the workmen's leader—a giant of an
Irishman—hidden somewhere beyond the wall of
bodies between her and the train.

A spy for the rival railroad? If James Joy had sent
a rabble rouser from his line, Adella had best learn
as much about him as possible. Starting with what
he looked like.

She pushed through the workmen. Each man
spun with a scowl, ready to berate whoever poked
him in the ribs or stepped on his toes. When they
saw her, they stumbled back, jaws dropping. She
reached the platform's edge just in time to see the
man on the stockcar leap to the engine, run across its
back and slid down the cattle guard to the ground.

The big Irishman shoved through his men with a
growl. "Why aren't you chasing after—?" He
slammed to a halt in front of her.

He hadn't touched her, but the sight of him
looming over her with a combination of anger and
disbelief twisting his mud-streaked face, pushed her

back. She teetered on the edge of the train platform, the weight of her valise throwing her further off balance. Many hands reached for her, including the giant's.

She refused to let go of her valise and accept them.

She fell with a shriek. Her rear end hit the mud with a bruising wallop. She gritted her teeth to stop any additional embarrassing outbursts then, valise still in hand, staggered to her feet. And promptly sank ankle deep in the muck.

A colossal groan rent the air. She jerked round to face the train, as did the workmen on the platform above her. The terrible sound came again, making the stockcar shudder with its force. A crack like gunfire echoed. Chains burst. Iron screeched against iron. And the mountain of rails toppled toward her. Trapped as she was in the muck below, she'd soon be crushed in a muddy grave. Fear devoured all further thought.

A broad hand clamped round her arm and yanked. Her feet popped from the mud, and she sailed through the air before landing on the platform. The hand released her. Shock rendered her legs useless, crumpling her like a rag doll on the boards beside her valise.

With the force of Thor's hammer, the first rail struck the earth. A shower of mud pelted the platform on either side of her. The clanging that followed left her ears ringing.

"Did I hurt you?" the giant's now familiar brogue whispered, so close it raised goose flesh.

Lifting her head, she stared into eyes as silver as newly minted dollars, the only difference in a face as muddy as the rest. The man's massive frame crouched protectively over her. She was bombarded with memories of her mother's stories, tales passed down for generations of legendary Celtic warriors. She had never dreamed of encountering one of those mythical men in human form.

How to Read *Adella's Enemy*

Adella's Enemy (the novella)

www.amazon.com/dp/B00EE1UW5E

Passion Prize (the anthology)
Features three interlinked stories: ***Adella's Enemy*** by Jacqui Nelson, ***Eden's Sin*** by Jennifer Jakes and ***Kate's Outlaw*** by E.E. Burke

www.amazon.com/dp/B00EDSCZK8

Turn the page to read an excerpt from
Between Love and Lies.

BETWEEN LOVE AND LIES – EXCERPT
(Nominated for the 2013 RWA®
Golden Heart® Award)

In a town ruled by sin,
will he earn her love or her lies?

South of Dodge City, Kansas—May 1876

The cattle were destroying everything: the tiny apple tree she'd sheltered in the wagon during the long, sweltering journey from Virginia; the fence she'd devoted weeks to repairing over the winter with scraps of deadwood; the vegetable garden she'd sown during the first whisper of spring and painstakingly coaxed to life every heartbeat since.

All trampled, devoured, gone.

Sadie glared at the beasts, eyes burning with tears of hopeless rage. They were thin, ugly creatures, spindly legs culminating in cloven hooves, heads wielding heavy horns that twisted out of their skulls in long spikes. Texas longhorns, the Devil's helpers. In the middle of them rode Lucifer himself, sent straight up from Hell to torment her and tear away everything she'd slaved to build.

She tracked the long-legged, solid-built cowboy as he steered his horse through the milling beasts, angling toward her and her father—and their sod house which, she realized with a jolt of dismay, was also in danger of being leveled by the heaving mass of cattle. The intruder, similar to all the other Texas drovers, was covered in a layer of trail dust so thick it hung on him like a second skin. But it was one of the only things he and the other men had in common.

While the rest hollered and cracked whips over the backs of the beasts in their charge—trying to persuade them to return to the trail—this man urged his mount through the river of hide and horn, making a beeline for her.

It infuriated her that he was so silent, that he could guide his horse with remarkably little effort. As the distance between them shortened, unease crept up her spine. His gaze was unwavering, never leaving her.

She swallowed, tightened her fingers around the ancient shotgun clutched at her side, and concentrated on her anger and frustration, transferring them from the longhorns to settle solely on him. She did not want him to come any closer. Yanking the shotgun up to her shoulder, she took aim. The cowboy straightened in his saddle but otherwise did not acknowledge her hostile action. Nor did he slacken his pace; if anything, he bore down on her even faster.

Damn him to hell. Her finger tightened on the trigger.

Something slammed down on her shotgun, pitching the rusted barrel earthward. The buckshot tore a savage gouge out of the clay in front of her, kicking up a cloud of dust. The blast rocked her and forced her to stumble back.

Her father's red face inserted itself between her and the cowboy. With a curse, he jerked the weapon from her numb hands.

As she stood gawking at him, the cattle, spooked by the shotgun blast, bolted—fast and in every direction. Her father sprinted toward their lone plow horse, vaulted onto its back and galloped away from her and the cattle.

Typical. She shouldn't have expected anything different from him. He'd thought only of securing his own safety. He'd abandoned her alone and unarmed in the center of the herd.

I'm going to be trampled. I'm going to die.

Time suspended as she contemplated her life ending. She felt nothing. All her hard work had been obliterated in a blink, and she could not summon the will to fight back, to face the prospect of starting over. If this was the end, so be it.

The bawling cattle and thundering hooves were deafening. The heat of their breaths hit her first, then their bodies. Walloped square in the chest, her lungs compressed and she was knocked off her feet. But the surge did not wash over her. Instead, a solid hand caught her about the waist, jerking her up until she crashed into an immovable wall.

She sucked in air and immediately wished she hadn't. Pain pierced her ribs. Dust billowed and shrouded the air, blinding her. Through slitted eyes she realized her leather-clad perch was already covered in a thick blanket of dust...and she was being pressed tightly against it. Frowning, she struggled to raise her head and discovered a square, beard-stubbled jaw directly above her.

Lucifer—in the disguise of a Texan cowboy— held her in his lap while waves of cattle buffeted his mount, his grip on her solid but not bruising as he guided them to safety. When they had cleared the beasts and the noise level dropped a notch, he peered down at her. Eyes like warm whiskey stared at her from an angular face etched with concern.

"Are you hurt?" His voice was low and ragged; his breath fanned out in bursts, caressing her face.

Her world tilted and the air once more left her lungs. She forced herself to remember he was responsible for destroying everything she held dear. Anger flooded her, pushing away all other thought, the same way his herd had swept away her dreams.

She curled her fingers into a fist and hit him as hard as she could in the stomach. Pain ricocheted up her arm. He didn't budge. He merely blinked, his brows lowering. Infuriated by his lack of response, she unleashed a flurry of hits, striking him with her fists, elbows and feet.

Beneath them, his horse spooked, whinnied shrilly and reared up.

Blind to everything but her need to make him hurt as much as she did, she launched her entire body at him. They tumbled from the horse and struck the ground hard, him landing first on his back, her on top of him. His breath left him in a grunt of surprise, but his hands remained locked around her waist. She scrambled to her knees before he pulled her back down. Twisting and turning, she struggled in vain to break free of his grip.

"Hold still. I'm trying to help you. You're gonna get us both killed."

His voice caught her off guard, stilling her. The tone was rough and demanding but edged with a note of pleading. Its undercurrent tugged at her.

Bewildered, she shook her head, refusing to yield to him. "Trying to help?" she yelled, slamming a fist down on his chest. "Do you know how long it took me to plant that garden? Or build that fence?" She hit him with her other hand. Exhausted, she wondered if he even felt her punches, which angered her beyond reason. "You've destroyed my entire life!"

She pounded out her fury on him until she couldn't lift her arms. When she stilled, he shocked her by gathering her close, drawing her into the curve of his body, pulling her head down onto his shoulder. His touch was gentle and reassuring; his palm cradled the back of her head, while his fingers smoothed the wild tangle of her hair.

His tenderness was her undoing. No one had held her with such care in a long time. Not since her mother had died. Great sobs shook her and she hid her face in his shoulder, unable to stop her tears.

He remained motionless until her shoulders ceased shaking, then stroked the rough pads of his thumbs across her cheeks and tucked her snarled tresses behind her ears. Her stomach squeezed into a knot and she hunched her shoulders, burrowing her nose into the tear-dampened wool of his jacket. The smell of him—masculine and earthy—infused her senses with longing.

"If I could undo the damage, I would," he whispered against her ear, his voice soft and husky. Silk and sand. Together with his breath, hot against her skin, it unleashed a storm in her belly, like a herd of pronghorn antelopes spying a mountain lion.

She jerked away, scrambling off him. This time he didn't move to stop her. She didn't go far, though. She didn't have the energy. Sitting stiff-backed beside him, she stared blankly at the rubble that had once formed her home. The salt of her tears stung her skin and her eyes ached, mirroring the pain in her soul.

His stiff leather chaps creaked as he stood and stepped closer. The din associated with the longhorn herd had faded, the cattle having returned to the trail, once again heading north toward Dodge. The drover didn't follow them, nor did he touch her. The heat of his body did, though, intensifying the strange fluttering in her stomach.

"It can be rebuilt." The words were spoken plainly, without a trace of doubt. Maybe such things were possible in his world, but not in hers.

A bitter bubble of laughter burst from her, and she bit down on her lip. She wouldn't let him see how much he'd hurt her. See that a scream was building inside her. One so big that, if she let it out, she was certain she would shatter. "Easy for you to say."

He sighed. "I know it won't be easy, but I can't undo what's happened."

You have no idea! her mind screamed as she watched her father steer the aging swayback mare toward them.

She lurched to her feet. Behind her, the cowboy placed a callused hand under her elbow but she shrugged off his hold, refusing to look at him. Instead, she glared at her father and dreaded what was certain to come. She knew him too well—his manipulative mind, his greed and his lack of love for her, his own flesh and blood.

But when her father reached them, it was the cowboy who spoke first. "It's a right shame, my herd moving through your homestead like that, Mr.—?"

"Sullivan. Timothy Sullivan. And yes, it is."

What her father lacked in stature, he made up for with a classically boned face and thick hair gone white before of its time. With looks like that and his smooth-talking tongue, he really should have pursued a career in the theater. Then maybe he could have made a contribution to their meager funds instead of being a drain on whatever she earned.

Unfortunately, he was more interested in drinking and gambling.

He eyed Sadie briefly, then turned to the man standing next to her, his familiar features settling into a look of mournful loss. "Me and my daughter worked hard building the place.

Liar!

He hadn't expended a single minute on their farm. He'd left that all up to her. She cringed at his charlatan nature, knowing he'd ply the cowboy with a consummate actor's skills, trying to extract as much compensation as he could for something he had no part in creating.

The cowboy surprised her again. "I'll compensate you fairly for your loss, Mr. Sullivan. It's the least I can do for you...and your daughter."

Not wanting to see any more, she turned away but couldn't block out the scrape of his footsteps, the jingle of his spurs, as he approached her father. They rang harsh against the tender earth of her home. He murmured something, deep and gravelly, that she couldn't catch. But she heard the surprise in her father's gasp.

"You are most generous, sir!"

She spun around. A tall stack of greenbacks rested on her father's soft, white palms. Her heart plummeted and the starch went out of her spine. She looked at the cowboy, her eyes burning with unshed tears.

His brows drew together and he took a step toward her. She took one back, shaking her head, forcing all the emotion from her heart and, she hoped, from her face. She turned and kept moving away from him, to where her home had once stood.

Giving that much money to a compulsive gambler was a sure-fire recipe for disaster. It would be gone come morning...and so would her future.

Look for ***Between Love and Lies***
in autumn 2014

Or sign up for my newsletter at
www.JacquiNelson.com
for a reminder on release day.

Made in the USA
Charleston, SC
25 April 2015